D1398677

Books by the author

The Vampire Awakenings Series:

Awakened (Vampire Awakenings, Book 1)

Destined (Vampire Awakenings, Book 2)

Untamed (Vampire Awakenings, Book 3)

Enraptured (Vampire Awakenings, Book 4)

Historical Romance

A Stolen Heart

Books written under the penname Erica Stevens

The Captive Series

Captured (Book 1)

Renegade (Book 2)

Refugee (Book 3)

Salvation (Book 4)

Redemption (Book 5)

Broken (The Captive Series prequel)

Vengeance (Book 6) Coming December 2015

The Fire & Ice Series

Frost Burn

The Kindred Series

Kindred (Book 1)

Ashes (Book 2)

Kindled (Book 3)

Inferno (Book 4)

Phoenix Rising (Book 5)

The Ravening Series

Ravenous (Book 1)

Taken Over (Book 2)

Reclamation (Book 3)

The Survivor Chronicles

Book 1: The Upheaval

Book 2: The Divide

Book 3: The Forsaken

Book 4: The Risen

Where to find the author

Website: **https://ericastevensauthor.com/home.html**

Mailing list for Brenda K. Davies & Erica Stevens Updates: http://visitor.r20.constantcontact.com/d.jsp?llr=unrjpksab&p=oi&m=1119190566324&sit=4ixqcchjb&f=eb6260af-2711-4728-9722-9b3031d00681

Facebook: www.facebook.com/BrendaDaviesAuthor

Twitter: @BrendaKDavies1

Blog: http://brendakdavies.blogspot.com/

CHAPTER 1

Kansas, 1890.

"Drop the pistol." The piercing sound of a hammer being cocked back was as loud as a gunshot on the eerily quiet back road. "Now!"

Alexandra's heart leapt into her throat, but her finger remained steady on the trigger as she held the gun tight within her grasp. The deep, husky voice was close to her ear, so close that she could feel his breath tickling the hair on the back of her neck. He was so close that she could feel the heat radiating off of him when he shifted closer to her. Suddenly, the cold barrel of a gun was pressed against her scalp, threatening to upset her cowboy hat.

"I said *now*!" the man behind her barked.

In spite of his shouting, her aim did not waver from the man directly in front of her, cowering against the wagon. His wide brown eyes rolled back in his head and to Alex's utter horror, and extreme displeasure, the driver of the wagon now had a wet stain down the front of his pants after having lost control of his bodily functions the second she'd brandished the gun. He'd been too scared to react fast enough to get the moneybox she knew was on the carriage before someone else had silently approached her from behind. Inwardly, she cursed the man's cowardice; he had put her in this position after all.

Jarett bit back a swear as he pushed his pistol more forcefully into the skull of the small man before him. His movement shoved the man slightly forward, but the man still didn't lower the gun he had aimed at the driver. Jarett didn't know how he'd gotten into this damnable position in the first place. He'd only planned to stop on the side of the road, relieve himself, and continue on his way. Instead, he had come back to find the driver cowering beside the wagon. The man had actually pissed himself, Jarett realized with disgust.

Frowning, he focused his attention on the small, slender man before him. Beneath the battered cowboy hat and faded red bandana, he could make out just a flash of copper colored hair. The hand holding the gun was small, rather delicate looking, and tanned. With a silent groan Jarett realized that this slight man before him was actually a young boy, and that he might be forced to pull the trigger. He had no qualms about killing a full-grown man, but a boy...

He didn't want to kill a young boy, but if push came to shove… Jarett shrugged his shoulders. He had been hired to do a job, and he was going to do it, child or no. The boy was a thief, not some innocent caught in the crossfire. The boy had chosen this life with the knowledge that he could die as a result of his poor choice. And if the boy didn't drop the gun he currently had trained on the now soiled man, he was going to die by Jarett's hand in the next few minutes.

The pistol was shoved painfully against Alex's head again, now causing the hat to shadow her eyes. "Don't make me tell you again, or I will put a bullet through your thieving head," the voice behind her hissed.

The sound of another hammer being cocked seemed even louder than the first. "I don't think so mister, put the gun down." Alex breathed a sigh of relief at the sound of her brother, Hugh's voice. "Are you ok?"

Even though she couldn't see Hugh, she knew the question had been directed at her. "Took you long enough," she growled, making sure to keep her voice deep and gravely.

Her brother's low chuckle seemed entirely out of place in this situation. "I'll take that as a yes. It seems, mister that you are in a bit of a predicament. I would suggest lowering your weapon."

Jarett grit his teeth, unable to believe that he hadn't heard the second man approaching. He had been so focused on the fact that he would have to kill a child, that he hadn't been paying attention to his surroundings.

"Drop your gun mister," the man behind him commanded again.

"I'll put a hole in your buddy's head first," Jarett grated. The boy before him took a small step forward; a whimper escaped him as Jarett jammed the gun against the base of his skull again.

"Don't move!" the man behind him barked.

Jarett dropped suddenly, shoving the boy down as he spun for the man behind him. He was rewarded with a grunt as he took the man's legs out from under him with his right leg. They fell to the ground together in a tumbled heap. The dust and dirt that their bodies caused to billow up around them temporarily blinded him.

"No!" the boy cried.

Regaining her feet, Alex raced forward as Hugh fell to the ground. The man that had held the gun on her was now on top of Hugh; his large hand was wrapped around Hugh's right wrist as he slammed it into the ground. Hugh grunted as the pistol flew from his hand and the man drove a fist into his stomach. The man turned suddenly, his knee on Hugh's chest pinning him to the ground, as he once again leveled his pistol on Alex.

Dust hung thickly in the air between them, but Alex wasn't fooled into thinking that he couldn't see her as well as she could see him. Fighting back the terror clawing at her chest, Alex gripped the pistol with both hands in order to keep it steady in her shaking grasp.

"Let him up," she grated through clenched teeth.

"Like hell!" the man spat.

The dust between them began to settle, and for the first time Alex was able to get a good look at the man that had thwarted their plans. She wished that she hadn't.

He was absolutely frightening and the size of a bear! He looked about as ferocious and deadly as one too. For a second her hands wavered before they raised up to level the gun at a chest easily twice the size of Hugh's. His shoulders were broad enough to block out the copse of trees behind him. His arms were the size of small tree trunks and the thick, bronzed muscles of his forearms were heavily corded as they bulged beneath the rolled up sleeves of his shirt.

Although he was still kneeling on Hugh's chest, Alex was certain that when he stood, he would be well over a head taller than her. Her gaze darted to Hugh pinned helplessly to the ground, wheezing for breath. With a small twist of his knee, the man caused Hugh to choke and gasp. Apprehension spurted through Alex, jerking her gaze immediately back to the formidable man before her.

A black cowboy hat shadowed his brow, but the high planes of his cheekbones, the straight blade of his nose, and the firm line of his full lips were clearly visible. Black hair curled down to the collar of his shirt, another strand had fallen forward to brush against the corner of one of the most amazing pair of eyes she'd ever seen.

Swallowing nervously, Alex forced herself to meet eyes the color of gold. A feral, predatory gleam sparked within his eyes as he unwaveringly held her gaze. It was highly unnerving, and for a moment Alex feared she might disgrace herself like the cowering man behind her had.

"It seems we are at an impasse boy," Jarett grated. "Your partner has been caught. Now, since I'd prefer not to shoot a child, and since I don't feel like being shot by one, I suggest you get out of here."

The boy's eyes darted to the man Jarett had pinned beneath him. He watched as a myriad of emotions raced through the boy's vivid, emerald green eyes before he turned his attention back to Jarett. The old bandana covering the lower half of his face and the low hanging cowboy hat obscured all of the boy's features except for those startlingly innocent eyes. It was obvious he had not been a thief for very long, for there was no sense of cruelty within their emerald depths. The boy seemed to waver slightly; his hands shook before becoming steady again.

"I can't do that." Jarett felt as if he'd been socked in the gut as he realized that the boy was actually going to choose death, for there was no way this boy would survive a gunfight.

"Go!" Hugh grunted out.

Hugh's word caused her to jump; her eyes flew to her brother. She would *never* leave him behind. Even if she did leave, it would only be a matter of time before she was caught. Murdock knew who Hugh was; it wouldn't take much time for him to put two and two together. When he figured it out, he would come for her. Alex shuddered at the thought; she knew just how much Murdock would love to get his hands on her, to punish her. The man would relish in it. And if he had Hugh, oh dear God if he had *Hugh*, he could force her to do anything he wanted.

Swallowing back her sudden nausea, Alex tried to ignore her rising panic. How was she ever going to get the both of them out of this?

"Don't make me kill you boy!" the man told her.

"I could kill you," she retorted with more bravado than she felt.

The man quirked a black eyebrow in amusement as a cruel smile curved his mouth. "Do you honestly think you can?"

No, and that was the whole problem. She could pull the trigger, take her chances, and hope for the best. She had never killed a man before though, never even shot one, and the idea alone made her stomach curdle with revulsion. Hugh stared back at her helplessly, his eyes pleading with her to leave him behind. Her resolve strengthened as she turned back to the man. For her brother she could shoot him, for her brother she would do anything.

The stranger seemed to read that truth in the sudden set of her shoulders, or maybe it was something in her eyes, for he stiffened perceptively and the sardonic smile slipped from his face. For a second they simply stared at one another, knowing that they had come to a standoff that neither of them wanted, but couldn't avoid. With a deep breath, Alex pulled the trigger at the same time that another shot rang out.

The force of the gunshot rocked her balance; the force of the bullet hitting her shoulder knocked her over completely. A shrill cry escaped her, not from pain because she didn't feel that yet, but from the knowledge that she had been shot. Grunts, snarls, and then a sickening thud sounded in her ears.

Alex tried to sit back up but the pain was coming now and it was even more searing, more excruciating, than she had ever thought it could be. Panting a little, she cried out as hands heedlessly grabbed hold of her body, jarring her wounded arm. The hat that had been knocked from her head when she'd fallen was suddenly shoved back over the hair pinned to the top of her head and she was brought up against a warm, solid chest.

"Hold on Alex, hold on." Relief coursed through her as she realized that it was Hugh holding her. She became aware of the fact that he was carrying her as he jogged through the trees, toward the horses they had left tethered within the forest. "What were you thinking?"

"I couldn't let him take you," she whispered weakly. "We'd have both been dead."

"Hold onto the pummel."

Alex gasped as she was thrust upward. Fumbling with her good hand, she managed to grasp hold of the saddle. Hugh had the reins of her horse in his hand when he swung up behind her. He made a loud clicking noise as he drove his heels into the sides of his horse. His grasp on her tightened as he led the horses expertly through the woods at a brisk canter. Alex felt the world slipping away from her as she labored to stay conscious. The blood seeping from the bullet hole tickled her skin as it seeped down her arm and coated her shirt.

"Did I kill him?" she whispered weakly. She had to know the answer to that. If she was going to die she had to know if there was going to be a mortal sin on her soul or not.

"No."

"Did I shoot him?"

"Yes, you did." Alex heard the wry amusement in his voice, but she was too weak to reprimand him for finding pleasure in the discomfort of others.

"Was it bad?" she asked worriedly.

She never knew what his answer was as she slid into a black wave of unconsciousness.

CHAPTER 2

The next thing that Alex knew was agony, pure and simple torture. She screamed loudly, jerking upright only to be shoved back down by a pair of strong hands as someone dug piercing, burning needles into her shoulder. Screaming again, she thrashed against the hands holding her down.

"Shh Alex, it's okay now." She fell back against the bed, shivers coursed through her as sweat coated her burning body. Opening dazed eyes, she just barely managed to focus on Hugh's face, hovering above her. "It's okay now," he repeated. "The bullet is out."

"Ms. Alexandra, you must drink this."

Alex was gently raised up. Recognizing Lysette's imposing figure, she knew that it would be useless to struggle as a glass was pressed against her lips. Lysette had come to work for their family before Hugh was even born, had helped her mother to care for them, and had taken over the care of the two of them after their mother had died. There had been many nights when Alex had crawled into Lysette's bed in search of comfort, and other nights when she'd been sick and Lysette had stayed with her, nursing her, loving her. Lysette was like a mother to her, someone that Alex loved and cherished, and that loved her in return, but right now all she wanted was for Lysette to leave her alone.

She opened her mouth, choking as the foul tasting liquid was poured down her throat. Alex was too weak to fight against it as she lay limply in Hugh's arms. Even though she sputtered and gagged, Lysette managed to pour all of the liquid down her throat.

Alex slumped back on the bed, once again unconsciousness slipped blessedly over her mind and body.

***

Jarett yelled belligerently at the doctor that had been called to remove the bullet from his leg. Grabbing a pitcher of water from the table beside his bed, he heaved it at the man that finally managed to extract the bullet from his upper thigh. Though the bullet was far too close to his manhood for his liking, it had thankfully managed to miss any major arteries. The doctor retreated hastily, spewing instructions so hurriedly behind him that no one in the room was able to catch them all. The only thing that was intelligible was the fact that he would not be coming back again.

"Well now, that wasn't very wise."

Jarett's eyes shot to the man lounging in the corner of his room. Resentment boiled through his veins, but he shoved it down as he grabbed the bottle of whiskey from his nightstand and took a long swallow. Normally he wasn't a fan of whiskey, but right now he relished in the burning sensation as it made its way down his throat, spread through his belly, and numbed some of the soreness from the doctor's inept attentions. He wiped his mouth as he slammed the bottle back down.

"The man was a complete fool," Jarett retorted.

Murdock studied Jarett impassively. "He might be thinking the same thing of you."

He glared at Murdock but the man didn't seem fazed by it as his face remained blank and impassive. "You have your money, leave," Jarett told him.

"I just had to make sure that my guard is healthy before I go. How's the head?"

Jarett winced as he relaxed against the pillows. He still couldn't believe that the boy, the boy he had thought so innocent, had managed to shoot him, in the thigh no less, and much too high up on the thigh for his liking. Half an inch more, and he would have been a eunuch for the rest of his life. That was bad enough, but to add insult to injury, his prisoner had smashed him over the head with his *own* pistol. His head throbbed like a festering wound, but he wasn't about to admit that.

"It's fine," he muttered.

Murdock chuckled as he moved forward and settled himself in the chair next to Jarett's bed. He sat back in the chair, his arms folded over his chest. Jarett glared at the man. He didn't like Murdock, hadn't liked him since they'd met during a poker game last year in St. Louis. The man had offered him a job guarding and transporting his money then, but Jarett had turned him down. There was something about Murdock that reminded him of a snake just waiting to strike. He'd been content guarding shipments of money between the states for other businessmen, and his reputation of always getting a shipment where it needed to go safely had provided him with plenty of work. He'd preferred not to get involved with Murdock. Until recently.

Recently he'd found himself quite discontent, in fact he'd become exceptionally bored with his life in St. Louis. It was the reason he'd finally agreed to work for Murdock. He'd had enough of St. Louis, and Murdock's money and the chance to move further west, had been too tempting to turn down this time. He'd had no intention of staying in Kansas but it was a good stop off point along the way to somewhere else.

He wasn't sure where yet but maybe he'd even buy himself some land somewhere and settle down to raise cattle. It seemed to have worked out well for Murdock if the size of the load Jarret had been escorting today was any indication. Plus, he'd worked a few cattle ranches over the years and he enjoyed the work more than he enjoyed being a guard, but he hadn't had enough money to make a start. He'd planned on just dropping off the money, getting the salary coming to him, and heading out further west to settle down and start a new life. But now, now, he had some pay back to distribute before that plan was fully implemented.

"You don't recall anything else about these two?" Murdock inquired.

"I told you all I know," he replied bitterly. "Trust me, I *will* find them, and they will be punished."

"No, they will be brought to me," Murdock replied. "I want to know who these bastards are. They've already gotten quite a large sum of money out of me before today, they will pay for that."

"They won't be bothering you for awhile, I shot one."

"You're sure?"

"Yes." That thought was the only thing that soothed his bruised pride a little. "I saw the blood on his shoulder."

"Hmm," Murdock said as he thoughtfully rubbed at his mustache. "There's a barn dance in two weeks. There might be a way to see if anyone there is sporting a bullet wound."

"They might not go," Jarett replied.

"Everyone in the community goes."

"They might not be part of this community."

"Oh, they are." Murdock's hazel eyes narrowed as he leaned forward. "They are."

Those words made Jarett realize the man was keeping something to himself, but he wasn't certain what it was. Not that he cared. All he wanted was his revenge. When he got his hands on that boy again, he wouldn't make the same mistake of feeling any kind of sympathy for him. No, he was going to rip the little son of a bitch limb from limb, right after the boy received a bullet in the same exact place that Jarett had gotten his.

"Are you sure you'll be able to find them?"

Jarett snorted. “Trust me, I’ll find them. You won’t have any more problems with moving your money; I’ll make sure of that.”

“I’m going to hire other men too.”

Jarett grabbed the whiskey bottle again. He didn’t care if Murdock hired half the county, *he* was going to be the one to bring them in. “Do whatever you want. How is the driver?”

“Uninjured and officially removed of his duty.” Murdock stood up. “I’ll send one of the women up to help you.”

“Don’t bother,” Jarett muttered.

He wasn’t particularly in the mood to be bothered right now as he watched Murdock make his way out of the room. The door closed out some of the noise of the revelry going on below. Even with the door closed the piano, loud shouts, and laughter was still easy to discern. Jarett stared at the ceiling as he thought over everything that he remembered about the two men from earlier today. There wasn’t one detail that he couldn’t recall about the boy; the details about the other man were a little vaguer, and what characteristics he could recall could describe a hundred men in this town. But in that last second, before the lad had pulled the trigger, Jarett had memorized the image of emerald eyes and coppery hair. He was certain that if he saw the boy again, he would know him.

Jarett propped his arm behind his pounding head as he studied the cracks above him. He would be out of bed tomorrow, and he would start his search then. He didn’t care about how many other men Murdock had hired to find the elusive thieves because come hell or high water he would find them first.

The whiskey was beginning to have its desired effect upon him as he drifted in and out of consciousness. The door creaking open caused his right eye to crack a little and his hand to instinctively move to the gun on the stand beside him. Jarett watched as a small, voluptuous woman crept forward. When she saw that he was awake a smile curved the corners of her full, painted mouth. Her brown hair had been swept into a coiffeur with delicate tendrils of it framing her pretty, heart shaped face. Her light brown eyes skimmed appreciatively over his body, a lusty gleam filled them as she once again met his gaze.

"How are you feeling?" she inquired in a husky voice.

Jarett stared up at her without expression as his eyes fell to her lush breasts revealed by the low cut gown. The dusky peaks of her aureoles were visible above the neckline; almost all of her charms were on full display.

"Is there anything that you need?" she inquired with a fluttering of her lashes.

"No. Not right now, thank you."

Some of the lust in her eyes dimmed at his stony expression. "I'll check on you again later then." She gave a brief bow of her head before turning and slipping out of the room.

CHAPTER 3

"I *am* going!" Alex declared firmly.

"Alex," Hugh grumbled.

Alex planted her hands on her hips and tilted her chin to defiantly stare up at her brother. She had spent nearly a week in bed, and she wasn't about to spend one more day there. She would go insane if she did. It was only a simple trip to town, surely that wouldn't harm her overly much, but Hugh was being a stubborn buffoon. They had been arguing for over ten minutes now and neither one of them were any closer to winning or relenting to the other.

However, she had no doubt that she would win this argument. "I saved your life, you owe me."

"By letting you kill yourself?" he retorted. "I also saved *your* life; don't forget who got your ass back home!"

Alex scowled at him. "I am perfectly capable of taking a wagon ride and shopping at the mercantile. I helped Lysette with dinner last night."

"Don't remind me."

"I'm going!"

"Fine!" he yelled throwing his hands in the air. "But if you hurt yourself it's on *your* head!"

He spun on his heel and stormed over to the wagon. Alex smiled over her victory but she hurried after him before he could leave without her. Scowling ominously at him, she strained to climb into the wagon without his help. He sat in the driver's seat, the drive lines in his hands, smiling innocently at her in return as he watched her struggle her onto the bench seat.

Alex didn't give him the satisfaction of upbraiding him for his lack of help, knowing that it was his way of proving a point. Instead, she adjusted her bonnet, smiled sweetly at him, and waited for him to move the wagon forward. His smile slipped away and he glowered at her before slapping the lines across the horse's rump.

Alex grimaced as the horse jerked the wagon forward, jarring her bad arm. She grit her teeth and turned her attention to the passing countryside before Hugh could see the pain on her face. It wouldn't matter that she had won the battle, if he even remotely thought she was hurting, he would pull the wagon over and remove her bodily.

That was not going to happen, she wasn't about to sit in the house for one more day. She had always been an active person; the four days she'd spent in bed had nearly driven her mad. When Hugh had refused to let her out of the room for yet another two days, she'd finally resorted to picking the lock on her bedroom door. She'd gotten the lecture of her life when he found her in the kitchen last night, but it hadn't mattered to her, she had been free. Now she was finally going to be out and about again.

Alex watched impassively as they took the familiar road into town. It was only a short, five-mile trip that she knew by heart. They passed by cottonwood trees, oaks and elms. The scent of the trees mixed with the sweet smell of the blossoming wild flowers covering the roadsides. Alex dabbed a bead of sweat from her brow. It was warm for May, and even though she only wore her wispy muslin walking dress, she was becoming uncomfortably hot but she knew it wasn't entirely from the heat of the day. Her arm was aching and she was sure that it was the source of her growing discomfort.

"Does it hurt?"

He may have been perturbed with her, but Hugh wasn't about to take satisfaction in the fact that she was in pain. However, they were still close enough to home that he would turn the wagon around, drop her off, and probably tie her to the bed in order to keep her there if he thought she were in pain. "No," she lied.

Alex kept her gaze focused on the road, ignoring the dust that the horse's hooves kicked up. The harness jingled melodiously as the animal plodded steadily down the road. The ruts in the road, and the jarring of the wagon, set Alex's teeth on edge. She tried to hold herself as still as possible as they passed over the bumpy way, but it didn't help much.

A flash of brown drew Alex's attention back to the forest. A smile played at the corners of her mouth as she spotted the doe with her tiny fawn. She was about to draw Hugh's attention to them, but they had already passed by.

"Do you think that man is still around?" Alex inquired as she turned away from the woods.

Hugh's shoulders became more rigid and a muscle twitched in his cheek. "Might be."

"You're sure that I didn't kill him?"

"Yes Alex, I'm sure," he replied impatiently.

Even though he had answered that question a hundred times over the past week, she still felt relieved by his answer. She couldn't help but feel guilty over shooting the man, and she worried constantly that he hadn't survived it. Although, from what little Hugh had told her, she had not inflicted a mortal wound, but she almost had. He always had a twinkle in his eye when he told her this, and an amused smile on his face that Alex didn't find the least bit funny. When she pressed him to explain what he meant, he never would, so Alex was constantly troubled that he was lying to her and that she had severely injured the man.

If Hugh was lying to her, and she had killed the man, she would never forgive herself, even if their lives had hung in the balance. They had been the thieves after all, and no matter what their reasons were for stealing Murdock's money, she had never entertained the thought that someone else might get wounded, much less killed. She had never even pondered the idea that she or Hugh might get hurt.

The first five robberies had gone so smoothly that she didn't think one could go wrong. She'd never thought that she would have to shoot someone, let alone be capable of doing it in the first place.

Her hatred and thirst for vengeance against Murdock had blinded her to reality. She was paying for it now with her own soreness and guilt.

The only problem now was that they had to figure out what they were going to do about Murdock. Alex wasn't going to commit any more robberies; it wasn't worth the risk to their lives, or someone else's. She wasn't about to let Murdock get away with what he had done to them either though. There had to be another way to make him suffer besides stealing his money. The only problem was that she didn't know what would damage him more than taking his fortune dollar by dollar.

"Hugh, what do we do now?" she asked.

"I don't know."

"I'm not going to be a part of anymore robberies."

"I wouldn't let you anyway."

Alex bristled over his arrogant tone. "If I *did* want to, you couldn't stop me."

He laughed as he cast a sideways glance at her; his sky blue eyes twinkled merrily. "Pa should have taken you over his knee more when you were younger, instead of letting you run wild."

"*You* were the one who encouraged me to run wild."

Hugh smiled fondly. "Not my fault that you weren't a boy. I needed someone to torment."

"And you succeeded."

"Yes I did."

"What are we going to do?" she pressed.

He turned his attention back to the road. "First, we're going to give you a chance to heal completely and then we'll think of something."

"But..."

"We're nearing town, keep quiet."

Alex shot him a nasty look but clamped her mouth shut as they turned onto the main road to town. Buildings came into view as the horse continued to plod lazily onward. Wooden sidewalks rolled out along the painted storefronts. Some of the buildings were more freshly painted than others, but none of them were run down. Women and men strolled down the walks, some gathered to talk in small groups.

Hugh pulled up in front of the mercantile and wrapped the lines around the wagon brake before climbing down. He didn't have a chance to come around to help Alex down for Paul Fitzgerald was already there. Alex accepted Paul's hand, smiling as he helped her alight from the wagon.
"Alexandra, it is always a pleasure to see."

"As it is you, Paul," she replied.

Which it was. For all of his over exuberant ways, Paul truly was a nice boy. Although, she supposed he really couldn't be considered a boy anymore. He was twenty-two, two years older than her after all, but try as she might she could only see him as the young boy that she'd gone swimming, fishing, and riding with as a young girl. Of course he had grown since then and was actually a good looking man with pale blond hair, twinkling blue eyes and refined features. She was well aware of the fact that Paul's feelings for her had changed a few years ago but hers had always remained the same. She simply wasn't interested in him.

He slid her arm through his as Hugh came around the back of the wagon. Hugh gave Alex an amused grin before clasping hands with Paul. Alex carefully slid her arm free of Paul's, grateful that it was her good one that he'd taken hold of. She cast Paul a rueful smile, she didn't want to upset him with her mild rebuff, but she also didn't want to do anything that would encourage him to show more interest in her than he already did.

"How are things going at the ranch?" Paul inquired.

"Just fine," Hugh replied. "How about yours?"

"Same as always," Paul replied but his eyes darkened. "Had some more cattle and sheep stolen last week, but nothing too major."

Alex concentrated on trying to keep her face impassive while inside she was seething. It was Murdock, they all knew that it was Murdock stealing livestock and knocking down fences. Poor Mr. Driscoll had had a barn fire last month that had destroyed three of his horses and a good amount of his grain. He had sold his land after that and moved back east, Murdock had been the only one that could afford to purchase it.

Unfortunately, even though they knew who the culprit was there was nothing that any of them could do to stop him. The sheriff was Murdock's man; he wouldn't raise a hand against him. Besides that, the only evidence against Murdock was the fact that all of the trouble had started shortly after he had arrived in the area.

That was no proof at all.

"We lost three last week," Hugh replied.

"Amazing how they just up and vanish, isn't it?" Paul asked sardonically.

"Yes, it is."

"There is an interesting piece of news running through town." Paul leaned forward as he prepared to share the gossip. "It appears that someone tried to rob Murdock's wagon again. Unfortunately, they failed in their attempt."

"Really?" Alex asked and made her eyes innocently wide as she stared up at Paul.

Paul gave her a goofy smile as he ran his hand through his hair. "Ah, uh yeah. Seems one of the thieves got shot in the process. Murdock's man has been staying in town, asking questions."

Alex's gaze turned to Hugh. He was leaning against the wagon, no hint of tension in his tall, lean frame. "Murdock's man?" Alex inquired.

"He was guarding the money when the wagon was held up. I guess there was a bit of a scuffle, he was shot too..."

"Is he okay?" Alex asked anxiously.

Hugh shot her a silencing look as Paul gave her a quizzical glance. Alex had never hid her hatred of Murdock, or his men, and had never before shown any kind of interest in their wellbeing. She knew that her question was highly unlike her but she hadn't been able to stop herself from asking.

"Well, yes," Paul answered. "He's well enough to be nosing around town, asking about a boy and a man."

Alex released the breath she hadn't realized she'd been holding until then. "Too bad they didn't get the money," Alex replied, her gaze went to the sidewalk as Megan came around the corner. "If you gentlemen will excuse me."

She didn't wait for a reply as she lifted the skirt of her dress and hurried across the street to her best friend. Megan broke into a dazzling, dimpled smile when she spotted Alex. "Alex, it is so good to see you!"

"I'd hug you, but I don't think I could get my arms around you. You are getting so big!" Alex cried.

Megan's smile grew even wider as her hand fell lovingly to her belly. "That's what Daryl keeps saying."

Alex laughed happily as she slid her good arm through Megan's, they chatted amicably as they leisurely made their way down the walk. Megan waddled more than walked now, but even though she was so big, Alex was certain she'd never seen her friend look so lovely. There was a permanent sparkle in her cornflower blue eyes, a rosy glow to her dimpled cheeks, her pale blond hair shone in the sun and an air of happiness surrounding her.

Although they were the same age, Megan's life was far different from Alex's shattered one. Megan had been married for over two years now to Daryl, whom she loved whole-heartedly. She was about to become a mother, and had settled into the joy of family life.

"Did you hear about the robbery?" Megan asked in an excited whisper.

"Yes, Paul told us the minute that we arrived."

Megan patted Alex's hand. "That boy is helplessly in love with you."

"Megan, don't start," Alex warned.

"He's a good man Alex, he would treat you well."

The only drawback of Megan's wedded bliss was that she was determined for Alex to have the same. Alex resigned herself to the same conversation they had every week. "I told you that I do not feel that way about Paul."

"Well, there are plenty of other eligible men around here that would be more than willing to take you on as a wife."

"I don't want anyone to *take me on* Megan. Plus, most of them would not want me as a wife anyway."

"That is not true." Alex refrained from arguing with her friend, they both knew that it *was* true. "Your father is gone Alex."

Alex was staggered; this was something that Megan never brought up, it was something that Alex never discussed. "I know that better than anyone!" she cried angrily.

"I'm just saying that he wouldn't want you, or Hugh, mourning him forever. It's been two years after all."

"I am well aware of that," Alex grated through her teeth. This wasn't a conversation she wanted to have, it upset her too much, however Megan seemed bent on continuing it.

"Or have either one of you getting hurt in an effort to exact revenge."

Alex almost stumbled over her feet, her mouth dropped open as she turned toward Megan. The happiness was gone from Megan's blue eyes as she scanned Alex's body. Alex's heart raced as Megan's eyes came back to her, suddenly sad, and knowing. "I don't know what you're talking about," Alex managed to choke out through her clogged throat.

Megan patted her hand again, gave her a half-hearted smile, and resumed strolling down the walkway. This time Alex was the one hurrying to catch up with her as her legs suddenly felt like wooden blocks. Megan *knew*, Alex was certain of that, somehow Megan had managed to divine that it was Alex and Hugh behind the robberies.

"We should get you a new dress for the dance next week," Megan said casually. Alex didn't know what to make of this abrupt change in conversation, so she didn't reply as Megan swung the door of the mercantile open. "We'll catch you a husband yet."

"I don't need a new dress, and I don't mean to catch a husband." Alex instinctively found her voice as they resumed their worn out and old argument.

"Of course you do, and since I can't buy anything for myself right now, you're going to let me buy something for you."

Alex shook her head so forcefully that it knocked her bonnet askew. She couldn't reach up to fix it, as her good arm was still hooked firmly through Megan's. Instead, she gingerly moved her hand up, undid the ribbons, and tugged it free. "You'll burn," Megan scolded.

"I think it's a little too shady in here for that."

Alex inhaled deeply; she loved the smell of the small store. Honey, oats, perfume, soap, leather, and a myriad of other scents all blended together to make the air almost refreshing. The store was cool compared to the outside and it took Alex's eyes a few seconds to adjust to the dim light. The only other person in the store was Suzanne Kensington, the daughter of the store's proprietor. Suzanne looked up as the bell signaled their entrance but no one exchanged pleasantries. Alex held Suzanne's glare before Megan gave her a tug toward the back of the store.

Alex followed behind as they passed by rows of jams, honeys, oats, flour, sugar and salt. Megan's step didn't falter as she bee-lined straight for the dresses. Alex sighed in resignation; she knew there would be no escape for her.

She chanced a glance back at Suzanne, but she had returned to flipping through the pages of whatever fashion magazine she had received this month. The familiar spark of dislike flowed through Alex as her eyes fixated upon the beautiful brunette. At one time, they had all been good friends, but that had changed when they were around the age of fourteen. When Suzanne had hit her teen years she had suddenly become mean spirited and cruel.

Megan swore it was because Suzanne was jealous of Alex, but Alex firmly disagreed. There was nothing to be jealous of after all. Suzanne was beautiful and there wasn't anything she wanted that she didn't get, including men. Suzanne's family was one of the wealthiest in the county. Alex's family had always struggled to make a profit from their wheat farming and their livestock. Things had actually started to become good for them, and they had finally started to turn a respectable profit when Murdock had arrived.

The unexplained thefts, and the deaths of their livestock had started to occur shortly after he moved into the area. Now they were fighting to survive again, a fact that had become worse since her father's untimely death. Unlike Suzanne there was no room for frivolities in her life, nor did she want there to be. She had never been one to covet new dresses, shoes, ribbons, or jewelry.

Even now, she would have rather been at home riding the fields with Hugh, than standing in front of a rack of dresses. Although, there would be no riding for her for awhile, she thought sourly, as she rubbed her damaged arm. Now that she knew the man she had shot was perfectly fine, her guilt wasn't quite as bad and she was beginning to resent the fact that he had put a bullet in her shoulder.

Megan pulled out a canary yellow dress that made Alex cringe even before Megan held it up to her and shook her head. Alex stood impatiently, tapping her foot as Megan held up a blue dress before sliding it back onto the rack. "Give your poor, extremely pregnant friend a little pleasure here Alex," Megan muttered as she lifted another yellow dress for Alex's approval.

"I don't want a new dress."

Megan slid the dress onto the rack. "You deserve a treat, and I'm sure that Hugh will agree with me. Besides, how else will you catch a husband?"

"Oh for goodness sakes Megan, let it go. I cannot leave Hugh to take care of the ranch, nor would I leave it. Why are you so determined to marry me off?"

Megan held up a forest green dress; she shook her head and returned it to the rack. The bell over the front door rang dimly in the distance as Megan pulled out a blue dress. "Maybe I aim to see you happy," Megan replied.

"I *am* happy," Alex insisted.

"Not like you used to be, besides maybe a husband will help tame your unruly ways," she mumbled.

Alex almost laughed but the sudden sadness in Megan's eyes stopped her. "That is not going to happen."

"That's what I'm afraid of. I can't lose you Alex."

She longed to wrap her arms around Megan and calm the sudden hurt in her eyes, but she couldn't do it with her bad arm. Instead, she settled for clasping hold of her friend's hand, and squeezing it. "You won't," she promised.

Megan took a deep breath as she pulled her hand away. "I am no bigger than last week Alex. You had no problem with hugging me then."

Alex inhaled harshly, unable to believe where this conversation was going. "Megan..."

"I know," she whispered as she moved closer to Alex.

"I don't know what you're talking..."

"Don't Alex, you've never lied to me before, don't start now. It was just time I told you that I *know* and that I'm concerned about you. I swear that if you get yourself killed I will never forgive you."

Megan's voice was so low that Alex had to strain to make out the words. When she did, tears sprang into her eyes. She blinked them away as she straightened away from her friend. Answering tears shimmered in Megan's eyes as she scanned Alex's face. "How?" Alex inquired in a hushed tone.

Megan wiped her tears away. "That man of Murdock's is asking about a slender, copper headed boy with green eyes, and a slender man with blue eyes. You are not the only redhead around here so I didn't immediately connect the two, until today. He said he shot the boy in the left shoulder." Megan's gaze went to Alex's shoulder, the arm that Megan hadn't taken hold of. "I know how you and Hugh feel about Murdock. It wasn't a difficult conclusion to come to."

Alex was stunned speechless as she gaped at Megan. Her mind spun as her belly cramped. "Has anyone else..."

"No, no one else even suspects, at least not that I've heard," Megan assured her. "They would never expect that a woman would be capable of aiding in the robberies, but they don't know you like I do. You put up a good front Alex, but I can see the anguish behind it. That man though, he won't give up, he is determined to find out who shot him."

Alex winced at the blatant reminder of the fact that she had shot a man. "I didn't mean too," she whispered fervently. "He had Hugh; I didn't know what else to do."

Megan nodded. "I know that Alex, I've heard the stories going around, you hate to kill flies for crying out loud let alone shoot someone. I am only saying that he will not give up, he interrogated me himself, and he's staying at Shelby's Tavern until he can find the robbers."

Alex swallowed heavily. If the man was staying at the tavern then there was a good chance they might run into him again. Alex felt the color drain from her face, and for a frightening instant she truly thought she might faint. She glanced around, but there was no one else near them. "The tavern?" she whispered.

"Yes. Of course I doubt he'll put two and two together, you are much too feminine looking for you to remind him of a boy if he should run across you."

"Still," she whispered, biting nervously into her lower lip. "We should go Megan."

"No, you *are* getting a new dress. Besides, the ladies over there love him; I doubt they've even let him out of bed yet for the day."

The color flooded back into Alex's face as quickly as it had left. Heat covered her from head to toe at the insinuation in Megan's statement. She knew all about the ladies at Shelby's, but still, to hear it put so bluntly was more than a little embarrassing. So was the fact that, for some strange reason, the thought disturbed her.

She had a sudden flash of golden eyes, bronzed skin, a chiseled handsome face, and a new flutter of disturbance shot through her entire system. It was an odd feeling, one that she had never experienced before, but it wasn't unpleasant. Then she recalled the deadly coldness of those eyes and she shivered involuntarily. How could those women not be scared of him when he was so obviously savage?

"They like him?" she choked out.

Megan laughed as she took in Alex's discomfort. "Another reason for you to marry Alex, you are truly missing out on the pleasures of a man."

"Megan!" Alex gasped, aghast at her friend's boldness.

Megan's laughter grew louder as she shook her head. "Oh, I am just teasing you, 'tis fun to do. But you *are* missing out you know." Megan went from laughing to serious at the drop of a hat as her hand clenched around Alex's. "Promise me that you will not put yourself in such peril again."

Megan stared up at her pleadingly, her grip almost bruising. Startled by Megan's abrupt change Alex remained unspeaking before squeezing Megan's hand. "I promise that there will be no more robberies," she swore.

Megan shook her head as she released Alex's hand and turned back to the rack. "That's not the same," she mumbled.

"Megan, he killed my father!" Alex hissed.

"I know that Alex, but your father wouldn't like you living in such a way. He would not like to see you so unhappy. I think this dress will do nicely."

Megan's mood was jumping around more than a tornado. Alex was having a tough time keeping up with her as Megan held up a pale lavender dress. "You confound me," Alex muttered.

Megan giggled. "Well you aggravate, annoy, and scare me half to death so we're even."

"Hardly," Alex snorted.

"I will not tell anyone," Megan vowed.

"I know you won't." Alex wrapped her good arm around her friend, and pulled her close for an embrace. She held her as she fought back tears of melancholy and dread. The last thing she intended was to put Megan in any kind of jeopardy, but now that she knew their secret, that was exactly what she was in.

CHAPTER 4

Jarett leaned across the counter of the mercantile and rested his arms on the glass surface as Suzanne flirted with him. She was a very attractive woman that oozed sex and she was well aware of that fact as she fluttered her curled black lashes at him and ran her finger across his arm. Knowing that the mercantile was the center of every town, he'd been coming in here every day for the past week. If Jarett was going to stumble across the boy, or if he happened to show up, this was the place that it would most likely happen.

It was the boy that he was gunning for the most. He had been a fool to think that the child wouldn't pull the trigger, and the one thing that he hated most was being made a fool of. He could have sworn that there had been innocence in the boy's eyes but he had been mistaken, a fact that hadn't happened often in his twenty-eight years.

However, it was exceptionally easy to read Suzanne. She leaned over the counter, displaying a good view of the plump breasts emphasized by her low cut dress. Although the dress was not as revealing as those worn by the women at Shelby's, it was enticing. Her full mouth parted as her chocolate eyes lazily perused him. If it had been any other time, Jarett may have been more aroused by this woman. Lately his thoughts were focused upon one thing and one thing only, finding the bastard that had shot him.

"Sorry handsome no redheaded boys today, unless of course, you count Alex," she purred.

Jarett's body became rigid as adrenaline shot through his veins. "Who's Alex?" he demanded brusquely.

Suzanne's eyes flashed with annoyance before she hastily covered the emotion up. "Alexandra Harris," she drawled as bitterly as if she'd just been forced to swallow lemon juice.

Jarett was instantly amused and intrigued. Until now, Suzanne had always played sweet and desirable. Underneath it though, he had sensed a conniving, manipulative woman who would do anything to get her way. He wondered about this girl that had finally caused Suzanne's perfect exterior to slip a little.

"Who is she?" he inquired.

Suzanne shrugged as she smiled sweetly and trailed her finger over his jaw. Jarett made no attempt to stop her, but he despised her touch. If Suzanne even suspected that she didn't have him wrapped around her finger as much as she thought she did, she would refuse to help him, and until he found his prey, he needed her help.

"No one for you to concern yourself with," she purred.

Jarett was growing more amused by the second. No matter how she tried, Suzanne couldn't keep her animosity at bay. Soft laughter turned his attention from her as an obviously pregnant woman came into view. Walking beside her was another woman with copper colored hair that hung over her shoulder in a thick braid that dangled at her waist. At the moment the woman's face was even redder than her hair. He recognized the pregnant woman; he had questioned her earlier in the week, but the other one he didn't know.

Jarett found himself fascinated by the girl as she ducked her head. Her hair shone like fire in the dim sunlight that filtered through the windows. It was the same color that the boy's hair had been but this woman was obviously no boy. She moved with grace, her rounded hips swayed in the modest walking dress she wore. The bodice clung to the swell of her full breasts but the scooped neckline was much too demure to reveal any hint of their flesh.

The pregnant woman, Mrs. Malloy he recalled, glanced up at him. Her eyes widened, her tiny mouth parted on a gasp as she abruptly stopped walking. The other woman stopped and turned toward her friend. "Megan, are you all right, it's not time is it?" she demanded.

Jarett frowned in puzzlement as his gaze met the obviously troubled pregnant woman's. "No, no," she said hastily and turned to her friend. "Just a small contraction is all."

Her gaze fell from Jarett's as she put her hand to her belly. "We must get you home!" The redhead said anxiously.

"No, 'tis fine I assure you, I've had them before."

Alex frowned at Megan; she knew there was something truly wrong with her. Megan had become as white as a ghost; a sudden chill swept down Alex's spine. She knew then that Megan was lying, that there had been no contraction. Alex took a deep breath to steady herself, she could feel his presence now, feel his eyes boring into the back of her head.

"Oh God," she whispered.

"Just false pains," Megan said, more loudly than necessary. "Come now, there is no reason to fret."

Alex stared pleadingly at Megan, she was certain that she couldn't do this. How could she possibly face the man that she had shot, and still act completely normal? "Are you sure?" she asked anxiously.

"Yes, yes," Megan said, squeezing her hand in an attempt to offer her a little comfort.

Alex straightened her shoulders and forced herself to turn back around. Those honey hued eyes immediately latched onto hers. Alex fought back a gasp of alarm as they seemed to bore straight into her soul, strip her bare, and reveal every horrible deed she had ever done.

For a minute she was too astonished to even breathe, let alone move. He was much the way she remembered, larger and more handsome than any man she'd ever encountered. There was also a remote air about him that she'd never encountered with anyone else. Even without a gun in his hand, she was certain that this man could kill anyone he chose if the mood so struck him. Judging by the look of him the mood struck him often.

His eyes leisurely scanned over her body, he studied her with a look that was both inquisitive and lustful. Alex shuddered as trepidation, and something that warmed her from head to toe, tore through her in equal measure. Pinned by the ravenous gleam in his eyes, she stood completely still as his gaze came back to hers and a cynical smile twisted his full lips. Resentment surged forward to drown out all of the other emotions rocketing through her.

Jarett enjoyed every second of his perusal of the magnificent woman before him. Her slender waist, gently flaring hips, and long legs were entirely enticing. A rush of heat blazed into his loins, hardening him instantly as he looked over her splendid figure again. He knew that beneath the modest gown was a body designed for bedding, a body that could give a man many, many hours of pleasure.

Meeting her gaze again, he was surprised to notice the color that spread through her cheeks, even as her eyes sparked with anger. Beautiful eyes that looked hauntingly familiar, but could not possibly belong to the person he sought. However, they were the same vivid emerald color, and they even seemed to hold that same odd glint of innocence. An innocence that was both intriguing, and disconcerting.

There was no way that a woman that looked like that was in the least bit innocent. For not only was her body perfection, but so was her face. Her beguiling eyes were fringed by black lashes that contrasted strikingly against the copper of her hair as they swept toward deep brown, finely defined eyebrows. Her nose was small and a little pointed, her cheekbones high and elegant.

But her best feature, besides her eyes, was her mouth. It was full and luscious, even when compressed into a disapproving line, as it was now. It was a mouth that would arouse lustful images in any man, and he wasn't immune to them. It was a mouth specifically designed for kissing, designed for wrapping around a man's cock...

Jarett cut the thought off abruptly as he realized the treacherous turn that his thoughts had taken. He was already becoming unbearably hard, which was a little unsettling considering the fact that he had been so completely unaffected by Suzanne, or even the more willing and less conniving women at Shelby's. But even more unsettling was that his thoughts had veered sharply off of his intended goal. Especially now when he suspected that this woman might just be an important clue, if not the key in his mission.

"Are you going to buy that?" Suzanne asked rudely.

The woman that had captured his attention tilted her chin as she turned toward Suzanne. He read the same animosity in her gaze that he'd heard in Suzanne's voice, and he realized that this must be the disliked Alexandra Harris. Alexandra made her way forward, careful of her friend's ungainly step. Mrs. Malloy laid a violet dress on the counter.

"For you Megan?" Suzanne inquired sweetly. Megan ducked her head as the hair on Alex's neck rose. She knew that patently sugary tone of Suzanne's voice. It was the one she always used before her claws came out. "Hoping to regain your girlish figure soon after birth?"

Alex forgot all about the man behind her as she focused upon the witch before her. She didn't care what Suzanne said about her, she never had. For some reason though, Suzanne had decided to focus her animosity on Megan, who had always been a little self-conscious about her normally plump figure.

"It's for Alex," Megan explained.

Suzanne smiled smugly as her chocolate eyes turned to Alex. "Oh, silly me," she replied. "I just never expected Alexandra to buy a new dress. It's been such a long time after all." Alex bit on her bottom lip, forcing herself not to say anything as she tried to remain calm. "If I do recall, it was right before your father died."

The color drained from Alex's face as Megan inhaled sharply. She and Suzanne may have traded barbs in the past, but there were places that Suzanne was not supposed to go, certain subjects that should always be off limits. But for some reason, Suzanne's claws were exceptionally lethal today and she seemed determined to draw blood. Alex took a shaky breath as she forced herself to maintain some semblance of control.

"Suzanne," Megan said quietly.

Suzanne tossed her deep brown hair back as she flashed that innocent smile again and began to neatly wrap the dress in tissue paper. "What's it been Alex, two years? Yes, it has, hasn't it? Such an unfortunate incident, you must miss him terribly."

Jarett watched and listened with a mask of indifference on his face, but inside he was beginning to seethe. It had been obvious earlier that Suzanne didn't like Alexandra, and it appeared that Mrs. Malloy was included in that dislike. However, he had a feeling that this conversation was even more antagonistic than usual. The sudden pallor of Alexandra's face, the firm set of her shoulders and the compression of her mouth were enough proof of that. The look of utter horror and hopelessness on Mrs. Malloy's face only confirmed it.

He noted the cruel curve of Suzanne's mouth and the smugness in her brown eyes as she bent behind the counter. He knew that a lot of this conversation was because of him. Suzanne had assumed that she had him wrapped around her finger, but she was too astute not to have noticed the way he had been staring at Alexandra.

"Such a shame," Suzanne muttered. "Now, where are those boxes?"

Alex was certain Suzanne knew exactly where those boxes were but was just trying to draw out her torment. Megan looked absolutely miserable as she shot glances back and forth between Suzanne and Alex, her tiny hand gripped Alex's arm.

"Of course you know how sorry I was to hear about it," Suzanne continued.

"Please hurry Suzanne, Daryl is waiting for me," Megan said hastily.

"I know the boxes were right here," Suzanne replied absently. "I can't believe that Hugh is allowing you to buy a dress Alex. I know how tight things must have been for you both since your father died."

"I'm buying it for her," Megan interjected. "For the dance next week. It's my birthday gift for her."

Alex silently thanked Megan. The last thing she needed was Suzanne spouting off about how poor they were while she was buying a new dress. They didn't keep the money they stole but distributed it among the distressed farms and ranches in the area. They only kept enough to replace the stolen or dead livestock on their property and the damaged crops. It still wasn't enough, but neither she nor Hugh were in the least bit interested in making a profit off of Murdock. They were only interested in ruining him.

However, if this man's suspicions were aroused enough, she didn't put it past him to put two and two together and pin her as the boy who had shot him. He seemed far too ruthless not to figure it out. The thought of what he would do to her if he did find out made her legs weak.

"That is so kind of you! A bit late as your birthday was last month, wasn't it Alex?" Suzanne inquired.

"It was, but the dance is this month," Megan replied.

"How thoughtful of you. Lord only knows how much Alexandra deserves it. I mean she works so much at the ranch that it's no surprise she has no time to behave like a proper lady."

Alex's forehead furrowed as she tried to figure out if Suzanne was trying to insult her. She found nothing wrong with working at the ranch. In fact, she was proud that she could rope, ride, and shoot better than most men. She exchanged a glance with Megan who seemed just as confused as she was. Then, a gleam came into Megan's merry blue eyes and she started to chuckle. Suzanne shot her a perplexed look from behind the counter. Megan assumed a look of innocence as she attempted to stifle her laughter.

Behind them both, Jarett was growing just as amused as Megan. Suzanne looked highly disgruntled. It was obvious to him that Alexandra had no idea that Suzanne had been trying to take away some of her womanly appeal in Jarett's eyes by claiming she behaved more like a man than a proper woman.

Oddly enough, her statement did quite the opposite, which was unexpected. He had always liked his women delicate, dainty, and very proper, in public at least. But Suzanne's statement, the bonnet clutched in Alexandra's hand, and her tanned skin showed him that this woman was anything but proper, and she didn't give a rat's ass what anyone else thought of her.

It intrigued him that such a beautiful young woman had not a care for clothes and other finery, but seemed more concerned about the ranch that her father had left behind. It was also clear to him that Mrs. Malloy had caught on as she sent a glance toward him, and placed her hand over her mouth in order to stifle another giggle.

Suzanne finally pulled the boxes out from beneath the counter. Alex breathed a sigh of relief as her shoulders slumped. She couldn't believe that for all of Suzanne's words her biggest insult had been that Alex worked the ranch. That wasn't something she was ashamed of, although she was well aware that many proper women would be.

However, she had been raised to help at the ranch. Her father had never been able to resist her when she pleaded for something, and she had constantly pestered him to take her out with him and Hugh. He had finally relented to her requests and allowed her to start working the ranch with them when she was nine.

She still didn't understand what Suzanne was trying to do, but Megan obviously did, so she would be informed as soon as they left the mercantile. Suzanne lifted the dress, placed it in the box, and smoothed down the pleats. "Then again, if your father hadn't been so foolish as to shoot himself, you and Hugh wouldn't have to worry so much."

The floor dropped out from under Alex, the world tilted alarmingly around her as everything in sight suddenly became blurred. Nausea rolled through her as a myriad of vivid, bloody images exploded in her head. They caused her whole body to tremble and tears to burn her eyes as she fought to see.

"Alex!" Megan cried.

Jarett took a swift step forward as he realized that Alexandra seemed about to faint. Placing a hand soothingly against the small of her back, he was shocked to feel the shudders that wracked her delicate spine. The look on her face was one of absolute devastation as her curling lashes blinked back the sheen of water in her eyes. For the first time in years, Jarett actually felt sorry for another human being.

He lifted his head to glower at Suzanne. She had done this because of him; he knew that. When her other insults hadn't appeared to affect Alexandra, or him, Suzanne had gone for something truly hurtful. The worst thing about the whole situation was that Alexandra seemed to have no idea why the little vixen had done it. Suzanne pasted a look of utter innocence on her face as she leaned across the counter and rested her hand upon Alexandra's arm.

"Alex, I'm sorry, I didn't mean to upset you."

To his amazement, Alexandra threw the woman's hand off, lifted her chin and leveled Suzanne with a stare that would have made many a grown man wither inside. Suzanne, however, maintained a look of utter innocence. "Don't touch me!" Alexandra spat.

Jarett could feel the tremors still running through her body, but he was fairly certain that it was sheer anger that shook her now. "I didn't mean to offend you," Suzanne protested.

"I don't know why you hate me so much, nor do I particularly care, but if you ever say one word about my father again I will rip that cruel tongue out of your mouth! Do you hear me?" Alex hissed.

Alex was fighting not to leap over the counter and throttle the vicious woman right now. For the first time, Suzanne actually revealed a true emotion as she took a fearful step back. Alex spun on her heel; she was certain that if she stayed one second more she would attack Suzanne.

She slammed right into something solid. It was only then that she realized the stranger had still been standing behind her and that his hand had been resting in the small of her back. Alex had completely forgotten he was even here. She had been right though; he was a good head and shoulders taller than her as she had to tilt her head back in order to meet his gaze. She was startled to find eyes that reminded her of leaves in the autumn staring down at her with a mixture of curiosity and unsettling concern.

Alex's breath left her. The heat of his body burned away her ire. He was so close to her that she could see the black bristles along his square jaw, smell his tantalizing scent of leather and soap. Never in her life had she been so aware of a male before. It frightened her as much as it enthralled her. It reawakened the new sensation that he had stirred in her earlier as her body remained pressed against his. She pondered what his lips would feel like against hers, what his fingers would feel like running through her hair and over her skin.

Then she recalled exactly who this man was, why he was here, and what she had done to him. Her heart slammed against her ribs as panic tore through her.

Jarett watched in amazement as the annoyance fled her eyes. She stared up at him with a mixture of confusion that rapidly turned toward desire. He saw it bloom in the crystal green depths of her eyes, turning them a darker shade of emerald. Yet the confusion remained, as well as that amazing depth of innocence that fascinated him. Then fear spurted forth, it cleared her eyes before she lowered her gaze.

"I uh… I'm sorry," she stammered. Though she wasn't apologizing for bumping into him, but for shooting him, although she still had no idea where. She couldn't see any place on him that appeared to have been damaged by a bullet, and yet she was sure that she had shot him, everyone said so. She stepped to the side, cast Megan a pleading glance, then turned and strode toward the door.

"Don't forget your dress Alex!" Suzanne called after her.

Alex didn't bother to reply as she hurried from the mercantile. She was desperate to escape the suddenly tiny store and the disturbingly large, revenge-seeking man.

Desperate to escape from the distress and longing he provoked in equal measures. Thrusting the screen door open she stepped onto the shadowed sidewalk and slumped against the wall. She gratefully inhaled the fresh air in heaping gulps.

"What is the matter with you?" Megan demanded the instant Alexandra was out the door. Jarett smiled in amusement as she planted her hands on her plump hips and glared at Suzanne.

"What?" Suzanne inquired.

"Don't you dare *what* me Suzanne! I've known for years what a wretched person you are, but that was the most despicable thing I have ever seen anyone do! I never thought that even you could stoop to such levels!"

"I don't know who you think you're talking too..."

"I'm talking to you!" Megan snapped. "There is only so far jealousy can go Suzanne, you have severely crossed the line today and you know it. You should be ashamed of yourself! Why I, I have never been so disgusted with someone in my entire life!"

With that, the extremely pregnant woman spun on her heel. Jarett grabbed her arm as she wobbled unsteadily for a second. She cast him a grateful smile before moving away as fast as her legs would carry her ungainly body. Jarett's amusement over her display of temper and defense of her friend vanished when she left the store.

"Of all the nerve," Suzanne muttered. She turned back to him with beguiling eyes. "Everyone knows about her father, I didn't think it would upset her so much."

"Yes you did," he replied crisply. "I can assure you that if that little display was for my benefit, it didn't work."

Her mouth dropped open as Jarett tipped his hat to her and strolled out of the store.

CHAPTER 5

"You shouldn't have said that Megan," Alex said when Megan appeared at her side.

"You heard me?" she asked as she glanced anxiously up and down the empty boardwalk.

"Oh yes," Alex replied with a smile. "You weren't exactly quiet."

"Yes well, she deserved it."

"She's going to hate you as much as me now, you don't deserve that."

Megan's chin tilted up. "She had no right."

"She doesn't know what you know."

"Are you defending her?" Megan gasped incredulously.

"No, of course not! I'm just saying that she doesn't know the truth."

Megan closed her eyes and tossed back her flaxen curls as she shook her head. "Never mind that, are you all right?"

Alex nodded, she felt anything but all right, but it wasn't Suzanne that upset her so much now. Now it was the man still inside with Suzanne. Alex stopped breathing as the screen door pushed open and he stepped outside. If he hadn't already seen her, she would have turned and bolted for safety. As it was, his icy stare pinned her to the spot, making it impossible for her to move.

The door slammed shut as he made his way toward them. Alex braced herself, she was uncertain what to expect from him. Inside the mercantile she had seen a flash of a compassionate man, but it had been so brief that she was beginning to think she might have imagined it. He stopped before them; his hat shadowed his brow as he surveyed her impassively.

"Do you feel better miss?" he inquired.

Alex swallowed heavily before answering. "Yes."

She did appear calmer to him now but before he could respond an enthusiastic voice interrupted him.

"Alexandra! I am so glad that I ran into you today."

Alex's head shot around as the familiar voice caught her attention. Beside her, Megan groaned as Henry barreled toward them. His haggard face was florid and his bloodshot brown eyes gleamed with excitement. Henry's gray hair was matted to his forehead; his spectacles had slid down his sweaty nose to perch precariously on the large, bulbous end. His breath reeked of alcohol, the scent of it oozed from his pores but she was well accustomed to the smell and didn't wrinkle her nose as everyone else did when he approached. Alex winced as he grasped hold of her hands, drawing them briskly forward and pulling at her injured shoulder.

Sweat broke out on her brow but she didn't think the stitches were torn. "It is good to see you too Henry."

He cast an abashed look at the two people behind her. "Megan, Mr. Stanton, how do you fair today?" he asked in his loud, high-pitched voice.

So the stranger's name was Mr. Stanton and he seemed to be making himself well known in town. A shudder ran through her as she thought about the degree of determination that revealed. Her mind was spinning as Megan and Mr. Stanton quickly answered Henry.

"Good, good. I suppose you wouldn't mind if I borrowed Alex for a bit?" Henry gushed on.

"Of course not," Megan replied.

Alex had no choice but to follow as Henry hooked his arm through her bad one, took hold of her hand, and pulled her forward. She was well used to Henry's overabundance of energy, and normally didn't mind it, but her arm was screaming in protest. She had to force herself not to rip her hand away from him. They turned the corner and he led her down the road to the cramped and leaning shack that he occupied behind the blacksmith's forge.

Flinging the door open he hurried her inside. When he finally relinquished her hand and arm, she released a breath of relief as it fell back to her side. She moved it tenderly back and forth to make sure that it wasn't bleeding before she focused her attention on the tiny shack. Henry did odd and end jobs like sweeping, running errands, and sometimes working in the kitchen at Shelby's tavern. He was content to work there for free drinks and enough money to buy some food.

There was never any money left over for luxuries and it showed in the sparse shack. Bottles of whiskey, some half full, some empty, lined the floor and had been kicked into the corners of the room. There were no lanterns or candles, the blanket on the cot was threadbare, and the place had the permanent aroma of sour booze.

This time Alex did wrinkle her nose as she walked around the room to thrust open the four tiny windows.

"Alex, don't worry yourself with that."

"Henry, you cannot expect me to sit in this room with you without some fresh air."

He snorted unhappily as she gathered the liquor bottles and dumped them into the large barrel outside the door. They had been going through this same ritual at least once a month for the past five years, ever since Henry's son, Charlie, had moved to California in the hopes of finding gold. Alex and Hugh had been good friends with Charlie, but Hugh had no patience for his drunken father. Alex had become like a daughter to Henry over the years. When her father had been killed, Henry had been a shoulder that she could cry on.

She made the bed and cast Henry a scolding look when he sighed impatiently. "I wish you would stop drinking so much Henry."

He reddened, as he always did, and shrugged. Picking up his soiled clothes Alex dumped them in a pile by the door. She would drop them off at Shelby's for Rachael to launder before she headed home. She glanced around the now tidy shack. It still stank of alcohol, was still unbelievably dingy but this was what Henry was happy with. She had tried many times to get him to change, to help him, but he was set in his ways.

"Come now, you must read me my letter," Henry urged.

Alex couldn't help but smile as she took Charlie's letter from Henry and settled into the wobbly chair in the corner.

***

"Isn't that the man that works at Shelby's?" Jarett inquired. He watched as the man disappeared around the corner with Alexandra nearly running to keep up with him.

"Yes. If you were planning on questioning Alex today Mr. Stanton, you have just lost your chance," Mrs. Malloy said.

Jarett turned back to her. "Why is that?"

"When Henry gets a hold of her, he's loathe to part with her again."

Jarett scowled ferociously, what a woman as beautiful as Alex saw in the tiny little drunk was beyond him, and he didn't particularly care. He frowned as he glanced down at the sidewalk again and realized that he *did* care. What was she doing with the man? They couldn't be sleeping together, well maybe they could, but he highly doubted it.

Footsteps on the boardwalk alerted him to the approach of two people. He turned to see a tall, lean brunette man with dark blue eyes, and a somewhat shorter blond man. The brunette's eyes were hostile as they landed on him. "Are you Murdock's man?" he demanded abruptly.

Jarett's temper instantly swelled to the forefront as he returned the man's glare. "I am no one's man," he replied coldly.

The brunette's scowl deepened. "Are you the man that was shot?"

Jarett was fighting against the urge to drive his fist into the man's arrogant face but it could turn the townspeople against him. He needed the help of the people in town if he was going to find out who had shot him. The only problem was that none of the townspeople seemed to be willing to help.

He was beginning to agree with Murdock, that it was someone in the community stealing from him, for they all seemed to hate the man. The minute he mentioned that he was trying to find the thieves, the people he questioned closed up tighter than clams. The only one who had been a little helpful was Suzanne and he had just burned that bridge.

His thoughts immediately returned to Alex, she was the best lead that he had. She was the female version of his thief; the boy he sought could quite possibly be a brother of hers. Unfortunately, she had just slipped through his fingers.

Cursing inwardly, he returned his attention to the men in front of him. He knew the blond man's name was Paul but he hadn't met the other one yet. His eyes narrowed as he took in the blue eyes and brown hair. The only problem was that a good portion of this town had the same color eyes and hair but the build was the same as one of the thieves.

Jarett studied the man more carefully; he very well could be the other thief he was looking for. The lips compressed into a firm line would have been completely obscured by the bandanna. He tried to recall the shape of the face and the upper bridge of the nose but it was only a blur. He supposed the high cheekbones and aquiline nose of the man across from him could have belonged to the thief but he couldn't be sure.

"Yes. Who are you?" he demanded.

"What business is that of yours?" the man retorted.

There was something about this man that was a little too hostile. "You fit the description of one of the thieves I'm looking for."

The man didn't even flinch, his eyes didn't waver, but Jarett's instincts were screaming at him that this was the man. "So do many others," he replied before turning away dismissively. "Megan, where is Alex?"

"Henry found her."

The man pulled his hat off and ran his fingers through his hair. "Great, we're going to be here all day now," he muttered.

"You could always go retrieve her," Paul suggested.

Jarett didn't miss the look of hopefulness that crossed Paul's features and lit his eyes. Apparently he would have more than the old man for competition if he decided to distract himself a little by pursuing her. He had no idea what kind of relationship the brunette man had with Alex; maybe they were married. He hadn't seen a ring on Alex's hand though and there wasn't one on the brunette's either. Siblings maybe, but they didn't really look anything alike.

How many men did Alexandra have in her life? He thought sourly.

"No, let's leave them be," the brunette said.

"Sure wouldn't mind knowing what they do over there," Paul said as he rubbed at his chin.

"Wouldn't we all," Megan said. "But trying to get it out of Alex is like trying to grab a star from the sky."

Jarett could guess at what they were doing over there but he didn't think his guess was right, which made him only more curious to know.

"Let's go over to Shelby's and wait for her there. I could use a few pints anyway. Would you like us to walk you home Megan?" his suspect asked.

"No, here comes Daryl now, though he'll probably drop me off at the doorstep and rush off to join you two," she replied.

"If you let him out," Paul teased.

"Of course I will; it gets him out of my hair for an hour or two. He's driving me crazy now with all of his fussing."

Paul and the other man were grinning when Daryl, a short, sandy blond haired man stepped onto the walk. "What is so funny?" he demanded as he wrapped his arm around his wife's round middle.

"Nothing at all darling," Megan replied happily.

Daryl frowned as he studied his wife. "I think you've been outside long enough, why don't I take you home?"

Megan rolled her eyes and stroked his cheek lovingly. "Yes dear. He'll be joining you boys shortly."

The suspect and Paul walked away without looking back at Jarett, Megan and Daryl crossed the street and went in the opposite direction. Jarett remained where he was as he debated what to do next. Alex would be meeting his suspect at Shelby's later. He could always follow them over there now, he was staying there after all, so it wouldn't be overly suspicious if he went back to have a few drinks and relax.

However, his quarry would still be there, waiting for Alex to arrive later on. Why would she be going to Shelby's in the first place? He'd thought her a respectable enough woman in the mercantile, but it seemed as if he had just met three of her men in less than five minutes. One of which was his best suspect, and she was definitely the best lead to his main quarry.

Growing more intrigued by the second, he glanced back to where Alex had disappeared. Curiosity winning out, he decided to investigate what she was doing with the old man and to follow her from there. One thing was for sure, if she were his, he would know exactly what she was doing and whom she was doing it with. He wouldn't simply walk away and leave her to her own devices.

CHAPTER 6

At first Jarett didn't know where they had gone and then he spotted the shack. The over flowing liquor bottles in the large barrel by the front door told him that it was the right place. He forced himself not to limp; he refused to show such weakness no matter how much his leg hurt, as he moved forward soundlessly. He told himself that the only reason he was doing this was because he was determined to question Alex. He was certain that she was involved in the robberies through one of her brothers, or through the brunette that had been looking for her.

However, as he stepped up to the side of the building he realized that he didn't know how he would react if he heard them making love in there. It was doubtful but still he hesitated, uncertain if he should go any farther. He was intruding on her privacy. Then he heard her voice and he found that he was unable to stop himself from moving forward as it flowed melodically out the open window.

"Send my regards to Alex, Hugh, Paul, Daryl, and Megan. Love always, your son Charlie."

Jarett's brow furrowed as he stepped closer to the building and tried to discern what he had just heard. He shifted his weight off of his wounded leg. It had been much better for the past two days, but when he stood up for too long it began to throb. He leaned gingerly against the wooden shack to keep it from groaning under his added weight.

"Do you really think he will come for a visit?" Henry asked anxiously.

Alex folded the letter and placed it on the nightstand. "He said that he would."

"When do you think he will come?"

Alex warmed at the eagerness in Henry's bloodshot eyes. She hadn't seen him look this happy in years; she knew how much he missed Charlie. For all his faults, Henry dearly loved his son. He'd always enjoyed a nip of whiskey but his drinking hadn't gotten out of control until after Charlie left. Alex knew it was because Henry was lonely but he would never admit it.

"Hopefully soon, we would all like to see Charlie again," she told him.

Henry was spryer than Alex had seen him in years as he hopped to his feet. "We must write him at once and find out!" He cried as he dug through his small nightstand. He pulled out a piece of paper and a fountain pen. "It has been so long!"

Alex didn't miss the note of melancholy in his voice as he handed her the supplies. She placed them on the bed before squeezing his hand. "Henry, you are more than welcome to stay with Hugh and I. Lord knows we could use the extra help."

"Rubbish, the two of you are more than capable of running that place."

"Yes but there is so much that we need help with. Crops always have to be tended. The fences forever require mending; livestock is always missing, or dying."

Henry snorted as he released her hand and settled in his chair. "Well, we all know the reasons for that Alexandra and there isn't anything that I can do to help with that problem."

"No, but you can help us with the aftermath, please think about it Henry. It would mean so much to me."

"Have I said yes to you yet?" he inquired.

"No, but I can always hope that one of these days you'll come to your senses and change your mind."

"Isn't going to happen gal, I'm set in my ways. Now let's find out when Charlie is coming."

Alex bent over the paper as Henry began to recite what he wanted to tell Charlie. When he got to the part about Megan being as big as house, she cut in. “Megan will have my head if she ever found out I wrote that!” she protested.

“You didn’t tell her you do this for me, did you?” he demanded. His wrinkled face tensed with anxiety.

“No, of course not, I promised you that I wouldn’t tell anyone and I haven’t, but well… I just can’t write that to Charlie.”

“Oh, very well, just tell him that she’s about ready to pop.”

“Henry!”

He laughed happily as he slapped his boney knee. Alex gave him a scolding look, but refrained from further reprimand. When he finally stopped laughing, he wiped the tears from his eyes and continued with his letter.

Jarett remained outside as he listened to the conversation. The more he heard, the more he felt like a bastard. He had briefly contemplated the idea of Alex sleeping with this man, but she was reading him letters and writing letters in return to his son Charlie. It was becoming clearer to him that their relationship was more like that of a father and a daughter.

His confusion about this woman continued to mount. He had seen Alex and felt the stunning effect of her beauty. A woman that looked like her was fit to be a queen. Yet, according to everything he’d heard she worked like a man and was far from pampered in any way.

Not only that, but there wasn’t a woman he could think of that would take the time to sit down with an old drunk, read and write his letters, and talk with him. She had even invited the man to come and live with her, and Hugh, whom he thought might be the elusive sibling he sought.

Plus, she was keeping her reasons for being in the shack a secret. No one knew what she did in there, and he was certain that many of the townspeople had suspected the same thing as him about their meetings. Still, instead of explaining what she did while in Henry's company, she kept Henry's secret that he could neither read nor write. Her relationship with the old man must have put her reputation at stake and started rumors and gossip. He knew how small towns worked; there was no way it hadn't.

The more he found out about her, the more intrigued and amazed he became. Jarett moved carefully away from the wall as chairs scraped and good-byes were exchanged. Moving back to the boardwalk, he leaned against the brick wall of the bank to await her arrival. He didn't have to wait long before she came around the corner. Her head was bent against the bright sun; her discarded bonnet hung from her dress pocket and an armload of filthy clothes was pressed against her chest.

She turned the corner and collided with him as he moved to block her path. With a startled cry, she took a stumbling step back and dropped the clothes. Jarett grabbed her arm to steady her before she fell over. Her skin was as soft as silk and he couldn't stop himself from caressing it briefly with his thumb. Lust slammed into him, hardening him instantly as her full mouth parted and her breath froze in her chest.

The moment was broken when she pulled her arm away. "I am sorry Mr. Stanton, I wasn't paying attention to where I was going," she apologized.

"It's my fault; I was trying to stop you."

Anxiety curled through Alex to push out that strange sensation she experienced whenever she was near this man. Now, with those words, he had reminded her of who he was. There could never be anything between them, not like she really wanted there to be anyway, her life was complicated enough without adding a man to it.

"Why?" she inquired.

“I’m sure you’ve heard that I’ve been asking around about the robberies.”

“Yes, I have.” Alex bent to gather Henry’s laundry in an attempt to distract herself from his presence, and his questions. When he bent down to help her gather them, she tried to shoo him away. “No, Mr. Stanton, they’re...” Alex’s face flushed as she tried to tell him that the clothes were filthy, but she couldn’t bring herself to say something bad about Henry.

Jarett held on as she tried to pull the clothes from his hands. They had a brief tug of war over a pair of overalls before she finally relented. When her eyes came back to his, he saw the protective gleam in them and he understood completely what she had been about to say. He fought the urge to wrinkle his nose and kept his face blank as he helped her to gather the smelly garments.

A tiny smile curved the corner of her luscious mouth as her gaze briefly met his again, approval and thanks shone in her eyes. For a second he couldn’t move. That smile had caused a stream of emotions to burst through him with yearning taking a strong lead. He suddenly had to learn everything he could about this woman; she intrigued him like no other he’d ever met. Her delicate appearance was completely deceiving. This woman was strong, proud, protective, and completely unpretentious.

Gathering the remaining clothes within his arms, he tried desperately to ignore the awful stench emanating from them. She hesitated before rising to stand beside him. He didn’t know how she could stand to be so close to the clothes when it was taking all he had not to gag from the stench.

“Thank you,” she said. “But you really don’t have to carry those.”

She attempted to take Henry’s clothes back; she knew that the smell had to be bothering him, even though he showed no signs of it. Many people, including Megan and Hugh, didn't understand her relationship with Henry. They surely wouldn't help her with his laundry, and if they did, they would complain every second of the time it took for them to help. That this man, this *stranger*, did not complain in the slightest was a fact that amazed her.

"That's okay, miss. You're still carrying quite a load."

"You're very kind Mr. Stanton."

Jarett was flabbergasted, no one had ever called him kind, nor was he even remotely close to being kind. "Trust me miss, I am anything but kind," he grated through his teeth.

Alex blinked at the sudden harshness that filled his face. Just a second ago there had been warmth in his eyes, maybe even a bit of compassion. Now, they were golden shards of ice. They were the same eyes of the man who had shot her. Alex shivered as she hastily averted her gaze from his.

"Where are you taking these?" he demanded gruffly, irritated by the effect that her comment had had on him. The girl was confounding to him in more ways than one. He was wading into dangerous territory here; territory that he'd had no intention of finding himself in.

"Shelby's."

Jarett's brows drew together as he realized that was why the two men had said they would meet her there. "Let's go then." She fell into step beside him, her head was down as they moved briskly down the boardwalk. "Do you have a brother miss?"

Her head shot up as she gazed at him in alarm. "Why yes, I do."

Jarett felt his heartbeat speed up in anticipation. He was close; he knew it. Her brother had to be the one that he was looking for. "Is he in town with you?"

Alex frowned at him as she tried to figure out where this line of questioning was going. "Yes, he is. Why do you ask?"

"May I meet him?"

Alex felt dread building in the pit of her stomach. This was definitely bad; she knew that in every fiber of her being. However, there wasn't any way that she could tell him no without raising his suspicions further. "Of course, I'm sure he's around here somewhere. This way."

Jarett turned to follow her down a small alley beside Shelby's. The surrounding buildings cast the alley into shadows, causing it to be much cooler than the street. The sounds of banging pots and pans reverberated against the walls. The heady scent of meat, potatoes, and baking bread wafted through the air and caused his stomach to rumble.

Alex was balancing the laundry in her arms when he reached around her to pull the screen door open. She hurried into the kitchen of Shelby's and called hello to Martha and Polly before making her way down a shadowed side hall that was cooler than the kitchen. She was aware of his presence behind her with every step she took. The heat of his body, so near hers, was having a strange effect on her. Inside, she was still nervous over taking him to meet Hugh, but his body heat was making her heart race with unfamiliar excitement.

After what seemed like an eternity, but couldn't have been more than a minute, she made it to the laundry room. Rachel glanced up at her and grimaced when she spotted the clothes in her arms. Then, Rachel's gaze darted over her head and a saucy smile curved her mouth. "Jarett, what on earth are you doing here?"

"Just helping with this load," he replied casually.

Rachel looked like he could have knocked her over with a finger. Then her eyes settled on Alex and she began to smile knowingly. Alex's eyes bounced between them, but though they knew each other they didn't seem *overly* familiar with one other. Not like it would matter, she told herself firmly, she didn't give one fig what he did in his spare time.

Jarett didn't say anymore as Rachel was beginning to look as if she were trying not to laugh out loud. "I assume they're Henry's," Rachel said.

"They are," Alex confirmed as she walked over and dropped the clothes on the center island.

"I'll have these washed and cleaned before Henry comes in tonight," Rachel promised.

"Thank you Rachel."

Rachel patted her arm as she gathered some of the clothes and turned to dump them into a vat of hot water. "Hugh poked his head in a little while ago, looking for you. He's in the tavern."

"Hugh's in the tavern?" Alex forgot all about the man behind her as Rachel dropped that bombshell. Her brother never went into the tavern, especially when she was around.

"He's over there with Paul and Daryl."

Alex frowned before an idea occurred to her and she began to smile. She had always speculated what went on in there, what it was like. Now, she would be able to have her curiosity satisfied. "I guess I'll have to go get him then."

"That isn't a good idea Alex." She ignored Rachel's caution with a wave of her hand. Her mind was already on what she would see when she got over there. "He told me to tell you to wait here if you showed up. He's going to be back in a few minutes."

"That's all right," Alex replied as she moved toward the door. "I'm sure he won't mind if I fetch him."

"Alexandra!" Rachel called after her as she moved hastily down the hall. She was in such a rush that she forgot about the door in the kitchen, that led straight into the tavern, and went out the door to the alley.

"Ah hell," Jarett muttered as he hurried to catch up with her. She was almost at the end of the alley by the time he caught up to her again. "Where do you think you're going?" he demanded.

She turned to look at him. "I was just going to find Hugh," she replied innocently.

He scowled down at her. "I thought you were going to introduce me to your brother."

"Hugh *is* my brother," she replied. "If you come with me, you can meet him."

Jarret found himself unable to breathe as his mind flashed back to the three men on the sidewalk that had been coming here. Paul and Daryl he had already known but number three, his number one suspect, hadn't given up his name. He was beginning to realize that Hugh was the other one now sitting in the tavern with Paul and Daryl.

His number one suspect was *her* brother. He still wasn't going to get out of her way though. "You are not going in there," he said firmly.

Alex planted her hands on her hips as she stared up at him. She had begun to like this man, no matter what the circumstances surrounding him were, but no one, not even Hugh ordered her around. "Look Mr. Stanton, I appreciate your help with Henry's things, but I am going into that tavern to retrieve my brother. Now, if you'll excuse me."

She didn't make it one step before he moved to block her. Alex's patience was waning as she haughtily stared up at him, her jaw locked as her scowl deepened. "Miss, I can't let you go in there, it's no place for a lady."

"Sir, I assure you that I am no lady," she retorted tersely. "Just ask any of the *good* ladies in this town."

Jarett didn't have to ask any of the good ladies, he could well imagine what they thought about the time she spent with Henry. Imagine what they thought about her working a ranch, and the fact that she seemed to know the women in the tavern pretty well. However, he wasn't going to let her into that place. He knew that the men would be all over her in two seconds flat. He didn't stop to examine his protective urges; he just knew that he wasn't going to let this happen.

"I will go get him," he told her.

Alex was fighting the urge to shove him out of her way. She wanted to see the tavern and find out what went on in there. Oh, she had a pretty good idea, but still it wasn't the same as actually seeing it. "You don't even know who he is."

"Actually, I met him this morning."

"But..."

He held up a hand to forestall her. "I didn't know he was your brother until now."

"I still have to go inside and get him. He may very well stay in there all day if I don't," she insisted.

Jesus she was stubborn, but he could see curiosity was the real reason that she was trying to go inside; her brother was just an excuse. "Does your brother usually stay in there drinking and leave you alone to fend for yourself?"

"Well no," she admitted reluctantly. "He has never done it before."

"Alex!" Alex braced herself and turned around. Hugh was scowling as he stalked toward her. "Where were you going?" he demanded.

She smiled at him as he stopped before her and planted his hands on his lean hips. "I was just coming to see if you were ready to leave," she said sweetly.

"Rachel said that you were coming to get me."

"Yes, I was..."

"You are not to go in there, ever! Do I make myself clear?"

Alex's smile slipped from her face as she glared at her brother. "I can go anywhere I please," she retorted.

"No you cannot!" he snapped.

Jarett watched in startled amusement as the two siblings faced off. As far as appearances went they were as different as night and day. However, their temperament was obviously similar. His eyes stayed mainly focused on Hugh as he awaited some slip up that would confirm he was one of the suspects. He was so focused on his sister that he hadn't even noticed Jarett's presence yet.

"You have no say over me..."

"I'm your guardian. I have every say over you," Hugh interrupted.

"Like hell!" she retorted with a snort.

"You found her," Paul said. They were both cut off as Paul and Daryl approached from the kitchen door.

"Yes," Hugh muttered as he shot Alex a scathing look. She glowered at him in return. She was angrier that she wouldn't get to go inside than she was about Hugh's highhanded manner though.

"I told you that she wouldn't go inside," Paul said.

"I would too," she argued. "I see no reason why I cannot..."

"There is every reason why you cannot. Think of the damage you would do to your reputation!" Hugh interrupted her.

"What reputation?"

"Alex," he said in warning.

"Well, it's true. So I see no harm in satisfying some of my curiosity."

"Over my dead body!"

"Don't tempt me!" she shot back.

"Hey guys, call a truce already," Paul inserted. "Alex, be reasonable."

Hugh snorted loudly. "She's never reasonable."

"Well if you weren't suck a jackass..." she started.

"Alexandra, watch you language. I swear if you finish that sentence, I will put you over my knee and spank you like you should have been years ago!"

"I would like to see you try it," she grated as she took a step closer to her brother.

"Enough!" Paul cried. "Give it up already!"

Jarett's amusement had grown with every passing moment. There was a spark of determination in Alex that he greatly admired, but he sure wouldn't like to be the one in charge of her. Hugh's eyes landed on him and narrowed with hostility. "What do you want?" he demanded.

Jarett's amusement faded as he met the man's antagonistic stare with one of his own. Alex tossed a look over her shoulder at him. "He helped me with Henry's things."

"Do you know who he is?" Hugh demanded.

"Yes, he's looking for the robbers. He asked to meet you," Alex replied nonchalantly as her eyes pleaded with her brother to take it easy. His demeanor was questionable in the extreme. Jarett was not a stupid man, and if Hugh didn't watch himself, he would become Jarett's prime suspect.

Hugh's scowl deepened as he ignored Alex's silent message. "He is Murdock's man."

"I told you earlier that I am *no* one's man," Jarett growled.

Alex felt the hair on the nape of her neck rise at the wrath radiating from Jarett. "He was trying to stop me from going into the tavern," she said.

She hoped to ease Hugh's resentment by giving him a reason to be appreciative of Jarett's presence; it didn't work. "You shouldn't be associating with him at all," Hugh said.

"Can we just go home now?"

"Yes." Hugh grabbed hold of her good arm and shot Jarett a glare as he started to tug her along beside him.

"Thank you for your help," Alex said. Jarett's attention was distracted from the man he was certain had been involved with the robbery as he turned his gaze down to her. "We'll see you two at the barn dance," she called over her shoulder to Paul and Daryl.

They nodded in return as Hugh pulled her forward, heedless of the fact that he looked even more suspicious by doing so.

CHAPTER 7

They could hear the sound of the fiddles just before the barn came into view. Due to all the whispered comments about her, Alex usually didn't like the social setting of the dances, but she found herself eager to attend this one. She didn't want to think about the true reason why she was excited to be here but thoughts of Jarett kept intruding on her days, and nights. No matter how much she tried not to admit it, she knew that her enthusiasm had everything to do with him.

Hugh stopped the wagon behind another one and wrapped the lines around the brake. He shot her a heated glance that she returned full bore. They'd gotten into a fight earlier over whether or not to come to the dance. Alex had insisted they attend, they rarely missed one and after his behavior last week not coming tonight would only cause more suspicion. Hugh had finally relented but he wasn't happy about it and he had let her know that by not speaking to her throughout the entire ride.

He climbed down from the wagon and came around to help her down. "You will behave," she whispered as he took hold of her arm.

"Of course," he muttered.

"Hugh..."

"Alex, I will not do anything suspicious," he interrupted. "Let's just get this over and done with. I would like to get out of here as soon as possible."

Alex allowed him to lead her through the barn doors. Half the town seemed to have arrived already as people mulled about the cramped barn. Alex's gaze instantly found Jarett standing by Murdock and talking with Shelly Fisher. Shelly was a cute brunette with an easy smile, temperate demeanor and a pristine reputation. In short, she was everything that

Alex wasn't and she was made acutely aware of that fact as Jarett smiled charmingly down at Shelly. Alex wasn't prone to jealousy, in fact she'd never experienced the emotion before, but now it ripped through her like a hot branding iron.

She averted her gaze and focused her attention on the rest of the crowd. She spotted Paul as he wound his way through the people toward them. A sunny smile lit his handsome face. Alex bit back a groan; she was going to have to ward off Paul's unsolicited attentions all night. Maybe Hugh had been right and they should have stayed home. For once, she wished that she had listened to her brother.

"She's here."

Jarett's attention was distracted from Shelly by Murdock's excited whisper. Frowning, he turned toward the man. He was astounded by the lust twisting Murdock's features and that had caused his fingers to curl into the arm of the chair he was sitting in. It was rare that anything made Murdock's stoic composure slip even a little. Jarett followed the direction of his gaze to Alexandra. His breath froze in his lungs as he drank in the sight of her. Even in the modest, faded green dress she wore, she was ravishing. Blood flooded into his cock as his gaze swept over her curvaceous figure, there were so many things that he would love to do to that body.

His lustful thoughts were doused when he noticed Paul's blond head bee lining toward her. "Excuse me," Murdock murmured, drawing Jarett's attention back to the man.

Jarett watched as Murdock made his way through the crowd. His resentment continued to mount as Murdock arrived at her side at the same time as Paul. He saw the fleeting look of loathing that crossed Alex's features when she looked at Murdock before she covered it up. His curiosity mounting, he took a step forward to join them when he recalled that Shelly was still at his side. She gave him a fierce stare before turning on her heel and disappearing into the crowd. With a dismissive shrug, he forgot all about her as he steadily made his way forward.

"Would you care to dance Ms. Harris?"

Alex fought her revulsion as Murdock stretched a hand out to her. She took hold of Paul's arm, she had just turned him down for a dance, but she would have taken the devil's own hand before Murdock's. "I have already promised Paul that I would dance with him."

Paul didn't give away the fact that she had just turned him down. He knew well how much she despised Murdock. Murdock's nostrils flared as he glared at the two of them but Alex wasn't at all cowed by the vehement look that he gave her.

Paul pulled her past the swirling couples dancing merrily to the fiddles. She caught a glimpse of Jarett in the crowd before Paul swung her into a rousing, fast-paced song. She threw herself into dancing; she laughed as she was spun into Joel Harding's arms. As the night moved on, she was claimed by one single man after another.

Murdock didn't try to ask her to dance again, she had never danced with him and he knew that she wouldn't. She didn't know what had possessed him to ask her tonight. He had stopped doing that last year, after she had turned him down for the third time. She'd hoped he'd thrown in the towel and decided she really wasn't worth the rejection, but for some reason he must have thought that this year would be different. It never would be though.

She caught glimpses of Jarett in the crowd as he danced with one girl after another. Occasionally she spotted him on the sidelines talking with other women, and some of the men, but she was well aware of the fact that most of the ranchers avoided him. Only some of the merchants, Murdock, and Murdock's hired men spoke with him. The blatant snub was a reminder that he was her enemy, that he was determined to help Murdock against all of them.

It was a reminder that she could have done without, but knew she needed. She was so swept up in her thoughts and tangled emotions that she didn't realize who was holding her until she was a few seconds into the dance. Her feet stopped moving instantly, causing a couple to bump into her and Murdock. The couple sent curious glances at them before swiftly moving around them.

Revulsion rolled through Alex as she stared into Murdock's passion filled hazel eyes. She supposed some would have found him handsome, not her though. From his cool skin, to the color of his eyes and the thinness of his lips, everything about him reminded her of a reptile. A cruel smile curved his mouth as his eyes traveled leisurely over her body. Alex recoiled and tried to pull away from him but his hand clenched upon her waist as he pulled her closer to him. The firm evidence of his arousal pressed against her abdomen.

"Let go of me!" Alex managed to get her voice free of the knot that had lodged in her throat.

"Come Alexandra, 'tis just a dance," he purred.

Alex fought a shudder as she finally managed to wrench her hand free of his. Placing both hands against his chest, she tried unsuccessfully to push him away. "If you don't release me, I will scream."

"And cause a scene, I think not."

A muscle began to twitch in her cheek as her jaw clenched. "I do not care about causing a scene, but I'm not sure that you feel the same."

His eyes filled with rage and fine lines pinched the corners of his mouth. Alex became truly concerned for her safety as she felt the tremors that rocked through him. "Let's get something straight right now, Ms. Harris, I've never made my intentions perfectly clear before but I am now. I want you and I will have you. I always get what I want. *Always*."

"Over my dead body!" she spat and wiggled to get free of him. "Let go of me!"

He released her so suddenly that she took a stumbling step back and bumped roughly into Joel. Mumbling a brief apology, she shot Murdock a hate filled look before turning and hurrying off the dance floor. Whatever pleasure she had managed to find in the evening had been effectively ruined. The last thing she wanted was to stay a second more, but she didn't feel like taking the time to try and find Hugh. She sought some fresh air in the hopes of ridding herself of the lingering revulsion that Murdock's touch had caused.

Making it to the barn doors, Alex stumbled outside and inhaled large gulps of fresh air. She moved forward blindly, heedless of where she was going as she stumbled around the corner of the barn. She bent over and rested her hands on her knees as shudders rocked through her. It took her a few moments but eventually she regained enough control so that she was able to stand back up. Leaning against the barn, she closed her eyes against the night; the noise of the fiddles was the only sound that penetrated the stillness.

"Are you all right?"

Alex jumped; her eyes flew open as the deep voice sounded close to her. Jarett was standing before her, his eyes were assessing as they searched her face. She was struck speechless by the aura of power that radiated from him. In the gloom of the night he seemed even more lethal than he had with a gun in his hand. He was also just as appealing and magnificent as she recalled.

"I'm fine," she forced herself to reply.

Jarett knew that was a lie. The moonlight spilling over her delicate features revealed that her face was paler than normal. Her hands were trembling as she wrung them before her. He'd seen the exchange between her and Murdock; he'd been on his way to intervene when Murdock had released her. He didn't know what had been said inside, or what had occurred between them in the past, but it was more than obvious that Alex despised Murdock, and that Murdock lusted for her.

"You don't look fine," he told her.

Her chin tilted proudly up. "I don't like your boss," she grated through her teeth.

A muscle jumped in his cheek. "He's not my boss."

"Then what is he?" she demanded.

"He hired me to bring his money safely in, but I stayed for my own reasons."

"To catch the thieves." He didn't miss the hostility that laced her voice, or the shuddered look that passed over her eyes.

"Yes," he replied coldly.

Alex released a bitter laugh. "Do you know anything about the man that hired you?"

"I don't care to know anything about him; I only care to catch the boy that shot me."

"Are you always so indifferent to other people's problems?"

"They're not mine."

Alex stared at him in disbelief as unreasonable hurt filled her. This was not the man that had so valiantly refused to acknowledge Henry's odor. This was not the man that had helped to steady her inside the mercantile when she was being verbally attacked by Suzanne. He wasn't even the man that had hesitated, unwilling to shoot what he thought was a boy. She didn't know this man, but she realized that he was callous and hard, and a complete stranger.

"You were right," she whispered. "You are not kind."

Jarett didn't like the brief sting that statement caused him. He didn't know why he cared what this woman thought of him, but for some reason he did. That realization only irritated and upset him more. "I told you that."

Alex continued to gaze at his emotionless eyes. "And when you find these thieves, what will you do then?"

"Murdock is offering a good reward. I'll turn them over to him, after I exact my own justice."

A chill raced down Alex's spine as she thought about what that justice might be. From the look of him now, it wouldn't be good. Apprehension coiled within her belly for herself, and for Hugh. He obviously hadn't figured out it was she and Hugh who were the thieves he was looking for, and she prayed he never would.

She was fairly certain that he suspected that something was off about them though. She had realized earlier in the week that he'd been asking to meet her brother because he'd thought that his coloring would be the same as hers. Hugh's blatant hostility hadn't escaped his notice either, she was certain of that.

"Well then, I hope you do not find them," she told him.

"I'm sure you do."

"And just what is that supposed to mean?" she demanded.

His smile was as chilling as snow. "It's more than obvious that you dislike Murdock."

"As does everyone in this area," she scoffed.

"So I've come to learn."

"That should tell you what kind of man you're trying to help."

He couldn't help but be amused by her feistiness as he propped a hand on the barn behind her. Her eyes widened as he leaned closer to her. He was suddenly more fascinated by her then the conversation, or his suspicions about her brother. That mouth was the most irresistible thing he'd ever seen. Without thinking, he reached up to run a finger along her full bottom lip. Her quick inhalation caused her breasts to brush tantalizingly against his chest.

Alex was mesmerized by his eyes and the delicious shivers his touch sent down her spine. She forgot everything they had been discussing, everything that she was afraid of and disliked about him. The only thing she could do was feel that tender touch all the way down to her toes. Her breath hitched in her lungs as he moved toward her. Her eyes crossed, she watched in fascination as his mouth brushed over hers. A bolt of lightning burned through her veins and caused her heart to leap.

The kiss was no longer than a second, but it changed something inside of her and made her aware of her body in ways that she never had been before as her nipples began to tingle. His mouth was only inches from hers as he hovered above her. She felt the loss of contact just as acutely as she felt the sun caressing her skin on a hot summer day. When his head bent to hers again she did nothing to stop him, she didn't even think about trying to stop him.

His mouth touched against hers again, but this time, Alex's eyes drifted closed. She responded to him as his mouth slanted over hers, demanding and hot as he sought to take more from her. She wasn't entirely sure what he wanted from her, but she was more than willing to give it to him right now. His hand left the barn wall to curl around the back of her head, drawing her more firmly against him as his fingers slid through her hair. The brush of his tongue against her lips thrilled her as much as it startled her. She gasped in response. To her utter astonishment, he slid his tongue between her lips and into her mouth.

Alex was overwhelmed by the heady invasion that rocked her senses at the same time that it melted everything inside of her. His tongue caressed the roof of her mouth, and then flicked against her own. She hadn't known that men could kiss women like this, let alone imagine the firestorm of sensations that such an intimate gesture would evoke. Without thinking, Alex responded to him and her tongue began to move against his. The low growl he emitted, and the tightening of his hand in her hair, told her that he enjoyed it as much as she did.

Jarett wrapped his other arm around her, crushing her against him as he relished in the taste and feel of her. She was warm and pliant in his arms as her body molded perfectly against his. The supple swell of her breasts pressed tantalizingly against his chest. He caught each of the delicious little moans she emitted as her obvious passion only served to heighten his. She whimpered a protest when his mouth left hers but her hands dug into his back as he left a searing trail of kisses down her neck.

Alex was trembling so badly she was certain that she would have collapsed if his arm hadn't been around her waist to support her. Clinging to him, she gave herself over to the delicious sensations coursing through her as he nibbled on her earlobe before swirling his tongue around it. Alex's knees buckled. A chuckle escaped him before his mouth reclaimed hers.

Stroking over her belly, he slid his hand up the front of her dress before clasping one of her full breasts. She instinctively tried to pull away but even as she thought it, her body arched closer to his. His hand caressing her breast sent a burning sensation through her; all she craved was to know what it would feel like against her bare flesh. His thumb circled her hardened nipple before moving onto her other breast.

Jarett's blood roared in his ears as his heart pounded rapidly. Grasping her waist, he pulled her flush against his erection and rubbed it tantalizingly against her. He relinquished her mouth again to move down the delicate column of her throat. Impatiently, he pulled the dress lower but it revealed no more than the upper swell of her breasts.

She was so responsive that it was taking all the control he had not to take her now, against the side of the barn. He desired her with an intensity that was beginning to border on the edge of insanity. If he didn't pull away from her now, then he never would. Tugging the edge of her dress up, he broke away from her and took a step back. He had to put some distance between them in order to calm some of his raging lust.

It didn't help to look at her, he decided immediately. In the moonlight, she was even more beautiful. Tendrils of her hair curled around her face, her lips were swollen and still wet from his kisses. Her brisk inhalations caused her luscious breasts to rise and fall temptingly. Her eyes had darkened to the color of oak leaves with passion as they met his.

Without even intending to, he bent his head and nibbled upon her full lower lip again. "Come with me."

Alex was too caught up in the new sensations coursing through her for his words to penetrate at first. A sigh escaped her as his tongue slid over the lip that he had just been nipping at. He pulled back again, his golden eyes were nearly black with need, and his handsome face was merely inches from hers. Her heart was thumping in her chest, her body still quivered.

He kept his arm around her waist as he turned her away from the barn and pulled her toward the shadows of the woods. Reality was like diving into the lake in January as it slapped her in the face. Digging her heels in, she attempted to stop his forward momentum. "Where are we going?" she demanded as she tried to escape his iron grasp.

"I have a room above the saloon; I find a bed preferable to the ground."

Alex's mouth dropped as she realized his meaning. She should have expected it; she had been behaving like a hussy after all, but the words still shocked her. Shame and humiliation threatened to choke her as she resumed her struggles to get free. "Let me go!" she cried in a choked voice.

He stopped moving and turned to face her. The shadows played over his face from the trees swaying in the breeze around them. "Would you prefer to do this outside?" he demanded hoarsely.

Color crept through her face. "No..."

"Then let's go."

She planted her heels in and refused to move as he took a step forward. "No! I mean we can't... I can't!"

He spun back toward her, his eyes narrowed as his jaw clenched. A chill slid down her back, she looked around frantically as she realized he could do anything he wanted to her. He was ten times stronger than she was and she *had* led him on. She was an idiot to have allowed things to go so far and in such an unpopulated location. She had allowed him to believe she was a loose woman. Plus, she was certain that he had probably heard that her reputation wasn't exactly pristine.

No matter how untruthful the rumors were, she knew that the people of the town gossiped about her incessantly. She knew that no one found her respectable, but until now, she hadn't really cared. Now she realized just how detrimental all of the unfounded rumors might be.

"What do you mean you can't?" he demanded.

Alex focused on the ground as she dug the toes of her boot into it. "I um... I can't do this," she whispered.

He grasped hold of her chin and tilted it up so that she had to look at him again. She hesitantly met his savage scowl. "And why not?"

Her lashes lowered to shadow her eyes. Even in the dim light illuminating her, he could tell that her face was nearly the same color as her hair. He was puzzled by her strange behavior, and even more disturbed by her sudden reluctance; she had been more than willing just moments ago. His fierce arousal was more than ample proof of that.

"I don't even know you," she muttered.

"We can remedy that now."

Alex tried to take a step back but his arm was still locked around her waist, his fingers still clasping her chin as he kept her rooted to the spot. "No." It was the only word that would get past her constricted throat.

"You were more than willing a minute ago." Her hands pressed against his chest as she attempted to pull her chin free again. He was unwilling to relinquish her when he had been so very close to satisfying the ardent lust she provoked in him. "Is it because of Paul; are you concerned that he'll be angry if he finds out that you've cuckolded him with another man?"

Alex's eyes flew back to his. She shouldn't have been staggered by the words, shouldn't have been offended by them, she *knew* what people said about her, but inexplicably she was. She opened her mouth to tell him that he was wrong, that there was nothing between her and Paul, but he was speaking before she could.

"He need never know, and if he happens to find out then I'll make sure that he doesn't hurt you. Come now."

Alex continued to plant her heels in as he attempted to draw her forward again. Her disbelief and humiliation was becoming suffused with anger. She knew that he had every reason to think this way about her, knew that she had given him no reason to think otherwise, and yet she was more than a little irritated by his callous treatment of her and his belief about the kind of woman she was.

"Let go of me!" she commanded as she twisted to break free of his grasp.

He spun back to her and thrust his face mere inches away from hers. Alex swallowed heavily as she attempted to take a step back in order to breathe. He didn't release her; instead he drew her closer and melded her body against his.

"I know you don't mean that. You want this as badly as I do."

It took all she had not to give into the clamoring demands of her body. His hand brushed over her cheek, she fought the urge to turn her head into that caress, to surrender everything she had to him. His hand slid over her shoulder, his fingers touched upon the healing bullet wound through her dress.

Ice flowed through her veins, freezing the fire that he had been stoking again within her. True terror gave her the strength to wrench backward. He was so startled by her burst of strength that he was unable to keep his hold on her. Backing up quickly, Alex almost tripped over a tree stump but managed to catch herself in time. He didn't move, didn't come after her, as his hooded eyes gleamed dangerously in the moonlight.

Alex wasn't going to hear what else he would say to her. Lifting her skirt, she fled through the trees and back toward the barn. Branches slapped at her but she barely noticed them as she leapt over a fallen tree and arrived at the front of the barn. Panting heavily, she bent over as she tried desperately to catch her breath. She had been so close to giving herself to him, to forgetting everything that she held dear. If he had found out, if he had seen...

Alex moaned as she wrapped her arms around her suddenly cramped stomach. "Alex!" She nearly jumped out of her skin as she thought that he had returned for her. Standing hurriedly, she was relieved to see Hugh making his way toward her. "Where have you been?" he demanded.

Alex fought to keep her face impassive as she nervously fiddled with her disordered, untidy hair. "I...I went for a walk in the woods," she stammered out.

"I can see that," he replied as he pulled a twig from her hair.

"Are you ready to go?" she asked hopefully.

"I was ready when we got here, but that's not why I was looking for you."

"What is it?" she asked nervously.

"It's Megan, she's in labor and she's asking for you."

"Oh God!" Alex cried. All of her guilt and shame vanished in the space of a heartbeat as concern for her friend blazed forth.

CHAPTER 8

Daryl was beside himself with worry by the time Alex arrived at the small house on the edge of town. "That harridan won't let me in to see my wife!" he shouted the instant Hugh pulled the wagon up.

Alex jumped down and hurried toward him. Megan's piercing cry echoed through the open windows and froze them all in place. Daryl moved first as he turned and stormed back toward the house. He banged loudly on the door. "Let me in, you old tyrant!"

Alex rushed forward, grabbed hold of his arm and pulled it away from the door "You know you cannot go in Daryl," she said firmly. "Hugh, why don't you take Daryl over to Shelby's and buy him a few rounds."

"I'm not going anywhere!" Daryl shouted. His round face was florid; sweat marred his brow and pasted his disheveled blond hair to his forehead. His blue eyes were practically bulging as they challengingly met Alex's.

"Daryl, you're not helping anyone right now. I'll be with Megan, everything is going..." Alex was cut off by another cry that froze the breath in her lungs. It seemed to pierce the night as efficiently as a knife sliced flesh. The silence after such a cry was almost as shocking as the sound had been. Dread clawed at Alex's insides and caused sweat to coat her skin. "All right," she finished in a whisper.

Daryl jerked his arm away but Hugh grabbed hold of him before he could start his pounding again. "Alex is right Daryl; you're doing more harm than good right now. We'll go to the tavern, have some toasts to your child, and smoke a few cigars. Come on Daryl; listen to reason. They're not going to let you in, and staying here isn't helping anyone."

"But..." Daryl started to protest.

"Go Daryl," Alex urged. "I'll stay with her, I promise. I won't leave her side, not for a second. I'll come and get you as soon as your child is born."

Hugh grasped Daryl's slumped shoulders and pushed him toward the road. Megan's next scream caused Daryl to freeze in the middle of the street. Hugh continued to usher him forward as he pulled Daryl's rigid body forward. Alex waited until they were out of view before turning to knock on the door.

"It's Alexandra!" she called.

"Let her in!" Megan cried.

The door was unbolted as Mrs. Landow, the town's midwife, swung it open. She gave Alex a disdainful glance that Alex chose to ignore as she swept into the cozy home. Alex hurried into the bedroom immediately to the left of her. The sight of Megan, propped up on the bed, her hair soaked with sweat and her face extremely red froze her in the doorway. Then, Megan stretched a trembling hand to her.

Alex's paralysis fled as she rushed to her friend's side, seized hold of her hand and fell onto her knees beside her. "If you're going to stay, be of some help," Mrs. Landow barked and tossed a cold cloth at Alex.

She raised it to wipe the sweat from Megan's forehead. "It hurts," Megan panted.

Mrs. Landow snorted unsympathetically as she hurried around the small room. She lifted the lantern off the old bureau and brought it toward the bed. She placed it beside the bed and pulled the blankets back to examine Megan. Alex turned away to focus her attention on Megan. "Not much longer," Mrs. Landow muttered, more to herself than anyone else.

"When did this start?" Alex asked anxiously.

"This morning," Megan gasped out.

"Why didn't you send for me sooner?" Alex demanded.

"The...da..dance..."

Megan broke off as another cry erupted from her; it was so loud that it shook her tiny frame and her hands clenched on the bed. Alex felt completely useless as she continued to wipe the sweat from her brow. Megan was panting when she slumped against the pillows and her eyes drifted closed. Alex took hold of her hand; she whispered words of encouragement for the future, and the joy that the baby would bring to them all.

Megan's cries became more frequent, the hand currently holding Alex's squeezed so forcefully that Alex was certain the bones would break. Alex was sweating almost as bad as Megan was as the heat of the cramped room became almost unbearable, even with the windows open and the spring air drifting in. Her knees began to ache, her back smarted unbelievably, but she refused to give up her spot at her friend's side.

"You're going to have to start pushing soon," Mrs. Landow muttered.

"I can't," Megan panted. "I just can't."

"Yes you can," Alex encouraged.

Megan shook her head, but then another contraction rocked through her and caused her to bear down. Alex bit back her cry of anguish as her hand was squeezed beyond its capacity for pain. Megan's scream pierced her eardrums and slammed through her skull. For a second her vision blurred as the soreness in her hand seared up her arm.

"Push," Mrs. Landow ordered.

Megan's face was vivid red, the veins in her forehead stood out. "Come on Megan, you can do this," Alex urged through gritted teeth.

Megan groaned before she fell back against the pillows; she was trembling as her body went limp. Alex didn't know what had just happened until a new cry filled the air. Her head jerked around as Mrs. Landow stood up, a rare smile on her wizened face. “It’s a girl!” she announced.

“Oh!” Alex freed her hand from Megan’s now limp hold and rose to her feet. Her knees cracked and her back protested the movement but she ignored them both as Mrs. Landow washed and swaddled the tiny bundle in her arms.

“Let me see her,” Megan whispered weakly.

Mrs. Landow hurried forward to place the tiny bundle in Megan’s waiting arms. Alex leaned eagerly over them as Mrs. Landow moved away. Her heart swelled as she took in the perfect little being in Megan’s arms. “She’s beautiful,” Megan breathed.

“Yes, she is.” Alex couldn’t stop herself from touching the tiny hand curled into a fist. “What are you going to name her?”

A beautiful smile lit Megan’s face as she leaned against the pillows with her daughter cradled to her chest. “What do you think we should name her?”

“Me?” Alex squawked.

“Yes, you. You’re going to be her godmother after all.”

Tears streamed down Alex’s face as she took hold of Megan’s hand with her good one. “What do you think of Caroline?” she whispered.

Megan shook her head no. “That was your mother’s name; you should give it to your own daughter.”

“And what do you think the odds of that happening are?” she asked laughingly.

Megan didn’t smile in return. “You will one day.”

Mrs. Landow made a rude sound that they both chose to ignore. “Megan....”

“No, think of another name,” she insisted.

Alex frowned thoughtfully as she studied the tiny bundle wrapped securely in Megan’s arms. “Faith,” she whispered.

Megan lifted her daughter to brush a loving kiss upon her brow. “Faith, I like that. I’m sure that Daryl will too. Oh, Daryl! Where is he?”

“Hugh took him to the saloon before he could bang the door down,” Alex replied.

“You have to get him Alex,” she said urgently.

“I will,” she promised. “Right now.”

She dropped a kiss on Megan’s forehead before hurrying toward the door. Mrs. Landow gave her a disdainful stare that she returned in full, unwilling to let another snide look go by. “Let’s get you cleaned up,” the old woman said to Megan. She turned away from Alex and hurried to Megan’s side.

***

Jarett tilted back his ale and gulped it down as he surveyed the packed saloon. The single men from the dance had made their way over; an evening of dancing with the upstanding single women had left them as randy as bulls. The working girls were being well used, and well paid for their services tonight. Services he was almost tempted to use. The young men from the dance weren’t the only ones who had been left unsatisfied this night, and the dull throbbing in his groin was a frustrating reminder of that fact.

His gaze traveled back to the three men in the corner. They had come in over an hour ago, confiscated a table, a bottle of whiskey, and cigars. Daryl kept glancing toward the door and running a hand through his already disheveled hair. Paul was sitting casually, his legs stretched before him as he tipped back another shot of whiskey.

Jarett’s attention, however, was mainly focused on the third man, Hugh. There was cool disdain in Hugh’s face as he drank. He had been studiously avoiding Jarett’s gaze as he surveyed the people around him. Jarett couldn't help but wonder what he was doing here and where his sister was.

At the thought of Alex, his cock instantly began to harden. He tried not to think of her but he found his thoughts drifting back to her every few seconds. She'd been openly receptive to his attentions, and more than eager, he was certain of that.

He just didn't know what had happened to change her mind, nor did he particularly care, he thought with a scowl. She had felt so good, been so unrestrained in his arms. He bet she would be just as eager and uninhibited as she strained beneath him in bed. He wanted to know what her voice would sound like as she called out his name when he brought them both to fulfillment.

He abruptly shut the vivid images of her naked body off as he forced his attention back to the men in the corner. He couldn't let thoughts of her ruin his concentration now. This was the first opportunity he'd had to study his quarry and see how he behaved. Daryl and Paul didn't fit the description of the second man or the boy, but he wondered if they were somehow involved with the robberies.

A flash of skirts caught his attention before Dolly slid onto his lap. She playfully wiggled against him as she tossed her arms around his neck. "I see you're ready for me handsome," she purred. "Maybe tonight you'll decide to give me a go."

Jarett almost groaned aloud from the firestorm of heat that filled his already hardened prick. It had been awhile since his last tumble. He'd been contemplating just such a go earlier but he found himself becoming turned off by the idea. "I don't think so," he forced himself to grate through clenched teeth.

She pouted prettily as she leaned forward to press her lush chest against his. "Could have fooled me."

Dolly's pout grew as she batted her eyelashes flirtatiously. His gaze traveled over her rounded figure and the full breasts revealed to her pink aureoles. Her brown hair was pulled into a loose chignon; spiraling curls of hair fell free to frame her round, pretty face. Even with all of her charms a vision of a slimmer figure, much more modestly covered, and shining copper hair came to mind. His hands tightened involuntarily on Dolly as lust surged through him. He was suddenly torn between shoving her off of his lap and carrying her upstairs to pound out his frustration.

He was so torn that for a moment the disturbance in the people surrounding him didn't penetrate. Then he noticed the men turning to stare and the sudden hush of the rowdy bunch that had been surrounding him. His forehead furrowed as he sought the source of their focus. His gaze landed on her immediately.

Frowning, he took in the dampened clothes clinging to Alex's slender frame. Her hair had slipped free of its knot. It cascaded down her shoulders in unkempt disarray to dangle about her breasts. Her face was flushed; the emerald of her eyes was unusually vivid as they landed on him before focusing on Dolly. A muscle twitched in her cheek, her jaw clenched before she turned away to search the raucous room.

The piano player in the corner continued to pound away at his keys, oblivious to the confusion that her entrance had caused. Jarett was not as oblivious; he could feel the lust oozing from the men surrounding him. Even rumpled and dirty, she was still the most enticing piece in the entire place and all of these men had taken her entrance as an open invitation. Unfortunately, her brother couldn't see her from his position, nor could his friends.

"Get up!" he commanded gruffly.

Dolly didn't argue with him, her own disbelief at seeing Alex was as evident as everyone else's. She slid from his lap quickly. "Now that's a woman I could get lost in," the man next to him announced as he eagerly slapped his friend on the back.

Jarett's irritation continued to mount as he made his way through the men. He didn't get to her fast enough. A middle-aged man grabbed hold of her arm and drew her toward the bar. Jarett saw her tugging at her arm as she planted her heels in, much the same way that she had done to him earlier. He saw the flash of discomfort that crossed her delicate features as the man's hand tightened on hers. Jarett's burgeoning anger turned into full-blown rage as he realized that the man was hurting her.

Alex strained to get free; she wished that she had never come in here. What had she been thinking? She hadn't, that was the problem. She had been so eager to tell Daryl the good news that she hadn't stopped to think that tonight, after the barn dance, most of the men in town would be here carousing for women, and she had walked right into their nest.

Into *his* nest.

Fresh fury filled her as she recalled the spectacle of Dolly curled up in his lap. She had known that what had transpired between them earlier had meant nothing to him, but she hadn't needed to be slapped in the face with the reminder that any warm, willing body would suit him just fine.

She glanced at the man holding her arm; she'd seen him with Murdock and knew that he was one of his hired hands. The idea of it made her nauseous. She attempted to pull free again as she searched for Daryl and her brother, but she was unable to find them amongst the thick throng. Her curiosity about Shelby's was being satisfied; unfortunately, she would have preferred if it hadn't.

There were half a dozen women, all of whom she knew, and all of whom were dressed so provocatively that the spectacle of their almost completely exposed breasts caused her to look away. Marty was pounding enthusiastically on the piano in the corner. Gaming tables had been set off to the side and a crowd of men was gathered around them, they were yelling encouragements or moaning sympathetically for their friends. The place was filled to capacity with a sea of crushing bodies that heated it and filled the air with their body odor. Two dimly lit chandeliers provided sparse illumination for the tables but the place was mostly in shadows.

The man suddenly grabbed hold of her injured hand, causing her to wince as he pulled her up to the large mahogany bar. Frank, the bartender, raised his gray eyebrows as he gaped at her. "Get the lady what she wants!" the man holding her hollered.

"I don't want anything!" Alex had to raise her voice to carry over the noise of the room.

"Of course you do gorgeous, get her a whiskey."

"No Frank, don't." She turned her attention away from Frank's astounded face to glare contemptuously at the swarthy man still holding her hand. "Let me go."

He laughed but he released her hand. Alex spun away as she took her opportunity to escape. A startled cry escaped her when the man slid his arm around her waist and dragged her against him. Revulsion shuddered through her as he pressed against her; his arousal was obvious as he jammed it into the small of her back. "Where ya goin'?" his words were somewhat slurred.

"Let go of me!" Alex dug her nails into the hand that held her.

He muttered a volatile curse that caused her ears to burn and his hand clenched on her waist. A cry escaped as her panic began to escalate. Surely, someone would help her.

Her eyes scanned the group of men surrounding her but their eyes were all gleaming with lust, and they were all Murdock's men.

"Is this the one that Murdock is after?" A tall blond inquired.

"Aye," the man holding her replied. "Though I don't think he'll mind if we get a taste before he does."

"Let go of me!" she cried as she tore into the strong, tanned hand holding her.

"Bitch," he grated.

"Here now," Frank interrupted. "Let the girl go!"

"What are you going to do about it old man?" the man demanded as he swung her around so that she faced the bar again. Frank's brown eyes were sympathetic before he turned his attention back to the man holding her.

"Let her go!" the forceful command caused everyone to jump a little.

Alex was spun in a full circle as the man wheeled around to face her rescuer. Relief filled her as her eyes landed upon Jarett. Then, fear began to trickle down her spine as she took in the fury radiating from him like a heat ray. His golden eyes were as bright as the sun as they ran disdainfully over her, before turning to the man holding her.

"Here now, there's plenty to go around before we give her to Murdock," the man holding her said.

"Let her go," Jarett grated again.

The man scowled as he shifted his hold on Alex and pushed her behind him. "What's it to you?" the man demanded as his hand moved toward the colt revolver at his side.

"She's mine, and if you move that hand one more inch I'll blow it off."

The man's eyes flickered briefly with apprehension before he moved to draw. Jarett pulled his gun free with a hiss of leather and leveled it at the man's chest before he'd even grabbed hold of his own gun. Stunned silence hung heavily in the air as the man's hand slid away from his side.

"Don't push me," Jarett told him. "Alexandra get over here, *now*!"

Alex hesitated; she was almost as afraid of him as she was of the men surrounding her. Never had she seen a man draw a gun so fast, she hadn't even had time to blink before it was leveled at the man. The deadly look in Jarett's eyes told her plainer than words that he wouldn't hesitate to pull the trigger. She shuffled out from behind the man that had grabbed her and cast a frightened glance at his group of friends.

"You're lucky Murdock wants you alive," the man said.

Alex winced at the blatant reminder that her rescuer was every bit as much her enemy as this raggedy group of men standing around her. "I was thinking the same thing about you," Jarett replied as he flicked an impatient glance at Alex. *Why was she taking so long?* He thought angrily.

He grabbed hold of her arm and pulled her against his side. "Murdock won't like you touching his woman," the man said.

"I'm not his woman!" Alex was unable to stop herself from retorting.

Jarett's hand tensed in warning upon her arm as he pushed her behind him. Alex nearly sputtered with indignation at his rough treatment but she realized that this was not the time to voice her opinion. "Murdock can have her when I'm through," Jarett replied as he holstered his colt.

Alex opened her mouth to protest that statement but he nudged her toward the door. She bristled at his highhanded manner as he thrust the door open and pushed her through. She tried to turn to face him but he continued to propel her toward the alley that led to the kitchen.

"Let go of me!" she yelled.

He pulled her into the dim alley and pressed her against the wall. "Did you satisfy your curiosity?" he snarled, his face mere inches from hers. The vehemence in his voice left her temporarily speechless. "Was it what you expected, do you want to work there too?"

An eyelid began to twitch. "How dare you!" she spat.

"How dare I?" He grabbed hold of her arm as she tried to turn away. Alex gasped as he spun her around, planted her firmly against the wall again and braced his hands on either side of her head. Alex's chest heaved with her breaths as she glowered at him. "Those men would have had you for dinner, unless that was your objective!"

Alex clenched her good hand into a fist. She meant to drive it straight into his arrogant, hateful face. He grabbed hold of it before she could swing at him; his hand was firm as he kept it within his grasp. "Don't," he growled.

The hair on the back of her neck stood up at the tone of his voice. He was so large and obviously infuriated with her but she didn't care, she was every bit as indignant as he was, maybe even more so. He had done nothing but treat her with disrespect and contempt. Although she knew that he was her enemy, that he thought her a shameless hussy, she could feel herself responding to his touch even now. She hated herself for it, hated the way he made her feel, and the complete lack of control she had over herself when he was around.

"Let me go," she managed to grate through clenched teeth.

"You didn't mind my touching you earlier," he taunted.

Alex thrust her shoulders back as she ineffectively tried to pull her hand free. "You arrogant, ignorant..." she sputtered, unable to think of a word suitable for him.

The sound of his caustic laugh sent a chill down her spine as she stopped trying to free her hand. “Come now Alexandra, certainly you know a few good curses.”

The sight of that man touching her was firmly emblazoned in his mind. It aroused more than just anger in him, but also a swell of protectiveness and possessiveness that bothered him more than he would care to admit. However, he couldn’t stop himself from taunting her, for Alex in a state was truly something to behold. Her vivid eyes fairly sparked and her full breasts heaved against the confining restraints of her modest gown. The savage desire she had aroused earlier was back in full force.

When he thought about what could have happened to her, before her brother even realized that she was there, his ire grew to astronomical proportions that he had never known before. He didn’t know why this woman affected him the way that she did but he knew that it was perilous. He realized that he was teetering on the edge of a treacherous precipice. His lust for her was clouding his judgment, yet right now, he couldn’t find it in himself to care.

Alex remained unmoving; she was unwilling to give him the satisfaction of watching her wriggle. When his gaze drifted down to her mouth, anticipation and trepidation warred to life within her. She didn’t realize she was holding her breath until her lungs began to burn. She released it on a rush of air that caused his eyes to flicker back to hers. A gasp, half protest and half need escaped her as his arm slid around her waist and drew her against him.

“Don’t,” she murmured but she knew the protest was only halfhearted.

“Make me stop,” he whispered.

She knew that she could, knew that he would let her walk away. He’d let her go earlier when he didn’t have to, and he would do so again now. His other hand twined into her hair, there was no anger in his demeanor now, only a powerful hunger that more than matched hers. A battle seemed to wage across his face as his eyes ran over her face. Alex was confused by the turbulent emotions that flickered across his features before his head bent to hers, and all thought fled. His kiss was just as exciting as she remembered. It swept her into a world of sensation that engulfed her whole body and consumed her with its intensity. Alex couldn't stop herself from molding against him as her lips parted to the probing of his tongue. He invaded her mouth with deep, penetrating thrusts that caused her to moan in pleasure.

Jarett growled low in his throat as her tongue entwined with his in an imitation of the mating dance that he was determined to have with her. He pressed himself firmly against her and used his thigh to part her quivering legs. She whimpered as he pressed his rigid arousal against her. He slid his hand over her slender body and grasped one of her breasts.

Alex would have collapsed if it hadn't been for his firm thigh braced between her legs. It was a gesture so intimate that it should have shocked her, yet it didn't. Instead, she found herself even more aroused. She knew that what they were doing was wrong, that she should put a stop to it, but she couldn't bring herself to care as his mouth left hers to trail down the delicate column of her throat. She relished in each new dizzying sensation, she arched against him and gasped as fire spread through her body when she rubbed against his thigh.

Trembling, beyond reason and thinking, she repeated the motion and nearly cried out in joy as the same fiery spurt of pleasure burst through her. Alex was nearly crazed with the need encompassing her as his mouth trailed over her neck to the edge of her collar. She threaded her fingers through his thick hair and winced as fresh pain flashed through her bruised hand.

A cry slipped out before she could stop it. "Ow!"

The small yelp took a minute to penetrate his lust-filled mind. When it did, he pulled away abruptly. He didn't know how he had harmed her, but he knew that the cry had been real. She blinked dazedly at him as her hands slipped away from his shoulders. She lifted the right one and clasped it by the wrist. Rage locked his jaw and caused his nostrils to flare as he recalled the look that had crossed her face when the man had grabbed her hand.

"Did he hurt you?" he demanded ruthlessly.

Alex blinked at the rage that suddenly vibrated from him. When he took hold of her wrist, his touch was surprisingly gentle. His eyes narrowed as he strained to see her wrist through the shadows. He spat out a curse when the dim illumination of the lanterns spilled across her badly bruised hand.

"I'll kill him," he grated.

Alex's eyes flew back to his face. His eyes were shuddered; his face seemed to be composed of granite. There was a brief flicker of warmth in his eyes as his fingers stroked the back of her battered hand. She was so touched by the tender gesture that she was struck speechless and unable to correct the mistake that he had made. The fact that he was irritated that the man had mistreated her was enough to take her breath away.

Then, reality returned with a thunderous crash. "Oh, Daryl!" she gasped.

Her free hand flew to her throat. Disgust swamped her as she realized that she had completely forgotten about him. He was probably sick with worry, and Megan was waiting for him to come home to meet their daughter. They were both counting on her and she was acting like a two-bit whore in an alley beside the saloon.

Jarett stiffened at the sound of the name. "It's Jarett!" he hissed and threw her hand away.

She blinked at him, her forehead furrowed at the sudden change that swept over his features. For a second she didn't understand what had happened, and then knowledge dawned. Straightening her shoulders, she tilted her chin angrily as she glared at him.

"I know your name!" she snapped and held her bruised hand to her chest. His gaze was indifferent as he met hers with an antipathy that rocked her.

"Sure you do," he drawled.

He took a step away from her; he couldn't stand to be near her anymore. His own self-loathing was almost as fierce as the abhorrence he felt for her. She had called him by her best friend's husband's name, if he had needed anything to dampen his lust for her that should have done it and yet he still felt a ferocious urge to posses her. That fact did nothing but enflame his burgeoning temper.

"That's right," she bit out. "I'm such a whore that I'm sleeping with my best friend's husband."

He shrugged as he ran a hand through his tumbled mass of hair. "It's none of my business."

To her absolute horror, she felt tears of frustration and shame burn her eyes. She fought them back as she drew on her pride to get her through this humiliating situation. "If you must know, the reason that I was in the tavern was to find Daryl..."

"I don't particularly care."

"To tell him that Megan delivered a beautiful baby girl, and that she would like her husband to see his daughter," she finished, heedless of his attempted interruptions.

She didn't know why she was attempting to explain anything to him, she didn't particularly care what he thought about her, but the last thing she wanted was some vicious rumor that she was sleeping with Daryl running through town. She knew that Megan would never believe it, but it would still be a needless upset that Alex wasn't about to let Megan experience. "Now, if you'll excuse me."

She spun on her heel and headed toward the kitchen. It was the door she should have used in the first place, the one that would have saved her from all of this humiliation. She hadn't been thinking when she had gone through the front door; she vowed never to let that silly mistake happen again, just as she vowed never to set eyes on Jarett Stanton again.

The strong hand on her arm caused her to release a cry as she was spun around. Without thinking, she struck out at him. Her hand hit pitifully against his well-muscled arm. He didn't even flinch, didn't even give her the satisfaction of some kind of reaction as he seized hold of her other arm and pinned them both to her sides.

"Let go of me!" she yelled and attempted to kick him. He braced his legs apart to avoid her fruitless attempts.

"Stop it!" he commanded and gave her a little shake.

Alex went limp in his grasp, her jaw clenched as she flung her head back to glower at him. "Get your hands off of me!"

He didn't enjoy the fire in her eyes right now. Beneath it, he could see the unhappiness he had caused, an unhappiness that touched him more than he cared to admit. "Alexandra..."

"I didn't give you permission to use my name! Get your hands off of me!"

"I didn't mean..."

"Yes, you did! If I'm such a despicable person then why do you insist upon touching me? If you think so little of me then why do you insist upon torturing me with your revolting presence? Leave me alone!"

She ripped herself backward and to her utter disbelief, he released her. She took a few staggering steps away as she fought against the tears threatening to blind her. Never in her life had she been this humiliated, she hated herself for letting him touch her when she knew who he was and what he thought of her. Which wasn't much at all. Trembling, she turned away and hurried toward the salvation that the kitchen offered her.

Jarett wanted to stop her and apologize for his mistake but he was unwilling to do it. She was right, if he did think so little of her then why did he keep bothering with her? Was it just because of lust? He'd felt that for many women before but he hadn't pursued them as relentlessly as he continued to pursue her. Though, she had eagerly returned his advances before reality had intruded upon them again.

Yet he couldn't stop himself from feeling like an awful cad. The distress in her eyes had been more than evident, the shame and resentment burning from them had been a blazing light. His feet remained planted where they were even though he still couldn't shake the sensation that he should apologize. He debated waiting for her to come back out but decided against it. She was too incensed right now to listen to reason. He would talk to her later.

Mumbling a curse, Jarett returned to the front of the saloon but instead of going inside he decided to take a walk to sort out his tangled emotions. Why did he care what she thought of him? He would be better off separating himself from her and putting as much distance between them as he could. She was a distraction to him; she clouded his judgment and aroused emotions that he couldn't control.

Yet, try as he might, he couldn't get the look of torment in her eyes out of his head. He had done her a grave injustice, he knew that, but he was certain that it hadn't been the first time someone had thought the worst of her and it probably wouldn't be the last. Then why did he feel so bad about it?

He paused to lean against the wall of a building. His gaze traveled toward the shack nestled within the shadows of the night. He recalled listening to her read the letter to Henry, the protectiveness that had lit her eyes as she had watched him grasp her friend's clothing. He was beginning to realize that there were many more layers to Alexandra than he had been willing to admit. There was pride, and a deep wealth of caring and strength within her that had all combined to wedge their way into his stony heart without him even realizing that it had happened.

He wanted her with an intensity that he had never known before and that was something he couldn't deny. She was more sensual and beautiful than any woman he'd ever met, and yet she worked like a man, took care of drunks, and didn't fail to excite and aggravate him all at the same time.

He pushed himself away from the wall. He would stay away from her; he had too. It was for the best. She was the sister of his prime suspect, a woman that would only hamper his investigation. He had upset her, and he was sorry for it, but the best thing was to stay as far from her as possible.

CHAPTER 9

Alex slammed the nail into the post with an air of finality before pulling another nail from the cluster in her mouth. She jerked the barbwire taut with her gloved hand and twisted it around the wood before positioning the nail and hammering it in. Although she had hoped that repairing the fences -that had been mysteriously knocked down again last night- would ease some of her pent up frustration, it wasn't working.

Instead, with every nail she drove in, she fumed more and more. She had told Hugh that she would repair the fencing, and that he should go tally up how many cattle they had lost, but she was beginning to regret having volunteered for it. She was sweaty, dirty, and not one iota closer to easing the constriction in her chest. Wiping her hands on the damp shirt she wore, she pulled another nail from her mouth, positioned it and began to hammer it in.

Her wrath was no longer solely directed at the idiotic, egotistical jerk from last night but also on Murdock. They couldn't afford to lose any more cattle and she was certain that more than a few had been herded away. She was half-tempted to go to Murdock's ranch and see if she could find them, but she couldn't take the chance of being caught there.

She drove the nail home and sighed angrily. Standing, she stretched her sore back as she glanced at the sun scorching her. She grabbed the strand of barbwire and moved over to the last pole. Hugh and Jesse had helped her dig the holes, and hammer the posts in before they'd left, a fact that she was extremely grateful for as the sun climbed higher into the sky.

After this was over, she would like nothing more than to jump into the lake and enjoy a refreshing swim in order to rid herself of the aggravation lodged inside her. She hadn't felt quite this empty since her father's death. She refused to think about the person that she had designated to the bleak recesses of her memory during the long, sleepless hours of the night. She swore she'd throttle him if she ever saw him again.

It didn't help that it was *his* boss that was causing this aggravation now. She'd throttle them both, she decided, unsure of who she hated more right now, Murdock or the jerk from last night, the one who's name she had conveniently forgotten.

Wrapping the barbwire around the post, she pulled another nail free and grasped it in her bruised hand. She began to pound it into the wood, though she would have liked for it to be someone's thick skull she was banging it into instead. The corral was eerily still except for the loud, enthusiastic banging of her hammer. Even the birds had flown away when the noise had gotten too much for them to take. Hugh and Jesse had herded the remaining cattle away from the holes in the fence so they couldn't escape before she fixed them.

They had taken the cattle down to the lower paddock and they wouldn't be returning to the high ridge today. She wasn't even remotely concerned that anyone would bother her while she was alone. No one other than Paul, Megan, and Daryl came onto their property -in the daytime anyway- and she had her colts holstered to her side.

She wasn't as fast of a draw as the jerk, but she was quick and a dead on shot. For a moment she daydreamed that she had wanted to shoot the jerk the first time she'd met him. She would have saved herself the offense of last night if she had. She briefly entertained the fantasy but she would have hated herself if she had killed him, no matter how much the arrogant oaf deserved it.

Driving the nail home she stood, stretched her muscles and wiped the sweat from her forehead once again. One more nail and then she could plunge herself into the cool water of the lake. It was fed by a natural spring that kept it cool even in the middle of the summer and had been her and Hugh's favorite place to go since they were children. However, she was glad that he wasn't with her now for she meant to rid herself of her filthy clothes before climbing into the soothing water.

She positioned the nail against the pole and tapped it to set it firmly into the wood. A shadow fell across her as she pulled the hammer back to slam the nail home. She glanced up sharply, fully intending to unleash some of her frustration on Hugh for ruining her solitude, and her blissful plan of diving into the lake.

Disbelief slammed through her at the same time she swung the hammer forward. With a loud yelp, she jerked her hand back as the hammer made contact with her thumb. Jumping back, the hammer tumbled from her grasp as she ripped her glove off. She stared at the red, throbbing thumb before sticking it in her mouth and sucking upon it in an instinctive attempt to ease the soreness in it.

She ripped the thumb from her mouth and spread her legs apart as she glowered at the jerk sitting on his horse and staring at her with a mixture of amusement and concern. "What are you doing here?" she demanded.

"Are you okay?" Jarett ignored the fiery glare she sent him as he glanced down at the hand she'd hit.

"What do you care?" she snarled as she bent to retrieve the hammer. She may not shoot him again but she had no problem with heaving the hammer at his offensive face. Hefting it up, she was reassured by its weight in the palm of her hand.

Jarett leaned forward to rest his arms on the pommel of his saddle. He had known that this wasn't going to be easy, but he hadn't realized just how tough it was actually going to be until now. A part of him still didn't understand what he was doing here, but the other part had wanted nothing more than to see her again and apologize for his mistake.

He'd vowed that he would stay as far away from her as possible, but somewhere in the sleepless night he'd realized that he couldn't leave it like this. She deserved an apology, and he was determined to give it to her. He didn't like to think about why he disliked the fact that she was cross and upset with him. It wasn't an area he was willing to venture into right now.

His gaze darted down to the hammer in her hand; he knew she was contemplating throwing it at him. An amused smile quirked his mouth as his gaze traveled back to her face. He was struck by just how much she looked like the boy that had shot him. The baggy and torn breeches she wore, the over large shirt with the sleeves rolled up to reveal her lean, tanned forearms. The large cowboy hat on her head shadowed her delicate features and brilliant green eyes. Sunlight glinted off of her coppery hair, bringing out the golden highlights that shimmered through the thick braid dangling over her shoulder. She was the same height, the same weight, the same build. Her coloring was *exactly* the same.

A cold chill swept down his spine as his eyes skimmed down her lean body, her curves were somehow hidden beneath the baggy men's clothes. His eyes returned to hers as she tilted her chin haughtily. Her brother was his number one suspect, she hated Murdock, she occasionally dressed like a man and carried a pair of pistols at her side. Pistols he was positive she was more than capable of using.

If she pulled her hair into a knot on top of her head and covered it with a hat...

"Are you here for a reason?" she demanded.

Jarett shook his head in an attempt to rid himself of his troubling thoughts. "I came to apologize."

She released a disbelieving snort and turned back to the last nail. With an aggressive swing, she drove the nail into the wooden board. Glancing at the vast expanse of field, she determined not to acknowledge his presence as her eyes scanned the rolling green pastures. Only small tufts of clouds marred the pristine clarity of the sky.

"I was wrong last night," he said.

Alex still refused to turn toward him. Her afternoon was already spoiled; she wasn't going to ruin it even more by talking to the jerk.

Jarett folded his arms and studied her rigid back. His gaze traveled over the new fence posts she had been stretching wire across. There were twelve new beams, evident because they were brighter than the weathered posts surrounding them. "What happened here?" he inquired.

The question aggravated her enough to jar a response from her. "Like you don't know!"

"I don't know."

In the brilliant light of day he wasn't quite as frightening as he was at night, but he still exuded strength and a raw sexuality that attracted her to him, no matter how much she hated to admit it and tried to fight it. Alex slid the hammer into the waistband of her breeches. Grasping the barbed wires carefully, she pulled them apart and slid in between them to his side of the fence. She didn't acknowledge him as she headed for the copse of thick grass where she had turned her mare, Chantilly, loose.

She wasn't surprised when she heard his mount move forward also. "What happened?" he demanded again.

"Your boss happened," she tossed angrily over her shoulder. "Just like he always does."

Jarett's thoughts continued to spiral into more sinister depths where she was concerned. "What makes you think Murdock did this?"

Alex sniffed haughtily as she turned back to face him, she ignored the horse that pushed at her shoulder for attention. "I told you before Mr. Stanton that you should learn more about the man that hired you. You told me, in no uncertain terms, that you didn't care. Why do you care now?"

"Let's just say that I've found my curiosity peaked, so enlighten me."

Alex didn't know if he was playing with her or not. His horse nudged her again and pushed her back a step. Absently, she stretched her hand out to pet his velvety muzzle. "I don't have all afternoon Mr. Stanton, and I'm afraid it would take far more than that to enlighten *you*."

He couldn't hide a smile at her snotty attitude, nor could he rid himself of his persistent suspicions. His gaze fell to the bandanna tied loosely around her throat; he tried to picture it over her face with only her eyes revealed. If only he could recall the shape of the eyebrows or the color of them. Frowning, his gaze returned to her face as her hand lingered upon Ricochet's black muzzle.

Kicking his foot free of the stirrup, he swung his leg over and slid to the ground. She took a startled step away. He stood with his hand resting upon Ricochet's high back. "Tell me Alexandra, why do you hate Murdock so much?"

"Everyone around here hates him," she replied a little too casually.

"Yes, but I sense that your hatred runs a little deeper."

Alex began to feel the first real coils of anxiety in her belly as she realized that he was studying her with a bewildered gleam in his eyes. She was suddenly well aware that the clothing she wore was much too similar to the clothing she had worn during the robbery. Alex pulled her hat off in an attempt to remove as many similarities between her and the boy she pretended to be as possible. She didn't put the hat back on; instead, she used it to fan herself.

"I don't know what you mean." She tried to sound airy but she sensed that she failed miserably.

He took a step toward her, but she refused to back down. "He knocks the fences down," he said.

"Yes."

"Steals the livestock."

"Yes."

He wasn't asking questions but she was answering him in an attempt to ward off his steady approach. "What else has he done?"

He stopped before her, his hands folded casually behind his back as he rocked on his heels. "There was a mysterious barn fire on another ranch; livestock has turned up dead, when it isn't missing," she told him.

"And all of this started to occur after he moved into the area?"

"Yes."

"He's trying to drive the ranchers off, trying to drive you and your brother off?"

Alex's jaw clenched as she eyed him. She didn't trust him or this line of inquisition. "Yes."

"And the sheriff won't help any of you?"

"The sheriff is his man, he's paid well to turn the other cheek," she retorted.

A sardonic smile curled his mouth as his suspicions were coming closer and closer to being confirmed. He didn't know how he hadn't seen it earlier, probably because she had been too alluring to be passable as a boy. However, he should have known that in her work clothes, with a bandanna covering the delicacy of her features, that much of her beauty could be concealed. All of the pieces had been there, but he'd been too blinded by lust to put them together. The realization incensed him beyond belief.

"Anything else Alexandra?" His voice was deceptively calm and controlled. "Has he done anything else to deserve such hatred?"

Alex clamped her mouth shut on the truth; only four other people knew it, and they were the only four that she trusted with her life. *This* man wasn't one of them. In fact, he was very much her enemy, almost as much as Murdock was. Maybe even more so, for Jarett wasn't as blind or stupid as Murdock was.

Unable to stop herself, Alex took a step back. Something in his gaze reminded her of a tiger stalking its prey. Her heart suddenly felt like a lump of lead in her chest as she took another step away.

"Isn't that enough?" she asked.

"I wouldn't think so. It's not enough to break the law, not enough to shoot a man, to shoot *me*. There are other ways of extracting justice."

"What would you know about it?" she demanded. "What would you know about having all of your hard work destroyed by one man's greed? What would you know about watching your friends suffer, watching families suffer because one man is determined to own all the land?"

"Why do you care so much? Most of the town has ostracized you Alexandra. I've heard the rumors, the talk. Megan, Daryl, Paul, Henry and your brother are the only friends you have. What does it matter to you what happens to the ones who have shunned you?"

How did Alex explain that they had all been her friends at one point in time? That it had only been after her father's death, when she had become unruly and stopped caring about respectability, that people had begun to talk about her? How did she tell him that it didn't matter if they shunned her as long as Murdock never succeeded in his goal of obtaining their farms? She would do anything in her power, fight until her last breath to make sure that he didn't succeed.

"I don't wish to see anyone hurt," she whispered. "Especially not by him."

"Oh, but anyone that works for him deserves to be hurt?"

"No!" she cried. "No one deserves to be hurt!"

"Except Murdock?" he inquired with bland innocence.

"Yes," she spat. "*Especially* him!"

"Such vehemence from a woman who doesn't want to see her neighbors upset, neighbors that have spurned her. Is there no other reason for your hatred of Murdock?"

He saw the flicker of doubt in her eyes. "No," she whispered.

The malice that filled his eyes should have cautioned her but even if she had heeded the warnings, she wouldn't have had enough time to escape. With a livid roar he was upon her, his hands grabbed her and he pulled her toward him. Too startled to fight, she was jerked forward with only a muffled cry of protest. It wasn't until she heard the rending of cloth, felt the fresh air upon the bare skin of her shoulder that she began to react, and by then, it was too late.

CHAPTER 10

"You bitch!" Alex recoiled as if she had been slapped. She winced as his fingers dug into the flesh of her upper arm with a bruising intensity that caused her to cry out in pain. "You rotten little *bitch*!"

Terror caused her mouth to go dry, her heart to hammer, and a burst of adrenaline to surge through her body. She wrenched backward but he clung to her. He lifted her feet off the ground as he thrust his enraged face into hers. There was actually a vein pulsating in his forehead as he shook her sternly. Alex cried out and kicked ferociously to get free as he spun her around and carried her across the ground.

"Put me down!" she cried, truly petrified about what he was going to do to her.

He completely ignored her. A red haze blurred his vision as his gaze once again fell to the fresh bullet wound in her shoulder. The puckered ugliness of the healing wound was stark against the creamy perfection of her skin. Its hideousness only served to reinforce the true depth of depravity in her soul. To think he had thought her different, thought her innocent. Like the boy he had mistaken her for, he knew that she was really a wolf in sheep's clothing. There was nothing good about her, she was a greedy, money hungry, conniving bitch.

Swearing, he thrust her onto the back of Ricochet. Ignoring her startled cry, he grabbed hold of the pummel and swung himself up behind her. She clawed at the sides of the saddle in an attempt to get free. He ignored the small yelp she emitted as he took hold of her waist and pulled her firmly against his chest.

"Let me go!" she yelled as she clawed savagely at his thickly muscled arm. He squeezed the breath from her in return.

"I'll beat you to a pulp if you don't stop!" he grated in her ear and spurred Ricochet abruptly in the side.

Her fight ceased, she gripped the arm that she had been trying to shred as they lunged forward. The horse pounded across the ground in a full gallop that caused her heart to lurch into her throat and her stomach to roll threateningly. They burst out of the small patch of woods. He reined the horse sharply to the left and across the open expanse of land with a reckless abandon that she would have found exhilarating if she hadn't been so frightened.

"Where are you taking me?" she demanded over the thundering hoof beats.

"Murdock's paying a nice reward for the thieves; I think he'll truly enjoy it when I hand you to him."

The world spun threateningly as a cloud of blackness descended over her. She struggled from its depths, determined not to succumb to the panic threatening to consume her. She would rather be dead than handed over to Murdock. Without giving him any warning, she wrenched herself to the side, determined to escape the iron hold on her waist.

She teetered for a moment, staring at the grass of the field as the ground loomed beneath her. A hand entangled within her hair and he wrenched her back to stop her from falling. Pain tore through her battered skull as she clawed at the hand holding her. Heedless of the agony in the hand Megan had bruised, she fought with a frenzy that bordered on insanity.

"Stop!" he barked.

Blinding lights filled her vision, despite it all, she didn't stop battling him. "Let go!" she screeched.

Jarett cursed and pulled back on Ricochet's reins, as her frenzied thrashing grew even worse. He released his hold on her waist, lifted her up and dumped her unceremoniously across his lap. She squealed as she kicked at him. He took satisfaction in the sight of her draped across his lap and he had to fight the urge to paddle her delicious backside. The thought had just entered his mind when she sank her teeth into his thigh just centimeters from where she had placed a bullet in him.

Amazement and pain coursed through him. Without thinking, he gasped hold of her hair again and ripped her back as he sought to free his leg from her vicious teeth. She was flung from his lap and landed upon the ground with an explosive exhalation of air. Remorse and self-loathing filtered through him, she'd most likely kill him if she got the chance, but that was no reason for him to have just handled her like that.

Jarett expected to find her lying defeated upon the ground when he pulled Ricochet up. Instead, she was on her feet and already running. Cursing, he turned and spurred Ricochet in the side as he raced across the field toward her. Leaning down in his saddle, he bent over to grasp her around the waist. He was almost to her when she threw herself flat on the ground.

He was incensed by the time he kicked his foot free and jumped down. She wasn't quite as nimble as she had been when she'd first fallen. She remained in place as he stalked toward her, determined to put her in her place. Her hand twitched toward her gun. Jarett froze as she leveled him with a steely gaze.

"Don't touch it Alexandra," he advised.

"You're faster than me," she panted. She was winded from her sprint and her body was sore from the fall, but she was still in enough control of herself to put up a fight to the death. Something she planned to do.

"Yes," he agreed.

"You'll have a bullet in me before I can even get my hand on my gun."

"Yes."

"Then do it."

Jarett was unable to believe what she had just said. Her hand twitched again, but there was a deep acceptance within the brilliant depths of her eyes. Dirt and sweat streaked her delicate features but she was still stunning. "Alexandra..."

"You'll have to kill me to turn me over to Murdock. I won't go alive. Do you understand me?"

"You're going to pay for your crimes."

"Then take me to the sheriff..."

"Murdock's man?"

"Hang me yourself. I don't particularly care. I will not give that man the satisfaction of getting his hands on me."

He contemplated her set demeanor. Her hand moved to the butt of her gun and rested upon it. He had no fear of her, not yet. He would have the gun out of her hand in one shot, she knew it as well as he. It was her obvious determination to die, rather than take the chance that Murdock might let her live that held him still.

"I didn't mean to shoot you, you know," she said. "I simply didn't know what else to do. I couldn't let you take Hugh, Murdock would have known then. Our lives would have been as good as over. If you had taken him, I would have had to go after him, simply so that Murdock wouldn't have the pleasure of torturing him, which he would have. If I had been captured, I would have found a way to take my own life before he got to me. So you see, I had no choice, you would have done the same."

"I wouldn't have broken the law by robbing from the man in the first place. I would never have put myself in that position."

Her jaw clenched as she tilted her chin proudly. "It's easy to judge people from your lofty position, isn't it Jarett?"

"I am not a thief. I've earned everything that I have."

"Draw the gun Jarett, but don't just shoot mine from my hand, do me the favor of killing me. Give me that mercy." It was the dry connotations of her voice that affected him more than anything she said. She was resolute; there was no doubt in his mind that she expected to fight to the death. "I have two guns, if need be, I'll use the other one on myself. Can you stop both of them?"

Astonishment filtered through him as she continued to stare resolutely at him. "What did he do to you?" he asked quietly.

Her eyes flickered as sorrow filled their stunning emerald deaths. Tears swarmed in them before she blinked them back. "Would you believe me if I told you?"

He shrugged absently. "Try me, what can it hurt?"

Alex hesitated; her eyes scanned his face as she debated the wisdom of telling him. What harm could it do? She decided. She was going to die no matter what. She truly wouldn't allow him to take her to Murdock; she only prayed that Hugh might have a chance to escape before Jarett could get to him. Although, she doubted it. Anguish speared through her chest at the thought of her brother, but there was nothing she could do for him now.

"Alexandra."

His voice drew her attention back to him. There was no emotion on his face; his eyes were remote and unreadable. He was not the man that had kissed her, not the man that had helped her with Henry's clothing. This man was an indifferent, analytical stranger waiting to hear her speak.

"He killed my father."

Jarett blinked as her words staggered him as much as a slap would have. He had truly thought that she would try to come up with a better lie than that. He already knew the truth of what had happened to her father. "Your father shot himself."

Alex winced at the lie that had spread rapidly through the town, a lie that she had done nothing to correct. It had destroyed her inside, had eaten away at her heart and her soul. It was a lie that Hugh had insisted she perpetrate for her own safety, and that Paul, Megan, and Daryl were the only other people that knew it was false.

"That is a lie," she replied coldly.

"Alexandra, you may believe that, it may give you a reason to justify your actions, and Hugh's, but I was there the day that Suzanne said your father shot himself and you did nothing to correct her. I've asked around town and many people have told me that his death was an accident. It was a tragedy for you, yes, but it was an accident."

Alex cringed at the reminder that she'd done nothing to defend her father's honor. "Suzanne doesn't know the truth."

"Oh, and who does know the truth?"

"I can't tell you that."

He was certain that he already knew the answer to that question anyway. "Why don't you tell me what you believe happened?"

She was incensed by his condescending tone. "It's not what I believe! It's what I *know*!" she retorted.

He quirked an eyebrow as he tilted his head. "Then what do you know?"

"I know that Murdock shot my father."

"And how did you come by this bit of information?"

"Don't patronize me!"

Jarett held his hands up in a gesture of surrender and peace. "Tell me what you know," he encouraged.

She wrapped her hand around the butt of her gun, more for something to hold onto than with any thought of drawing it. His eyes went to her hand, but he made no move toward his gun. She wasn't fooled into thinking that he couldn't beat her anyway, and he knew that as well as she did.

"I saw him do it," she admitted. She waited to see the disbelief that she knew was coming, but his face remained impassive as he studied her. "My father often took me or Hugh with him to ride the fences, sometimes we both went, but at other times it was just one of us. He loved to show us the property; he had worked hard to make the ranch successful and he was proud of all he'd accomplished. He tried to instill that pride in us, share it with us, and he succeeded."

Alex drew a deep breath to steady herself. "That day, it was just me. Hugh had spent the night in town. A fact that I'm sure Murdock knew. He probably never suspected that my father took me with him sometimes. Believe it or not, I was prim and proper at the time, or at least I was when I was around town."

He remained silent as he watched pride, wistfulness, and sadness spread across her face. He wasn't even sure she was aware of the tears in her eyes. "However, my father had reconciled himself to the fact that he wasn't going to be able to leave me behind when he and Hugh went out riding together. When my mother died, they were all I had, and I trailed after them like a lost puppy. In the beginning, I even went so far as to sneak a horse out of the stable and followed behind them until they were far enough away that they wouldn't send me back.

"After that, my father gave up on trying to keep me in the house, like a proper lady, and allowed me to learn how to work the ranch too. He also taught me to shoot, to hunt, and to rope. I set out to learn everything and I was very adept at it. After a time he became just as proud of my accomplishments as he was of Hugh's.

"However, in town I was the epitome of respectability. Only Megan, Paul, Daryl, and Hugh knew that I worked the ranch as well as any man, so not even that was a blemish on my reputation. My father went with me to Henry's; they were good friends. When Henry's son Charlie left, I knew that Henry was lonely so I never refused to go visit him like Hugh did. After my father was killed, Henry and I grew even closer and I started going to his home by myself."

Alex had to pause to take a breath. A knot had begun to form in her chest, making it difficult to breathe. It had been years since she had told the truth to anyone; she had never expected to reveal it again in her lifetime. She closed her eyes, her hand clenched on the butt of her gun as a shudder swept through her.

"My father rode the fences every day at the same time. I hadn't been with him in almost a month. Megan and Daryl's wedding had been coming, and I'd been helping her with the millions of little details that entailed. They had been married the day before. It was why Hugh was in town; he'd done a little too much celebrating the night before and slept at the tavern. I was late; I had meant to get up early to ride with my dad. I'd greatly missed the time that we spent together, the conversations that we had shared, but it had been a long night and I had over slept.

"I was coming up to the southern ridge, the one below where you found me today." A shudder swept through her, racking her body as memories began to assail her. "I saw them before my father did," she continued, unaware that her voice had become a choked whisper. "I was on the other side of the fence, in the tree line. I had planned to surprise him and give him a good scare; I liked to do that sometimes. I knew he would yell at me, but he was never truly angry with me for scaring him."

Jarett stared at her, a part of him melted as tears slid down her cheeks to leave a clean trail through the dirt covering her cheeks. He was certain that she didn't know she was crying. Certain that she had no idea she had begun to shake so fiercely that her hand had slid off the gun. Her eyes were distant, swamped with woe and turned inward to her memories.

He fought the urge to go to her, to wrap his arms around her and comfort her, but he knew that she would freeze up if he did. So he remained where he was, not telling her to stop, even though it was obvious that her memories were shattering her.

"They came from the trees. My father stopped to greet them. I stopped where I was; I knew my father would be cross with me if they saw me in a pair of breeches and a man's shirt. He may have been proud of my accomplishments, but I was his little girl, and I was to behave as such around people.

"I waited impatiently for them to leave, moving further into the shadows of the woods. The first hint that something wasn't right came when my father started to gesture enthusiastically, his voice high and irritated, but I was unable to make out the words. I've always been curious, so I started to make my way forward, careful to stay hidden. I recognized Murdock's men first, and then I saw him at the front of the group. I froze, unable to go any closer. I had *never* liked Murdock. The way that he looked at me made my skin crawl.

"I heard my father shout and then I saw the gun, it was only a flash in the sunlight, almost blinding. The shot itself was deafening. I remember that. I recall that clearly, for the world suddenly went still. No sound penetrated my ears after that shot was fired. I saw my father's mouth moving, but I couldn't hear the words.

"Murdock grinned pitilessly as he slid the gun back into its holster. Then, I saw the vivid stain spreading across my father's chest, his hands clutched at it and then he was sliding, falling. I thought I screamed, but I realized afterward that I didn't. I just sat there, unable to move as Murdock left with his men. I could have done something to stop them, could have gone after them, but I didn't. I couldn't..."

Jarett took an involuntary step toward her. He moved cautiously, troubled that her hand would go back to her gun, but she was still lost in her memories and grief. Her tears were rolling more freely now, streaking down to wet the ground in front of her booted feet. Her shoulders shook, but she seemed unaware of it all.

"I went to him," she whispered. "Eventually I found the ability to move and I went to him. He was on the ground, barely breathing; the awful rattling coming from him somehow managed to pierce the deafness that had descended upon me. I knelt by him and drew him against my chest, I was unaware I was crying until my tears landed on his face. He was so limp by then, so lifeless, but his beautiful green eyes were open."

Her hand came unconsciously up to touch a corner of her eye, a gesture that was more telling of her love for her father than any of her words. "I begged him not to leave me. Begged God not to take him, but no one was listening. He didn't live long, but his eyes never left mine, even after he died. I don't know how many hours I stayed there. I know that it was night before Hugh, Daryl, Megan, and Paul found us. The look on Hugh's face was heart wrenching. The look on Paul's and Daryl's almost as bad. Megan couldn't even speak. My father was a good man. He loved us. He..."

Her words were cut abruptly off as strong arms swept around her and pulled her against something warm and solid. She blinked in dazed confusion as she tried to recall who was holding her and where she was. Her mind was still locked on a past that she had worked hard to keep blocked out. Then, her gaze settled upon the tender golden eyes staring down at her. Amazement jolted through her but she didn't try to pull away from the security of his arms.

Jarett didn't know what had possessed him to grab her, she had just looked so broken that he had been unable to resist. He wiped the tears from her face. She looked down in bewilderment before touching her cheek. Color suffused her face as she bent her head and turned her face away from him.

"Here." Jarett handed her a handkerchief.

She took it with an unsteady hand and wiped the tears from her face. "Thank you."

Jarett glanced down at her bent head. He placed his hand under her chin and nudged her face up. She was paler beneath her tan, her eyes more dazzling from her tears, and her black lashes were stuck together from their wetness. "Why does everyone believe that your father shot himself then?"

A shudder rocked through her. Unable to stop himself, he began to rub her back in an attempt to ease some of the sadness that was shaking her. "When I finally told Hugh what I had witnessed he went into a frenzy," she whispered in a choked voice. "Daryl and Paul had to hold him down to stop him from going after Murdock. When Hugh finally calmed down, it was Daryl that suggested that no one else be told what I had seen."

"Why is that?" he prodded when she stopped speaking.

"I was the only witness," she whispered. "We couldn't go to the sheriff and tell him what I'd seen; we knew he would just tell Murdock. Murdock never would have let me live if he knew what I had seen. So Daryl suggested that we never mention it. I fought against doing that with every ounce of my being but Hugh finally convinced me. We were all the other had left, Murdock would have done whatever it took to silence me, and then Hugh would have been alone.

"I know my brother, if something had happened to me, no one would have been able to hold him down and no one would have stopped him from going after that monster. I hated the lie, I still hate it," she spat bitterly. "To have people thinking that about my father is something that I cannot stand, but we didn't know what else to do."

Jarett recalled her reaction to Suzanne's words that day in the Mercantile. Things were beginning to make more sense now. "So you decided to take your revenge out in another way?"

Alex winced at the reminder. "Yes."

"I see."

"No, you don't," she gushed out. She had to make him understand. "I truly did *not* want to shoot you. I didn't know what else to do. I was scared. I never thought that anything would go wrong, I never allowed myself to contemplate such a possibility. If I had..."

Her voice trailed off as she looked away from the burning intensity of his eyes. "If I had, then it never would have started. I never would have done it. But everything had gone so smoothly before. It won't happen again, not for the reasons that you're thinking, but simply because..." she swallowed convulsively. "Because I could not shoot a man again. I feel wretched about what I did. I hate myself for it. I was no better than Murdock that day."

Jarett stared at her. The intensity of her gaze, the self-hatred within their depths all served to make him believe that she was telling the truth. He wanted to believe her, he did believe her about her father, but had she truly felt trapped, and remorseful, after shooting him?

"I kept asking Hugh if you were okay. He told me that you were, but it wasn't until I saw you that I felt any measure of relief. He told me it wasn't a mortal wound, but he wouldn't tell where it was." Her eyebrows drew together as her gaze ran over his toned body. "I still don't know where it was."

Jarett had to bite back a smile. He could well imagine that her brother hadn't told her where the bullet had gone in. She lifted her gaze back to his, confusion and curiosity was evident on her face. "Where *did* I shoot you?"

"Somewhere no man would like to be shot," he replied. When she still looked confused, he decided that he wasn't going to elaborate on his statement. "What do you propose to do to Murdock now?"

"There isn't much that we can do," she said. "Steal some of his cattle maybe, knock down his fences, but that doesn't help us and it doesn't help the surrounding ranchers. It will just aggravate him; make him angrier and more determined for pay back. So that truly isn't an option. The only thing that distressed him, and helped all of us, was stealing his money."

Jarett frowned in confusion. "How did stealing his money help the other ranchers?"

Exasperation settled over her features as her jaw clenched. "We didn't keep the money," she said coldly. "Oh, we kept some of it, enough to replace our own wounded, missing, and dead livestock but the rest we gave away. Going into town every week it's easy to learn about people's losses. The money shipments came in once a month, we kept a record of losses and divided it the best that we could to the people who could use it."

More pieces of the puzzle began to click into place at this revelation. He finally understood the rancher's and townspeople's unwillingness to help him catch the thieves, even though Murdock's reward was quite large. If the ranchers had suspected Alexandra and Hugh, they still wouldn't have turned them over. They were the two people helping to keep the ranchers afloat.

However, with Murdock's reward money they would receive a large sum, but their fences and livestock would still go missing, and the money would dwindle away. Not only that, but they all suspected, no they all *knew,* that it was Murdock causing the destruction in the first place. The ranchers would do what they could to protect the people that had become a thorn in Murdock's side and the only help they had against him.

"I see," he said.

Alex didn't want to ask the next question but she had too. "Are you still going to take me to him?"

Jarett thought over her story and the reasons behind what she had done. He was jolted to realize that he no longer harbored any resentment toward her for shooting him. His thirst for revenge had been drowned beneath her grief and distress.

"I meant what I said," she whispered. "I would prefer it if you kill me now."

His hands clenched around her waist as he pulled her against his chest and slid his hand into her thick hair. He couldn't stand the thought of anything happening to her, and he knew that if Murdock ever realized what she had seen, what she had done, he would destroy her and her brother. "I won't take you to him," he promised.

She slumped against him, suddenly weary and more than a little beat down. All of the aches in her body blazed to life at once. Her tailbone hurt, her legs felt like limp noodles, her back was a mass of knots and bumps and her hand throbbed like the devil. Her good hand dug into the thin material of his shirt. She buried her face against the muscular wall of his chest and took comfort in his solid, reassuring presence as she gave herself over to the solace that he offered.

Jarett's head dropped down to rest on top of hers. She smelled of earth, horse, leather, sweat, and something utterly feminine, something entirely Alexandra. It was sweet and reminded him of strawberries as it tickled his nostrils. Her hair was damp with sweat, tangled and dirty, yet it still felt like silk as he rubbed his cheek against it.

Beneath the thin cotton of her shirt, he could feel the delicate curve of her spine as he rubbed at the knots he discovered along the way. The supple swell of her breasts pressed tantalizingly against his chest as she breathed. Realizing that he was growing aroused, Jarett grit his teeth and pulled slightly away from her. Even he was not so coarse as to take advantage of her when she was so vulnerable. "Come on, let's get you home."

His voice was gruffer than he had expected, but the heat stiffening his cock was becoming unbearable. She blinked up at him and her hands slid away from his waist. He missed the loss of contact instantly as she took an unsteady step back. A grimace twisted her face before she pushed it aside and composed her face into a mask of indifference. Jarett was not fooled. She was injured and it was his fault. He had lost his temper, but then to be fair he hadn't known then what he knew now. That fact didn't make him feel any less like a miserable bastard for what he had done.

With a muttered curse, he bent and swung her easily into his arms. A startled sound escaped her and her arms latched around his neck. He crossed the ground to Ricochet and carefully placed her in the saddle before swinging up behind her.

CHAPTER 11

"Where have you been?" Alex winced at Hugh's callous tone of voice as he pulled up beside them. His face twisted into a scowl. "We've been looking all over for you!"

Jarett's hands tightened around her waist as she leaned into him. "Hugh..."

"What happened to you?" he barked out. "You look like crap!"

"Hugh..."

"What are you doing with *him*?" he exploded.

"If you'd shut up for two seconds I could tell you!" Alex snapped back.

Hugh's scowl grew even more threatening. Alex returned it ferociously. He took a deep breath and his brown eyes turned hatefully toward Jarett. "I suppose you had something to do with why she looks as if she was drug behind a horse."

"Yes," he admitted.

Indignation slashed across Hugh's face, his hand instinctively moved to his gun. "Hugh don't!" Alex cried. "Just listen to me!" She glanced around the field before her eyes fell on the house in the distance. "Actually, let's go home so we can sit and talk."

"Alex," Hugh growled.

"Hugh," she returned. Jarett watched in amusement as he was reminded of the scene between them outside of the tavern. "Trust me."

His scowl faded, but his eyes remained hatefully locked upon Jarett. "Fine," he muttered before turning his horse away.

Jarett followed behind and pulled Ricochet up when they reached the two-story log house. The screen door burst open and an older, heavyset black woman came rushing out to the large, wraparound porch. "You found her!" she cried. "Jesus child you look a mess!"

"Good to see you too Lysette," Alex mumbled.

"What did you do, get in a fight with a bear?"

"Feels like it." She spoke so softly that only Jarett could hear her. His mouth quirked in amusement as he slid off the saddle and pulled her down to him. "Jarett, put me down."

He ignored her command, Hugh's irritated gaze, and Lysette's wide-eyed amazement as he climbed the porch steps with Hugh following behind. "I'll fix ya a bath," Lysette mumbled, her eyes darted to Jarett as she shook her head in confusion.

Alex sighed blissfully at the thought of hot water. "That would be wonderful Lysette, thank you."

Lysette mumbled something about children and disgraces as she held the door open for Jarett. He stepped into the dimly lit foyer. His gaze ran over the large staircase before him, the worn red rug beneath his feet, and the fine layer of dust that covered the tiny table to his left.

"This way," Hugh commanded as he moved down the hall and pushed open a set of sliding doors on the right.

Jarett moved into the large library. His step faltered as he took in the collection of books lining the dark wood walls. The curtains were flung open to reveal the setting sun that was the only illumination in the room. His footsteps became muffled on the hardwood floor as he stepped onto the worn green, silver, and gold carpet. He settled Alexandra onto a sofa; the cushions were so thread bare that stuffing was beginning to show through the deep green material.

Standing away from her, he took in the matching chair and love seat that were in the same condition as the sofa. The small table beside the sofa, and the one in between the chair and love seat were both scratched. The curtains had been yellow, but time and neglect had faded them to a dingy cream color. There was a massive, ornate desk at the head of the room with a ledger lying open upon it. The room had once been nicely appointed, it hadn't been a wealthy man's office but it was the office of a prideful man. Whatever money that had been used to originally decorate the room was now gone. No, they most certainly were not keeping the money they stole, he realized.

"Is someone going to tell me what is going on?" Hugh demanded.

Alex shifted on the sofa and tried to ignore the discomfort of her body. Jarett shot her a warning look. Confusion swirled through her as she turned her gaze from him, to the irritated countenance of her brother. "Perhaps we should have some drinks first," she suggested.

Hugh's scowl grew. "I don't think now is the time for drinks!"

"Well I do. I could use some brandy." Hugh looked as if she had said she could fly, but he nodded and turned to the bar in the corner. He pulled the top off the decanter and poured her a small splash. "I need more than that. Jarett would you like something?"

Hugh crashed the decanter off the bar as he spun around. "Jarett is it?" he barked.

"Scotch, if you have some." Jarett ignored the obvious fury that blazed from Hugh.

"Yes, we do," Alex replied. "Pour yourself something too Hugh, you're going to need it."

"I already figured that out," he muttered and turned away again.

Alex waited for Hugh to bring her drink to her. He shoved it unceremoniously into her hand as he gave her a scathing look, one that he turned on Jarett as he all but threw the glass at him. Alex was amazed by the amusement that crossed Jarett's face before he took a sip of scotch.

Hugh stood stiffly by the bar, his arms folded over his chest as he glared at the two of them.

"Well," he prompted.

Alex took a sip of brandy to wet her parched throat. The liquor burned its way through her body, warming her from the inside out and relaxing her tensed muscles. Taking a deep breath, she decided to plunge right in. "He knows Hugh."

"Knows what?" Hugh grated from between clenched teeth.

"Everything, and I do mean *every*thing."

Alarm flickered across Hugh's features before he was able to cover it up. "Dad?"

"Yes."

"Alex!" he roared, causing her to jump. "Are you insane?"

His hand flew to his gun as he spun on Jarett. "No!" Alex cried. She lurched awkwardly to her feet and winced at the discomfort the movement caused her. Jarett caught her as she stumbled and brandy splashed from her glass.

"Sit down," Jarett ordered gruffly. Alex's eyes flew to Hugh. His gun was drawn; the expression on his face was remote. The sound of the pistol cocking rang loudly in her ears yet Jarett didn't even turn to look at him. "Sit, before you hurt yourself."

Alex glanced between them; she refused to sit while Hugh had his gun drawn. Jarett swept her up and deposited her on the sofa again. Sputtering in indignation, she tried to stand back up but he pushed her shoulders down. She glowered at him before turning her attention to her brother. "Put the gun down Hugh," Alex pleaded. "Please."

He didn't move; his eyes never left Jarett. "He'll tell Murdock."

"If he was going to tell Murdock, then I would be there by now or I'd be dead. Think Hugh, he brought me home."

Jarett released her shoulders and turned away from her. He wasn't surprised when he heard her stand up behind him. "She's right," he said calmly.

There was love and fear evident in Hugh's eyes as he looked at his sister. Confusion marred his brow as he turned back to Jarett. "You've done nothing more than try to find us for weeks now. Why aren't you taking us in?"

Unable to stop himself, Jarett's gaze returned to Alexandra. He had no doubt in his mind that Hugh would pull the trigger if he felt that Jarett was a threat to her. It had only been her faint plea that kept him from pulling it now. He really didn't want to have to kill the man, he understood where Hugh was coming from, and it would destroy Alex if something happened to her brother. He would defend himself if he had to though.

"I understand why you did it," Jarett told him.

"She shot you."

"Yes, she did, but I can understand why."

"I told him everything Hugh," Alex admitted. "About dad, about the money, about where it goes. He knows it all, and I am still here."

"He hurt you," Hugh said.

"I gave as good as I got."

Hugh grinned. "I'm sure you attempted to."

Alex huffed angrily; she knew that Hugh didn't believe her. "I bit him."

"Where?"

"Upper thigh," Jarett answered.

The amusement that lit Hugh's face completely confused Alex. "What is so funny?" she demanded.

"Nothing Alex," Hugh replied. The smile slipped from his face as he turned his attention back to Jarett. "You're Murdock's man."

"I told you before that I am no one's man," Jarett replied. "Murdock hired me to make sure the money was delivered safely from St. Louis. I did that. If it weren't for the two of you, and me getting shot, I would have been out of here that night. Murdock is not paying me to stay here now; I did that for my own personal vendetta."

"So you no longer carry your vendetta?" Hugh asked.

"No."

"And why is that?"

It was *Alex*; he knew that. He wasn't about to let her get hurt again, wasn't about to let Murdock get his hands on her, and he wasn't going to be the one that allowed it to happen. He didn't want to think about what that realization meant, not yet anyway, and he wasn't about to admit it.

"I'm not going to let a man get away with murder," he said.

"But you'll let the person that shot you get away?" Hugh inquired.

"There are certain circumstances in this instance."

"You would have done the same?" Alex asked.

"No, I would have killed Murdock years ago." Jarett's tone of voice indicated that he would have done that and not felt any regret.

Hugh's eyes went to his sister. "There is a reason why I didn't do that," he muttered defensively.

"I understand that reason." Jarett was startled to realize that he *did* understand. If Hugh hadn't been killed outright, he would have been arrested and hung. Alex would have been left to fend for herself. If he had been in Hugh's place, he might have made the same decision, once he had cooled off enough to think clearly.

"So you believe that he killed our father?" Hugh inquired.

"Yes, I do."

Doubt still haunted Hugh's eyes though as they ran over Jarett. "He brought me back Hugh," Alex said softly. "He was taking me to Murdock." The rage that suffused Hugh's features caused her to rush onward. "He didn't Hugh, he brought me back here!"

Without realizing what she was doing, she grabbed hold of Jarett's solid arm. She took comfort in the strength that radiated from him. She didn't miss the steely look that came over Hugh's face, but she didn't care right now. The idea of anything happening to Jarett was more than she could tolerate. She didn't want to lose him and she was petrified that Hugh might do something rash.

"And you no longer want the reward money?" Hugh asked coldly.

"I never wanted or needed the reward money, nor would I take it from a murderer."

Hugh sipped at his drink as he seemed to debate Jarett's words. He glanced back at his sister and placed his gun back in its holster. Alexandra's grip on his arm loosened, but she didn't release him. He glanced down at her, oddly comforted by her touch.

"So, now what?" Hugh asked as he downed his scotch.

"Now, I am going to help you," Jarett told him.

"Why would you do that?" Hugh inquired as he turned to refill his glass.

"Like I said before, I don't want to see a man get away with murder."

"I see, and how do you plan to help us? Our father was killed over two years ago; all evidence that it was a murder is gone. No one would believe Alex if she came forward now."

"Was there evidence?"

"Yes. There were at least half a dozen hoofmarks around our father's body from Murdock's men," Hugh told him.

"Not much evidence there," Jarett said thoughtfully.

"My father's guns were fully loaded," Alex said. She suddenly realized that she was still clasping Jarett's arm and released it. His eyes gleamed with amusement as he smiled at her. Heat flushed her face; she looked quickly away and drank her brandy.

"So there was no way he accidentally shot himself," Jarett said.

"No," Hugh answered and turned back to face them.

"And you're sure the sheriff won't help you?"

Alex finished her brandy and thrust the glass out to him. Jarett took it and handed it over to Hugh. "Another one?" Hugh blurted.

"It's been a grueling day Hugh," she whispered.

"You'll get drunk."

She refrained from saying that that was exactly what she planned to do. She felt like a mass of raw nerve endings right now and all of them were exposed to the world. They weren't just raw from the pain in her body, but also from the pounding that her soul had taken today. The memory of her father's murder was still far too close to the surface right now. It threatened to consume her within its depths. She tried to bury it back where it didn't fester so much, but she couldn't seem to do that right now. She hoped the liquor would help.

Jarett handed her the glass of brandy, she accepted it with trembling fingers. "The sheriff has never been any help to us before," she whispered. "No one knows that my father's guns were fully loaded at the time, except us. The townspeople and ranchers must have assumed that some bullets were missing, if we were the ones that started the lie," she said bitterly and took a gulp of her drink. "I hate that lie."

"Alex..."

She waved off Hugh's words. The liquor was beginning to have an effect on her. Her body wasn't as tender and there was a strange fuzziness filling her skull. "I know, 'twas necessary," she mumbled.

"How do you plan to help us?" Hugh inquired, seeming to have decided to leave her be.

"First things first, I'm moving in here."

"What?" they both shouted.

"If I'm here then Murdock's attention will be diverted from the two of you. My questions stirred up enough curiosity; he has the descriptions of the two men. No one but Alexandra fits the one, trust me, I know. However, if I move in here he's not going to think that I'm cavorting with the person that shot me. Plus, I'll be able to do some investigating about the broken fences, and missing livestock so that I can gather enough proof that it is him." He didn't add that he would be added protection for Alex, but he knew that was his true reason.

"You can't move in here," Hugh said firmly.

"And why is that?" Jarett inquired.

"Alex's reputation..."

"I have no reputation Hugh," she interrupted. "It's been in shreds since father died."

"I don't care!" he snapped. "It's not that bad now, if he moves in here you'll never be able to salvage it. You'll never find a suitable husband."

"Oh for crying out loud, now you sound like Megan! What does it take to get it through your thick skulls that I don't want to find a suitable husband? That I enjoy *my* life!"

"You deserve a better life."

"I have the life I want! Besides the only man that would have me is Paul."

"He's a good man," Hugh said quietly.

Alex grit her teeth as her hand clenched around the glass. She was well aware of Jarett's intense scrutiny. "I have told you, and I have told Paul, that I do *not* think of him that way," she hissed. "Let it go Hugh, I am begging you, let it go."

Jarett didn't miss the sudden sadness that flashed through Hugh's eyes before he turned his gaze away. He opened his mouth as if to say something more, then he thought better of it and closed it. Her glass was suddenly thrust forward again. Alex leveled him with a look that dared him to argue with her. He decided that he wasn't about to. She'd had a rough day and he understood that right now the only thing she truly wished was to feel nothing. He knew well how she felt as he took the glass from her and handed it to Hugh.

"I still can't allow you to move in here," Hugh decided not to comment on his sister's drinking as he refilled the glass. "I know what people think of Alex now; I can't stand the thought of them thinking even less of her."

Jarett took the glass from Hugh and passed it onto Alex. "After last night..."

"Last night," Hugh interrupted him crossly. "What happened last night?"

Alex glowered up at Jarett as she considered shooting him again. "You didn't tell him?" he inquired.

She continued to glare at him before turning away to mumble 'no' into her glass. "Tell me what?" Hugh demanded.

When it became apparent that Alex wasn't going to tell him, Jarett did. Hugh's face grew redder as the story progressed; his eyes remained glued to his sister as she returned his gaze with the same intensity. "What were you thinking going in there?" he exploded as soon as Jarett was done.

"Now do you see why I didn't tell him?" she muttered.

"Like I wasn't going to hear about it anyway! Jesus Alexandra, you could have been *raped*!"

"Hugh!" she cried. "Enough!"

"It's *not* enough! One of these days your recklessness is going to get you killed. And don't think I don't know about the trip you made to Murdock's last week." Alex's mouth dropped open as she gazed at him. "Yeah, I followed you. The only reason I didn't stop you was because I had to know where you were going, and then you didn't do anything stupid so there was no reason to show myself. I'm not as blind to your antics as you think I am. I was planning on having the trellis taken down this week, but it's coming down today."

"No, it's not!" Alex cried. "Besides, if you'd stop watching me like a guard dog, I wouldn't have to climb down the trellis whenever I need some time alone!"

"To get yourself killed! Father would have had a fit if he knew about any of this behavior."

"Well he's not here, now is he?" she bit out.

"It ends now. You are to stay away from Murdock. You're to stay out of town or so help me I will lock you in your room until I think it's safe for you to emerge. It's done Alex, it's all *done*!"

She climbed to her feet and slapped away Jarett's hands as he tried to steady her. "It is *not* done," she grated as she took a step toward her brother. "You may know my secrets Hugh, but I also know yours."

"What are you talking about?" Hugh inquired.

"Don't you dare play stupid with me! I was outside the day that Murdock came here to speak with father, and the window was open. I heard everything that he had to say to the both of you. I saw the rage he was in when he left."

Hugh's face had grown paler with every word she spoke but Alex didn't care about his opinion. She wasn't sure if it was the liquor that had caused her tongue to loosen, or if it was the resurgence of memories that couldn't be repressed again. She was going to finish what she had to say, and she was going to make sure that Hugh realized that no matter what he did, he wasn't going to stop her from getting her revenge on Murdock.

"It's not a coincidence that he killed father less than a week later," she said flatly.

"Alex, I don't know what you thought you heard..."

"Don't!" she yelled. "Don't *lie* to me!"

Jarett reached out to steady her, he was confused by the turn the conversation had taken but he instinctively sought to ease the torment that twisted her features. She tried to slap his hands away again, but this time he didn't release her arm as she swayed a little.

"Why didn't you say anything before?" Hugh inquired.

Alex took a steadying breath before continuing. "I wondered if you would say something," she whispered. "Or if you would hate me."

He took a step toward her. "Alex no," he breathed. "It wasn't your fault."

"It *was* my fault!" she exploded. "That bastard killed him because of me!"

With a violent wrenching motion, she ripped her arm free of Jarett's grasp and took an unsteady step backward. The library doors slid open and Lysette's face appeared. Her troubled gaze ran over them before settling on Alex. "Your bath is ready Alexandra."

Hugh was staring at her with a mixture of horror and pity that was her undoing. She turned on her heel, walked out of the room and up the stairs. Unable to stop her sobs, she closed her bedroom door behind her and fell against it. She slid to the floor and drew her legs up against her chest as sobs ripped through her.

CHAPTER 12

"Let her go." Jarett stopped moving at Hugh's command. He turned back to him as Hugh began to refill his glass of scotch; he downed it and refilled it again. "She'd prefer to be alone right now."

"But..."

"I know my sister," Hugh said. "She hates to cry in front of people, she'll only get angrier if either of us witnesses it. I haven't seen her cry since the day we found her in the field with our father."

Jarett glanced to the doors that Lysette had closed behind Alex. He was torn between wanting to go to her and knowing that Hugh was right. Besides, there were things that they had to get straight between them. "What did Murdock, and your father, argue over in this house?" he inquired.

Hugh gave a harsh laugh as he slammed his glass down. "I can't believe she knew," he muttered more to himself than to Jarett. "Murdock wanted to marry her, my father said no. We all knew that Murdock was the one causing the trouble around here. The bastard didn't even wait a month after he moved here to start harassing people. There was no way that my father was going to let him marry her. Murdock would have crushed her spirit and destroyed her."

"He didn't like being told no," Jarett said more to himself.

"God no," Hugh replied. "My father was dead a week later."

"I understand why you didn't tell her."

"If I had known that she knew..." Hugh's voice trailed off as he stared out the window.

"Has he been back to ask for her hand again?"

"No, but I have no doubt that the man still wants her, I see the way he watches her, and I'm not a fool. It's obvious that Alex wants nothing to do with him, but I think he's biding his time and waiting for his opportunity to come after her again."

"Like discovering that the two of you are the elusive thieves he's been looking for?"

"Like that," Hugh agreed.

Jarett frowned at him as he folded his arms over his chest, his irritation rose as he realized the peril that Alexandra was in. "How could you have left her alone up there today?" he demanded.

Hugh lifted his glass again. "Old Willy was watching over her but he had to step away for a minute to relieve himself. He usually stands guard over her from a distance. If Alex doesn't at least have a notion that she's being left alone, then she rebels. Trust me; I tried keeping her under constant guard. She always managed to slip away from them, and then we would spend hours looking for her, hours in which she purposely stayed hidden in order to make a point.

"I've found that it's easier to let her think she's got her freedom. I know she climbed down the trellis last week because I have men that stand guard every night. They came to get me when they spotted her. Today, Willy had been watching her from the woods but by the time he returned she was gone." His eyes shot accusingly toward Jarett. "He came to find me immediately. You know if you had taken her to Murdock, he would have destroyed her."

"She would have destroyed herself first."

Hugh huffed as he leaned against a shelf and absently swirled the scotch in his glass. "Yes, she probably would have."

Jarett sat on the arm of the sofa and stretched his legs before him as he thought over everything that he'd learned.

The thieves that he had been determined to destroy were suddenly the ones that he was sympathizing with. The woman upstairs had somehow managed to work her way beneath his skin and wedge herself into a place that he hadn't even known existed.

She wasn't the conundrum he'd thought she was. She had her secrets, but they were necessary for her survival. The sorrow and guilt that she had been living with would have destroyed a lesser person, and yet she cared for people with an openness that was astounding. Instead of shutting out the world, she continued to give of herself in every way that she could.

He longed to help her heal and bring her fully back to life again. He just didn't know how, nor was he sure that he would be capable of such a thing.

"She didn't want to shoot you, you know," Hugh said.

"I know."

"She drove me insane while she was healing from her own wound, pestering me to know if you were all right. It was the first thing that she asked when she regained consciousness. It would have destroyed her if she had killed you."

Jarett didn't doubt it for an instant. "I *am* moving in here. You're going to need my help with Murdock, and Alex. She obviously does not know what's best for her and is heedless of her own safety."

Hugh placed his glass down as he folded his arms over his chest. "I know what they say about my sister in town and what you've probably heard. I hate it, but there's nothing I can do to stop it. She insists upon seeing Henry alone, she insists upon working on the ranch, and she insists upon talking with the women from Shelby's. I know that I could deny her all of these things, but she doesn't have much happiness in her life. I won't take away what little she does have.

"If their cruel gossip really distressed her then I would stop her, but she cares nothing for what people think about her, their words bother me more than they bother her. She's been visiting with Henry for five years now, it's only since my father died that the rumors about the two of them sprang up. I don't even know what they do in that little shack, but I would stake my life on the fact that my sister is not carrying on an illicit affair with the man. How anyone could ever think so is beyond me."

Jarett refrained from saying that he had thought so too, that he had gone so far as to follow her because of those thoughts. It wasn't a fact that he was proud of. "And Paul?" he inquired of the young man that followed after her like a puppy.

Hugh laughed but there was no amusement in his eyes. "Ah yes, Paul. He's been our friend since we were children, his feelings for Alex may have changed but she still sees him as a boy. It's a shame actually, Paul would make her a good husband and he knows that the gossip around town isn't true."

Jarett felt a flash of annoyance at the thought of Alexandra marrying Paul; it wasn't a thought that sat well with him. "I see," he said.

"I hope you do," Hugh said. "Because I see the way that *you* look at her too." Jarett's gaze returned to him and he scowled viciously. "But I also see the way that she looks at you. I assure you that I've never seen her look at a man like that and it worries me."

"I don't understand what you're getting at."

"I agree that we need you, that you will help deflect Murdock's suspicions from us, and that your presence here may even deflect his attention away from her in some way. I could always use a hand with Alex, and around the ranch. We've lost a lot of our workers over the past couple of years. Loyalty usually goes about as far as the paycheck, which is something that I understand, but if you think that you're going to move in here and have the added bonus of seducing my sister than you are sadly mistaken."

Jarett was irritated by Hugh's words but he kept his face completely blank. "What they say about her isn't true," Hugh said coldly.

"I know." And he was amazed to realize that he did. His glance returned to the closed doors as he fully realized that everything he'd thought about her was completely wrong. He recalled all of the things he'd said and done to her. A simple apology wasn't going to cut it, he owed her more than that and he was going to do everything he could to protect her. "I am going to help you, and that is it. I do think my presence will help to keep Alex safe from Murdock's intentions. If he thinks that she is with me, he may stay away from her."

"For as long as you are here anyway," Hugh replied bitterly.

"He'll be in jail, or dead, before I leave."

"And Alex's reputation will be beyond all repair."

"It is now," Jarett said. "However, I am certain that Paul would still have her."

"Yes, Paul will always take her, and maybe one day she will see him differently." Jarett hated the wistfulness in Hugh's voice. His hands clenched into fists at the thought of Alexandra with Paul. It took all he had to keep his face impassive as Hugh met his gaze again. "Can I trust you around her?"

"Yes," Jarett answered, but for the first time in his life he'd just given his word without knowing if he could keep it.

Hugh studied him before nodding sharply. "I'll have Lysette prepare a room for you."

Jarett stood abruptly. "I have to go into town to gather my things."

“Jarett.” He halted at the doors and glanced back at Hugh. “If you hurt my sister, I will kill you. I’m not Alex; the only tender spot in my heart is her. I will have no problem putting a bullet in your head.”

Jarett knew he meant it and if their roles had been reversed, he would have told Hugh the same thing. He pulled the doors open and walked out.

***

Jarett didn’t let himself think about the decision he had just made, or the situation that he had placed himself in. This was a no win situation, especially since he wasn’t going to touch Alex again. He would help her, he would keep her safe, but he’d be damned if he ever laid hands on her again.

The thought did nothing to ease his increasingly foul mood. What had he gotten himself into? And why?

All he had to do was picture her, standing across from him with unknowing tears streaming down her face as she spoke about her father, and he knew exactly why. He just didn’t like it.

He had come to care for her more than he had thought possible. Murdock wanted her; Jarett had seen that quite clearly at the dance. With everything that he had learned about Murdock today, there was no way that he would ever let him get his hands on Alex.

The only problem was how badly he *also* wanted her. It was a problem that he was going to have to get over, and fast. He was not about to take a virgin when there was nothing that he could offer her for her future. He had no security, no home, and no intention of getting married. He didn’t even expect to stay in the area after Murdock was dealt with.

Jarett pulled up in front of the saloon and tossed Ricochet's reins over the hitching post after dismounting. Entering the building, he tipped his hat to Frank in greeting. "Oh Jarett, you're back!" he paused on the stairs as Rachel came hurrying up to him. She was already dressed for the revelry of the evening. "Murdock was looking for you."

"Was he?" Jarett inquired casually.

"He was here a few minutes ago. I'm sure he'll return." Her eyes were troubled as they turned back to Jarett. "Have you seen Alexandra today?"

"Yes," Jarett replied briskly, he didn't know if Murdock had put Rachel up to asking.

"Is she okay?" she inquired. "Dolly and Frank told me about what happened last night."

"She's fine," he assured her.

Rachel glanced around the room again. "Good, that's good. Will you be joining us this evening?"

Jarett was sorely tempted to. He didn't know when he would get a chance to come into town again, and living with Alex was bound to be pure torture on his libido, but he *had* to get back to the ranch. He knew that nothing was going to happen tonight, but he didn't like being apart from her and not knowing if she was safe. She had managed to survive the last two years without him, and yet he felt certain that she needed him now. He knew that by robbing Murdock this past year, they had stirred up a hornet's nest.

"No Rachel, I've found another place to stay for awhile," he finally answered.

Her eyes twinkled as she smiled knowingly. "We're sure going to miss you around here."

"I bet you will," he replied with a wink. "I had better go pack."

He was halfway up the stairs before she called to him again. Turning, he glanced at her over his shoulder. "Alex is a good girl Jarett. Good heart on her."

"I know."

He hurried on up the stairs, shaking his head over the fact that even Rachel saw the good in Alex and only wanted her to be happy. He didn't know why he had tried to deny it to himself when he had known the truth about her all along. He supposed it was his own need to believe the worst in people and no one had ever proven him wrong.

Until now.

He packed hastily and was on his way back down the stairs when he spotted Murdock leaning casually against the bar with his gaze focused sharply on him. Hatred rose up in Jarett as he moved rapidly down the stairs. He fought the urge to pull his gun, and put a bullet in Murdock's head to end it all. However, getting himself hung right now wasn't one of his goals.

When he had enough evidence against Murdock, he would take that evidence to Topeka and let the law enforcement there deal with the man. Until then he had to remain calm, and keep his dislike of Murdock hidden. It was too soon to make him his enemy. Jarett swung his saddlebag over his shoulder as he strode over to him. The smile that was plastered on Murdock's face didn't make it to his hazel eyes.

"Like a drink?" Murdock inquired.

"No. I'm heading out."

Something sinister flashed through Murdock's eyes before he quickly covered it up. "Are you any closer to catching the thieves?"

"I haven't learned anything new."

Murdock frowned at him. "Maybe I was wrong after all; maybe they aren't part of the community." Jarett shrugged absently. "No matter. I came because I heard you had some trouble with some of my men last night."

Jarett had suspected that this was the real reason Murdock had been looking for him so he was prepared for the abrupt change in topic. “Nothing I couldn’t handle.”

Murdock’s eyes narrowed. “I hear you were with Alexandra Harris.”

Jarett leaned his elbow casually against the bar. “Word truly does travel fast in a small town.”

“Usually it’s just gossip,” Murdock replied.

“Not in this case.” He felt no compunction about lying to the man, or for delivering another killing blow to Alex’s reputation. By the time he left this bar, Murdock was going to know that Alex was completely under Jarett’s protection.

For a second Murdock seemed truly close to losing all control as his hand moved toward his gun and his casual demeanor slipped. In that instant Jarett saw the true depth of his obsession, and yearning, for Alex. Truly saw the man that lurked beneath. If he’d had any doubts about what Hugh and Alex had told him, they would have vanished right then.

“Where are you going?” Murdock nodded toward Jarett’s full saddlebag.

“Hugh Harris has offered me a job. I need to make some money until I can catch the thieves.” The hatred reappeared again but this time Murdock was quicker to suppress it. “Then I’ll be moving on.”

Murdock’s jaw clenched. “And if you don’t catch them?”

“I will. It’s only a matter of time.”

“Suppose they’ve left the area, maybe you should see if you could trail them.”

Jarett would have laughed at Murdock’s poor attempt at trying to get rid of him if it hadn’t annoyed him so much. “No, they’re still here. I think you were right about them being a part of the community. The townspeople aren’t willing to help me in any way. Those thieves are around here, right now they’re just laying low. They’ll slip up eventually, and when they do, I'll catch them. Now, if you'll excuse me."

"Of course," Murdock replied.

Jarett tipped his hat as he moved past him, all the time listening for the sound of a pistol being drawn to shoot him in the back.

CHAPTER 13

Jarett propped his hands up on the pillow behind his head and stared glumly at the ceiling. He was used to going without sleep, his body was more than trained for it after his nights spent guarding money shipments and in taverns, but for once in his life he would have preferred that it wasn't. He would love nothing more than to succumb to the darkness and find a few blissful hours of peace where he could completely forget about where he was, and who was in the room next to his.

She had still been locked in her room when he'd returned, and she hadn't made an appearance for the rest of the day. Hugh had insisted on leaving her be, but it seemed wrong to let her wallow in her melancholy. He'd seen the suffering that she endured and he would do anything to ease it. He just didn't know how to do that.

Helping them with Murdock was one thing, but he knew that sometimes when revenge was accomplished it didn't always ease the unrest in a person's soul. In fact, sometimes it did just the opposite. There had been very few friends in his life, he'd always been a loner. He'd never known his parents; he'd been dropped off at an orphanage in Boston as a baby and raised there until he'd struck out at twelve to make his way in the world. He'd taught himself how to shoot, had practiced it until he was better than anyone else he knew, and he was lucky enough that he grew larger than most men by the time he was seventeen. At eighteen, he had left Boston, looking to use his skills for something, and to get away from the more crowded coast.

Though he'd kept mostly to himself, he'd encountered a few people over the years, looking to avenge a loved one's death, and finding themselves with nothing left to live for after they succeeded. He'd even known one that had lost his life in the attempt of avenging his wife's murder. Jarett wasn't about to let that happen to Alex and he hoped that she was different. That once Murdock was taken care of, she would have enough in her life to keep her going afterward. From what he had seen, she did have a lot of people that cared for her and that she cared for in return.

A muted sound penetrated the still of the night. Jarett frowned as he strained to hear if it would come again. There was a small thud, and then silence. Sitting up, his gaze darted to the door that led to the room next to his. He knew it was locked; Hugh would have made sure of that before he moved Jarett into this room. If there had been room in the one remaining bunkhouse, Jarett knew Hugh would have moved him out there, but the building was full with the rest of the ranch hands. There had been another bunkhouse at one time, but it had been mostly dismantled for lumber over the past couple of years.

Another thud brought Jarett to his feet. Grabbing his breeches, he hastily slipped them on. He didn't bother with a shirt as he made his way to the door. He crept down the hall soundlessly and paused outside of her door. A muffled cry had him moving before he could think. Thrusting the door open, his gaze searched for a threat as he scanned the dimly lit interior of the room. There were two candles placed upon the nightstand, both of them were more than half-gone. Alexandra was lying in the middle of the large bed; her copper hair shone in the flickering flames. Her beautifully tanned skin was vibrant against the white sheets she lay upon.

The window had been left open; a cool breeze wafted into the room, carrying with it the scent of roses, grass, animals, and spring. He stood, uncertain as to what had drawn him here. Everything seemed perfectly fine.

He took a step back, meaning to exit discreetly when she released a muted, heartbreaking sound that froze him in his place. She turned over; her cry was muffled by the pillows as she curled her hands into them. He knew that he should leave, that she was only dreaming, but try as he might he couldn't force himself to move.

When she cried out again, he broke into motion. He noiselessly closed the door so that she wouldn't wake anyone else in the household. He was certain that she wouldn't want the others to know she was having a nightmare.

He made his way toward her. The candles flickered over her face and illuminated the tiny blue lines in her eye lids, emphasized her delicate features, and the heart wrenching tears that slid down her cheeks. He didn't know what possessed him, but he slid onto the bed beside her. She released a low wail that was pitiful in the extreme.

Looking to comfort her, he pulled her into his lap and cradled her against his chest as he soothed her hair from her forehead. His fingers twitched, he had to fight the urge to undo the tie holding her braid together so that he could allow her hair to spill free. Then she whimpered and her hand curled into his chest. His attention was immediately distracted from the long plait. Small shivers coursed through her as another muffled cry escaped.

"Alexandra, wake up," he coaxed. "Wake up."

His hand wrapped around her legs as he pulled her more firmly against him. Her silken, tan thighs burned into the flesh of his palm. He tried not to think about how she had gotten her thighs so tan; it brought forth an image that he was desperately fighting against as her taut buttocks settled firmly against his engorged cock. He knew the instant that she woke, felt the startled stiffening of her body and the brush of her lashes against his bare chest.

Alex blinked in confusion, uncertain of where she was and who was holding her. The enduring nightmare with its images of her father's blood on his shirt burst across her mind. Then she felt the slightly coarse hair beneath her cheek, the firm chest that her head was resting upon and the large palm against her thighs. His scent enveloped her, masculine and earthy beneath the subtle aroma of soap and leather. She knew instinctively who was embracing her so tenderly, but even though she knew she should be angry at finding him within her room, she felt oddly safe and comforted.

Instead of pulling away like morals and propriety told her she should do, she nestled closer to him and buried herself against the solid warmth of his chest. She could hear the reassuring beat of his heart; feel the steady pulse of it beneath her fingers. She knew she should be ashamed by her behavior, but she felt none. He helped to chase away her nightmare and brought her solace where there had been none. She wasn't even embarrassed by the fact that he knew about the nightmare, or that he had come here because of it. If it had been anyone else that had come to wake her, she would have been mortified.

"Did I wake you?" she asked.

"No," he replied, his voice oddly hoarse. She sighed as he brushed back strands of her hair from her forehead. "Do you have nightmares often?"

"I haven't had one in awhile, but after today..."

She broke off as she shied away from recalling the events of *this* day. Events that had left her so raw that she had let the nightmares slip back in. She used to have them every night for nearly seven months after her father died. They had tapered off to the point where she now had them only every couple of months.

"Does your brother know?" he inquired.

"No one knows."

Jarett dropped his cheek to her hair and inhaled her tantalizing scent. He rubbed her back up to her neck before traveling leisurely down again. The thin, white cotton gown she wore was little barrier against his hand and her skin. He was well aware of the fact that he should leave, but for the life of him, he couldn't bring himself to move. She felt so good cuddled in his lap. He held her until the excruciating pressure in his loins became too much for him to handle.

"I think it's time that you get back to sleep," he whispered against her ear.

Alex didn't want to leave the cocoon of security that he offered. His arms were a safe haven in a world of chaos and suffering. Her fingers slid through the sprinkling of hairs that covered the broad expanse of his chest. She savored in the solid strength of the muscles that flexed beneath her palm.

She became aware of an increase in the rate of his heartbeat. His hand stopped moving as his fingers curled into her back. She tilted her head back; she was so close to him that she could see the black bristles lining his jaw. His eyes were the color of honey as they met hers. A shiver worked its way through her as she recognized the carnal gleam in his beautiful eyes. Involuntarily her gaze dropped to his lips, memories of what those lips had felt like on hers exploded inside of her head in a rush of vivid, wicked images.

She tore her gaze from his mouth and her eyes instantly came back to his. His breath was warm against her cheek, minty as it filled her nose. She stared breathlessly up at him; she needed him to kiss her as badly as a flower needed the sun. He let out a low groan before lowering his head to hers. Alex's eyes drifted closed as her mouth parted in anticipation.

A tremor of delight swept through her as his mouth touched upon hers in a butterfly caress that warmed her insides. For a moment, she worried that he was going to leave her as he pulled back but his lips still brushed against hers. Then, his mouth reclaimed hers with an urgency that was far more demanding. Alex melted under the onslaught of his mouth; her bones seemed to dissolve as everything inside her liquefied.

She opened her mouth to the probing of his tongue against her lips. He swept inside, tasting her in long deep pulls that stole her breath. Her arms wrapped around his neck and held him close as she met his questing tongue. Her heart beat rapidly against her ribs as shivers wracked through her.

The world she tried so hard to hide from disappeared; she was swept up in him as surely as any tree within the path of a tornado. She forgot everything as her senses were swamped with the taste, smell, and feel of him. His hair was silky and thick when her fingers slid through it; the bristles on his jaw were rough against her skin, but not unpleasant. She didn't want this amazing feeling of belonging and safety to end.

She didn't quite know how it happened, but somehow she wasn't in his lap anymore and was now lying upon the bed. His body was heavy and hot as he settled himself over her and pressed her into the soft mattress. She savored in the feel of the muscles that bunched and flexed beneath her hands when they ran over his back.

His callused hand ran up her thigh. Alex gasped as it came tantalizingly close to the junction between her thighs, so close to the place that was throbbing with need. She didn't know what it was her body craved so badly but she was certain he would have the answers for her.

His mouth left hers to press feathery kisses across her cheeks. He nibbled at her earlobe before drawing it into his mouth to suck on it. Alex gasped and her fingers curled into his back as he moved steadily down the slim column of her throat and lower across her collarbone. His mouth and tongue left a searing trail that made her squirm beneath his steady ministrations.

Jarett pulled the collar of her nightgown down low to bare the lush breasts that he had longed to behold from the instant he'd first seen her. They were just as perfect and luscious as he'd imagined they would be. He took a minute to appreciate them as he ran his thumb over her pert, strawberry colored nipples. Her body arched beneath his as he bent his head to draw her nipple into his mouth. He rolled his tongue around it while he fondled her free breast.

The delicious sensations he aroused caused Alex's toes to curl as fire seared through her veins. She dared to open her eyes, her breath froze in her lungs at the erotic sight of his dark head bent over her, tasting her as his other palm kneaded and massaged her. The breath exploded from her when he nipped at her, her eyes closed and a moan escaped as pleasure swamped her.

He knew that he should stop this now, while he still had some semblance of control over himself, but her responsive cries and eager movements drove him onward. He would stop soon, he told himself but he knew that he lied. He wouldn't stop unless she told him too.

Her skin was as smooth as silk as he explored every one of the curves and hollows of her body. The nightgown that had seemed so unbelievably thin before now seemed as if it were a giant barrier that had to be removed immediately. He *had* to feel every inch of her.

Pulling the gown slowly off of her shoulders, and down over her breasts and belly, he waited almost breathlessly for her to tell him no, for her to come to her senses and realize that this was not what she wanted. He moved unhurriedly as he lifted himself a little off of her and continued to push the gown lower.

He allowed himself the pleasure of gazing upon her slender body that was amazingly tan everywhere. Even down around her loin area where her inviting folds were shielded by auburn curls. He was marveling over that fact when her hands slid from his neck to shield her breasts. His eyes returned to hers, he was dismayed to see reality returning to her emerald eyes. She parted her swollen lips but before she could speak, he took hold of her wrists. Pulling her arms gently away, he revealed her to him again.

"You're beautiful Alexandra, let me look at you."

Alex shuddered as his gaze traveled over her again. It was only the fervent tone of his voice that held her completely motionless, that stopped her from shielding herself again. When his eyes came back to hers, they were filled with a fire that stole the breath from her lungs. Suddenly she realized exactly where this was going, that kisses weren't going to be enough for him tonight. She had known that since she had woken in his arms, she realized with a jolt, she had *wanted* it.

"Tell me to stop," he grated. "I will if you tell me to, but you have to tell me to stop Alexandra. I don't have the strength to stop myself."

She should tell him to stop, she realized. This was wrong. It went against everything she believed in, every moral that had ever been instilled within her. It would earn her the reputation that she had so wrongly been given, but try as she might, she couldn't get the words past her constricted throat. She wanted this more than she had ever wanted anything in her life. The fact that he was willing to stop, that she was sure he would stop if she asked him too, only served to make the decision easier for her.

She tugged her wrists free of his grasp and wrapped her arms around his neck. Torment blazed over his face, there was a flash of emotion that was so fleeting she didn't have time to name it before he surrendered. The force of his kiss was even more demanding than before. His tongue swept into her mouth in deep, plunging movements that left her trembling and breathless as his caresses built a fire within her that made her writhe upon the bed beneath him.

His hand slid over her belly, down her hips and slipped in between her thighs. She gasped as his fingers brushed over that most intimate part of her and caused heat to course through her entire body. She forgot all about her shock at what he was doing when he stretched her apart and slid a finger into her. He ground against her as he moved deliberately in and out in a motion that matched the tantalizing thrusts of his tongue. Instinctively, her hips began to rise and fall with his driving motions. Something began to build inside of her as a quickening in her body started to spread from her belly, moving like liquid fire into her extremities. She felt as if she were on the precipice of something fantastic, something just out of her reach but coming closer.

He caught her whimper of disappointment with his mouth as he slid his hand away from her, but he was going to be inside of her for her first orgasm. Shoving off the breeches he'd slid on so hastily earlier, he kicked them aside impatiently.

Nudging her thighs apart, he settled himself between them. His rigid cock jumped in enthusiastic anticipation of what was to come as her thighs pressed against his sides. Grasping hold of her hips, he forced himself to move slowly as he parted her delicate folds with the head of his cock and eased himself into her. She was so warm and deliciously wet and tight that he had to grit his teeth against the savage urge to drive himself forward and end the torture that was wracking his body. Her hands clenched on his back as he reached the barrier of her virginity and her eyes fluttered open to reveal the clouded haze of her passion filled eyes. He was so struck by her beauty, her trust in him, and what she was giving to him that he couldn't move.

She inhaled a hitching breath and gave a small nod. His cock jumped in anticipation, he hesitated for a second before driving himself forward. Breaking through her barrier, he caught her startled cry of distress with his mouth. Her nails dug into his back as a whimper escaped her, and it took all he had not to spill into her immediately. It had been months since he had been with a woman and the feel of her was almost more than he could bare.

"The worst is over Love," he grated against her lush mouth as he struggled to maintain his control. "Just relax. It will feel better soon."

Alex bit into her bottom lip. She fought back tears as she tried to obey his words. His lips brushed against her temple as his hand rubbed her relaxed nipple back to life. Gradually, the pain began to recede and her legs loosened their hold on him. He pulled out of her before sliding slowly back in. The friction the motion caused sent a new spiral of pleasure throughout her body. When he pulled back again, her hips instinctively rose to meet his. A gasp of pleasure escaped her as the motion brought him deeper into her body.

Her world became filled with him again, her body was consumed by the feel of his muscles as they flexed and bunched beneath her hands. A sleek sweat began to coat his skin as he moved in and out of her. His hair-roughened chest against her nipples created a delicious sensation that helped to stoke the fire even higher within her. His powerful body between her thighs was a feeling that she had never thought to experience, and she relished in it. She held onto him as he swept her into a world that consisted only of pleasure, sensation, and him.

Jarett was certain that he had never felt anything as magnificent as her. He ground his teeth against his fierce need, determined to bring her to fulfillment as he patiently rebuilt the passion that she had exhibited so willingly earlier. He felt it when her body eased and her pleasure returned completely. Felt it when she lost all inhibitions and eagerly began to meet each of his penetrating thrusts.

"Jarett."

His name on her lips, uttered in that husky tone was nearly his undoing. Something inside of him snapped. Something primitive and feral burst forth as he touched upon an emotion within himself that he had never known existed. His world became centered upon her, and all of the pleasure that she gave as eagerly as she received.

The spreading warmth through her limbs, the growing pleasure in her belly and loins was becoming almost more than she could bare. She was so close to something she couldn't describe and yet she was frightened by the fact that she was unable to control the new sensations rolling through her body. A tingling sensation shot through her that caused her toes to curl, her heart to race, and her body to arch off the bed.

A low cry escaped her as her muscles contracted around his cock. Her powerful climax ripped his own release from him in endless waves that seemed to go on forever. His shout of pure pleasure was muffled against her full lips as he reclaimed her mouth.

Shudders racked his body as he collapsed on the bed. He just managed to catch himself from falling on top of her and crushing her. Wrapping his arms around her, he pulled her sweat slickened body on top of his. He felt the shivers still coursing through her as her hair cascaded around him.

He was aware of the fact that something inside of him had just changed, that things were never going to be the same and that he didn't want to let her go. He was astonished to note that the realization didn't frighten him at all as he inhaled the scent of their lovemaking. He didn't even mind the fact that he had spilled his seed in her, which was something he had managed to avoid since he was fourteen, but tonight, with this woman, he had lost complete control of himself.

Alex was still drifting in a state of euphoria that she never wanted to end. She had never known that such a feeling of being utterly complete could ever exist and she would be perfectly content to spend the rest of her life exactly where she was. Megan's words about discovering the pleasures of the wedding bed drifted back to her and she had to stifle a laugh. She wasn't married, but Megan had been completely right, she'd been missing out on something extraordinary. She wasn't going to let the fact that she had just committed a sin intrude upon this moment. Nothing this wonderful could be wrong, and for as long as she lived, she would never regret this night.

It would be a beautiful memory that she would cherish for the rest of her days alone, she knew that she would never share this intimate act with anyone, but him. Sadness at the thought of him leaving threatened to creep into her blissful mood. She closed her eyes against the sorrow threatening to envelope her.

"Alex."

She smiled at the sound of his voice. "Yes?"

"Dare I ask how you got this tan?"

A laugh escaped as her finger made a circle around his small nipple. It was so similar to hers as it stiffened beneath her ministrations yet so different. She wanted to explore all of him and learn all of their differences. His large hand clutched hers and held it flat against him. His heart beneath her hand was still pounding faster than normal. He gave her hand a squeeze to remind her of his question.

"There's a lake out behind the north pasture that I enjoy swimming in," she answered.

Jarett bit out a curse that brought her head up. Exasperation and frustration coursed through him as he realized that she was swimming nude, while her brother's men watched over her. He couldn't think about the fact that others had seen her in that state and beheld her exquisite beauty; if he did he might kill them.

Alex frowned at the stormy look that descended over his handsome face. “It’s very sheltered, few people know about it,” she told him.

His scowl deepened. “Your brother has men that follow you.”

Alex laughed when she realized what had caused his sudden burst of anger. “He usually has Willy follow me.”

“You knew?”

She smiled as she propped her chin on her hands to stare down at him in amusement. “Of course I knew.”

“And you didn’t say anything to your brother about this?”

Her smile grew as she began to stroke the chest beneath her hand. “It’s almost always Willy. He can’t do much around the ranch anymore, watching over me gave him a purpose, and it helps him feel useful again. Don’t get me wrong, he may not be as spry as he used to be, but he can still shoot an eye out of a fly from a hundred feet away, that’s why Hugh assigned him to me. Hugh knows about my dips in the lake, and he knows that Willy is probably the only one of our hands that would never be tempted to look.”

“And why is that?”

“Willy’s been here since before I was born, he watched over me when I was a baby, helped me learn how to shoot, rope, and herd. He was best friends with my dad. He was the ranch foreman, and still would be if he hadn’t resigned because he wasn’t feeling as young as he used too. I’m more like a daughter to him. When Willy isn’t the one watching me, I don’t go to the lake. Not that I don’t trust everyone else here, but most are young and there is no reason to tempt them.”

“Wise choice,” he muttered. He still didn’t like the idea of her stripping and diving into a lake, even with an old man that she completely trusted as her protection. From now on, he would be the one keeping an eye on her. She may trust this Willy, but he wasn't about to take any chances. "How many hands are left here?"

"Five."

He lifted an inquisitive eyebrow. He'd seen part of the ranch today; the expanse of it was massive. "That's all?"

"There used to be more, but when all the trouble started my father had a tough time paying people. Understandably, they moved on. The people left are the ones that have been here their entire lives. They're happy here and even if their pay isn't regular, they have a place to sleep, food to eat, and we're all like family here. Before my father died, he had begun to expand on the ranch and had started to add some wheat farming and horse breeding. We still make most of our income from the cattle though and that is where Murdock attacks us the hardest."

Jarett was sorry he had asked. The happiness she'd shown as a result of their love making was gone as the reality of the world crashed back upon her. Grasping her chin, he lifted his head to kiss her full lips. He only meant to try and push the world back again, but when she moved over him, he instantly hardened inside her again. It was too soon for her, he tried to tell himself.

Rolling her over, he tried to pull out and away from her, but she wrapped her legs around his waist and held him in place. "It's too soon Alexandra." He had to force the words out. "You'll be too sore."

She smiled seductively up at him, her hand trailed over his lips before sliding over his cheek. "I want you Jarett."

He groaned at the words. "Alex..."

"Shh," she whispered, drawing his head down to hers and nibbling on his lower lip.

His heart trip hammered in his chest as her tongue flickered over his full bottom lip before slipping in to tease his. He stifled another groan as her persistent ministrations began to melt his resolve. Her mouth moved over his jaw to lick playfully at his earlobe. His hands clenched upon the sheets as he fought against the urge to take her again. She was a fast learner, and a temptation he couldn't resist as she continued to kiss him and her hands ran over him. Her hips rose to draw him in deeper before sliding back down.

He tried one more time to argue with her, to tell her that it was too soon but she lifted her hips again and wiggled beneath him again. His resolve melted completely as he began to meet her titillating movements. He kept his pace slow and easy as the world around them receded once again.

CHAPTER 14

Alex was exceptionally grateful that the dining room was empty when she stepped into it the next morning. Now that it was daylight, her actions last night seemed much worse than they had when Jarett had been holding her in his arms. A dull heat suffused her face at the memory of it. She didn't know what was going to happen when she saw him again, what he would say, or how he would react, for he had been gone when she awoke.

If it hadn't been for the soreness between her legs, the lingering scent of him on her skin, and the blood she had found on her sheets, she would have been certain that last night was a very pleasant dream. At first, she had been mortified by the blood and uncertain of what to do with the ruined sheets. She had stripped them from the bed, buried them in her trunk until she could get rid of them, and retrieved a new set from the linen closet.

Now she was running late, which was something she never did. She didn't know how she would react when she saw Jarett again, but if she wasn't careful Hugh would know what had transpired, and that was something that couldn't happen.

Hurrying to the sideboard, she heaped a pile of eggs, bacon, and toast onto her plate. Her appetite was bigger this morning than usual. She was in the process of wolfing down her meal, eager to get to work, when Lysette came strolling in. Alex nearly choked on the bacon she had been shoving into her mouth as Lysette shot her a scolding look.

She forced herself to slow down. "You'll choke if you keep eating like that."

"Sorry Lysette," she mumbled around the bacon. She received another scolding glance for talking with her mouth full and swallowed heavily. "Where is everyone?"

"They were up with the sun, been out for hours now." Alex winced at the reprimand she heard in Lysette's words. "Your brother and that man went up to the north pasture." Alex took *that man* to be Jarett and she was briefly grateful that she wouldn't have to see him right away. Then, disappointment filled her. She was a little nervous to see him again, but she was also eager to. "Took Darren and Jesse with them."

Alex ignored Lysette's reproachful look as she forked the last of her eggs into her mouth. She walked across the room to drop a kiss on Lysette's round cheek. "What's got into you child?"

Alex shot a grin over her shoulder as she hurried from the room. Stepping onto the porch, she inhaled the fresh spring air and felt the sunlight flowing over her. There was a sense of happiness inside her that she'd thought forever destroyed by loss and betrayal. She knew that its reappearance had everything to do with Jarett.

Doubts flickered in, would he want to see *her* again, or what if what had happened last night meant nothing to him? The realization that she knew little about him slid through her like an insidious snake. He was harsh, and she had thought him unforgiving, but he'd proven yesterday that he could forgive, that he could be understanding and tender. He was also impossible for her to resist. She knew those things about him, but she knew nothing of his history. The realization left her feeling slightly hollow and even more uncertain of herself and the events that had transpired last night.

She wondered about his time with the women in the saloon and if he would consider her like one of them now. It was what he had thought about her in the beginning after all, and she had proven him right last night. A shiver of unease worked its way through her. She may have been a virgin when he'd taken her, but she was a fallen woman now. She had given herself outside the bonds of wedlock and the sanctity of marriage. It was a sin. She didn't know what she would do if he looked at her with revulsion. It would destroy her, she was certain of that. She expected no future with him, but she wouldn't be able to stand it if he looked down on her now.

Then she recalled the way that he had held her afterward, the tender words he had whispered to her, the gentle touch of his large, callused hands. She knew that she had drifted to sleep in his secure arms. He wouldn't have done those things if he'd thought that she was a disgrace, would he?

Her happiness from the night was beginning to evaporate as doubts swirled up to choke her. Last night had been special, to her, but to him it was an act that had probably been played out many times, with many women.

The sounds of bawling cattle interrupted her thoughts. Grateful for the distraction, she pushed her hat onto her head and hurried down the porch steps. She couldn't dawdle over her doubts anymore; they would destroy her if she did. She would know soon enough what Jarett thought of her, but for now work still had to be done.

Willy and Jasper were inside the corral helping Perry with a young colt ready for breaking. Alex smiled as her day suddenly picked up. She had forgotten that the young pinto colt was to be broken today. Slipping easily through the fence, she hurried to join Willy as Jasper and Perry led the horse around the ring, a saddle and bridle were already in place on the horse.

"Try to mount him yet?" she inquired.

Willy was scowling as he turned to her. "No, and you're not about to."

Alex smiled sweetly at him as she clasped her hands behind her back and rocked on her heels. She watched the spirited colt as it began to buck wildly. "I think I'll give him a shot."

"Hugh left standing orders that you're to stay away from him," Willy informed her.

"When was the last time I obeyed Hugh?" she inquired.

"Never, and that's the problem."

Alex patted Willy on his bony shoulder as the colt made another loop around. Sweat had begun to mar his fine coat; he tossed his head back and forth and fought against the bridle. Alex waited until the colt made three more circles before she called a halt to his leading. She cautiously approached the horse so as not to startle him. The colt's eyes rolled in his head as he snorted loudly and followed her movements.

Alex rubbed his muzzle as she talked softly to him and waited for him to calm down. It took minutes of patience and understanding but eventually his sides weren't heaving so forcefully, his eyes stopped rolling, and his ears came forward as he leaned into her touch. Alex moved along his side, rubbing him constantly and never failing to talk to him as she grasped hold of the pummel and lines.

"Alex!" Willy hissed.

"Shh Willy, you'll upset him." She tossed a sly grin over her shoulder as she slipped her foot into the stirrup. The colt's ears flickered back in alarm. "Stay away," Alex told him as Willy made a move to grab his bridle. "Leave him be."

Alex waited patiently for the colt to come to terms with this new feeling before gradually lifting herself up. He didn't move, but his nostrils flared. Alex patiently waited for him to adjust to each new move she made. Eventually she was settled into the saddle, both feet in the stirrups and the reins in her hands. She patted his sweaty neck and whispered words of encouragement as he stood, trembling beneath her.

"Hugh's going to throw a fit," Willy muttered.

"He'll get over it," she told him.

"He specifically did not want you on this colt."

"I've broken horses before."

"But this one's rowdier than the others, and you know it."

"Willy I'm on him, aren't I?"

He spit on the ground, his displeasure evident as he planted his hands on his hips. "You are, now why don't you get on down."

Alex smiled at him as she continued to rub the colt's neck. "I don't think so. In fact, I think I'll take him for a spin."

Before Willy could protest more, she signaled Jasper to start moving as she gave the colt a nudge. In the beginning she was so sore from last night that she wanted to climb back out of the saddle, but she wouldn't give Willy or Hugh the satisfaction, and eventually her body adjusted to the familiar motion. Time passed quickly as she moved the colt from a walk, to a trot, before easing him into a moderate canter. The young horse took every new stride with an easy acceptance and grace that amazed her. Alex barely moved in the saddle, his stride was so swift and true. There was a lot of speed vibrating through his muscles just waiting to be released.

After a little bit, she called a halt to the lead lining. She remained in the saddle as she waited for the colt to cool down and ordered Perry and Jasper to remove his lead lines. They did so reluctantly as they cast troubled glances between her, and a scowling Willy.

When she thought that he was calm enough, she nudged the colt back into a walk around the circle. They moved easily through his paces again, until he was once again flowing into a smooth canter.

***

Jarett tilted his head back as he glanced at the clear blue sky warming the earth. Beside him, Hugh and Jesse quietly discussed the twenty cattle they had recently lost. They still had over a hundred head, but any loss was detrimental to the ranch. Tipping his head back down, he glanced at Alex's brother. He felt no compunction about having broken his promise to Hugh, on the same day that he had given it. He couldn't bring himself to feel bad about something that had felt so right, and so good.

He would feel bad if Hugh found out though, as Hugh would more than likely try to fight him. A fight between them would only upset Alex, and that was something that he was loathe to do. He wanted her happiness more than anything else. He'd only known her for a short time, but he'd grown to care for her more than anyone else he'd ever known.

This realization didn't scare him as it had before, but he didn't know what to do with it yet either.

"I'm going to kill her."

Jarett turned at Hugh's statement. Hugh was glowering as he gazed down the crest of the hill. Behind Hugh, Jesse and Darren were trying to hide their grins but failing miserably. Jarett followed Hugh's stare, his gaze instantly latched onto Alex as she rode the colt with the easy grace of one born to the saddle.

His heart leapt into his throat. He had seen the colt earlier, untamed and crazed, as they tried to bridle and saddle him. It had taken three people to hold the horse's head and one more to keep a leg off the ground to stop his kicking long enough to get the saddle on. Jarett had thought it would be impossible to break the colt, Hugh had vowed he was going to sell him the first chance he got, and the men they had left to work with the horse looked as if they had just been told they were going to have to dance with the Devil.

Yet, there she was, leading the colt into a fluid canter. As much as they appeared to be getting along well, he fully agreed with Hugh, he wanted to strangle her and the men they had left behind. The men that were now leaning against the corral gate, watching her, instead of keeping her away from the crazed horse like they had been told to do.

"Then I'm going to kill them," Hugh said as he nudged his horse forward.

Jarett rode by his side as he approached the small corral at an easy trot, hoping not to spook the colt. The men by the gate looked up and their eyes widened. They had the grace to look chagrined as they exchanged glances. The two younger ones made a move to slip through the fencing, while the older one folded his arms over his chest and glanced at Alex.

"Alex," Hugh called out. His voice was filled with tension, and it was obvious by the vein throbbing in his forehead that it had taken everything he had not to bellow her name.

She glanced up at him and smiled sweetly as she eased the colt to a trot. "Yes?" she inquired innocently.

Alex thought the top of Hugh's head was going to blow off as his face turned red. "Get down!" he commanded.

"I think I'll stay here for a while, he's doing very well."

To prove her point, she stretched down to pet the colt's sweaty neck. She was well aware of another set of eyes burning into her as she moved past the fence, eyes that she was suddenly hesitant to meet. She was grateful that her face was already flushed from exertion; otherwise everyone would have seen the blush that was beginning to heat her skin from head to toe.

"Alex," Hugh said in a warning tone.

She eased the colt to a walk and Perry hurried to grab his bridle. The colt backed up restlessly and tossed his head. "Don't," Alex said tersely.

Perry took a small step back. Alex could feel the tension and distress in the quivering muscles beneath her. She stroked his neck and whispered to him until he settled down again. With the endless patience she had exhibited in mounting the colt, she began to cautiously dismount. She had one foot still in the stirrup, her hand braced upon the pummel when the pounding of hooves caused her head, and the colt's, to shoot up.

Alex felt the colt tense and knew that he was going to bolt. Forgetting all about patience, she kicked her foot free as the powerful animal sprang forward. Off balance, she stumbled back and landed on her butt. She cursed and she slammed her hands on the ground; she was determined to let into whoever was pounding up the driveway at such a reckless, breakneck speed. She was still sitting, incensed and annoyed, when hands grabbed hold of her.

"Are you all right?"

She blinked in surprise as Jarett knelt before her. His face was tense with unease as his gaze scanned her body. "Yes," she mumbled.

The heat of his body against hers caused her breath to catch in her chest as she surveyed his handsome face. His eyes came back to hers and an easygoing smile curved his full mouth. An answering smile sprang to her lips and she almost flung herself into his arms. She remembered the people watching them before she did so though. He seemed to sense her thoughts as he winked at her before helping her to her feet.

"Thank you," she mumbled, suddenly uncomfortable again as she self-consciously wiped the dirt from her backside.

"I told you to keep her off of him!" Hugh snapped.

Alex turned to her brother, who was now holding the reins of the heaving colt. He was glaring at Willy, Jasper, and Perry. "And I told them that I've never listened to your orders before, and I'm not about to start now!" she yelled at him.

Hugh turned his ferocious glower on her. "Besides, we were doing just fine together until..." Alex trailed off. Turning away from Hugh, she shaded her eyes against the sun to look up at the rider who had come barreling down the lane. Paul was sitting upon a heavily breathing bay, a grimace on his face as he met Alex's censuring glare. "He was spooked," she finished.

"And how many times did he throw you before that?" Hugh demanded.

"Not once."

"Yeah right," he snorted.

Alex folded her arms firmly over her chest. "He didn't throw me once, did he Willy?"

They both turned to look at the older man, who seemed reluctant to answer. Alex knew he was angry at her but he would never lie. Finally, he spit on the ground and turned to Hugh. "She was never thrown."

"There!" Alex cried triumphantly.

"This horse is a lunatic," Hugh declared.

"Not if you know how to handle him," she retorted. "Which I do, and his name is Satan."

"Fitting," Jarett mumbled from behind her.

She shot Jarett a look but her brother's question pulled her attention away from him again. "I suppose you plan to keep him?"

"Yes, I do," Alex said.

Hugh shook his head as he thrust Satan's reins at Perry. "Dad really should have paddled your ass more when you were younger," he muttered. Alex grinned happily, fairly bouncing with excitement as her brother capitulated to her wishes. Satan took a step back as Perry went to get him and his eyes rolled. Hugh's scowl grew deeper as he spun back to Alex. "If you want him, then you take him!"

Alex smiled triumphantly as she made her way over to Satan. Taking the reins easily from Hugh she soothed the colt with a caress. "You just have to know how to handle him."

Jarett watched in amusement as she calmed the undisciplined creature with her hands and gentle words. He knew well how her ministrations could calm a beast; she had succeeded with him after all. His pride in her grew as the crazed colt relaxed against her and rested his muzzle on her shoulder. He was certain that his heart had stopped when he realized that the colt was going to bolt. In that instant, he knew that if anything ever happened to her, it would destroy him.

Jarett feasted upon the vision of her in her dirty clothes, damp with sweat. Her hat had come off when she'd tumbled to the ground and her copper hair gleamed in the sun. Strands of it had straggled free to frame her beautiful face. He had always thought that he would never enjoy a dirty, unkempt woman, he knew now that he had been completely wrong. He relished in the sight of Alex, no matter what she was wearing. Her smile tugged an answering one to his mouth.

His attention was distracted from her as Hugh appeared at his side. Hugh glared at him as he continued to keep his body in between Jarett and Alex. "What brings you here, Paul?" Hugh inquired.

Jarett had completely forgotten about the young man, the one that had almost gotten Alex hurt. He turned to Paul, not at all put off by the hostility in the clear blue eyes that met his. He was certain that Paul had already heard the rumors, though he was likely to disbelieve them, even with Jarett's presence here.

Jarett began to seethe; he wanted to declare to her brother and his friend that Alex was his, and that there would be no more talk of Paul marrying her. However, he couldn't. He wasn't prepared to make the commitment that such a statement would inevitably bring, nor did he want for her brother, or Paul, to have any hint of what had passed between them last night.

Paul kicked free of his stirrups as he dismounted with ease. A rush of hot air against his neck caused Jarett to glance over his shoulder. Alex had moved to stand behind them; Satan's nose was only inches from Jarett's shoulder. Her earlier amusement was gone as her emerald eyes warily met his. Instinctively, he moved a little closer to her as a powerful surge of possession swept through him.

"We had some trouble at the ranch last night." Paul's mouth was pinched at the corners as he spoke. "Somehow the barn caught fire."

Alex's hand flew to her mouth as her annoyance with Paul vanished in a heartbeat. "Was anyone hurt?" Hugh demanded.

"Pa's got some burns on his hands, and Sherman burnt his leg, but other than that we were lucky."

"Did you lose any livestock?" Hugh asked.

"Four horses and two milk cows."

Nausea welled up inside her. "Those poor animals."

"You don't know how it was started?" Jarett inquired.

Paul's eyes had a callous gleam in them as they met his. "I have an idea how it was started it, and who, but I don't think *you* would appreciate my suspicions."

Jarett leveled Paul with a brutal glare. "Jarett's working for us now," Hugh said firmly.

Paul's gaze zipped past Jarett to Alex. "I see," he muttered. Jarett took another step in front of her in an attempt to block her from Paul's view. "We're going to have a barn raising tomorrow, if you can come."

"Of course we'll be there," Alex replied.

Paul smiled at her before turning his attention back to Hugh. "I must talk with you, privately."

Hugh nodded briskly. "Jarett, why don't you join us?"

Paul's eyes flashed with resentment, at the same time that Alex started to protest. She was silenced by Hugh's terse reminder that she had to take care of her new pet. Simmering with indignation at purposely being left out, she turned away from their retreating backs and led Satan toward the barn.

CHAPTER 15

Alex was restless and antsy as she slipped from her bed and paced across the floor to the window. She could feel the wood grains of the floor against her bare feet. The night was clear, the stars and quarter moon were vivid in the vast sky. She stared out at the road, wondering for the hundredth time where Jarett, Hugh, and Paul were.

Shortly after their private meeting, Hugh had come to inform her that they were going to Paul's farm to see what help they could offer. That had been hours ago. It was now past midnight, and there was still no sign of them.

The only answer she could come up with was that they were at the saloon. Seething with impatience and jealousy, she restlessly paced away from the window. She hated Jarett for doing this to her. She hadn't expected anything from him, but she had at least hoped that he wouldn't turn to another woman so soon after what they had shared. Now she knew that her hopes were for naught.

An owl hooted in the distance, its forlorn cry echoed the hollow loneliness that resided in her heart. She couldn't take much more of this. Walking back to the window, she scowled at the empty space where her trellis used to be. Well, she'd show them. If they were going to spend a night out on the town, then she was going to experience a night out herself.

Grabbing hold of her robe, she pulled it over her nightgown, and slipped on a pair of worn slippers. She knew the ranch like the back of her hand and knew exactly where she was going. Slipping out of her room, she hurried down the stairs as quietly as possible. She had no doubt that Hugh still had people on watch, but no one would be behind the house.

Hitting the ground noiselessly, she glanced around to make sure that no one was lurking about before she slipped into the shadows of the forest. She clutched her robe closed against the cool air of the night as she moved easily through the thick woods. The heat of the day had evaporated with the descent of night, but it was still the lake she headed for. She had to clean herself and purge her soul of the heart wrenching agony clawing at her and she hoped that the cool waters would help accomplish that.

Tears were burning the backs of her eyes, tears she refused to shed as she reminded herself that she had expected nothing from him. She had made her bed, now she was going to lie in it. She just wasn't ever going to lie in it with him again. There was no way that she would welcome him back into her bed, but then it didn't seem as if he wanted to be in her bed anyway. He'd gotten what he wanted from her already; that much was clear.

A hand shot out of the night, it wrapped around her waist as another one slammed over her mouth to stifle the startled scream that rose in her throat. Struggling wildly, she was hauled against a massive chest and pinned firmly to an unrelenting body. Her fingers clawed at the hand at her mouth.

"What are you doing?"

Alex went instantly limp as Jarett's incensed whisper registered in her terrified mind. He released her and spun her around to face him, his hands dug into the flesh of her shoulders as he shook her roughly. "Let go of me!" she cried.

"What are you doing out here?" he snarled.

Alex blew a strand of hair out of her eye as she met his glare. "I could ask the same of you," she retorted.

His nostrils flared as his jaw clenched. "I'm making sure that there is no trouble tonight, do you wish to lose your barn too?"

"Of course not!" she cried, and then an awful thought occurred to her. "How long have you been out here?"

"Since before sunset."

"Where's Hugh?" she demanded.

"On the other side of the pasture, now what the hell are you doing out here?"

Alex felt like the lowest form of human life. She'd been thinking such horrible thoughts about him, and her brother - she had partially blamed Hugh for their absence- and all this time they had been sitting outside making sure that no harm came to the ranch. Hugh did it often, but Jarett had no reason to, other than helping them out.

"Why didn't you return to the house first?" she asked.

His breath expelled on a rush of air that pushed the hair off of her forehead. "It wouldn't make sense to have Murdock seeing us post guards, would it? Now, answer me!"

He gave her a sharp little shake that caused her teeth to rattle. Alex jerked out of his grasp; she gave him a scathing glare as she took a step back and pulled her robe closer around her. The look on his face was cold enough to freeze fire, and it was directed solely at her. A chill raced down her spine as she realized just how furious he was.

"I was just going for a walk," she informed him in a haughty tone of voice.

She didn't have time to move before he grasped hold of her again, he moved much faster than she would have thought for a man so large. A small gasp escaped her as he hauled her up against him. "Are you insane? You know that Murdock comes here at night! Are you trying to get yourself killed? Raped?"

Alex winced at every word as if she had been struck with a whip. "I just wanted to be alone!" she cried as she pushed at his massive chest with her hands.

"You wanted to be *alone*? Hugh's right, you should be locked in your room!"

"I should not!"

He bit out a curse as he swung her around, lifted her effortlessly off the ground and threw her over his shoulder. Alex's hands dangled at his waist and the blood rushed into her head. She pushed herself up his back with her hands and rested her palms on his shoulders. "What are you doing?" she demanded.

"Taking you back."

"But I planned to go for a swim!" she sputtered lamely.

He stopped walking. "Oh, a swim?"

Alex should have known by the tone of his voice that she should be wary, but she hated his highhanded manner. "Yes," she replied.

"Very well."

He changed directions and pushed aside the thick branches of the trees as his stride ate up the short distance to the lake. She could feel the tension in his body, from her angle his face seemed set in stone. The bristles on his jaw were fuller than yesterday and added an aura of danger to him. She shivered, not from the cold, but from the lethal man holding her.

"Jarett..."

Her words were cut off as she was released unceremoniously from his arms. She squealed as she clawed for purchase at his shoulders, but it was useless as she plummeted downward. Cold water swelled over her head; it filled her mouth and nostrils. Choking and sputtering, she broke free of the water and tossed her wet braid over her shoulder as she shot to her feet. Her foot got caught up on the wet hem of her robe and caused her to stumble back a few steps.

Finally getting her balance, she turned to let him have it, but her words died as her eyes landed on him. He had already stripped out of his shirt and was kicking off his breeches. Alex's throat went dry as she drank in the sight of him. Even after everything they had shared last night, she had never truly gotten a good look at him nude. Like a thief, he stole the breath from her lungs.

The corded muscles of his shoulders and chest rippled as he tossed his breeches aside. The ridged muscles of his abdomen glistened with droplets of water from her splash into the lake. A blush swept over her as she took in the hardened shaft jutting out from a dark nest of curls between his thighs. It was unbelievably large as it pulsed with blood and need.

Alex's gaze traveled down his powerful thighs. For the first time she saw the bullet wound that marred the flesh of his upper thigh. She understood some of Hugh's sly smiles and words now as she stared at the puckered red mark that had almost made him less of a man. She was unable to look at his face again for fear she would burst into flames.

"Come here," he ordered gruffly.

Alex's eyes flew back to his; she shook her head and wrapped her soaking robe closer around her. She was being silly, she knew, but she couldn't seem to help it. She was suddenly rather unnerved as he waded gracefully into the cool water. Her lips parted as he stopped before her, she had to tilt her head back to look up at him. Just him being this close to her caused her body to become aroused. A smile curved his mouth as the hungry gleam in his eyes caused her heart to lurch into her throat.

Jarett reached forward and pulled the robe away from her body. The gown beneath was nearly transparent from the water. Her nipples were erect; the wet hair that had escaped her braid clung to her face. He was amused that she was still a little shy with him, but he planned to have that come to an end after tonight.

He was amazed by how swiftly she could make his anger turn into a profound hunger for her. A hunger he was beginning to think would never be satisfied, no matter how many times he possessed her. He clasped hold of the braid and began to unravel the thick plait. Her breathing was shallow as she watched him free her hair and spread it around her shoulders.

He admired the gleam of her skin in the dim light of the moon as he slid the robe off her shoulders and tossed it onto the bank. When he began to slide the clinging nightgown up, she lifted her arms for him. He slipped the wet material over her head and threw it up by the robe. Her hands went to cover her exposed breasts but he pulled them gently away to drink in her splendid body.

Color began to suffuse her cheeks as his gaze came back to her face. Wrapping his hand around her neck, he pulled her to him and claimed her mouth. All of his pent up frustration at being kept away from her broke free as he slid his arm around her waist and drug her against his body. She came with an eagerness that more than matched his own. Her arms slipped around his neck as she eagerly met the deep, penetrating thrusts of his tongue.

His hands traveling over her back sent shivers of delight down her spine and caused her skin to break out with goose bumps. All of her shyness vanished as the warmth of his body enveloped her. Desire blazed forth and shook her with its intensity. His hand cradled her breasts; a low moan escaped her as his thumb fondled her sensitive nipples.

His hand clasped her waist; he lifted her and led her from the water to lay her on the moss-covered bank. She had only a second to glimpse the trees overhead, and a spattering of stars, before he was on top of her. Her body ached for him as he enfolded her within his embrace. She didn't hear the rhythmic hum of the crickets, the clicking of the tree branches, didn't feel the chill of the mossy bank, or the air around them, as everything became centered upon him and the heat he created in her body.

His mouth and tongue created a trail of searing kisses across her body. She was gasping and moaning as her body arched up in an invitation to take her again, to fill her but he annoyingly ignored her as his mouth steadily moved lower. His tongue dipped into her belly button and swirled around it as his hand parted her thighs. His thumb rubbed tantalizingly against the part of her that was already wet for him.

Alex's eyes flew open as he bent his head between her thighs. Her legs instinctively tried to clamp shut as astonishment coursed through her. He ignored her protest as she tugged at his hair and tried to pull his head away from her. She was suddenly very aware of what he aimed to do, and the realization was horrifying. People didn't do that, did they?

Then his mouth was on her, hot and questing as it replaced his hand upon her most intimate area. She no longer cared if people did this or not as she had no semblance of rational thought left. All she could feel was the pleasure his mouth gave her as his tongue delved greedily into her. She couldn't suppress a cry of ecstasy as she writhed upon the bank. His mouth stoked her passion to heights she hadn't thought that she could attain. Spasms racked through her, a low moan escaped as her body found the release that only he could give to her.

He moved over top of her and stifled her cry of ecstasy with his mouth as he drove his large shaft into her. She had thought that she'd reached her peak before, but as he filled her, she knew at once that she'd been wrong. She never wanted to part with him as his fast, demanding thrusts pushed her ever higher. Her orgasm came again, swifter and fiercer this time. She bit into his shoulder to keep from screaming as her entire body shook and her fingers dug into his back.

Jarett absorbed the tremors that racked her body as her tiny teeth clamped down on his shoulder. He plunged deeper into her as he lost himself to the feel of her body and the bliss that she gave him. With a low cry, he drove forward again and found his release on a stream that ripped a yell of satisfaction from him.

It was awhile before he finally came back to earth and recollected where they were. He bit back a curse as he realized that he'd forgotten all about his purpose for being here and that he'd left them both vulnerable to an attack. Reluctantly, he eased himself out of Alex. He was amused to realize that she had fallen asleep. He propped his head on his elbow and watched her until she shivered and curled herself into the fetal position.

He walked over to his horse, hidden in a copse of trees, and pulled the saddle blanket free. He knew that he should take her home tonight, but he was unwilling to let her out of his sight. Rage suffused him at the thought that she could have been kidnapped tonight or possibly even killed. His anger abated as he draped the blanket over her slender frame and his hand lingered against her silken cheek. The feel of her helped to ease the wrath that had bloomed so powerfully in him. She was truly incapable of sensing any hint of jeopardy to herself. It was a fact that he was going to remedy, but for now, she wasn't leaving his side.

CHAPTER 16

Alex pulled at the annoying strings of her bonnet. "Stop it," Hugh scolded.

She scowled at him, but she released it and folded her hands in her lap. She was determined to stop fidgeting as the wagon rattled down the road. It wasn't the bonnet that was truly bothering her though; no it was the man at her side. Jarett's thigh was pressed against hers; the heat from his leg radiated into her body and reminded her vividly of every touch and every caress of the intimate act they had shared last night.

Unthinkingly, her hand came up to pull at the bonnet strings again; she was finding it increasingly difficult to breathe. Hugh slapped at her hand. "What is the matter with you?" he demanded.

Jarett's chuckle did nothing to ease her extreme discomfort and the stifling heat of her body. How was she ever going to get through this day if she couldn't get through a carriage ride? Her hand fell back to her lap but she refrained from snapping at Hugh. It wasn't Hugh she was mad at rather it was the smug oaf sitting on her other side.

He had brought her back to the house this morning, but instead of letting her go to her room in peace, he had followed her up there. Once there, he had continued the lecture that he had expounded on during the seemingly endless ride back to the ranch. By the time he had finished issuing his orders about what she was *not* to do from now on, she had been so irate that she couldn't even speak.

She would have followed him from the room, letting him know exactly what she thought of him if Lysette hadn't chosen that moment to knock on her door. Then, the only thing she had been concerned with was unlocking the door between their rooms, and shoving him out. Unfortunately, she had been unable to slam the door in his face like she'd longed to do.

Now, she had to sit here, torn between enduring rage and mounting hunger for him. Never in her life had she looked forward to one of these barn raisings, but now she desperately wanted out of the stifling wagon. Her hand fluttered to the bonnet again, but she dropped it when Paul's ranch came into view. Tables had been spread across the lawn; drinks and food were already set upon them. The women of the town bustled about, placing out the rest of the food as people continued to arrive.

Wagons and horses were gathered around the yard, a good deal of the town had already arrived. Some of the men were gathered around the ruined barn, busy tearing down the remaining boards. The rest of the men were cutting and carrying new boards across the lawn.

A sigh escaped her at the reminder that she would be relegated to the ranks of the refreshment table, a position she hated. The women had all stared and talked about her before. It would only be worse now that Jarett was staying at the ranch. She couldn't begin to imagine how awful this day was going to be. She wouldn't even have Megan here to help her get through it, but at least some of the girls from the saloon would probably be here, and would offer her some companionship. Shelby always donated a large quantity of food and drinks to these kinds of charity events. The women in town didn't like it, but the women that worked the saloon were the ones that brought the refreshments, and served them.

Hugh pulled the wagon to a halt and flung the lines around the brake. Jarett dismounted immediately and turned to offer her his hand. She met the challenging gleam in his eyes and took hold of his hand to allow him to help her down. Hugh frowned at Jarett, but he didn't release her hand as he returned her brother's glare with one of his own. Alex was confused by their blazing animosity toward each other as she looked back and forth between them. Jarett was only holding her hand after all. Then she looked past them, and saw to her consternation that everyone was watching them. She tugged on her hand until Jarett finally released it.

Casting them both a scornful look, she moved past them but realized only too late that they had been her sanctuary. She had just tossed herself to the wolves. All of the women at the refreshment table deliberately turned away as she approached. Alex grit her teeth against the blatant snobbery. She had expected it after all, she should be used to it, but it was even worse today. Before at least the women would say hi to her, some would even inquire as to how she was, but no one did that now. She was now officially a social pariah.

It was Rachel that came to her and locked her arm through one of her own. Rachel cast a scathing look at all of the women but unfortunately none of them looked up to receive it. "How are you doing Alexandra?" Rachel asked.

"I'm well."

"Just ignore all these fine *upstanding* women," Rachel whispered. "I never understood how being fine and upstanding gave someone the right to be deliberately cruel."

Alex smiled at her, grateful for her company. She didn't care that it only lowered her further in the eyes of the men and women around them; she wouldn't have been able to get through this day if she'd been completely alone. "Thank you Rachel."

"There is nothing to thank me for Alex, I may only be a whore but I stick by my friends."

"You're more than that Rachel," she assured her. "You're a good person."

Rachel smiled at her as she led her over to where the other women of the saloon were gathered. Alex had to stifle a bitter laugh as she realized that she was exactly where Jarett had once accused her of wanting to be, and where he had actually made her belong. There was no resentment in that realization, only a simple acceptance. He would leave, and she would spend the rest of her life with the fallen women of the town.

The fine ladies of the town may find them disgraceful, but they were the only ones who truly seemed to care about other people. Rachel did Henry's laundry every week, Dolly donated money to children's orphanages, a fact that few people knew. Amy, a small blond with doll like features, took in injured animals, nursed them back to health, and set them free again. These were all things that the good women of town would never lower themselves to do, and yet the social lepers were the ones that did them. This *was* where she belonged, and she didn't give a fig what anyone else thought about that.

Dolly and Amy waved in greeting and ushered her over to the large bowl of lemonade. The day passed in a rush of idle chitchat, banging, loud cheers, and raucous laughter, the latter of which came from the men as they assembled the barn.

Try as she might, Alex couldn't stop her gaze from straying to Jarett as he worked. He had stripped off his shirt to bare his solid back, thick arms, and massive chest. She enjoyed watching the play of sinew as he hefted boards, cut through them, or hammered them into place. The sun shone on his bronzed skin and the sweat trickling down his back. He was the largest man there, the most heavily muscled, and she could clearly recall the feel of him as he moved over her. Alex had to look away before her thoughts continued to travel down pathways that would only make her even hotter.

At first, the other men had avoided him, and they barely spoke to him. However, as the day wore on, and he worked just as vigorously as they did, they began to relax around him. Alex was grateful for that, but she couldn't help feeling a little resentful too. She'd done nothing more than he had, in fact she'd probably done far less than him if his past was brought into the equation. She couldn't have been his first and though she didn't want to think about it, he may have even been with one of the women gathered around her now. He had been staying at the tavern before moving in with her, and Dolly had looked *very* comfortable in his lap the other night.

Yet she was being completely snubbed, and the men of the town seemed to consider her fair game now. Many of them had come to the lemonade stand to offer lewd comments, or stares. Alex didn't know what to say or do to fend them off. By lunchtime, even with the support of Amy, Dolly, and Rachel, she wanted nothing more than to go home, jump in the lake, and scrub herself clean.

She was fantasizing about that delightful prospect when another wagon pulled in. Alex stifled a groan as she watched Suzanne and her father alight. The day had been bad enough, now it was only going to get worse. Tugging at the string of her bonnet, she pulled it free. It didn't matter what people thought about her, the blasted thing had to come off if she was going to breathe.

"She would show up when most of the women's work is done," Dolly muttered as she clucked her disapproval.

"Probably took her this long to decide what she was going to wear," Amy replied.

Alex cast a glance at Suzanne and winced involuntarily at how perfect, cool, and poised Suzanne appeared to be. She wore a form fitting lavender walking dress that emphasized her pale complexion, brown hair, and chocolate eyes. It was cut low to reveal an almost indecent amount of her breasts. The bonnet covering her hair was the same shade of lavender, and not one hair was out of place.

Alex didn't have to look down at her worn and faded yellow dress to know that she couldn't compare. Suzanne's flawless skin showed no hint of a tan, she would never be caught dead in a pair of breeches and a shirt, and she didn't behave more like a man than a woman. Alex was rumpled and sweating beneath the glare of the sun, and she was completely out of place in a dress to begin with.

Alex recalled the way that Suzanne had been flirting with Jarett and the admiring gleam in his eyes. There was no way that she could compete with Suzanne. It was a thought that had never crossed her mind before, as she had never cared, until now.

"Don't look so worried Alexandra." Rachel patted her arm reassuringly.

"I'm not," she mumbled.

Rachel's brown eyes were sympathetic, and although Alex was grateful for it, she also resented it. The sympathy told her that she had revealed far too much of her emotions. Suzanne's cheerful laugh felt like a knife slicing down her spine as Alex walked rigidly to the nearest bench and sat down. She pulled at the modest collar of her gown that now seemed too constricting. Dolly sat beside her and offered her a glass of lemonade, which she gratefully accepted though she would have preferred something stronger to ease the jealousy ripping through her.

The lunch bell was a loud tinkling that pierced through the sounds of the hammers, sawing, laughter, and girlish talk. "Come on, I picked out a perfect spot for us," Amy said happily.

Dolly grabbed hold of Alex's arm and hauled her to her feet. She felt like a wooden marionette as Dolly led her toward a grouping of trees where Amy was unfolding a blanket for them to sit on. Alex slumped gratefully to the ground, not in the least bit hungry, but more than happy to be away from the censuring stares of the women, and the lewd stares of the men.

"This is the perfect spot Amy," she remarked.

Amy smiled as she opened a basket of food and began to spread its contents of chicken, bread, and cheese on the ground. Dolly and Rachel dispersed the plates and silverware. Alex accepted their offerings, but merely stared at the contents on her plate. The lump that had been in her throat all day would surely choke her if she tried to get anything past it.

Glancing around, she spotted Hugh, Jarett, Paul, and Daryl by the tables gathering food from the plates that had been set out. Other men had settled by the barn to eat and drink. She knew that her brother and Jarett would join the men, but she couldn't help but hope that they would come over here.

Turning back to the women, her face began to turn red as they gave her knowing smiles. Alex became very focused upon the fine stitching of the colorful blanket they were sitting on. "Who made this?" she inquired.

"I did," Dolly answered. "I was going to send it to an orphanage, but Amy insisted I keep it for a day such as this."

"It's beautiful," Alex answered truthfully. "Would you make me one Dolly?"

Dolly broke into a beautiful smile. "I would love to Alexandra."

"Would you please call me Alex," she said, not for the first time that day.

"Alexandra." Chills swept up her spine, the hair on the nape of her neck rose as the familiar voice pierced her ears.

Turning, she shaded her eyes to look up at Suzanne. "Well, doesn't this look cozy," she purred.

"It is," Rachel replied with an edge to her voice. "Or it *was*."

"I see you've finally found where you belong, Alex," Suzanne continued as if she hadn't heard Rachel. "I always suspected you'd become a working girl."

Hot color suffused Alex's face as she became riled by Suzanne's words. "I could say the same to you Suzanne," she replied crisply.

A cruel smile twisted the edges of Suzanne's full mouth as she cast a disdainful glance at the women behind Alex. "How is Jeremiah Benchley these days Suzanne?" Dolly inquired sweetly. "Haven't seen him around town in awhile, or at least he hasn't been to visit me for some time now. Actually, now that I think about it, I had heard that he'd moved on to Abilene. But surely, you would know."

Alex was amazed at the red wash of color that suffused Suzanne's face. "I assure you that I would have no idea where such a low life could be," Suzanne grated.

"Oh, that's odd," Dolly replied as she thoughtfully tapped her chin. "From what he said, you two were close, *intimately* close in fact."

Alex bit on her bottom lip to keep from bursting into laughter when Suzanne spun on her heel and stormed away. "Dolly, you're incorrigible!" Rachel cried as tears of laughter spilled down her cheeks.

"Well, someone had to knock that girl off her high horse. She may have her daddy, and a good chunk of this town fooled, but she's no better than us," Dolly replied.

"Is that true?" Alex hated to be involved in the gossip, but she was unable to stop herself from asking.

"Oh yes," Dolly replied. "Jeremiah was quite talkative in bed."

Alex quickly diverted her gaze. "Corrupting my sister?" Hugh inquired as he appeared at the edge of the blanket.

"Of course we are," Rachel replied with a laugh.

"Well don't corrupt her too much; I can barely handle her now."

"I don't think anyone can handle her," Amy said.

"Think again." Jarett settled onto the blanket beside her. His eyes twinkled as they lit on her. He had donned his shirt again, but the buttons were undone to reveal a good patch of his bronzed, hair-roughened chest. His black hair was wet, and water trickled down the chiseled planes of his face from the dunking he had taken in the trough. It took all she had to force her hungry gaze away from him as her brother sat on her other side. Paul and Daryl sat between Dolly and Amy.

"What did Suzanne have to say?" Jarett inquired. Alex wasn't fooled by his casual tone; his body beside hers was rigid.

"Oh, her normal junk," Rachel replied nonchalantly. "But Dolly put her in her place."

Alex chuckled as she recalled the seething look on Suzanne's face. Jarett leaned over to poke at the chicken on her plate. "Eat, you'll need your strength for tonight," he whispered.

He smiled in amusement as Alex colored prettily and her lashes fell to hide her eyes. He didn't know why he was provoking her, but he found himself unable to resist. Just as he found himself unable to move his arm away from hers, he needed the contact with her, no matter how small. He'd noticed the way that the women had treated her today, knew it was because of him, and he was determined to offer whatever comfort he could.

She may still be riled at him about earlier, but it was high time that someone laid down the law with her. Although he didn't expect her to obey him, he had every intention of watching her like a hawk, and ensuring that there were no more nights spent creeping out of windows. Mainly because he planned to have her so tired every night that the last thing she would think about was sneaking out and getting into trouble.

Now he just had to think of a way to keep her from being so openly ostracized, and criticized, by the good women of the community. He also had to find a way to stop her from being openly pursued and lusted after by the men.

Out of the corner of his eye, he watched as she absently pushed her food around her plate. She looked lost and vulnerable, not at all like the proud woman that he had come to know. No matter how much she tried to convince herself that she didn't care what people thought, it still saddened her that they thought so little of her.

Without thinking, he wrapped his arm around her waist and pulled her close to his side. He ignored Hugh's dagger stare, and the startled looks on the faces of the people surrounding them. Her mouth was pursed as she turned toward him. "Jarett," she hissed.

Her eyes shot to Hugh who looked about ready to start spitting fire. Paul had an unhappy look on his face that tore at her heart and Daryl's lips were quirked in amusement. She knew he was dying to run home and tell Megan everything. Dolly, Amy, and Rachel smirked knowingly. Rachel winked at her before delicately peeling the skin off a chicken leg.

"Relax Love," Jarett murmured in her ear. "People will think we're carrying on an illicit affair."

Alex's distress was wearing off as her ire began to mount. "We are." She made sure to keep her voice pitched low so that the others couldn't hear her.

"It's not illicit," he whispered.

Her eyes narrowed as she glared at him; her temper rose even more as he smiled sweetly in return and brushed back a strand of her hair. "Stop it."

"I'll stop if you eat."

Alex sent him another fulminating look before grabbing a piece of chicken and biting into it. Jarett's chuckle did nothing to diffuse her anger as she swallowed heavily. She refused to look at him again or even acknowledge his presence. "We have to talk!" Hugh barked. "Now!"

Her brother jumped to his feet and planted his hands on his hips as he glowered down at Jarett. Jarett's hand tightened on her waist before he released her and leisurely climbed to his feet. Alex was unable to watch as the two of them walked away, but she could feel the curious stares of the five remaining people boring into the top of her bent head. She didn't look up again until it was time for everyone to go back to work.

She accepted Daryl's outstretched hand to help her to her feet. He was smiling at her, but there was an odd look in his eyes. She glanced over at Paul, but he wouldn't even meet her gaze as he stiffly walked by. "I hurt him," she whispered.

Daryl squeezed her hand reassuringly and held her back as Amy, Dolly, and Rachel hurried past. "We all knew how you felt about Paul, Alex. You made it perfectly clear. He'll get over it. I'm more concerned about you right now."

"I'm fine," she murmured.

"Are you?"

"Yes." His head tilted as he stared at her with concern. "Don't tell Megan, I plan to talk to her myself, please Daryl."

"I won't, but she's going to be asking a million questions about today. She's already heard the rumors flying around town. In fact, I think she's started working on a wedding dress."

"Tell her to stop!" Alex cried in horror.

Daryl laughed as he led her forward. "I think you're going to need it sooner than you think."

Before Alex could tell him how very wrong he was, he'd left her at the tables and hurried away. She stared after him in dismay but she would have to correct his misconception later. Her gaze fell on Hugh and Jarett as they emerged from a group of trees. Hugh was still scowling, but Jarett looked as happy as the cat that had swallowed the canary. Jarett caught her staring at him and winked before turning away. Alex gaped at him; her eyes darted back to her brother who was glaring at Jarett's back.

Alex turned away from them; she was determined not to think about anything except getting through the rest of this day as quickly as possible. It was sometime later that she became aware of Suzanne's high, flirtatious laughter. She looked down the tables at the other women, but Suzanne wasn't there. Slowly, with a feeling of dread, she turned toward the rapidly rising barn.

Suzanne was standing by Jarett, entirely too close for what was proper. She was leaning forward so that her breasts brushed provocatively against his arm. To his credit, he did step away, but not far enough for her liking, and certainly not far enough for Suzanne to get the hint. It took everything Alex had not to storm over there and rip out *every one* of Suzanne's perfectly groomed hairs.

"That girl is a tramp," Dolly muttered.

"And they call us the bad element," Rachel snorted.

Alex turned away, unable to watch anymore as Suzanne laughed again. Alex suspected that the high laughter was done on purpose, but she couldn't summon forth her anger again. It seemed as deflated as the rest of her. "You have nothing to worry about Alex, he's a sensible man, he'll see right through her," Amy assured her.

“I don’t care what they do.” She knew that she lied though as the tightness in her chest had everything to do with the scene she had just witnessed.

“He wants you Alex,” Dolly whispered.

Alex snorted inelegantly. “I’m sure he wanted all of you too.”

The minute the words were out of her mouth, Alex hated herself for saying them. It wasn’t their fault the man was a hopeless womanizer, or that they had to survive. It wasn’t their fault that she had done the same thing as them, without the necessity of survival that they had. She had done it because of the man himself. She was weak, immoral, and every bit as bad as Suzanne.

She had sworn that she would never let it bother her, but at that moment, she realized exactly how upset she was at herself. Her father would be so disappointed in her, she knew that Hugh was, and that realization on top of everything else today was just too much.

“I’m sorry,” she moaned as she stared at the three faces surrounding her. “I am so sorry, I didn’t mean it. Truly I didn’t.”

“Hush Alex,” Dolly said as she took hold of her arm. “You didn’t say anything that offended us.”

“Yes I did, you’ve been nothing but friendly to me all day...”

“Just as you’ve always been nothing but nice to us,” Rachel interrupted. “You treat us just as you treat everyone else. But you’re wrong about Jarett.”

Alex was baffled by her statement. “I don’t understand what you’re saying.”

Dolly sat her on a bench and Amy handed her a glass of lemonade. “We didn’t have any relations with him,” Rachel said.

“We did try though,” Dolly said. “That is one good looking man but we weren’t what he desired.”

Alex couldn't find words as she sat and stared at them. "Well at first all he was concerned with was finding the thieves," Rachel said. "But then he came walking into the laundry room with you and I *knew* we would never get our chance."

The three women exchanged smiles before focusing on her again. "It doesn't matter, I'm just a ah… I don't know what I am, a convenience perhaps. I don't want to talk about this anymore," Alex said.

"Well, we are going to talk about it," Rachel said firmly. "You have to get that misconception out of your head right now Alexandra. That man cares for you..."

"He does not!"

"No wonder Hugh is always so aggravated with you," Dolly muttered. "You are stubborn."

Rachel knelt before her and took hold of her hands. "I know men a lot better than you do, and I know when a man cares for a woman. That man cares for you. He may not be ready to admit it yet, but he does. You didn't see him sitting next to one of us today did you?" She motioned at the small group of women standing around her.

"No but..."

"No buts, he could tell you were upset and he was trying to comfort you in his completely inept way."

Alex bit into her bottom lip as she lowered her head to stare at the ground. "You love him."

"No!" she cried in ardent denial of Dolly's statement. "No, I don't!"

Then, her brow furrowed and her hands clenched upon her lap. She did love him, she realized with a horrifying, sinking sensation. There had always been an intense attraction to him, but somewhere along the way she had made the horrible mistake of falling in love with the oaf. She suspected it had happened the day that she had told him about her father, and he had held her so tenderly and believed her without hesitation. It had started then, but it was complete now. The realization should have been pleasing; instead, it made her want to run away screaming.

Her gaze involuntarily went to where he stood with Suzanne, except now he had moved further away and Hugh was by his side. He turned toward her and his eyes settled upon her face, which she knew had to mirror her distress. Alex looked away before he could see too much.

"I think I do," she whispered. "But I feel like I don't even really know him."

"You do," Rachel said. "He's a good man Alex, he cares for you, and that's a lot to know about someone. Now come on, up you go."

Alex let Rachel pull her to her feet, she was still shaking and a little confused by her sudden revelation. She couldn't seem to assimilate the little pieces of information they had given her befuddled mind.

"What's the matter?" Jarett's strong hand wrapped around her arm, his eyes were icy and dangerous as he scanned the women surrounding her.

"Nothing," she assured him. "I'm just overtired."

His eyes narrowed on her face. "You should have left your bonnet on; the sun is getting to you. Did you eat your lunch?" Alex opened her mouth to answer, but it was pointless. "Of course you didn't. I'm taking you home."

Alex's jaw dropped. He had just referred to the ranch as home. "We can't just leave," she protested.

"Watch us. Dolly, would you let Hugh know that I'm taking Alex home."

"Of course," Dolly replied. She threw a victorious smile at Alex before hurrying away.

Alex was scowling after her when Jarett wrapped his hand around the back of her neck and began to massage the knotted muscles there. She looked up at him, astounded and pleased by the gesture. He smiled down at her and pulled her close to drop a kiss on her lips. Alex didn't have time to react before he was pulling away from her.

"Hugh's going to kill you," was the only thing she could think to say.

His grin widened as he slipped his arm around her waist and turned her toward the wagon. "Bye Alex," Rachel called and grinned triumphantly as she waved.

"Good bye," Alex said and smiled shyly at them.

Jarett led her past the other women. He returned their horrified looks with a scowl that caused them to turn away. "They're going to be talking about me for the rest of my life," she muttered dismally.

"No, they won't," he replied firmly.

"Jarett, I know this town, I grew up here. Long after you're gone, they're still going to be talking about this scandal."

His hand clenched on her waist. "Is that what you want?"

"What?" she asked in confusion.

"Do you want me to leave?" His voice was so frosty that she didn't even recognize it. She had the sudden image of a hawk hunting its prey as he pierced her with his gaze.

"No, I don't," she admitted, even though she hated to do so. She didn't like him having the slightest clue as to how she felt about him but she'd never been a liar. "But you're going to, you said so yourself."

A muscle in his cheek twitched and Alex found herself holding her breath, hoping that he would say that he had decided to stay, that he *wanted* to stay, for her. However, he said no such thing as they made it to the wagon and he helped her up. His hand loitered upon her thigh; his eyes were unreadable as he stared at her for a minute before moving away.

Alex's shoulders slumped and it took everything she had not to start crying. He was going to leave. Rachel, Dolly, and Amy had been wrong; he didn't care about her, or at least he didn't care about her enough to stay.

CHAPTER 17

"Let me see her!" Alex cried as she hurried to her friend.

Megan laughed as she held out the tiny bundle in her arms. Alex took the baby and cradled her as she peeled the blanket back to look at Faith's tiny, perfect face. "She's beautiful," Alex breathed as she touched the strands of fine blond hair on the baby's head. Faith slept soundly, her small hands curled into delicate fists.

"She's an angel," Megan said. "Sleeps soundly through the night already." Alex looked up at Megan who had her hands clasped behind her back as she smiled at Alex. "So, are you going to tell me what's going on, or do I have to pry it out of you?"

Alex settled into the chair beside Megan with Faith still in her arms. She rocked back and forth as she told Megan everything. When she was done, she braced herself for the censure she was certain she was going to receive. Megan simply leaned back in the chair and smiled.

"I told you, you were missing out on something," she said with a chuckle.

"Megan!" Alex was aghast at her friend's words.

"Well I did. Oh Alex, don't look so miserable it will work itself out."

Alex shook her head as she glanced down at the infant in her arms. "I love him Megan."

"I know, 'tis obvious."

"He's leaving as soon as all this is over."

Megan leaned out to clasp Alex's arm. "Even if he does, which I don't think he will, you've done nothing wrong."

"How can you say that?" she demanded.

"Because it's true."

"My father would be so disappointed in me," she whispered.

"Alex, your father loved your mother, I'm sure that he would understand. What has Hugh said?"

"He's been surprisingly silent."

Megan's brow furrowed as she leaned back in the chair. "That *is* surprising."

"The worst part is that I can't turn him away," Alex admitted in an embarrassed whisper. It was the most horrible part of her shame. In the three days since the barn raising, she had continued to welcome him with open arms into her bed. She needed him with a desperation that bordered on insanity.

She was going to spend as much time with him as possible before he left. Megan's laugh caused Alex to shoot her a scathing glare. "It's not funny."

Megan immediately sobered, but her blue eyes twinkled merrily. "Alex, you're a woman, you have needs too."

"I'm not supposed to."

"Rubbish," Megan said firmly. "That's a load of hogwash and is the farthest thing from the truth. I don't care what anyone has told you, but the act is truly pleasurable when done right, and women have the right to enjoy it."

"Megan!"

"Oh, stop sounding so horrified," Megan scolded. "It's true, and I won't have you thinking less of yourself for enjoying it."

"Megan it's different, we're not married."

"So what?" Megan demanded. "You love him Alex; that is all that matters."

"Even if he doesn't love me?" she whispered.

Megan's eyes became sad and distant. "Things will work themselves out, I'm sure of it."

Alex wasn't so sure, but she was unwilling to dwell on it anymore. She safely steered the conversation into less treacherous waters. They spent a pleasant hour together before she climbed to her feet. "I have to go visit Henry."

"Are you ever going to tell me what the two of you do over there?" Megan asked hopefully.

"No," Alex answered with a smile as she eased Faith into Megan's arms. Megan didn't press her further. "I'll be back next week, take care of yourself and my little goddaughter."

"I will," Megan promised with a smile.

Alex slipped her bonnet back on and hurried out the door.

***

Jarett entered the small house after the faintly spoken bid to come in. It took a minute for his eyes to adjust to the dim interior after the bright sunlight of the day. When they did, he immediately noticed that Alex wasn't with Megan, where she was supposed to be. His teeth clenched in annoyance as his heart kicked up a beat with worry. She had promised that she would stay here, it was the only reason he had let her out of his sight for the past hour and a half. He should have known better.

"Where did she go?" he asked.

Megan quirked an eyebrow at his abrupt greeting, but a smile played across her lips. "She went to see Henry."

Jarett ran a hand through his hair, only then realizing how rude he was being, but he hated the idea of her walking around town unprotected. "Thank you."

"Mr. Stanton." He paused in the doorway and turned to look at her. "Can I talk to you for a minute?"

"I really have to find her."

"She'll be okay, no one will bother her in town, and nothing is going on between her and Henry."

"I know that."

She studied him with a perplexed look on her face. Then, her face lit up, and a delicate laugh escaped. "You know what they do over there!" she cried.

He found himself unable to resist returning her smile. "I do."

"You must tell me!"

"I can't, Alex doesn't even know that I know."

"You spied on her?"

"Yes, but it was before I knew her."

"I see," Megan said. "Come in for just a bit, Mr. Stanton."

"Call me Jarett, and I really have to be going."

"I suppose you do, but there's something that I would like to say to you. It will only take a minute, I assure you."

Jarett cast a glance at the tranquil road but he stepped into the house and closed the door behind him. Curiosity drew him across the room to inspect the tiny bundle in Megan's arms. "Alex named her Faith." Megan pulled the blanket back to reveal the sleeping baby. "She tried to name her Caroline after her mother, but I told her to save that name for her own daughter. Of course, she told me that she wasn't going to have children, or a marriage. And of course, I got the lecture to leave her alone on the subject, but the only thing I want is to see Alex happy. There's been so much unhappiness in her life, as you know."

Jarett didn't know where this conversation was going but Megan's normally merry blue eyes had taken on a tough look that he had never thought to see there. "She did tell you about her father?"

"Yes," he confirmed.

"That had to be extremely difficult for her, she doesn't talk about it to anyone, or at least she hasn't since it happened. She told you that she doesn't remember how long she was there before she was found?"

"Yes," he answered slowly.

Tears bloomed in Megan's eyes. Jarett rocked back on his heels, he wasn't sure that he wanted to hear what Megan had to tell him. "That's because she tries not to remember," Megan said sadly. "I've never told her, and I don't think Hugh has either. Near as we can figure, he was killed around nine thirty in the morning. Alex had left the house a little before nine, and it would take her about that much time to ride to that area of the ranch at a trot. We didn't find her until two thirty in the morning. She had sat there with him all day, and most of the night. It took a good ten minutes for Hugh, Paul, and Daryl to pry her away from his body. She put up a fight like a feral cat, kicking and screaming at them as she held onto her father's cold body.

"When they finally succeeded, she stood there shaking uncontrollably, covered in blood, and numb with shock. As long as I live, I will never forget the look on her face. I've never seen that much agony on a human's face before, and I hope to never see it again. She had no idea what was going on, what had happened. When we got her back to the ranch, she wouldn't talk to us for almost a day. For a while I was desperately afraid that I had lost my best friend."

Tears slid down Megan's cheeks as she turned her head to look down at her baby. "In some ways I did lose her that day, or at least I lost the Alex that she used to be. She never got over it, but I suppose no one would. She'll still laugh and talk and put on a happy face, but inside she's not the same. Alex used to want a family and a good husband; she used to make plans for her future. She doesn't do that anymore."

Unable to stand anymore, Jarett slid into the chair next to Megan; he closed his eyes and rubbed at his temples. He couldn't get the image of Alex clinging to her father for sixteen hours, holding him as he grew cold and rigid, out of his mind. Bile rose in his throat as an aching hurt clutched at his chest. He could well imagine the look on her face when they had pulled her away, frightened and broken.

"Why are you telling me this?" he muttered.

Megan's eyes were intense as they met his. "Alex stopped making plans for her future that day, because she truly doesn't believe she'll have one. Since that day, she has only ever intended to get even with Murdock, no matter the cost. She believes that she will die in the process, and that's a fate she willingly accepts. She's never said that to me, but I've known her our entire lives. It's why Hugh watches her so closely, I think he suspects the same thing but isn't willing to admit it."

Jarett stared at her as a dawning knowledge bloomed inside of him. Megan was right; Alex had every intention of getting revenge on Murdock, even if it meant her life. He should have realized it that day when she'd told him to kill her before taking her to Murdock. Indignation swept through him as he rose to his feet.

"Wait!" Megan cried. "I'm not telling you this so you go charging after her. If you start yelling at her, or become too controlling with her, she *will* rebel. If she rebels against you, then all hope is lost. She will only become more reckless."

"Then why are you telling me this?" he inquired.

"Because for the first time, in years, I see some hope in her again. She is actually thinking about something other than revenge for a change. You are the reason for that change, and I believe you are the only one who can keep her from destroying herself with this crazy need for revenge. I *need* you to stop her. I can't lose her, and I truly wish for her to be happy again. You can't tell her what I've just told you; she doesn't know how I feel about the way she's been living her life. Please, please, don't say anything."

"I won't," he promised through gritted teeth.

“Don’t hurt her.”

“I’m not going to hurt her; I’m going to kill her.”

He spun on his heel and stormed out of the house. He was oblivious to the jubilant smile on Megan’s face. “He loves her,” Megan whispered to Faith after the door slammed closed.

***

By the time Jarett made it to Henry’s house, she was already gone, as was Henry. He slammed the door open as he stomped into the laundry room of the saloon. Rachel glanced up at him and immediately froze when she saw the look on his face. “Where is she?” he nearly roared.

Rachel took a startled step back. “I don’t know. She and Henry just dropped off his clothes and then left. Try the mercantile.”

Jarett was fuming as he turned around and stalked back through the kitchen. He hurried down the alley and stepped onto the boardwalk, he truly was going to kill her. He had told her to stay at Megan’s, now he was following her trail from one place to another like a dog. From now on, she wouldn’t be left alone, at all.

Striding purposefully across the road, he was like a bull on a rampage by the time he entered the mercantile. Suzanne gaped at him from behind the counter. “Is she in here?”

“Who?” Suzanne squeaked.

At the same time, he heard Alex’s soft laughter. Sending Suzanne a scathing glance, he heard Alex speaking as moved toward the back of the store. “This hat makes you look wiser, Henry.”

“My dear, I have never been wise, and a hat certainly isn’t going to help.”

Alex laughed as she adjusted the jaunty hat on Henry's head and tipped it over his wrinkled face. "I've always found you wise," she assured him. She brushed her hands over the shoulders of his new jacket and stepped back to inspect him with a critical eye. "You look so handsome. Charlie will be pleased."

Henry clutched her hand; there was a hopeful look in his eyes that tugged at her heart. "Do you truly think so?"

She nodded reassuringly as she squeezed his hand in return. The sudden heat at her back made her heart thump in anticipation as she recognized Jarett's scent and presence. She turned to him but her smile faltered at the fury that was etched into the lines of his face.

"Didn't I tell you to stay at Megan's!" he snapped as he moved closer to her.

Alex was forced to tilt her head back to meet his gaze. "I had to see Henry."

His jaw clenched so forcefully that a muscle jumped in his cheek and a vein began to stand out in his forehead. "I would have taken you to see Henry."

"I assure you that I don't require a bodyguard. I can take care of myself."

He continued to stalk her until she had backed herself into the wall. "Oh yes, you've been taking care of yourself just fine by getting into all sorts of trouble, but that's over with now. You will do what I say, you will start obeying *me*."

"Like hell!" Alex retorted as she rebelled against his commanding demeanor. "You have no say over me, or how I choose to live my life!"

His eyes were golden fire as he clutched her shoulders. Apprehension surged through her as she realized she may have pushed him too far. "See here," Henry interjected.

"Stay out of this!" Jarett commanded. "When it comes to your safety I have every say over you Alexandra Harris."

Alex grappled to break free of his grasp, but he refused to relinquish her. Glaring up at him, she ceased her useless struggles as she fought the childish urge to stick out her tongue and kick him. "No you don't! You're not my brother; you're not my father..."

"You are going to listen to me! It's your safety that I'm concerned about!"

"Why? What do you care?" No, *now* she had gone too far. Something inside of him seemed to shatter as his eyes turned nearly black.

"I care about *you*," he hissed. "That's why I care."

Alex's eyes widened as his expression took on the startled look of someone that had just seen an albino deer. He shook his head and released her as he took an abrupt step back. "Finish what you were doing and meet me outside," he ordered crisply.

Alex stared in bewilderment after his retreating back. A part of her soared at the realization that he did care for her, another part felt utterly cold and empty. The look on his face had been one of horror at the realization, not one of joy, but then she imagined that's what her face had looked like when she'd come to the same realization. Alex shuddered as she turned away, she was unable to meet Henry's sympathetic gaze. "I'm all set Alexandra, if you have to leave..."

"No Henry, that's okay," she whispered. "Let's pay for these."

Henry took hold of her arm; he didn't bother to remove his new clothes as he led her toward the counter. Alex wouldn't meet Suzanne's gaze as she patiently waited for Henry and dreaded going outside to meet Jarett. She didn't know what she was going to say to him or what he was going to do.

Things were far more complicated then she wanted them to be. Wasn't loving someone supposed to be easy? She wondered woefully. It was easy between Megan and Daryl; it had been since they were children. And even if loving someone wasn't always easy, it certainly wasn't supposed to be this painful.

"Come Alexandra, I'm ready."

Henry took her arm and led her toward the door. Jarett was leaning against the wall, his face impassive as he turned toward them. He took her arm from Henry and bowed his head to him.

"I'll see you next week Henry," Alex promised.

"Of course dear."

Henry whistled happily as he made his way toward the tavern. "Henry!" Alex called after him. "You have to change first."

He cast a bashful grin over his shoulder before he changed direction and headed for his tiny shack. "Is there anywhere else that you need to go?" Jarett inquired, his voice as oddly detached as the rest of him.

"No," she mumbled.

He gave her a curt nod then led her toward the wagon. Hugh and Paul were standing by it and conversing, they stopped speaking as she and Jarett approached. Hugh's eyes were distant and troubled while Paul was wearing that upset, confused expression she was beginning to hate. "You look lovely today Alex," Paul complimented her.

"Thank you Paul. Is the barn finished?"

"Yes, thanks to all the help that everyone gave. I hope you're feeling better."

Alex blushed at the lie that had been told to explain their abrupt departure. "Yes," she mumbled.

Jarett's gaze bored into Paul as he saw the open adoration and hurt in his eyes. It grated on him to have a man looking at her like that. He had thought he'd made it abundantly clear that she was *his*, but it was obvious that Paul didn't care about that fact and was more than willing to overlook it.

Jarett knew that if he left town, Paul would still be willing to take Alex as his wife. The thought of another man touching her, sharing his life with her, was one that nearly sent him spiraling into a fit of rage. If he had anything to say about it that would *never* happen.

His hand clenched involuntarily on her arm. She glanced up at him before looking away. He released her arm only to slide his own around her waist possessively. Paul and Hugh both glared at him but neither said a word. Alex tried to step away from him but he only pulled her rigid body closer to his large, possessive one.

"Well, I must be going," Paul said. "I'll see you tomorrow night."

Alex frowned as Paul hurried away. "Tomorrow night?" she inquired of Hugh.

"I invited Paul for dinner." Hugh answered her while glaring daggers at Jarett.

CHAPTER 18

Alex sat at the table stiffly, hating the dress she wore and the pull of her intricately pinned hair. Lysette had somehow managed to get the thick mass into a knot but small, delicate, annoying little curls fell down to frame her face. She absently shoved a strand aside and wished that she hadn't allowed Lysette to do her hair but Lysette had insisted upon it. Alex hadn't had the energy to fight her. After last night, she'd barely had the energy to get out of bed this morning.

Her glance strayed to Jarett sitting beside her and casually leaning back in his chair as he took a sip of scotch. She couldn't help but blush as she vividly remembered the things he had done to her last night, the things that *she* had eagerly done to *him*. She should have been mortified by the wanton way that she had behaved, but she wasn't. There had been a desperation in his lovemaking, a passion that had touched the passion inside of her. She had spent many pleasurable hours in his arms and had fallen asleep when exhaustion had finally overtaken her sometime around dawn.

Sensing her stare, he turned toward her and locked eyes with her. For the life of her, she couldn't bring herself to look away from him. His breath was sensual against her ear as he leaned close; his strong scent of soap, leather, and male enveloped her in a warm cocoon as the heat of his body pressed against hers.

"You look beautiful tonight Love; I hope that it's for my benefit and not Paul's." There was an edge to his voice that caused goose bumps to break out on her skin.

"It's not for anyone's benefit," she whispered. "Lysette saw an opportunity to dress me up and took full advantage of it."

Her answer didn't seem to please him, but it satisfied him enough that he moved away from her. She studied him before turning her attention back to Paul and Hugh who were engrossed in a deep conversation about the livestock and damages that had been accrued. Alex knew she should be paying attention; it affected her as much as it affected them, but she couldn't seem to keep her focus on the two men as her gaze kept straying to Jarett. He looked unbelievably handsome tonight and completely desirable. Biting into her lower lip, she forced herself to think of the cows and horses, to think of anything but him, but she found it impossible.

Jarett glanced at Alex again as her gaze drifted to the night beyond the windows. Her brow furrowed as if she were troubled by something. She looked exquisitely beautiful with her hair up like that; the artfully curled tendrils accentuated the delicate contours of her face. She was wearing a forest green dress that wasn't as old as most of the others he'd seen her in, or as modest. The collar dipped down to reveal the upper half of her full, tanned breasts. It revealed far too much to Paul's amorous gaze for his liking, a gaze that was beginning to set Jarett's teeth on edge.

She may not have dressed up to catch Paul's attention, but she had it anyway. Jarett was going to have to set everyone right, and soon. There would be no more men mooning over her, no more men thinking that they could bed her. Taking another sip of scotch, he glanced at her again as she turned back to the conversation. Her eyes were turbulent as she gazed at her brother, something was obviously bothering her, but he didn't know what. He would find out later. Thoughts of later instantly turned his mind in a more lustful direction.

Alexandra may have been inexperienced when he had first taken her, but she was becoming much more sure of herself. She was infinitely willing and eager to please him as well as herself. Her fascination with him made up for any lack of experience. As did her sexual appetite, which more than matched his own, and her stamina, which he thought might actually exceed his own.

When he was with her, he felt like an untrained youth, unable to control himself. She brought out a part of him that he had never known existed. A part that no longer had anything to do with lust and everything to do with the fact that he cared for her, deeply. He had never been as happy as he was when he was with her. There was no one, and *nothing*, that could take her away from him.

Unable to resist touching her, he pushed back a lock of her hair. Her smile and sparkling eyes warmed his heart. Jarett's hand stilled on her cheek as she tipped her head into his caress and her lashes fell over her eyes. Then, her eyes flew open and she straightened in her chair. She cast a furtive glance at Paul and her brother. Jarett removed his hand from her cheek, but he clasped hold of her hand beneath the table. He hated not being able to touch her any time he chose to, hated the fact that what was between them was socially unacceptable. Hated the fact that he knew she was ashamed of herself, even though she never said a word about it and never led him to believe that she regretted anything.

Rubbing her delicate hand with his thumb, he was relieved to note that Paul and Hugh were so focused upon their conversation that they still weren't paying any attention to them. He thought of his conversation with Hugh the day of the barn raising, and knew that it was time to put everything to rights. He was about to start speaking when Jesse burst into the room. The young man was panting heavily and so distraught that he was heedless of the filth and blood covering him.

Alex's heart was in her throat as she jumped to her feet. "We've got a problem in the south pasture!" Jesse cried. "There's at least ten steer caught up in the barb wire!"

"What?" Hugh demanded harshly as he rose from his chair. "Jesus, how did that happen?"

Jesse's eyes landed on Alex before whizzing away. "They were herded into it," he admitted.

"Son of a bitch," Hugh snarled and shoved his chair in so forcefully that he knocked his glass of bourbon over.

"I'm coming with you!" Alex cried.

"No, you stay here." Jarett grabbed hold of her shoulders as she took a step after her brother. "This isn't something that you should see."

Alex could well imagine that it had to be awful, but she couldn't stay here and do nothing. "I'm good with wounds, just ask Hugh."

"Stay here Alex," Hugh commanded. "If there are any worth saving, I'll come get you."

Trembling with frustration, Hugh's words sliced into her deeply. *If there are any worth saving*, she shuddered as she took a step back. She wrapped her arms around herself in a useless gesture to ward off the sudden chill in the air. Those poor animals were probably suffering horribly, and there was nothing that she could do to help them.

Jarett drew her into his arms. He ignored the looks he received from the other men in the room as he held her against him. He kissed the top of her head before taking a step back and tilting her chin up so that she had to look at him. "Promise me you'll stay here," he said forcefully.

She looked about to protest as her eyes sparkled with defiance, and then it was gone. A weary slump came to her shoulders; a vulnerable look filled her eyes. “I promise,” she said. “I don’t want to see.”

He pulled her against him one more time. He didn’t like the idea of leaving her behind but he knew that they would need all the help they could get with the bulls and he had to see for himself. If there was any evidence that Murdock had done this, he would find it. Reluctantly pulling away, he dropped a kiss on her trembling lips before releasing her.

Alex hugged herself as she watched them leave. She listened to the door open and close; the sounds of rushing feet on the porch stairs, but she made no move to follow them. She’d meant what she said; she didn’t want to see.

***

It was some time later that Alex moved out to the porch, her gaze was trained on the pasture but she was unable to see much in the night. They would have to come back soon. Shivering, she wrapped the shawl tighter around her as the cool breeze floated over her. Lysette came outside and handed her a cup of tea before retreating into the house again.

Alex leaned against the post and prayed that they would come back soon or at least send someone to tell her what was going on. Actually, she knew what was going on. She just wanted Jarett to come back to hold her and let her know that he was there.

Clutching the shawl, her gaze turned back to the open pastures but nothing stirred in the night. The only sounds were the restless movements of a horse in the stable, and the chirruping of the crickets. Deciding to see what horse was so unsettled tonight, she walked down the steps and made her way to the stable.

Slipping into the barn, she lifted the lantern from its hook and made her way down the aisle. Satan poked his head out; his ears came forward as she approached. "I should have known it was you," she whispered.

He nickered as she hung the lantern on a hook and turned to a bin of carrots. Fishing one out, she held her hand out for him to accept it. His velvety muzzle and stiff whiskers tickled her palm as she stroked his forehead. She talked to him as she fed him another carrot before picking the lantern back up and looking around the large barn.

She inhaled the familiar scents of hay, horse, and leather. Scents that were normally comforting did nothing to ease the lump in her throat or the aching in her chest as she walked out of the barn. She hung the lantern back up, and huddled deeper into her shawl as she anxiously scanned the horizon again. There was still no sign of them.

She turned back to the house and was almost to the porch when she became aware of the horse tied to the post. Confusion swirled through her before her gaze shot to the man leaning casually against the house. She couldn't see his face, but instinctively she knew who it was, just as she knew that he was watching her. The shawl was suddenly useless against the chill that rattled her bones and set her teeth on edge.

"Ms. Harris." Murdock's voice was oddly husky, almost purring.

Alex swallowed down her rising disgust as she straightened her shoulders. She forced herself to move toward the sanctuary of the house before he decided to come to her. Her hand went to her side, but she hadn't brought her guns out with her. She didn't care that they would hang her; she would have gladly put a bullet in his head to end all of the anguish that everyone in the community suffered because of him.

Climbing the porch steps, she tilted her chin as she defiantly met Murdock's gleaming hazel eyes. They were filled with lust as he leisurely scanned her body with an insolence that made her itch to drive a fist into his face. "What do you want?" she demanded haughtily.

His gaze came back to hers. "I think you know what I want Alexandra."

Alex's stomach turned over, but she refused to give him the satisfaction of lowering her gaze from his. "I'd rather be dead."

A cruel smile twisted his mouth. "Come now, I know that Stanton's not the only one that has pounded out his lust between those thighs. The only difference is, I can offer you much more than he can."

It took everything Alex had not to throw up. She inwardly cringed at his words, but somehow managed to keep herself from vomiting on him. "You're repulsive. I want nothing to do with you, never have, and *never* will."

She took a hesitant step back as he approached her with a malicious gleam in his eyes. Taking another step back, she realized too late that she had backed herself into the banister. Casting a glance around, she sought some route of escape but found none. His hands locked on the banister on each side of her as he leaned toward her. The stench of whiskey, onions, and something even more foul washed over her as he exhaled. Alex cringed away as she breathed shallowly through her nose.

"Get away from me!" she spat. She resisted the urge to attempt to get free of him; she didn't want to do anything that would put her closer to him.

His hand moved to grasp hold of her waist; it burned into her skin like the fires of Hell. "I'll take good care of you Alexandra. Better care than Stanton will. You don't need him, he won't offer you any kind of future, but I'll set you up as my mistress. Come Alexandra, I just want a chance to taste what so many others have."

A gasp escaped her. Without thinking, her hand shot up and her fist connected solidly with his jaw. His head shot back as he took a stumbling step away from her. Seizing the opportunity to get away from him, she shoved him forcefully in the chest with both of her palms. He bounced into the wall of the house as she jumped to the side. She made it three feet before his hand snagged her skirt and he ripped her backward.

She opened her mouth to let out a bloodcurdling scream, but his hands wrapped around her throat and he choked the scream from her. She clawed at his hands as they cut off her air supply. Panic threatened to overwhelm her, stars exploded before her eyes and the world began to blur.

He released her suddenly and shoved her forward. She was gasping for air as she landed upon her knees. Trembling, she raised a hand to her brutalized throat. Tears burned the backs of her eyes as her vision began to clear. She jerked away from him as he knelt beside her. His hand curled into her hair, he jerked her head around to plant a punishing kiss on her mouth. Alex cried out against the gnashing of her lips against her teeth that caused blood to spurt into her mouth. She shoved against him as she tried desperately to break free. Strands of her hair were pulled from her head as she fought him but she ignored the pain that lanced through her skull.

"I will have you Alexandra, willing or not." He muttered against her mouth.

"Get away from her!"

Murdock finally released her at Lysette's bellow. Alex looked up as she heard the click of a revolver being cocked. Willy stood beside Lysette on the porch, a colt leveled at Murdock as he rose to his feet. "Easy old man," Murdock muttered.

“Get out of here before I kill you!” Willy growled.
“I have men in the woods, if you shoot me, the three of you will be dead in an instant.”
“Get out of here!” Willy snapped.
Murdock held his hands up as he edged his way across the porch, and down the steps. “Murdock.” He stopped and turned toward the sound of her coarse voice. “I *will* kill you.”
“I don’t think so my dear.”
She watched as he mounted his horse and turned toward the road. Murdock’s men emerged from the woods and fall into line behind him as he rode away. Rage burned through every inch of her as she climbed unsteadily to her feet to watch their retreating backs. Turning back to the house, she shrugged off Lysette’s hands as she grabbed for her.
“Alex, you’re bleeding!” Lysette cried.
Alex ignored her as she hurried into the house and took the stairs two at a time. Stepping into her room, she walked over to the guns resting on top of her trunk. Hefting them up, she strapped them around her waist. She would like to take the time to change out of her dress, but she didn’t have time to waste as she hurried out of the room again. Lysette was standing nervously by the door, her eyes widened as she took in the gun belt at Alex’s waist.
“Where do you think you’re going?” she demanded.
Alex glanced briefly at her before shoving open the screen door. Willy leapt up from the banister as Alex strode down the stairs toward the stable. “Alexandra Harris you get back here right now!” Lysette bellowed.
Alex jerked her arm free of Willy when he grabbed hold of it. He didn’t relent as he came back at her. The arthritis in his knees kept him from being as nimble as he once was and she deftly dodged him. Lifting her skirts, she ignored the banging weight of her guns as she ran to the barn. She was determined to escape before Willy could stop her.

Bursting into the barn, she didn't bother with the lantern as she grabbed a bridle from the tack room and raced for Chantilly's stall. She would have loved to take Satan, for he was faster, but she didn't have time to bother with a saddle and he wasn't broke enough for bareback. Thrusting open the stall door, Chantilly lifted her head as Alex hurried to her and slipped the bridle on.

"Alexandra!"

Willy's booming voice echoed through the barn as she took hold of the reins, and a large handful of white mane. It was a difficult undertaking with the dress, and the dragging weight of the guns, but she managed to lift herself onto the mare's back. She awkwardly settled the tangle of voluminous cloth from the dress around her. She didn't give a moment's thought to the expanse of calf she bared all the way to the knee as she led Chantilly to the door and gave the mare a nudge with her heels.

Clearing the stall doorway, Alex kicked harder. She ignored Willy's startled cry as he dove after her and tried to snatch her leg. Alex knew Willy would have no problem with dragging her off the horse if he got a hold of her. She jerked Chantilly's reins to the right, a maneuver she had never attempted with the gentle mare before. Chantilly shied and gave a frightened cry as Alex kicked her again. Willy's hand came up empty as the mare barreled past him.

"Alexandra!" Willy's loud shout was completely drowned out by the rush of wind that engulfed her as she exited the stable.

CHAPTER 19

Jarett, Hugh, Paul, Perry, and Jesse broke over the top of the lower ridge just as Willy burst out of the barn on horseback. Clinging to the reins of a large bay, Willy rode over the road and cut into the woods at a break neck speed that was deadly to any man, but especially so for old Willy. "What is he doing?" Hugh muttered, he sounded more baffled than angry though.

"The old man's finally lost his mind," Perry mumbled.

"I suppose we should stop him before he kills himself," Paul said tiredly.

Jarett had no intention of going after the old man. His only thoughts were to rid himself of the blood and filth covering him before crawling into Alex's warm bed, where he intended to try and forget everything he had just witnessed. *Such useless slaughter*, he thought with disgust. *Such a waste of life.* None of the steer could be saved and all of them had been bawling in distress. The echoes of their cries still sounded in his head. It had been a relief to put them out of their misery, a task to get them all disposed of, and an endless ride to get back to the house.

Perry and Jesse broke off to follow Willy when Lysette raced up, panting heavily. "Hugh you have to stop her!" she gasped. Jarett looked up as a growing feeling of dread began to work
through him. "She went after Murdock! She's gonna kill him Hugh!"

"What?" Hugh cried.

"Alex took her guns! We tried to stop her but we couldn't!"

"Shit!" Jarett exploded as he wheeled his horse and spurred him in the side.

"When did she leave?" Hugh demanded.

"Five minutes ago, she took to the woods. I think she's going to Murdock's ranch!"

Jarett just barely heard this last bit of conversation as his horse raced forward with the same breakneck speed Willy had departed with. He was going to kill her. He should have known better than to leave her alone. Megan had warned him that Alex cared nothing about her own life. Not when it came to making Murdock pay for what he had done to her father, but he hadn't listened to her. He hadn't wanted to believe that Alex would be so careless with her life.

Behind him, he could hear the thunderous crashes of the others as they raced through the woods. They were as heedless of the branches, briars, and trees that impeded their progress as he was. Ahead of him, he could barely make out the moving form of Willy. Jarett swore vehemently as his horse stumbled and it took all he had to keep Ricochet on his feet as he pulled back sharply on the reins.

"I'm going to kill her!" Hugh barked.

"Not if I get to her first," Jarett snarled.

Willy's horse disappeared from view as he rode on. Ricochet lurched forward and seemed to sigh with relief as they burst onto open ground. Jarett didn't hesitate to take in his surroundings as he followed Willy over the crest of a hill. He leaned low over Ricochet's neck as he urged the horse faster. There was still no sign of Alex as they rode relentlessly over the open field. Murdock's ranch was close, too close for his liking.

With her head start...

He was unwilling to consider what her head start could mean as they gained on Willy. Jarett finally spotted her, sitting atop her mare as she stared at the ranch set up on a bluff less than a hundred yards away. Men were moving about outside the ranch, their voices were loud in the serene night. Relief washed through him as she turned, her hand went to her gun when she spotted them, but it dropped back to her side. She made no attempt to escape though as she watched them come closer. Jarett reined in beside her and kicked free of Ricochet.

"What were you thinking!?" he bellowed as he stormed toward her.

"Jarett..."

"Don't you dare 'Jarett' me! I'm going to shake some sense into that thick skull of yours! Do you hear me?"

"I think the whole world hears you," she murmured.

He frowned at the hoarse sound of her voice but he didn't take the time to think about it as he grabbed hold of her waist and hauled her from her horse. His fury mounted as he realized that she hadn't even bothered with a saddle. That she had taken *that* ride without a saddle only made him want to throttle her more.

"Goddamn it Alex, you could have gotten yourself killed! I've had enough of this; I'm putting my foot down. You're to be locked in your room until you grow a brain, or you get over this insane death wish of yours!"

He was shaking as he held her, he was unable to let her go and yet he wanted to get as far away from her as possible before he really did choke her. "I don't have a death wish," she grated and then winced.

"You don't have a death wish! You don't even have a saddle! Were you going to go in there with guns blazing?"

"Yes," she admitted.

His fingers clenched on her waist as his eyes blazed with golden fire. The vein in his forehead was throbbing; a muscle in his cheek jumped from the force of his clenched jaw. She thought that she should be afraid of him, but she wasn't. She'd never seen him this cross before, but she knew that he wouldn't hurt her no matter how much he may be tempted too.

"I've had it Alex," he told her. "There will be no more of this, do you understand me?"

"I'm fine Jarett," she croaked out.

"Fine!" he exploded. "Look at you, you're bleeding!" Alex winced as he pressed his bandanna against her broken lips. "You're lucky you didn't fall off that horse. What were you thinking?"

The frustration in his voice touched her deeply. Not caring about their audience, she took hold of the hand pressing the bandanna to her lips. "I was thinking that I was going to kill him," she croaked out. "Then I thought about you, and Hugh, and everyone else, and I stopped. I couldn't go through with it. I knew he would kill me..." She had to take a minute to get more words past her parched and damaged throat. "And I didn't want to lose you."

Her words gradually penetrated his rage. His hand on her waist trembled at the implication of those words. Megan had said that he could change Alex's outlook on life, that he might give her hope for the future. He had thought that Megan was wrong on the ride over here, but now he knew that she had been right. The utter joy that suffused him at the realization caused a smile to tug at his lips. She wasn't hell bent on dying for her revenge anymore. Instead, she wanted to live for *him*.

He pulled her forward a step and brushed a kiss over her forehead. "Good, because you're stuck with me."

Her gaze was confused, yet hopeful, as she searched his face. "Stuck with you?"

"Yes, you're stuck with me, for good."

"What does that mean?" she whispered.

His breath was warm as his mouth brushed over her ear. "It means that I may have no say over your life now, but I will when you consent to be my wife."

As far as marriage proposals went it wasn't romantic, but she couldn't stop the huge smile that spread over her face, or the tears that sprang to her eyes. "Are you serious?" she choked out.

He stepped back to look down at her. "Yes. What do you say?"

She let out a strangled cry of delight as she flung her arms around his neck. "Yes," she grated. "Oh yes!"

Tears of joy streaked down her face as she buried her head in the hollow of his shoulder. He held her for a minute longer before lowering her to her feet and wiping the tears from her cheeks. There was a bright gleam in his glorious eyes as he smiled warmly at her. "Let's get you home, you're a mess."

She smiled brilliantly up at him as she leaned against his chest. "That would be fantastic," she admitted and winced again at the soreness of her throat.

Jarett turned to look at her inquisitively. "What is the matter with your voice?"

The dazzling emerald color of her eyes turned nearly black. Her jaw clenched as her nostrils flared. Taking a step back from her, he lifted her chin as he attempted to search her throat in the moonlight. His gaze shot to her swollen and split lips. A branch could have caused it, but it wasn't a branch that was causing her to sound like she had a frog in her throat.

"What happened?" he demanded.

Alex's gaze went nervously to her brother as he dismounted and strode over to them. "Jasper, get the lantern!" Hugh commanded.

"It's nothing," Alex assured them. "Truly, let's just go home. Jarett has asked me to marry him Hugh…" She had to break off as she swallowed convulsively. "We should be celebrating."

She knew that they would see her neck eventually, but she would prefer if it happened when they were far from Murdock's property. Or at least far enough away that someone could stop Jarett and Hugh before they came back here to kill Murdock.

"'Bout time," Hugh muttered as he snatched hold of her chin. "You were supposed to do that after the barn raising if you do recall."

Jarett shot him a quelling glance before turning his attention back to Alex as she jerked her chin free of her brother's grasp. "You're making him marry me?" she croaked angrily.

Hugh seized her chin again. "No, it was his idea. Why else do you think I haven't said anything about the two of you?" Color suffused Alex's face as she lowered her gaze from his. So her brother did know what was going on between them. She was certain that she had never been more mortified in her life. "Though, I was about to say something."

Alex couldn't look at him, and it wasn't until light burst over them that she recalled the situation she was in. She took a defensive step back, but she came up against the steel of Jarett's arm on her waist. Hugh took hold of the lantern and brought it closer to her as she pressed against Jarett. She knew that she would receive no sanctuary from him though.

"What happened to your throat?" Jarett roared.

Alex jumped as he grabbed hold of her chin and lifted it up. Hugh's jaw clenched as his gaze shot to hers. Alex cringed away from them as she uselessly tried to pull her chin free. "It's nothing."

Jarett's eyes narrowed as he took in the red marks surrounding her delicate throat and the ugly bruises already appearing. His eyes snapped back to her lips and then down to her throat again. Anger, pure and simple, began to shake his bones as he took in those marks. His gaze moved to the scratches on her breastbone and the tear in the neckline of her dress. Those marks could have also been caused by tree branches but he highly doubted it.

"What happened?" he demanded.

Alex knew there was no hope of getting out of this without telling them what had happened, but she preferred to do so at home. She wanted Murdock dead, but she couldn't have Hugh and Jarett going crazy while they were here. "Murdock's coming," Paul whispered.

Alex spun around to find Murdock and some of his men riding down the hill toward them. She grasped hold of Jarett's shirt and pulled impatiently at him when he kept his attention focused on the men coming toward them. "Don't do anything!" She ignored the rawness of her throat as she rushed to get the words out. "Please, both of you don't do anything."

Knowledge bloomed in the depths of Jarett's eyes as they came back to hers. "Son of a bitch!" he exploded.

"Jarett no, please don't, please! Hugh!" She turned toward her brother and grasped his arm when she saw the wrath that blazed through his entire being. "Please, both of you, I can't lose either of you!"

"Be quiet, Alex," Hugh spat.

"Hugh..."

Her plea was cut off as Murdock and his men arrived. "What are you doing on my property?" Murdock demanded, he pointed a rifle at Hugh as his men fanned out around him with their guns drawn.

Alex could feel the rage in Jarett's taut muscles as he stood with his gaze locked on Murdock. "My horse spooked," Alex said quickly in her hoarse voice. "They came to help me."

A malicious smile twisted Murdock's features as his gaze swept her. Jarett took a step forward but he was unable to dislodge her from his shirt. "You looked like you were in for the night when I last saw you Alexandra. You certainly weren't wearing your guns," Murdock said.

"I always wear my guns when I ride. It's not safe to do otherwise."

Murdock smirked at her. "No, it's not," he agreed. "Amazing that your horse came here, and without a saddle."

"I wasn't planning on riding far," she lied with ease.

"I see. Well then, I think it best if you all leave, now." Alex tugged at Jarett's shirt as she tried to back up. His gaze remained locked on Murdock as the man sent him a challenging grin. "Better go with your whore Stanton, I think she's eager to take *you* for a ride."

"I'll kill you Murdock," Jarett promised.

"Funny, that's what she said no more than an hour ago. After she got done begging for mercy."

"Bastard!" Jarett sprang forward so rapidly that Alex didn't have a chance to try and stop him.

Murdock's rifle leveled on Jarett's chest. "No!" she screamed.

Hugh and Willy moved to intercept Jarett as Paul and Jesse sprang from their mounts. Hugh took hold of Jarett's arm, he said something that Alex couldn't hear, but whatever it was it froze Jarett in his tracks. Alex stood breathlessly, her hands clenched together as she nervously watched them. "Unless you want a bullet in your chest Stanton, I would listen to the man," Murdock said.

Jarett seethed inwardly as his fists clenched and unclenched. The thought of ripping the man limb from limb was truly pleasant, but he would be dead before he ever got his hands on Murdock, and Alexandra would be left vulnerable. He now understood completely what it was that Hugh had gone through when he'd discovered the truth about his father. Hugh's fingers dug into his arm, his words still echoed in Jarett's mind. They were the only thing keeping him still.

"Let's go," Hugh said and tugged on Jarett's arm.

Jarett's gaze never left Murdock's as he moved back to Alexandra. Her eyes were pleading as he took hold of her arm and led her to the group of horses. He stopped beside Perry and grasped hold of her waist to hand her up to him. She gave him a confused look as she settled into the saddle. He was reluctant to let her go but he knew that he had too. Turning away, he grasped Ricochet's reins and swung himself into the saddle.

"Stay away from her Murdock," he growled at the man.

Murdock grinned at him as he leaned back in his saddle. "I take it you've stopped looking for the thieves."

"Oh, I'm looking for them, but I won't be collecting your reward money. They'll be going straight to the sheriff," Jarett informed him.

"I see."

It took all Jarett had to turn his horse away, he spurred him in the side. He waited for the sound of a gunshot as he sat stiffly in the saddle. When they reached the woods, he pulled up and turned to Perry as the man halted beside him. Jarett eagerly took Alex into his arms and cradled her within his lap. He was unable to stop himself from kissing her forehead, her cheeks, and chin.

"Did he hurt you bad?" he whispered as he nuzzled her neck.

"No." She shivered from the delicious sensations his attention sparked as she pressed closer against his chest. "Why did you give me to Perry?"

"Because if he shot me in the back, I didn't want the bullet to go through me, and hit you."

All of her pleasure vanished as she gasped in shock. "Jarett..."

"Shh Love, everything is fine."

Tears filled her eyes as she rested her head against his chest. Her happiness from earlier was gone. As long as Murdock lived, he would do everything in his power to make sure that their lives were wretched.

CHAPTER 20

Alex draped her arm across Jarett's chest and snuggled closer to his side as he leisurely rubbed her back. It had taken some persuading on her part, but eventually he had capitulated to her and agreed to sleep beside her in the bed, but he refused to make love to her.

"We'll get you a ring tomorrow," he whispered as he brushed the hair back from her face.

Alex's heart soared at the reminder that he wished to marry her, but along with it came the reminder that there was more she wished to learn about him. She lifted her head and rested her chin on his chest as she looked at him. "I know so little about you."

His hand stilled in her hair as a troubled look came into his eyes. "Anything you wish to know, just ask."

Alex frowned thoughtfully as she thought of the dozens of questions she'd wanted to ask him. "Where are you from?"

"I was born in Boston, as far as I know."

"As far as you know?"

Jarett smiled as he returned to running his fingers through her silky hair. "I was left on the doorstep of an orphanage as a baby. I was taken in by the nuns that ran it and raised there until I left at twelve. I have no idea who my parents were and I gave up all hope of ever meeting them by the time I was eight."

Alex's heart ached for him, it seemed like such a lonely childhood, but she tried to keep her face impassive as he spoke. He would hate it if he thought she pitied him. "Why did you leave when you were so young?"

He shrugged as his hands slid down to trail over her back. "The nuns were kind enough, oh there were a few we all avoided, but I didn't want to be known as an orphan any longer. I was convinced I was capable of taking care of myself. I got into more than a few brawls, and had a lot of close calls with the law on the streets, but I learned how to keep myself alive. I taught myself how to shoot with deadly accuracy, and eventually I became strong enough that most people were too afraid to confront me, and they left me alone. Well almost everyone." He smiled at her as he poked the end of her nose and she grinned back at him.

"Do you shoot everyone that confronts you?"

He chuckled as he twirled her hair around his finger. "Not everyone, but I've shot more than a few men in my lifetime. You were my first woman."

"It's an honor I'd rather not have," she teased. "Have you killed anyone before?"

His face became somber, his eyes distant as he nodded. "Two, both were in self-defense and when I was still living on the streets."

The torment in his eyes made Alex sorry that she had asked the question. She stroked his chest as she sought to soothe him. "How did you end up here?"

Some of the tension eased from his body at the change of subject. "At eighteen I left Boston and moved to Pennsylvania. I worked a farm there for a couple of years before moving onto Ohio for a year. When I'd had enough of that, I struck out for Missouri. I worked a ranch on the border of Illinois for a couple of years before deciding I wanted to return to some city living. I was twenty-three when I reached St. Louis; I started working as a guard for money transport and remained there for five years. It was also there that I encountered Murdock."

Her face darkened. "Were the two of you friends?"

"Not at all. I turned down his first job offers, but eventually I'd had enough of St. Louis and decided that it was time to move on. The money from Murdock was too good to turn down so I agreed to work for him."

"Will you have enough of here too?" she asked worriedly.

His fingers were tender as he took hold of her chin with them. "Never," he vowed. "All that moving was because I had been searching for a place to settle down my whole life, and a reason to. I've found both in you." The heartfelt sincerity of his words caused tears to brim in her eyes. "I've never felt this way about someone before. I have enough money to buy some property around here; as soon as Murdock is gone we'll be able to start our own ranch."

Alex's eyes darkened at the mention of Murdock's name. "Jarett you can't do anything foolish when it comes to him, promise me you won't."

"This coming from the queen of foolishness," he teased.

"Please Jarett," she whispered. "He already took my father from me; I couldn't stand it if he took you or Hugh too."

"I promise to be careful."

She rested her cheek on his chest again and savored in the sound of his steady heartbeat beneath her ear. She understood now why he had been so pitiless and untrusting toward her on more than a few occasions. He'd never had anyone steady in his life before, he'd never had anyone to count on, or anyone to love him. He'd never had anyone to believe in, other than himself. She was going to make sure he never felt alone again and that he knew every day that she would always love him.

"He'll make our lives dismal for as long as he's alive, and to kill him in cold blood makes us no better than he is," she said. "I don't want that Jarett; my father wouldn't want that."

His eyes were resolved as he scanned her face. "We'll get him Alex."

“You’re not listening to me!” She winced as the words tore at her raw throat. His eyes were dangerous as his gaze went to her neck. A sinking feeling started in the pit of her belly as she realized that it wasn’t just her, or Hugh, that sought revenge now, but Jarett too. “Please,” she whispered.

His hand tensed minutely in her hair as he rubbed the base of her skull. “We’ll get him Alex.”

“He’s not worth dying over.”

“The only one that is going to die is Murdock, and it won’t be in cold blood, it will be lawful. He hurt you Alex and he would have done more if Lysette hadn’t come out. He won’t get away with that.”

“But...”

“It will all be fine Alex. I promise that nothing will happen to me.”

She choked back a sob. “I love you Jarett.”

His hand stilled on her back, his eyes gleamed as a smile curved his mouth. “Do you now?”

“Yes, I do.”

He pulled her head down and kissed the tears from her face. “Good,” he murmured. “Because I love you too.”

Alex half sobbed with joy as she flung herself onto his chest and buried her head in his shoulder. He held her close as he absorbed the tremors that racked her. He closed his eyes against the ecstasy, and anguish, that twisted his soul. He did love her, he would do anything in the world for her, and he would make sure that Murdock got exactly what he deserved. Not only had Murdock hurt her tonight, he had made her life a living hell for the last two years. He had stolen her innocence from her, hurtled her into a world of misery, and he would pay for it. Jarett was going to make sure of that. Just as he was going to make sure the man never touched her again.

"Shh, just relax now, it's been an exhausting day, and you're going to need your rest for tomorrow. Just think what your day will be like when Megan gets a hold of you."

Alex groaned at the thought. She turned her head to brush a kiss across his cheek. The evidence of his arousal pressed firmly into her belly. She stifled a giggle as she squirmed on top of him in the hope of breaking his will. "Stop it you little minx, or I'm going to sleep in my room," he scolded.

Alex stilled instantly. "No fair."

"You're hurt Alexandra, go to sleep."

She closed her eyes in contentment as she determined to be happy with the knowledge that he loved her and that they were going to spend the rest of their lives together. Yet she was unable to shake her lingering apprehension and dismay. Murdock had taken so much from her already. She couldn't stand to lose anymore to him. It would destroy her if she did.

"I love you." He had needed to say the words again, no matter how odd they sounded to him.

He had never said them to anyone in his life, never even imagined that he would. But with her, they seemed right. They *were* right. She was his life now and he loved her with every fiber of his being. Something had been missing from his life, something that he hadn't known about until he'd met, but he did now. He couldn't even remember what it had been like without her in his life and he didn't want to.

"I love you too," she murmured.

***

"My God Alex, what did that man do to you?" Megan cried as she tugged at the high collar of Alex's dress.

Alex's hand flew to her bruised throat; a self-conscious heat flooded her face as Megan succeeded in pulling it down a little. Lysette had put a poultice on her neck this morning, to take some of the swelling and soreness out of it, but she knew that it still looked awful. Jarett stiffened beside her, his hand tightened on her waist. She hoped he didn't slip back into the fit that he had erupted into this morning.

By the light of day, her throat had been bruised with the clear imprints of Murdock's fingers on her skin, and she'd barely been able to speak. Alex had truly feared that he would go after Murdock then and there, but she'd been able to calm him down enough to think clearly. Mainly by clinging to his neck, and refusing to let him leave the room until he had regained control of himself.

It had been the first time that she had awoken to find him still in her bed, and although they were engaged, she knew that Hugh wouldn't be appreciative if he found out. She also knew that Jarett had stayed to see how she would feel when she awoke. It definitely hadn't been pleasant, and she worried that Megan's words were going to send him into a fresh frenzy.

"It looks worse than it is," she whispered hoarsely and tugged the collar back into place.

Jarett mumbled something, but she couldn't make out the words over Megan's anxious clucking. "Paul told me what happened, but I didn't think it would be this bad!"

"Megan, I'm fine." She grasped Megan's questing hands and pulled them away from her.

"Listen to you!"

She could feel Jarett's ire mounting by the second. His eyebrows were drawn together over the bridge of his nose as he met her gaze. She tried to smile reassuringly at him but her split lip didn't allow much give. "I'm fine Megan, truly."

Megan huffed; she shot an anxious glance at Jarett before grasping hold of Alex's hands and dragging her forward. "We'll be awhile," Megan called to him.

"I'm not going anywhere," he told her.

"You can't see the dress," Megan replied firmly. "It's bad luck."

Jarett ran a hand through his hair. "I'll be on the porch."

"Go to town Jarett," Alex murmured. "We'll be fine, truly. I won't leave, I promise."

He mulled over her words before shaking his head firmly. "I'll be on the porch."

Alex sighed in surrender as she watched him walk out the door. She hated the thought of him standing out there for hours, but she knew that he would. "Stubborn man," Megan commented.

"He was in a state this morning. I thought you were going to set him off again."

Megan winced and gave her a sheepish look. "I wasn't thinking," she admitted. "Sorry. Let me show you the dress!"

"I cannot believe that you've been doing this."

"Of course I have. I knew this day would come."

"Really, and who did you picture as the groom?"

"I've known who the groom was since that day we were in the mercantile. It was the first time I ever saw you look at a man like he was a man, and I *knew* he would be the one."

"You did not," Alex protested.

Megan smiled as she pulled Alex into the bedroom. "Yes, I did. Not to mention the man had enough sense to see right through Suzanne. Plus, he looked like he'd been hit over the head when he first saw you."

"That's because I resembled the thief he was looking for."

"You *were* the thief he was looking for," Megan replied laughingly. "But that's not how he looked at you Alex. I'm surprised he didn't strip you and take you then."

"Megan!" Alex gasped.

Megan released Alex's arm to walk over to her closet. "You're no virgin anymore, stop being so shy. Tell me, is he good?"

"You're incorrigible."

Megan laughed as she flung the doors open and pulled out a white satin dress. Alex gasped in delight as she recognized her mother's beaded wedding dress. "Lysette had it brought over after I sent her a message explaining my need for it. You and Hugh didn't even know."

"Oh," Alex breathed. "Oh Megan, I can't believe you did this."

Alex held the dress against herself and admired the fine lines of the delicate cloth. The sleeves were long and off the shoulder, the bodice was form fitting with little glass beads stitched into it, and the neckline was cut low. Holding it to her, Alex had a clear image of what her beautiful mother must have looked like in this dress, with her deep brown hair piled on top of her head and her brown eyes shining with happiness.

"I'd forgotten how beautiful it was," she whispered.

"Some of the beads had to be fixed, and the seams around the neckline had come loose, but other than that it's in excellent condition. Put it on so we can see if it has to be altered."

Alex stripped down to her undergarments and slipped the dress over her head. She relished in the feel of the exquisite satin against her skin. Except for the hem being a little short, the dress fit beautifully. "It's perfect."

Megan hurried around her, fluffing the skirt and adjusting the sleeves with a critical eye. "It is perfect," she said thoughtfully. "I'll just take the hem down a little and it will be all set."

"You don't have to do that Megan."

"Who's going to do it then? You? No offense Alex, I've seen you sew. It's not good." Alex smiled sheepishly as she nodded her agreement. "Come, stand on the stool and I'll do this as quickly as possible. As long as you stand still," she added pointedly.

Alex laughed as she climbed onto the stool that Megan pulled out. Twenty minutes later, she was twitching anxiously and eager to escape as Megan shot her threatening glances, and muttered scolds around her mouthful of pins. After another twenty minutes, Megan deemed her able to get off the stool before she purposely started stabbing Alex in the legs.

"Be careful taking that dress off, if you knock those pins out, I'm going to knock you out," Megan threatened.

Alex chuckled as she carefully removed the dress. She couldn't wait for Jarett to see her in it; he wouldn't even recognize her. She knew that he wanted the wedding to take place as soon as possible and that their next stop was the church. However, she still wasn't sure what day it would be, and she found herself antsy with anticipation.

Moving into the living room, she laughed as Faith let out a very inelegant burp. "She's just like her mother."

Megan stuck out her tongue as she rubbed her daughter's back. "Wait till you have one."

Alex's head tilted to the side as she studied them. For the past two years, she'd never considered the possibility of having a husband and children. Now, all of those old dreams were rushing back to her.

"Yes, just wait," she said.

Tears filled Megan's eyes. "I am *so* happy for you Alex."

Alex felt answering tears fill her eyes as she hurried across the room to envelop Megan and Faith in a warm hug. "You're the best friend anyone could ever ask for."

Megan patted her back. "So are you. Now go let that poor man in before he thinks that I've kidnapped you."

Alex had completely forgotten about Jarett standing on the porch. "Alex." Alex paused on her way to the door and turned to look at her friend over her shoulder. "You never answered my question. Is he good?"

Alex flushed to the roots of her hair as she nodded and turned away. "I thought so," Megan declared.

Alex was eager to have someone cut into Megan's blunt teasing as she pulled the door open. Jarett was smiling slyly at her as he stood in the doorway. "What was your answer?"

"Ah I… I don't know what you mean," she stammered.

He tilted her chin up with his finger. "The windows are open."

Closing her eyes, she silently cursed Megan. Megan's loud laughter echoed through the house as she strode over to join them. "You're embarrassing her," Megan scolded playfully.

"You started it," he reminded her.

"Yes I did, but we're ladies, we're allowed to tease each other."

"From everything I know of you two; you are far from being ladies."

"That's one of the finest compliments I've ever had," Megan replied happily. "Now you two, shoo. My daughter needs her rest and I have to finish the dress. Let me know what the reverend says after you see him."

With that, Megan placed a hand in the middle of Alex's back and shoved her across the threshold. "Oh, and Jarett, she nodded yes!"

Jarett's loud laughter effectively drowned out Megan's girlish giggles. Alex turned to shoot her friend a fulminating glare, but Megan knew better than to stick around as the door closed in her face. She turned her glare on Jarett instead as he continued to pull her toward the church. "It's not funny," she muttered.

"Yes it is Love." She looked away from him, unable to meet his gaze through the humiliation burning in her veins. "If it makes you feel any better, you're good too, very, *very* good."

"Don't tease me Jarett, and please don't patronize me."

He stopped walking and pulled her up beside him. Alex refused to look at him as she stared at her worn shoes. "I'm not teasing you, or patronizing you. Look at me." Swallowing heavily, she forced herself to look up at him. "Why would you think such a thing?"

"Jarett, I'm no fool," she whispered. "I know there were other women before me and they were probably more experienced than I."

She lowered her lashes again before she saw the confirmation in his eyes. He grasped her chin and forced her to look up at him. "There were other women but *none* of them have ever meant to me what you do, and *none* of them have ever made me feel the way that you do," he said firmly.

"Jarett..."

"No Alexandra. I'm not lying to you, I'm not humoring you; I *am* telling you the truth. No woman has excited me or pleased me as much as you do. There isn't one woman in my past that I would ever care to see again, nor is there another woman that I would ever want to be with. You are it."

"Truly?" she breathed.

"I'm marrying you, aren't I? I take those vows very seriously Alex. I love you, and that is that." Her heart soared with happiness; she didn't have time to respond before he hugged her against his chest and brushed a kiss across her forehead. "Good thing we're getting married, otherwise the reverend would be scandalized."

Alex gaped at him before turning around to meet the Reverend White's scandalized gaze. Wrapping his arm around her waist, he led her over to the speechless Reverend. "Reverend," Jarett greeted.

Alex fumbled with her bonnet strings as Reverend White's pale gray eyes pierced her. "Hello Reverend," she murmured.

"Ms. Harris, Mr. Stanton, how are you today?" Reverend White greeted.

"Fine Reverend," Jarett replied. "We would like to talk to you for a few minutes."

"Of course, what can I do for you?"

"We would like to be married, as soon as possible," Jarett informed him.

"Oh, this is fantastic news!" The reverend took hold of Alex's hands and pulled her closer to him. "I can marry you as soon as you would like, tomorrow even."

"That's good," Jarett answered.

Jarett frowned at Alex as she shook her head. "Not tomorrow," she said. "I am not feeling all that well Reverend, and I would like to be at my best for our wedding."

"Oh, of course dear, I understand that. When would you like the wedding to be?" the reverend asked.

"Two weeks," Alex answered.

"Good, good!" Reverend White cried. "You can come to the chapel..."

"At the ranch."

The reverend blinked in surprise at the location but rebounded quickly. "Of course, the ranch! How silly of me.

That will be perfect! I'll be there in two weeks, at what time?"

Alex looked to Jarett for help on that question. "Ten, Reverend," he answered.

"Delightful!" His word drew her attention back to him. "It will be my pleasure to marry you Ms. Harris. I am always eager to welcome a stray lamb back into the fold."

Alex had to stifle the urge to burst out laughing, as Jarett's face became a thunderous red cloud of anger. "I can assure you Reverend," Jarett said as he slipped his arm through hers, and pulled her hands free of the reverend's. "Alexandra did *not* stray from the fold."

Reverend White quickly recovered. "Of course not," he said. "I meant no offense. It will be my pleasure to perform the ceremony. I am sure that the whole town will be there to celebrate!" Alex refrained from saying that she highly doubted it, but she decided to keep her mouth closed. "Will I see you and Hugh in church this Sunday?"

She and Hugh were lucky if they attended church once a month, there was too much work at the ranch to do. The reverend looked so hopeful though, and it would probably be best if she did attend, she had committed a sin after all.

"Yes Reverend," she agreed.

"Wonderful! We'll announce the blessed day then! Of course I will see you too Mr. Stanton."

"Of course," Jarett muttered.

Alex had to fight back a smile at his disgruntled tone. "Good then, until Sunday. Congratulations to the both of you."

"Thank you Reverend," Alex said.

He nodded before strolling away. "Two weeks?" Jarett inquired.

Alex leaned into his side and rested her head on his chest. "I'm not getting married with his marks on me."

She could almost hear his teeth grinding together as he began to lead her forward. "I understand."

Hugh was placing flour into the back of the wagon when they arrived. He barely looked up at them as he lifted another flour bag and tossed it into the wagon, but she sensed something in the set of his jaw and the rigidness of his body. "Hugh, what is it?" Alex inquired.

He shook his head as he tossed the last bag on and straightened. He wiped his forearm across his sweaty brow. "Nothing Alex, did you speak to the reverend?"

"Yes, he'll be at the ranch in two weeks," Alex answered.

"Two weeks?" Hugh blurted and shot Jarett a threatening look.

"It was my decision; I will speak my vows, clearly," Alex said pointedly. Something sinister slid across Hugh's face as his gaze darted to the high neck of the dress covering the marks on her throat. It was too hot out for the dress, but it was the only one she had that covered the clear handprints on her completely.

"Trust me, that is not the worst part, your sister has volunteered us to attend church on Sunday," Jarett said.

"Oh Alex," Hugh moaned.

"It won't kill us to attend; we haven't been in a month," she defended.

"It was a perfectly good streak that did *not* need to be broken."

"Hugh..."

He waved her words off as he leaned against the wagon and folded his arms over his chest. "You ready to go?"

"Not yet," Jarett said. "Alex, stay with your brother, I'll be back in a minute."

She didn't have time to protest as he pulled away from her and headed across the street to the mercantile. "Care to tell me what is wrong?" she asked her brother.

"I told you Alex..."

"I know you Hugh."

The tension in his body was making him as taut as a bowstring. He glanced up and down the street before turning back to her. "There's a money shipment coming through tomorrow."

A pit seemed to open in her stomach. "Hugh no, we said that we weren't going to steal anymore."

"That was before..."

"Before what?" His gaze fell to her neck again. "No Hugh. I won't help you."

"You're not going to."

"You can't do it alone." He refused to meet her gaze. Alex turned toward the mercantile before looking back at Hugh. Nausea twisted through her as a cold chill swept down her spine. "He won't help you either."

Hugh shrugged negligently.

"Hugh please." She grabbed hold of his arms in a desperate attempt to try and make him see reason. "Don't you see that this can be a new beginning for all of us? We'll get Murdock eventually, but there is no reason to risk our lives for it. Please Hugh."

He glanced down at her, but she saw the resolution in his gaze. "Leave it be Alex."

"I'll tell Jarett, he'll stop you."

He pulled his arms free of her grasp. "No, you won't."

Frustration mounted as she tried to make her brother see reason. "I'll follow you. I can't let you go alone and you can't make me stay behind."

"I'll lock you in your room."

"Then Jarett will know that something is wrong!"

Hugh continued to stare blankly at her. Alex was suddenly freezing cold; even her bones seemed frozen solid as the realization that the both of them planned to do this slammed into her. Her arms fell limply back to her sides as she took a step back. "Damn you," she hissed. "Damn you both!"

She spun on her heel, she had to get away in order to think and be free. Hugh grabbed hold of her arm and pulled her back. He imprisoned her against his side with an arm around her waist. "You're not going anywhere Alex. Just stand there and look like the happy bride to be."

Tears threatened to choke her as she shook her head and refused to look at him. "You mean the bride to be that may never get married, don't you?"

"Alex..."

"Stop talking Hugh; I don't want to hear it."

CHAPTER 21

Alex refused to speak to either of them on the ride home, refused to acknowledge their presence as she climbed out of the wagon. She purposely ignored Jarett's hand as she glared at him and turned to go into the house. Shedding the heavy dress was a weight off her shoulders and she eagerly pulled on her familiar breeches and light cotton shirt. She tied a bandanna around her neck, grabbed hold of her hat and guns, and made her way outside to the stables.

"I'm going for a ride Willy," she called to the man lurking in the shadows.

He scowled at her as he stepped forward. "Why would I care about that?" he demanded as he spit on the ground.

Alex didn't answer him as she grabbed a saddle, saddle blanket, and bridle. She made her way to Satan's stall; she needed his speed and unruly energy today. She saddled him, pulled the bridle over his head, and gathered the reins before nudging him out of the stall and into the daylight. Her gaze drifted over the pastures as she tried to decide where she was going to go, and then she *knew*.

She spurred Satan forward and directed him toward the north pasture. She didn't open him up, not right away; she wanted to give Willy enough time to head out after her. Today was the first time she'd ever acknowledged his presence and she knew she'd wounded his pride by doing so, but her temper had gotten the best of her. That wasn't a good excuse though, it wasn't Willy's fault the men in her life were idiots. She was extremely tired of high-handed men telling her what she could, and could not do. Of thinking that they knew what was best for her, when they obviously didn't even know what was best for *them*.

Alex opened Satan up, and relished in the feel of his easy gate as he galloped forward. His muscles bunched and flexed beneath her as he ate up the land. Her mind shut down as she let her spirit become swept up in his, allowed herself to be free. The wind tore at her hat and hair as she leaned low over his neck, and inhaled his powerful scent.

When they made it to the top of the north pasture, she eased Satan into a graceful canter. She led him down the hill, following a trail that she had once traveled often, but she hadn't traversed it in two years. The small family cemetery came into view; there were only three graves there. Pulling Satan up outside of the wrought iron fence, she sat as she gathered her courage.

Releasing a harsh breath of air, she finally slid from Satan's back. She was breathing shallowly as she walked to the gate, released the latch and swung it open. The hinges creaked from lack of use and care. Alex felt a twinge of guilt as she took in the weeds that had sprung up where none had been before.

When her father was alive, he would come often to visit her mother's grave, and Alex and Hugh usually made the trip with him. There had been no weeds then, no squeaking hinges. Until now, she hadn't realized that Hugh had also been avoiding the cemetery.

Moving steadily forward, Alex held her hat down against the rising wind. There was a storm coming, she knew that, just as she knew that it would be a bad one. Ever since she was a child, she had loved the wild storms that swiftly rose up to blast over the land before disappearing almost as swiftly. Somehow, the threat that other people found in the howling wind, driving rain, and sizzling lightening had never frightened her. She found it exhilarating.

She knelt before her father's grave and pulled the weeds away from the small headstone. She trailed her fingers over the name engraved on it, *Bartholomew Harris*. The last time she'd been here was when they had buried him; she had vowed not to return until his death was avenged. She realized now that she hadn't thought herself worthy of being here while his murderer was still alive, and he was here, beneath the ground, no more than bones.

Tears slid down her face. She had been wrong, Megan had been right all along. Her father had loved his life so much, and he had loved her mother, Hugh, and herself, with every fiber of his being. All he had ever wanted for them was their happiness, and for the past two years, there had been very little of that. Things were finally getting better, but now...

Now she was petrified that she would be visiting Hugh, or Jarett's, grave too.

The ground crunched beside her, but she didn't look up. She already knew who was there; she would know him anywhere. "I haven't been here since we buried him."

He didn't touch her as he knelt beside her, but the heat of his body was still palpable against her skin. "Why now?" he inquired.

She lifted her head to look at him. "Because I was wrong," she whispered.

His head tilted to the side as he studied her. "What were you wrong about?"

The wind whipped his words away from him and tore at his clothes, but he seemed oblivious to it. "My father wouldn't want me or Hugh to be living the way we have been. He loved my mother so much; after she died, we were all that he had. All he wanted was our happiness and we haven't been happy; we've disgraced his hopes for us. Hugh hasn't been here any time recently either, I suspect for the same reasons as I."

"Which are?"

"I didn't think I deserved to be here," she whispered. "Not while Murdock still lived."

He leaned forward as he strained to hear her words over the rising wind. “And now?”

Her eyes were deep wells of sorrow that tore at his heart. “Now I realize that I never would have returned here, unless it was to be placed in the ground beside him.”

He moved toward her but she shied away and shook her head as she held up a warding hand. “Alexandra,” he groaned as his arms fell limply back to his sides.

“I’ve been living to die,” she told him. “I didn’t realize how much until last night. I realize it now, and I don’t want it anymore, my father wouldn’t want it. I want a future and happiness, love and life, and children.”

“You’ll have all that,” he promised.

“Will I? Or will I be burying you and Hugh here next?”

“Alex...”

She stood and absently brushed the dirt from her knees as she glanced up at the darkening sky. Thick black clouds had rolled in to block out the sun and the air held the heavy scent of rain. It crackled with energy and an impending sense of doom. For the first time in her life, Alex didn’t look forward to the storm.

She turned away from him and walked over to remove the weeds from her mother’s grave. “How did your mother die?” Jarett inquired.

“Influenza,” she replied absently as she rose again to move onto the smaller grave beside her mother. Pulling the weeds away, she revealed the name on the tiny grave, *Jacob Harris*.

“Who is this?”

“My little brother,” she whispered. “He was born too soon, he didn’t survive a week. I was four, but I remember how sickly he was. It was difficult for my parents and Hugh when they lost him. Hugh had been looking forward to having a little brother; a sister simply wasn’t any fun.”

There was a hint of amusement in her eyes as they met Jarett's. "Not that I blame him," she continued. "I was disappointed Jacob was a boy, boys were even less fun than I was."

Jarett simply stared at her as he fought the urge to take hold of her, but she still wasn't ready for him. It was one of the most frustrating moments of his life. She stared at him before rising to her feet. "You're going to go with Hugh tomorrow?"

He didn't even pretend not to know what she was talking about. "Yes."

Her gaze settled once again on the ominous clouds. "Why?" she whispered. "It's not your battle."

His eyes were as turbulent as the sky as he took a step toward her. "It is now."

"Because he hurt me?"

Something cruel flashed through his eyes as his gaze drifted down to her neck. "Yes and not just yesterday. He'll pay for everything that he's done Alex, everything."

Tears of hopelessness filled her eyes as she looked away from him. There had already been so much death, so much loss; she knew that she couldn't handle anymore. "Don't make me bury you, don't make me bury my brother."

"I won't."

She suddenly needed him more than she had ever needed anything in her life. Moving forward, she wrapped her arms around his waist and tilted her head to look into his eyes. Eyes that were ablaze with yearning and drove deep into her soul, they pulled at her heart, and turned her body into liquid heat. "Take me home Jarett."

He swept her up easily; his mouth claimed hers as he cradled her against his chest and carried her from the cemetery. The first fat drops of rain began to fall as he lifted her onto Ricochet's back. He took hold of Chantilly's reins and swung into the saddle behind her. Gathering her within his lap, his powerful body pressed firmly against hers.

She removed the hat from her head and lifted her face to the sky. In that instant, she had never looked more alluring, and he wanted her with an intensity that he had never experienced before. He dropped his head to hers and kissed the rain from her face, he savored in the taste of it upon her skin as he spurred Ricochet forward. He kept hold of her horse's reins as the mare followed behind them.

She turned to him; her fingers entwined in his hair as she pulled him down to her. "I need you," she breathed.

His hand spanned the expanse of her ribcage as he stroked over her. She cried out in ecstasy when he cupped her swollen breast and his thumb rubbed tantalizingly over her aching nipple. Her entire body was on fire, tremors shook her as his mouth seared over her neck before nipping at her earlobe.

"Jarett!" she gasped.

"Shh," he whispered hoarsely in her ear. "We're almost home."

He stopped in front of the house and brushed her wet hair back from her forehead. "Get inside Love, you're soaked through. I'll be up shortly."

She gave him a lingering kiss. "Hurry." She slid from the horse and ran up the steps of the porch.

Jarett didn't need her whispered word to urge him on. His cock was throbbing; the feel of her body was burned into his. Her persistent subtle scent of strawberries adhered enticingly to him; he could still taste the fresh rain from her skin. He was barely able to walk as he grit his teeth against his growing erection. The thought of her upstairs, waiting for him, was almost more than he could stand.

Jarett put the horses away before hurrying from the barn. The rain was coming in driving sheets that drenched him instantly, but did nothing to quench the passion tearing through his body. Lightening split the sky as thunder rumbled so loudly that the earth shook beneath his feet.

He threw the screen door open and ignored the scent of dinner as he hurried up the stairs. Pulling his guns and hat off as he went, he jerked impatiently at the buttons of his soaked shirt before he even reached his room. He needed her too ardently to be hampered by anything now. He entered his room, only to keep up appearance's sake, no matter how pointless it was. He paused to toss his guns, shirt, and hat onto the trunk and pulled his boots off as he moved. They clattered to the ground, but he was heedless of the puddles of water they formed on the carpet as he strode to the door adjoining their rooms and pulled it open.

He knew that he was feral with his desire and greatly afraid that he might hurt her, but he was unable to stop the primitive force growing inside of him. She stood beside the bed, her clothes were gone; the curling wet hair tumbling over her shoulders was the only thing shielding her from him. He was struck breathless by the tantalizing vision of her lithe, tanned body.

Then she came toward him with a natural grace that was hypnotically seductive. Her emerald eyes mirrored the burning intensity that was raging through his body as she stopped before him. He wanted to bury himself inside of her and pound out this savage hunger inside of him. A low growl escaped from him as he grasped for her, a part of him was concerned that he might frighten her; the other part was beyond thought.

"No," she whispered.

He froze. He had scared her, he had revealed too much of the beast inside of him that was clamoring to mark her as his over and over again. He frowned in confusion as she took a step toward him instead of fleeing like he had expected. She gave him an alluring smile that dazzled him as her hands slid across his skin and drifted over his chest.

Her lips left a trail of heat as she licked over his nipple, arousing it to life with her luscious mouth. He inhaled abruptly, his fists clenched at his sides as he realized that she meant to explore and seduce him. He was so bewitched by her actions that he couldn't bring himself to stop her, no matter how hotly the blood clamored through his veins.

His breath rushed out of him as her delicate fingers brushed over the edge of his breeches. He groaned as her small hand cupped his hardness and kneaded him through the wet, clinging cloth. His breath came faster as she slid the button free and pulled the zipper down. She was always eager in bed, but up until now, she had never taken the lead in such a way. No matter how badly he wanted her, he wasn't going to stop her.

She slid the breeches down his thighs and rose to stand before him again. He ground his teeth so fiercely that for a moment he thought they might shatter. Her hand encircled his rigid shaft and squeezed him as she moved up and down his erect length. She looked up at him, her eyes were dusky with lust, but there was an odd spark of wicked amusement in them that should have warned him, but didn't.

He watched in amazement, breathless as she knelt before him with her eyes still locked upon his. Her tongue flitted out to lick over his engorged head. Jarett jerked as a spasm of pleasure racked through his whole body. He was vividly reminded of the first time he'd seen her, of the images that had burst into his head, images that could never compare to the actual sight of her before him. A guttural moan escaped him, his hands entangled in her hair as she drew him deeper into her hot mouth. Her hands clenched his ass, her movements became more confident and demanding as her mouth ran up and down the length of him.

His head tipped back as the pleasure became almost unbearable. He pulled away from her, unable to endure anymore without spilling his seed. She blinked up at him as he lifted her from her knees. "Did you like that?" she asked.

"God yes," he admitted. "Too much. Where did you ever learn such a thing?"

His hands spanned her ribcage as he lifted her up; his thumbs brushed the underneath of her breasts. "You did it to me," she panted as the tip of his cock brushed against her wet center.

"Wrap your legs around me," he commanded gruffly.

She obeyed instantly; a startled cry escaped her as he gradually lowered her onto him. Trembling, she wrapped her arms around his neck and gripped him as he filled her. "Jarett," she gasped as he lifted her hips up before sliding her back down.

"You're so tight and warm," he grated in her ear.

Alex shivered at his words; her body quickened as she rode him with reckless abandon. The tempestuous mood she had sensed upon him when he'd entered her room was back upon him and it was taking her over too. The desire was all-consuming, making her completely heedless of the fact that she was clawing at the skin of his back in her urgency.

Her body seemed to splinter apart and a cry erupted from her; it was drowned out only by the hoarseness of her voice. His fingers dug into her waist, waves of pleasure continued to course through her as he prolonged her ecstasy by repeatedly driving himself into her. A groan of pleasure echoed in her ears, his back clenched beneath her hands as he found his own release.

Alex slumped against him, his body was sleek with sweat and the enticingly masculine scent of him enveloped her. She gradually became aware of the thunder echoing through the night and shaking the windows in their frames. Goose bumps broke out on her flesh as she shivered involuntarily.

“Cold?” He nuzzled her neck and carried her to the bed.

She moaned in protest at the loss of him inside of her as he lifted her off and laid her upon the bed. He smiled down at her as he turned away; he was heedless of his nudity as he gathered the blankets that had been turned down. Alex’s hand flew to her mouth; heat flooded her face as she spotted the claw marks marring his bronzed back. Though they were mostly just surface marks, she spotted a few spots of blood in some of the scratches.

He turned back to her, an eyebrow raised inquiringly as he paused with the blankets in hand. “What is it?”

“Your back,” she whispered.

He laughed as he crawled onto the bed beside her. He pulled the blankets around them, drew her into his arms and fit her body against his. Alex buried her head in his chest; she was unable to meet his gaze. The vivid images of her extremely wanton behavior were seared into her mind. He lifted her chin as he seemed to sense her sudden mortification.

“You must think me...”

“Beautiful, desirable, sensuous, and utterly irresistible,” he said she he ran his thumb across her lips.

“But the way I behaved was shameful.”

“Never. I wouldn’t change you for the world. I love the way you respond to me, the way that you become so uninhibited. I love that wild side of you Alex and I crave it like I crave water on a hot August day.”

“But I hurt you.”

He brushed her lips with his own; it was a tender kiss that melted her heart. “They are your marks on me, a reminder to me of where I belong, of where my heart is,” he whispered.

“If you need such a reminder then I will leave them on you every night,” she retorted.

He laughed as he rolled over so that his body covered hers. "I need no such reminder," he murmured against her mouth.

Her hands entangled in his hair, she pulled him back when he would have claimed her mouth again. He stared down at her, his desire evident in his gaze, even without the proof of it pressing against her inner thigh. She memorized every detail of him as tears began to burn the backs of her eyes. "Promise me you'll come back to me tomorrow," she whispered.

He hated the tears that shimmered within her eyes. "I promise Alexandra. I will never leave you."

"Promise you'll bring my brother back to me."

He wanted to close his eyes against the heart wrenching anguish in her gaze, but he was unable to do so. "I promise."

She bit back a sob as she tugged his head down to hers. His mouth burned over hers, heating her from the inside out. Hours after the storm had burnt itself out; he was still inside of her.

CHAPTER 22

Alex restlessly paced back and forth on the porch. There was a constant ache in her chest, and a knot in her throat that was making it difficult to breathe. She had awoken this morning to find Jarett and her brother gone. The dazzling light of the day had seemed somehow cruel in the face of her misery this morning. It seemed even crueler now that morning had slipped away to afternoon.

She had given up all attempts at normalcy hours ago, when she'd found herself staring at the road instead of focusing upon the steers being herded into the western pasture. Her concentration was not on her work, and because of that she was a menace to herself, and to the ranch hands. Realizing this, she'd returned to the house on the pretense that she wasn't feeling one hundred percent.

She had tried to stay in her room after uttering the lie, but the walls had seemed to close in on her and made the knots in her chest and throat even worse. Fleeing back outdoors, she had taken to the relentless pacing that she exhibited now. It was getting late, the sun would set soon, surely they should be back by now. *If* everything had gone right.

Her chest constricted even more as tears began to burn her eyes. She and Hugh had never stayed out this long, not even when she'd been shot. Something had gone wrong. She was certain of it. She lifted her head and scanned the horizon, but it was still empty, *too* empty.

She prayed silently as she resumed her pacing. She was unable to tolerate the feel of her own skin much more. If something had happened to them…

She felt like clawing her hair out, felt like screaming her fear and agony to the heavens. Felt like running until she couldn't run anymore. It took all she had not to collapse onto the porch and wail out the terror in her veins.

Lysette came onto the porch; the creaking screen door announced her presence. "Something's gone wrong," Alex whispered.

"You can't know that child," Lysette said soothingly. "Come inside."

Alex shook her head and clutched her hands before her. "I can't."

Lysette's eyes were caring as she walked over to stand by the railing. "I'll stay with you then."

Alex found a measure of solace as she took hold of one of Lysette's strong, callused hands. Even before she'd been shot, Lysette had known about the robberies. For her own safety, she and Hugh had never told Lysette the truth about their father's death. Alex knew Lysette had always suspected something more about the event, but she'd never pressured them, and she had never judged them when they had turned to stealing.

"This is what we put you through isn't it?" she whispered.

"It is."

"I'm sorry Lysette."

Lysette's doe brown eyes were warm and loving as she pushed back a stray tendril of Alex's hair. "I understand more than you realize child. There is nothing to be sorry for."

There was though, there was plenty to be sorry for, but Alex knew that Lysette didn't want to hear any of it. "I'll tell you the truth…"

Lysette shook her head and pressed Alex's hand against her belly. "I don't need to hear the confirmation of what I've always known in my heart. I understand why you tried to keep the truth from me though."

Alex searched Lysette's steady gaze but she saw only undying love shining back at her. She bent to brush a kiss over the older woman's soft cheek. "I love you Lysette."

"And I love you."

Alex squeezed her hand before turning away from her to resume her restless pacing. If they didn't come back soon she was going to go after them. She didn't care what Jarett and Hugh would do to her if she did, didn't care that she would be breaking her promise to Megan and herself by aiding in one of the robberies again. Didn't care anymore that she might be putting them in peril by pursuing them; that was the main reason she had stayed behind and not gone after them when she had discovered them gone. She had been concerned that she would come upon them at the wrong time, that she would somehow interrupt the robbery, or alert the people guarding the money to their presence. Now she wished that she had gone right away, that she hadn't let common sense rule for a change.

She wouldn't do so again.

She paused in her pacing as the distant sound of hoof beats caught her attention. A cloud of dust appeared on the horizon and rose into the sky. She took a step forward, and then another, she flew down the steps of the porch as the pounding hoof beats and the dust cloud drew steadily closer. "Please," she whispered. "Please."

Three horses appeared on the horizon. Alex's gaze swept over them, a cry of relief escaped her as she started running toward them. Jarett dismounted swiftly, Ricochet was still moving forward as he landed upon the ground and she flung herself into his open arms.

"Don't cry," he whispered.

"I was so worried," she managed to choke out. "If you plan on doing this again, I won't stay behind next time, and you can't make me!"

Jarett despised the tremors that wracked her and the tears that soaked into his shirt. “Shh Alexandra, everything is fine. I promised you we would come back, and we did.”

“I won’t stay behind!” she insisted as she buried her face in his shoulder. Her hands searched over him, she was unable to get enough of the feel of his body. “I mean it!”

“I know,” he whispered.

He held her until she calmed down enough for the sobs to stop shaking her, and her tears to dry. Her eyes were bloodshot when she pulled back to look up at him. She turned away from him to search for the riders that had come with him, but there was no sign of them.

“They’re in the barn,” Jarett said.

“Who else is with you?”

“Paul.”

“Paul?” she blurted.

“Yes. Do you remember the day that he came here after his barn had been burned down and he wanted to talk with Hugh alone?” Alex nodded. “He suspected you and Hugh were the thieves, my questions had aroused his suspicions, just as I’m sure they’ve aroused countless others. After what Murdock did to his barn, he decided to confront Hugh on it. He wanted in.”

Alex closed her eyes and rested her head against his shoulder. “Why didn’t you tell me?” she moaned.

“You were concerned enough about the two of us, never mind three.”

She wanted to be annoyed but she found she couldn’t get the emotion to grow within her. They were all safe, and that was all that mattered. “Did you succeed?”

“Yes.”

“Will you do it again?”

He nuzzled her hair with his nose as he planted a kiss on her neck. “I don’t know Alex, we’ll see what happens. What I have to do is catch Murdock breaking the law.”

"And if he catches you first?"

"That's *not* going to happen."

"And I didn't think I would ever be shot, or shoot someone else. *Anything* is possible Jarett."

"Yes, but look at how well that worked out for us."

She wasn't at all amused by the laughter in his voice, or the mischievous smile curling his lips. "It's not funny!" she protested.

He groaned at the anguish in her gaze and wrapped his hand around the back of her head. "I'm sorry," he whispered. "Now why don't you go inside and get cleaned up. I bet that you haven't eaten yet, have you?" She shook her head no in confirmation. Jarett bit back a curse at the torment that they had put her through today. "I know that you must be hungry, we'll be in to join you in a few minutes."

His gaze landed on Paul and Hugh as they appeared in the doorway of the barn. There was an oddly resigned look in Paul's eyes as he watched Jarett and Alex together. Paul walked over to Ricochet, who had stopped by the water trough. Seizing hold of Ricochet's reins, Paul tipped his hat to Jarett and led the horse into the shadowy interior of the barn. Hugh waved to him before turning to follow Paul.

Jarett bent down and swept Alex into his arms, he carried her up the steps of the porch. Lysette opened the door for him; there was a concerned look in her eyes as he swept past her. He gave her a brief nod before climbing the stairs and carrying Alex into her room. He set Alex on her feet and lifted her chin gently.

"I need you Jarett," she whispered.

His planned good intentions of getting her cleaned up, comforted, and fed flew out the window at her fervent words. Forgetting everything else, he pulled her against him and took hold of her mouth.

***

It was some time later before he led her back downstairs. A light coming through the closed library doors, and the muffled sound of voices, told her where Paul and her brother were. Jarett dropped a kiss on her forehead as he left her by the doors to gather dinner for the both of them. Alex hesitated, suddenly feeling shy to see her brother and Paul. They had to know what had just transpired between her and Jarett.

She reached for the door, but her hands fell limply back to her sides. She was still standing there when Jarett returned. He raised an inquiring eyebrow, his mouth quirked in amusement as her face flamed red. She looked away, unable to meet his mirth filled gaze.

"Standing there won't open the door."

"Jarett," she moaned.

"They know what's going on."

"I know, but it's so obvious now, and I..."

Her voice trailed off as she became focused on her shoes. "Here," he held a plate out to her. She took it with trembling hands as he bent to place a kiss on her forehead. "It's all right."

Alex bit into her lower lip as he slid the doors open. Paul and Hugh stopped speaking as Jarett nudged her into the room and used his free hand to close the doors behind them. Alex was unable to meet their gazes as her eyes strayed to the windows. The night pressed against the panes as Jarett subtly nudged her again.

She stared at the floor as she made her way to the sofa and settled herself on it. Jarett handed her a plate as he sat next to her. She suddenly wasn't hungry and the last thing that she wanted was food. Finally, she lifted her gaze to her brother and Paul. Both of them were staring at her with a mixture of amusement and discomfort. Alex's gaze darted to Jarett; his face held the same amusement as the others and sparked her temper.

Her eyebrows drew together as she gave him a stern look that caused him to smile even more. She tore her gaze from his to meet Paul and Hugh's again. "Everything went well?" she inquired.

"Yes," Hugh answered.

"Why did you get involved in this?"

Paul met her gaze directly as something sinister slid through his eyes. "For the same reason as you Alex."

Alex placed her plate down and moved toward the edge of the sofa. "I understand."

"Now what do we do?" Paul inquired.

"The next money shipment won't come through for another month, at least," Jarett said quietly.

Alex's hands clenched in her lap as an impending sense of doom descended upon her once again. Jarett rose to his feet and dropped his empty plate on the sideboard. He poured himself a glass of scotch before turning to look at her again. "Are you thinking about doing something else?" Hugh inquired.

"Aggravating him is one thing. What we have to do is catch him doing something illegal. The money that was stolen today is going to cause him to lash out at someone. We need to think about who that person might be," Jarett said.

"More than likely it will be us," Hugh said and folded his arms over his chest.

"No, it will be someone that's close to selling out. He'll want the property, and the power, that it will bring him. The money you've taken has hurt him, but it's only a piece of the money he has. The robberies strip him of his power though and he's going to want to exert his power over someone weaker, and soon."

"This is why you stole the money today," she whispered. The knowledge growing inside of her made her sick to her stomach. "You did this to try and rile him up."

He met her gaze unflinchingly. "Yes."

"You're going to get yourselves killed, and then what will you have accomplished?"

"Nothing is going to happen to us Alex," Hugh said.

"And I wasn't going to be shot," she retorted.

Hugh had the grace to look abashed, but his gaze never flickered from hers. "That was an unfortunate consequence."

"But it happened, and no matter what you say, it could happen again."

"No, it won't," Jarett said coldly.

She turned to him. "If you want him so badly, why don't you just offer him the one thing that will bring him forward? Why don't you use me as bait?"

Jarett's hand clenched upon his glass as he straightened away from the wall. "That will never happen," he growled.

"Why not? You're so desperate to catch him in the act, why not use me and get it over with?"

"Alex, I don't know what you're thinking, but get it out of your head right now," Hugh said.

She turned toward him, an innocent expression plastered on her face. "I don't know what you're talking about Hugh."

"I know you Alex; I know when you're up to something. Whatever it is, don't even think about it!"

"Well, why not? I helped to start this. I *will* help to finish it."

Jarett grabbed hold of her arm and spun her to face him. "You will do nothing to put yourself at risk!"

Alex jerked her arm free of his grasp. "If the three of you insist upon doing this, then I am going to help. You can't watch me constantly; I'm good at escaping when I want too. Give me the opportunity..."

"I will tie you to your bed!" he shouted.

"And I will get free!"

Jarett took a step closer to her. Her jaw was set firmly as she met his glare. "You will stay away from him."

"I will do what is necessary to keep my loved ones safe!" she retorted.

He grasped hold of her arms and pulled her against him. "I am telling you that I will tie you to your bed and that is no idle threat. I will lock you in that room. I will do everything in my power to keep you safe."

"And I will get free. Do not push me Jarett..."

"Do not push *me*!" he roared, causing her to flinch involuntarily. "In this matter you will listen to me!"

Alex tried to tear free but he refused to let go. "You're not my husband yet!" she retorted. "I can still change my mind!"

His nostrils flared as his eyes blazed fiery embers of anger at her. "I will bring the reverend here right now..."

"And I will refuse!"

Jarett's hands tensed upon her arms as annoyance and trepidation burned hotly inside of him. She would refuse him; he could see it in her gaze, in the firm set of her jaw. She would do anything she could to stop them; even it meant hurting him and herself. "Alex," Hugh said.

"If the three of you are going to be fools, then that is fine, but I will not stand by and watch you destroy yourselves. I would rather remain a whore than become a widow to a man who will get himself killed for a matter that has nothing to do with him!"

"It has everything to do with me!" Jarett snapped.

"The hell it does!"

"Damn you!" Jarett hissed.

"No damn you!" she shouted. "Damn you all! Let go of me!"

He continued to cling to her as he refused to release her. Frustration warred up, and before she could stop herself, she kicked him soundly in the shin. He didn't even flinch, but his eyes took on an ominous look that made the hair on the nape of her neck stand up.

"I think we all should settle down," Paul said calmly.

"Let me go," Alex said.

"You are not going to do anything crazy, I mean it Alex," Jarett said, the mellow tone of his voice was somehow more frightening than if he had yelled at her.

"And neither are you."

His jaw clenched to the point that it caused a muscle to twitch violently as he released her and took a step away. "We won't do anything," he said coldly. "Except guard whoever Murdock's most likely next victim might be. Do you want us to leave them unprotected?"

"Of course not, but..."

"There are no buts! We will not leave someone defenseless."

"I know you Jarett! You intend more."

His eyes were callous as they locked on hers. "Unless something illegal happens, I intend no more." Alex fought back a bitter smile as she shook her head in disgust. "You have to eat Alex."

She glanced at her plate but didn't move to take it. The lump in her throat wouldn't allow food to go down. "I'm not hungry," she whispered. "I'm tired; I'm going to sleep."

"Alex..."

"Please Jarett." She held up her hand to ward off his protests. "I can't eat right now."

He moved forward to slip his arm around her waist. She buried her head in his chest and took comfort in the steady beat of his heart, even as her mind raced ahead. There had to be something that she could do to protect them, even if it did mean using herself as bait. She was the one thing that Murdock truly wanted that he couldn't have. It was time that she used that to her advantage.

CHAPTER 23

Alex brushed Satan's mane as she tried to distract herself from the fact that her brother and Jarett had gone over to the Carpmen's farm to keep an eye on it. At least if they were at the farm they wouldn't be getting into any trouble, or at least that's what she told herself. She really didn't think Murdock would do anything right now. Not in the daylight, not even *he* was that arrogant.

The colt snorted and shifted beside her but he returned to munching on the oats she had just given him. She pulled the brush through his mane one more time before stepping out of the stall and dropping the brush into the open trunk.

They'd been gone for almost an hour now, plenty of time for them to be settled into their positions for a few hours. She glanced at the shadows but Willy had become better at keeping himself hidden ever since she'd called him out about following her. Guilt pulled at her for hurting his feelings but she turned away from the shadows and closed the door on Satan's stall.

She walked down the shedrow and grabbed a saddle and saddle blanket from the tack room before making her way to Chantilly's stall. She looked around for Willy again but her guard was being extra secretive today. She knew they'd left Perry behind to watch over her too; apparently, they no longer trusted her, and they had every reason not to. Perry was stationed in the woods that led toward town and Murdock's property. He wouldn't be able to see her until she left the barn, but even then, where she was going would seem harmless enough that Perry wouldn't stop her.

Opening the stall door, she tossed the saddle blanket and saddle onto the back of Chantilly. She'd stayed up late into the night trying to think of a way to lure Murdock out without being obvious about it. In the end, the answer had been simpler than she had expected. It had been a couple of years since she had gone fishing; it was one of the things that she'd lost interest in after her father's murder. But now that she had returned to her father's grave, and agreed to get married, it may not seem so odd that she was also returning to something that she had once loved to do.

Everyone in the area knew that the best trout fishing spot was a river that ran between her property and Paul's. To get to the river though, she would have to cross a section of land that bordered on a ridge above Murdock's property. She didn't expect to be noticed right away by the people on Murdock's property, but if she continued to go to the river every day, she would eventually be spotted and remarked upon by someone. She was certain that Murdock would eventually come to her, and when he did, she would be ready for him. It wasn't coldblooded murder if it was done in self-defense, she told herself.

Just days ago she had intended to move on with her life, it was what she wanted more than anything, but there would be no point in moving on if Jarett and Hugh were dead. Murdock wouldn't hesitate to destroy them, he *would* hesitate with her though, and he didn't know just how accurate she could be with a gun. She would have no doubts about pulling the trigger when it came to Murdock.

It was a risky plan, one that put her in jeopardy, but it was a risk she was willing to take if it meant keeping everyone she loved safe.

Taking a step out of the stall, she reached for the bridle hanging on the end of the door when she froze. Her head tilted to the side as she realized that it was unusually calm in the stable. Alex took a step back as a cold chill slid down her spine and the hair on the nape of her neck stood on end.

"Willy?" she called nervously. "Are you there?"

She was turning to look behind her when a hand slid over her mouth and she was forcefully jerked back against a chest. A scream rose in her throat but the palm pressing against her mouth quashed it as lips brushed over her ear. It took everything she had not to heave up her eggs from this morning as she recognized Murdock's awful scent. Her heart beat out a rapid staccato against her ribs as her hand slid toward her gun belt.

He had been arrogant enough to come out in the daylight, and she had been foolish enough to underestimate him. It didn't matter though; he had come to *her.* He was on her property and if she could get to her gun she was going to end all of this *now*.

Murdock snatched hold of her wrist as her fingers brushed over the butt of her revolver and slammed it down against her side. "Now now," he whispered in her ear. "There's no need for that."

Frustration gripped her, she didn't want to scream from fear anymore but from the futility of her situation. She struggled against his grip, but she wasn't strong enough to stop him from lifting her right hand and slamming it against the barn wall. An involuntary cry of pain escaped her as pain lanced down her arm. He lifted her hand and slammed it against the wall a second time. She was unable to stop the tears that formed in her eyes as a bone or two in her hand broke with a loud crack.

"Now there will be no chance for you to fire a gun," he breathed as his tongue flickered over her ear. Yes, she was definitely going to lose her breakfast. His hand eased on her mouth as he pulled her a few feet back.

"I'll kill you," she breathed. "And if Jarett catches you here, he'll kill you."

Murdock's chuckle was low in her ear. He spun her around to face him and grabbed hold of her shoulders. "Your thief of a fiancé has enough to worry about right now. The sheriff is on his way to arrest him as we speak." His laugh grew as the breath rushed out of her. "Oh yes, I know. I've known for awhile now, especially about *you.*" His finger wrapped around a tendril of her hair and he tugged it toward him. "There aren't that many redheads in these parts Alexandra."

The ground seemed to drop out from underneath her as her stomach plummeted into her feet. She'd never been more shocked in her life and it was taking everything she had to keep her wits about her. That was the only way she was going to make it out of this alive. "Just as I know that they're at the Carpmen's farm right now and you're all alone. They won't be coming for you Alexandra, not once those cell doors slam shut."

Panic for her brother and Jarett gave her more strength then she'd realized she could have. A snarl escaped her and she jerked back in Murdock's hold. His hand slipped on her arm as she threw the full force of her weight behind the motion. She staggered back and just managed to keep herself from falling on her ass. Spinning on her heel, she turned and fled down the shedrow toward the open barn door at the end. Her left hand fumbled for the gun at her waist but she gave up on reaching it as the motion of her running kept bouncing it away from her.

Her breath came in brisk pants as she honed in on the door. She was almost to it when she felt arms wrap around her waist and his body pressed against hers. The air was knocked out of her as she was slammed mercilessly into the ground. The scream that rose in her throat died there as something solid met with the back of her head and the world went dark.

***

Jarett shifted on top of Ricochet and climbed down from the saddle. The Carpmen farm had been undisturbed when he, Hugh, and Paul had left it behind under the watchful eyes of Jesse and a couple of Carpmen's farmhands. He was about to step toward the barn when the sheriff emerged from the shadows.

He'd met the man before, when he'd been running his investigation into the thieves, but he hadn't seen him in a couple of weeks. The sheriff's head was bowed as he held his hat before him. His thinning gray hair was brushed to the side, sweat beaded across his forehead as his brown eyes focused upon Hugh. He pulled a handkerchief from his front pocket and dabbed at his pudgy face with it.

"What are you doing here Sheriff Stacks?" Hugh demanded crisply as he led his horse toward the barn.

Jarett bristled over Hugh's attitude, the same attitude that had drawn his attention to Hugh and Alex in the first place. The sheriff twisted his hat in his hand as he glanced nervously between the three of them. "I know you and Alex are the thieves, Hugh." Hugh stopped walking toward the barn and Jarett pulled up abruptly. "I suspect Jarett and Paul joined you on this last robbery."

"I don't know what you're talking about," Hugh replied.

"Yes, you do. I'm not here to arrest you Hugh, nor am I here to argue with you."

"Then what are you here for?" Hugh demanded. "To tell us you're going to hand us over to Murdock?"

"He already knows," the sheriff replied quietly. Jarett's hand clenched around the reins, cold terror crept down his spine. His gaze shot past the sheriff to the interior of the barn and then toward the house. "I've turned my back for that man more times than I can count…"

"Where's Alex?" Jarett demanded.

"I have a wife, my children. He threatened my children if I didn't do what he asked. I didn't know what else to do.

Who was going to protect them if something happened to me?"

"Where's Alex?" Jarett barked at the man as he steadily approached him.

"But I simply cannot turn my back on this. I didn't know he was going to kill your father Hugh, I truly didn't. But the girl, what he intends for the girl, I can't stand by for…"

Jarett seized hold of the man's shirt and jerked him forward. "*Where is she*?" he bellowed.

The man's hat fell from his hands; his eyes bulged from his head as he met Jarett's incensed gaze. "Murdock took her."

Jarett thought his legs might actually give out on him. He was so consumed with terror that he could barely speak his next word. "Where?"

"He has a… a cabin out by Arcane… Arcane Falls," the sheriff stammered out.

"I know where it is," Hugh said as he grabbed the pummel of his saddle and swung himself into it.

"Wait!" the sheriff cried. "He has at least two dozen men with him!"

"I'll get help, don't do anything until I find you again," Paul said. Jarett didn't think that was going to be possible as panic compressed his chest and the driving urge to get to Alex consumed him.

"I'm coming with you," the sheriff told Paul.

"You better hope she's ok," Jarett growled at the man.

The sheriff paled visibly before he turned to the horse standing by the side of the building. Paul turned his horse away from them when the sheriff joined him. Kicking his horse in the side, Paul galloped down the road at a rapid pace that kicked up dust behind him and covered his progress.

Hugh's face was strained, his eyes troubled as they met Jarett's. "Lead the way!" Jarett shouted at Hugh.

Jarett's hands were shaking as he turned Ricochet and spurred him in the side. They had to get to her, *now*. No matter how fast Ricochet galloped though, he was certain that they weren't going to get to her in time; that they would be too late to save her from the man she despised most. He was going to destroy Murdock for daring to touch her again. He was going to make the man wish that he had never been born.

***

Alex fought to open her eyes but they refused to cooperate with her. Her head felt like there was a woodpecker inside of it just pounding away against her skull. She longed to fall back into the blissful world of unconsciousness again. She cracked a lid and quickly shut it against the light that flared over her eyes and the suffering that exploded through her already abused head.

She gave up on trying to open her eyes and see where she was and decided to focus on something else. Her right hand throbbed and though she knew she probably shouldn't, she tried to open and close it. She grit her teeth as bones grated against each other and her fingers had a difficult time moving due to the swelling in her hand.

Her head spun as she tried to piece together the details of everything around her. Whatever she was lying on was hard, and as her nose and cheek pressed against it she realized that she was on a wooden floor. Her mouth felt as if she had been chewing on cotton, her tongue was thick and heavy. Her mind spun as she tried to sort through her memories, and then, everything flooded back to her.

She bit back a groan and kept her eyes shut as she tried to figure out if she had any other injuries. Her right hand was definitely broken, she didn't know what Murdock had hit her with but she could feel a welt forming on the back of her skull. Her hands had been tied together behind her back at the wrists and she her skin was chafed from the tight bonds.

She was tempted to try and open her eyes again in order to take in her surroundings but she didn't know if someone was standing over her, watching her. The thought made her skin crawl, she wanted to leap to her feet and run from the room but she wasn't so sure she was up to running right now. Plus, she didn't know how she was going to defend herself and she would like for the pounding in her head to recede just a little bit before she was forced to do so. Alex continued to take shallow breaths as approaching footsteps sounded on the hardwood floor. The footsteps stopped just before her face and the creak of bones popping sounded as whoever it was knelt before her.

Murdock's onion scented breath tickled her cheek before his fingers brushed over her skin. Alex forced herself to remain unmoving but something must have given her away as he chuckled. "It's about time you woke up."

This time when she cracked her lids she didn't have to instantly close them again. However, the face before her was blurred into two and she found it almost impossible to focus on either one. Both Murdock's were giving her a leering grin that made her head pound even more and her heart leap into her throat. She was here, with him, and she was completely vulnerable. She found it increasingly difficult to breathe but she knew that only strength and determination were going to save her from this hideous situation. No matter what though, she would fight to the death before she ever allowed him to violate her.

His hand trailed down her cheek to her collarbone and over to her breast. She tried to jerk away from him but he only laughed as he followed her squirming movements away from him. "Don't touch me!" she shouted.

He laughed as he grabbed hold of her breast and twisted viciously. A startled cry escaped her as she jerked against the rope binding her. She tried to get her feet in front of her so that she could kick at him but he knocked her legs back before she could get a blow in against him.

Grabbing her legs, he rolled her onto her back and pinned them down. Alex bucked against him, a strangled cry escaped her; she would have given anything for her hands as he wedged his knee in between her legs and pushed them open. The agony in her head and hands was forgotten as she fought to get him off of her. His laughter only made her struggle even more, but he managed to level himself over top of her and began to jerk at the button on her pants.

"No!" she screamed. "No!"

He grabbed hold of her face and squeezed her cheeks as he jerked her face toward him. "Oh yes Alexandra. Oh yes."

She despised the hot wash of tears that burned her eyes, the helplessness that filled her as she remained pinned beneath his body. "Just kill me," she panted.

"Oh no, I plan to keep you alive for many, *many* years to come."

"Jarett, my brother…"

"The sheriff will take care of them. They may even be hanging from the gallows as we speak." Anguish lanced through her chest, her heart broke into jagged shards within her chest at his words. "That is what happens to thieves after all."

"You murdered my father!" she spat at him.

Murdock's eyes narrowed upon her, his hand clenched more forcefully upon her cheeks as he leaned closer to her. "I don't know what you're talking about."

She'd spent the past two years hiding the truth from him but it made no difference now. In fact, he was going to *know* that she'd been keeping this secret these past couple of years. That she and Hugh had just been playing with him, just biding their time until they could exact their revenge.

"I *saw* you," she told him with a smile. "I saw what you did. We've always known the truth you pathetic piece of crap!"

His grip on her increased but she didn't feel the pain as she relentlessly held his stare. He'd do everything he could to try and destroy her, but she would never give him the satisfaction of seeing her break. Before she knew what was happening, he lifted her head up and smashed it off of the floor. A whimper escaped her; the woodpecker in her head had brought along a friend and they both went into a frenzy that made her eyes water and her vision blur even more.

"Pathetic!" he snapped. "I'll show you pathetic!"

His mouth descended upon hers, blood spilled from her split lips as they were smashed forcefully against her teeth. Her brutalized lips were forced apart. Her gag reflex kicked in as his tongue was forced past her teeth and into her mouth. She was reminded of a worm squirming through the dirt as it ran over the inside of her mouth. Trying not to vomit, Alex bit down as forcefully as she could.

A gurgled, startled cry escaped Murdock as his blood pooled into her mouth. Satisfaction filled her; she refused to relinquish his tongue as he attempted to jerk it free of her mouth. She'd bite the thing off if she had to and choke on the blood pooling at the back of her throat. A forceful blow against her cheek startled her and knocked her hold on him lose.

A low moan escaped her as her head turned to the side and she spit out the vile blood filling her mouth. "You *bitch*!"

To her own amazement, a bubble of laughter escaped her at the lisp-like sound of his voice. Perhaps it was the numerous blows to her head or perhaps she was just cracking up, but she took great pleasure in the childish sound of his voice. He lifted his hand to slap her across the face when a knock on the door froze him in place.

"Murdock!" a voice boomed from the other side of the door. "We have company!"

"Tell them to go away!" he shouted back.

There was a brief hesitation on the other side before the person spoke again, "That's not going to be possible."

Murdock frowned at the words, his hand lowered to his side. He pushed her shoulders back and grabbed her throat. Alex kicked out as he pressed down on her windpipe, cutting off her air. With the back of his hand, he wiped the blood from his face and flicked it at her. She winced away from the blood that splattered over her as she squirmed beneath him. A merciless smile curved his mouth as her lungs began to burn and she fought to draw air into her lungs.

A chuckle escaped him before he finally released her throat and rose over top of her. Alex choked and gasped in air as she curled on her side. A harsh round of coughing escaped her as she spit the last of his blood from her mouth.

"I'll be back," he promised her.

Alex was still struggling to breathe as she watched him walk out the door. The instant the door shut she began to frantically search the room for anything to help her escape the ropes binding her. A sinking feeling settled in the pit of her belly as all she saw was a rocking chair in the corner, and a trunk at the foot of the massive, red-canopied bed.

She was in his room, she realized, and he had still dumped her on the floor rather than in the bed. That said more about what he thought about her than his brutal treatment of her had, she realized. There had to be some way out of here. Trying to ignore the numerous aches in her body, she squirmed like a caterpillar toward the nightstand sitting beside the bed. Hopefully there was something in the drawer that she could use to either help her escape, or kill the bastard. At the very least she could use the bed to help her to her feet.

CHAPTER 24

Jarett rode over top of the hill and pulled Ricochet up to look down upon the cabin nestled within the valley below. At least twenty men were outside of the house, they walked back and forth with their guns against their shoulders. Jarett would kill every last one of them if he had to in order to get to Alex. If Murdock had injured her in any way he was going to take great pleasure in drawing out the death he planned to give to the man.

"I think kidnapping my sister constitutes something illegal," Hugh muttered as he shifted on his horse and surveyed the people below.

"I think it constitutes a death sentence," Jarett growled.

Hugh snatched hold of his forearm when he nudged Ricochet forward. "I want her back as badly as you do but we have to wait for backup. Riding down there and getting ourselves killed isn't going to do anyone any good, least of all Alex. This way."

Jarett followed as Hugh disappeared into the woods and led the way through the trees. Jarett kept his eyes on the cabin and the men patrolling the outside. He shifted restlessly in the saddle, unable to sit still as he fought the urge to turn Ricochet and gallop down the hill to the cabin. It would be the wrong move to make, he knew that, but he couldn't shake the feeling that they were hiding within the trees while Murdock was doing something to Alex that may very well destroy her.

He tried to distract himself from his growing desire to murder by focusing on Hugh. "Do you think we can trust the sheriff?" he inquired.

Hugh contemplated this before turning in his saddle to face Jarett. "I think he may be trying to get out from under

Murdock, but I don't trust him as far as I can throw him. Paul will do everything he can to get help and bring them here though."

"How much longer?"

Hugh shook his head and though this waiting was nearly impossible for him, he knew Hugh was just as eager to get to his sister. "I don't know."

Jarett's hand slid to his gun. "I'm not waiting much more."

"Death isn't the better option here," Hugh said.

Jarett felt like ripping his own skin off as he stared at the house and waited. The crack of a twig behind him shot his head around as he ripped his gun free of the holster and cocked it. His finger was on the trigger but he stopped himself from firing seconds before he would have shot Daryl. Daryl threw his hands up as Jarett was already sliding the gun back into its holster.

"How many of you are there?" Jarett demanded.

Through the trees he spotted a group of men gathering amongst the foliage. He recognized most of them as local ranchers, and in the back he spotted Henry in the crowd.

"Fifteen," Paul answered as he emerged from behind Daryl. "And the sheriff."

Jarett turned his attention to the older man who had his head bowed. He had to fight the urge to pull his gun again and shoot him. "You're going down there first, Sheriff," Jarett said crisply to him.

The sheriff's head shot up, his eyes darted crazily around. The other ranchers scowled at him as they pressed closer against him, cutting off any hope he may have had at escaping. The sheriff's shoulders slumped as he gave a brief nod. "I owe her that."

"Like you had a choice. You owe *all* of us more than that," a rancher in the back grumbled.

The sheriff spurred his horse forward and emerged from the trees. Jarett followed closely behind with Hugh and Paul by his side. They were only thirty feet away from the house when Murdock stepped onto the porch. Jarett smiled grimly as he pulled his guns free, he'd never enjoyed killing a man, but he was going to savor in Murdock's death.

***

Alex had managed to caterpillar herself almost to the nightstand when she felt fingers brush against her wrist. A startled cry escaped her but before she could react, hissed words reached her. "Shh, Miss Alex, it's only me."

Her breath rushed out of her, her clenched muscles relaxed as she recognized Willy's voice. Tears of relief burned her eyes as her gaze went nervously toward the door. She had no idea where Murdock had gone, or why, but he could come back any second now. "What are you doing here?" she whispered as his fingers scrambled over the ropes binding her.

"Hopefully getting you out."

"You should go Willy, he could come back any…"

"I'm not going anywhere without you," he interrupted.

Her heart thumped against her ribs as she kept her gaze pinned on the door. "Where did you come from?"

"There's a window in the back of the room. I didn't hear Murdock coming up behind me in the stable. He knocked me out, but I regained consciousness in time to see him leaving the ranch with you draped over his horse. I'm so sorry Miss Alex."

"It's not your fault Willy," she assured him. *Just hurry*, she pleaded silently as he tugged at the ropes holding her. Her breath caught in her throat as his hand brushed against her broken one but she didn't protest. The ropes tightened upon her before blessedly giving way.

"Come on Miss. Alex, this way," he urged as she brought her hands before her to rub her raw wrists together. The sight of her already swollen and bruised right hand caused her to wince, but it would heal and it was the least of her troubles right now. Using her left hand, she pushed herself to her feet. The room tilted sickeningly for a second, Willy grabbed hold of her arm as she took an unsteady step. "Are you ok?"

Taking a deep breath, she regained control of herself before risking another step forward. "Yes," she whispered.

"This way."

He kept his hand on her arm as he led her toward the open window at the back of the room; they were almost to it when she heard the first gunshot erupt outside. Alex's hand instinctively went to her waist but her gun belt was gone. "Wait!" she ordered. Willy stopped trying to drag her behind him and turned back to face her. "Give me your gun."

"Miss Alex…"

"Please Willy, give me your gun." She held her left hand out for the gun. "He's done enough damage over the years; it's time for this to end."

Willy frowned at her but he pulled one of the revolvers free of his gun belt. Her hand wrapped around the butt of the gun as she took it from him and cautiously approached the door. Grabbing hold of the knob, she pulled the door open an inch and stuck her eye against the crack. She didn't see or hear anyone outside of the door so she pulled it further open and stepped into the hall.

Making her way into the hallway, she crept toward the front of the house. She'd just entered the front room when bullets shattered the window to the right of where she stood. She bit back a scream as she jumped back and threw her hands over her head. Willy released a startled curse before scurrying into the shadows behind her. More bullets flew through the window and pierced through the door. Wood frayed and splintered around them as bullets tore into the walls around them.

***

Jarett stayed low against Ricochet's neck as the horse raced across the field toward the front of the house. He fired rapidly at the men standing before the house, preparing to defend it, and the monster inside. Grass shot up around Ricochet's hooves as bullets pierced the ground but Ricochet didn't shy away from them as Jarett steered him through the fray. The piercing sound of gunshots reverberated through the smoke and dust clouded air, but he kept his eyes on Murdock as the man hastily retreated to the door of the house.

Jarett aimed at Murdock but another horse slammed into Ricochet's side, knocking him off balance and pushing Ricochet over a few steps. His shot was knocked off; instead of going through Murdock's forehead, it hit the front door. Cursing, Jarett pulled Ricochet over a few steps, but his chance at Murdock had been taken from him as Murdock's men converged upon them.

Jarett lifted his gun and fired at the men approaching them. He'd never aimed to kill before, but he did so now. Fiery rage burned through his veins as he took first one man out and then another. He didn't know if they were dead or not and he didn't care, the only thing he cared about was getting to Alex, and he didn't care who he had to go through to do that.

Hugh was close by his side, his jaw was clenched and a muscle throbbed in his forehead. His expression was as lethal as Jarett felt right now. Behind him a loud grunt sounded and a rancher Jarett didn't know tumbled from his saddle. Jarett ducked low as the man that had shot the rancher spun toward him and fired. The bullet passed so close to him that Jarett could hear it whistling by his ear as he fired his own shot. The man's body was flung backward as the bullet pierced him dead center in his forehead. The guilt Jarett had felt over taking a man's life when he was younger did not swell forth. Instead, he found only grim satisfaction as the man crumpled to the ground.

As far as he was concerned as long as these men were helping Murdock than none of them deserved to live.

***

Alex grabbed hold of Willy's arm and yanked him down to the floor beside her as wood rained down around them. She threw her right arm over her head as she sought to protect herself from the debris pelting them. Grabbing hold of Willy's arm, she pointed back to the room they had just exited. The front door was *not* going to be an option and neither was trying to get at Murdock right now.

Scrambling across the ground in a low crabwalk, she kept her hand in Willy's back as bullets continued to slam into the walls around them. *Jesus, how many men were out there?* She thought frantically. *And who were they?*

Was it possible that her brother and Jarett had somehow managed to evade the sheriff and find her here, or had Murdock been lying to her about having them arrested? She prayed that it was them outside the house, but she was afraid to get her hopes up too much in case they were in jail, or dead. She didn't know who else it could be though.

Willy crawled through the door of Murdock's bedroom; Alex followed behind him and slammed the door shut with the heel of her foot. She awkwardly lurched to her feet as her legs had become cramped from her position and her head was still a little fuzzy.

"This way!" Willy grabbed hold of her arm and pulled her toward the window again.

He shoved aside a velvet red curtain and helped Alex out of the window before following behind her. She staggered a little when she landed on the other side, but quickly regained her balance by leaning against the side of the house.

She frowned as she took in her surroundings and glanced at the building behind her. This wasn't Murdock's house. His house was larger than this and a rust red color. He also had fencing behind his house and not an open field. It took her a minute to realize that he had brought her to his cabin near Arcane Falls. He'd been planning to keep her hidden away here until Jarett and Hugh had been taken care of, maybe even Daryl and Paul too. She fought back the bile that rose in her throat as she focused on her escape.

Willy pulled his other gun out and held it before him as they both poked their heads around the corner of the cabin. In the front yard, at least ten men were sitting on top of their horses. Even more men were around the other side of the cabin near the woods. There were also more than a dozen men lying upon the ground. Screams of agony resonated though the air and she spotted two men writhing upon the ground. Her brother and Jarett might be somewhere out there, and if they were than she *had* to get to them. She also had to get to Murdock.

"Stay here Willy."

"Like hell," he retorted.

Alex shot him a look but she didn't argue with him as she kept the gun in her good hand and prepared to move forward. A man suddenly leapt off the side of the porch and started running across the open field. Willy and Alex flattened themselves against the cabin but the man paid them no attention as he fled toward the woods.

The man disappeared without alerting anyone to his or her presence beside the cabin. There was a small trembling in her legs. She'd never been so petrified in her life. Not even when Jarett had been sitting on top of Hugh holding a gun had she felt this deep quaking in her bones, but there was no way she was going to leave them, and whoever else was from the town, up there alone.

She took another deep breath and bent low so she could move along the porch without being spotted. She had only made it three feet when Murdock leapt off of the side of the porch. Alex's heart leapt into her throat, fury tore through her at the sight of the man that had caused so much misery to so many people. Stumbling back, she pushed Willy behind her as she flattened herself to the side of the house again.

Willy grabbed hold of her right arm when she took a step away from the building and lifted the gun in her left hand. She shook him off though and stepped further away from him. "Murdock!" she shouted across the field.

The man awkwardly stumbled forward as he turned toward her. With unflinching aim, Alex smiled as she pulled the trigger. Murdock released a startled cry as the bullet slammed into his right shoulder; the force of the impact spun him around before knocking him on his ass. Alex didn't pay any attention to the bullets flying back and forth in front of the house as she strode purposely across the field toward the man she'd been longing to kill for the past two years of her life.

A cruel smile twisted her mouth as she arrived at Murdock's side. He grabbed for the gun that had fallen a few feet away from him when she'd shot him, but she stepped onto his wrist, pinning it to the ground. His lips curled into a sneer as he lifted his head to scowl at her. "You missed bitch!" he scoffed.

"Oh I hit where I was aiming," she assured him. "My father taught me to shoot just as good with my left hand as I do with my right, but this…" She leaned over him as she pressed the barrel of the gun against his forehead. "*This* I wanted to do up close and personal. I had to see the look in your eyes when I killed you."

Murdock's eyes bulged as she pressed his head firmly against the ground with the gun. "Alex no!" The sound of pounding hooves approached her, her arm shook as her finger tensed on the trigger. It was Jarett shouting at her, she knew that, but she didn't even glance at him as his horse pulled up beside her and he jumped off the back of it. "Don't do this Alex, it makes you no better than him."

"So he can walk away again?" she demanded as she kept her eyes pinned on Murdock's.

"No," Jarett said. "There is no more walking away for him."

"The sheriff will just let him go again."

"The sheriff is the one that told us where to look for you. You're not a coldblooded killer Alex, revenge is one thing, but this is something you won't come back from. Don't do this."

She knew that he was right but she so badly wanted to pull the trigger, to end all of the misery, to finally put Murdock exactly where he deserved to be. "My father…"

"Wouldn't want this, you know that. Step aside Alex," Hugh said quietly from behind Jarett. "Please."

A scream of frustration built within her chest, she shoved the gun more forcefully against Murdock's forehead. Her arm trembled as she was torn between finally getting everything she had been striving for these past couple of years, and walking away from all the gloom that had enshrouded her family for so long because of this man.

They would still love her if she pulled the trigger, she knew that, but she would be going to a bleak place, one that she may never come back from if she crossed this line.

A strangled cry escaped her; she jerked the gun away from his forehead. The satisfied smirk that crossed his mouth only infuriated her more. Pulling the gun back, she slammed the butt of it as hard as she could against his temple. His head shot to the side, but instead of coming back at her, or trying to get away, Murdock remained stock still as she had rendered him unconscious.

"My father would have approved of that," she muttered as she stepped away from him.

Hugh laughed as he hurried forward. "Yeah he would have."

Jarett wrapped his arms around her and pulled her against his chest. Alex melted against him as she inhaled the sweat and horse that clung to his body. His hand cradled her head as he held her firmly against him, she could feel the tremors that rocked through his powerful arms. The overwhelming urge to cry engulfed her; she buried her head in his chest and wrapped her good hand in his shirt. She'd never been so relieved or overjoyed to see anyone as she was to see him and her brother.

"Thank God you're alive," she choked out.

His breath tickled her ear as he pressed his lips against her. He kissed her tenderly before stepping back to look at her. His jaw clenched, his golden eyes darkened as a muscle began to twitch in his cheek. She'd never seen him look so irate, not even when he'd realized that she was the one that had shot him.

Jarett held her firmly against him as joy and fury tore through him in equal waves. She was the most amazing thing he'd ever felt in his arms, but he wanted to kill Murdock. Her face was shadowed in bruises; her lips were swollen and bleeding, her clothing torn and dirty and that was only what he could see of her. He didn't know what was beneath her clothes or what else had been done to her.

He didn't know what consequences the events of this day would have on her, but he would be there every day for the rest of her life to help her get through whatever trauma lingered. Even if she had been raped, even if she shied away from his touch and spurned him for letting her down, he would stand by her side and love her.

"Jarett..."

"Look at what he did to you," he said from between his clenched teeth.

Alex winced and slightly turned away as he went to touch her mouth. His eyes went toward Murdock's still frame. "No Jarett," she whispered. "No more illegal activity, no more stealing, and *no* more killing. He'll get what he deserves. I'll heal and be as good as new in no time."

Jarett continued to glower at Murdock as the man released a low groan. His hand went to one of the guns at his side. "Please Jarett," she whispered. "I walked away and so should you."

His gaze finally came back to hers; his hand fell away from his gun. Paul and Daryl hurried past them, along with a few other ranchers to help Hugh with Murdock. Hugh and Paul took hold of Murdock's arms and jerked him to his feet. Murdock's head lulled down, his feet dragged across the ground as Hugh and Paul pulled him toward a waiting horse. One of the ranchers had rope with them and they swiftly tied Murdock's hands and feet together before throwing him unceremoniously across the back of the horse.

Jarett pulled her closer again and kissed her forehead. "Are you sure you're alright?"

"I'm fine," she assured him. She kept her broken hand hidden from him, frightened that it would only push him over the edge. She'd deal with his wrath when he noticed it later, but not right now. His gaze ran over her again as he seemed to be trying to see into her soul. She touched his stubble roughened cheek with her good hand.

"Alex…"

"I'm fine Jarett, you all arrived here before he could do anything more to me. Willy was able to set me free before he could violate me."

His shoulders slumped; he pulled her closer against him and tenderly kissed her forehead. "I'm so sorry I wasn't there. Please forgive me. He'll never touch you again."

"It's not your fault. He's terrorized everyone around here for years; he wasn't going to stop until he was finally forced too. Where are they taking him?"

"He's going to stand trial and he's going to hang," Jarett said. "The sheriff…"

"The sheriff is dead," Daryl said as he stepped forward.

"Then the new sheriff will see to it that justice is carried out," Jarett continued. She placed her head against his chest as relief flowed through her. "Till then he's going to be kept securely locked behind bars."

"That's the best news I've heard in years," she breathed.

Jarett rubbed her back as he turned her away from the cabin and led her toward Ricochet. With ease, he placed his hands on her hips and lifted her onto the saddle. Her eyes were haunted as she looked down at him but the smile she gave him melted the rest of the ice that had encased his heart ever since he'd discovered that she'd been taken. His hand lingered on her knee, before he grabbed hold of the saddle and swung himself up behind her.

He pulled her into his lap and pressed her firmly against his chest. She felt so small and fragile in his arms, but he could feel the steel rod of strength that kept her back rigid and her chin jutting forward as she stared at Murdock. He turned the horse to take her back to the ranch but she seized hold of his hand on the reins.

"No, I'm going to be there when the cell door closes on him," she said.

He knew that this was something she had to witness, but he didn't like the idea of exposing her to even more people in her condition. "Alex, the people in town…"

"They've talked about me for years. They're going to talk about today for years to come. If we have a child within the next nine months, they will talk about it, but it will be *yours*."

"I know," he said as he kissed her temple.

"Then you know there will be no stopping the gossip, no matter if they see me now or not. I've waited years for this Jarett, I *will* see it."

Jarett released a sigh before turning the horse to join the others. "Yes, you will," he agreed.

CHAPTER 25

The people of town were already beginning to gather around even before they arrived. Alex kept her shoulders thrust back as all the eyes followed her and Jarett down the street. They turned to whisper as soon as they passed, but she refused to acknowledge any of them as they headed toward the red brick jailhouse.

Jarett dismounted from behind her and pulled her tenderly down from the saddle. She took hold of his hand with her good one before following Paul and Hugh up the steps of the jail and into the building. She'd never been in here before but as she looked around she realized it was much as she'd pictured it over the years. A simple wooden desk was set against one wall, and there were two small cells at the back of the building, both of them had their doors open to reveal a small cot within.

She pulled her hand free of Jarett's as Hugh and Paul led Murdock into the cell on the right. Her heart thumped eagerly in her chest as they dumped a conscious, but dazed, Murdock unceremoniously onto the cot and walked out of the cell. There was a victorious smile curving Hugh's mouth as he closed the bars with a click of finality that caused a shiver of pleasure to slide down Alex's spine.

She threw her arm around Hugh's neck after he turned away from the cell. A small laugh escaped him and he hugged her against him. "It's over," she whispered in relief.

"It is," he agreed.

"Let me through! Let me through!"

Alex lifted her head at Megan's exasperated shout. Her friend appeared amongst the crowd of men gathered within the door. Megan elbowed her way past the last two men and stepped into the room. She flung herself into Daryl's arms as he stepped forward to intercept her. "You had me worried sick!" Megan cried.

"I'm fine," he assured her.

"Alex?" Megan pulled away from her husband and turned to search the jailhouse. Alex stepped away from Hugh as her friend barreled toward her. "What did that man do to you? Are you ok?" she gushed out.

"I am," she assured her, but even still Megan eyed her up and down.

"That evil, hideous bastard!" Megan cried before throwing her arms around Alex. "Thank God you're ok! How is everyone else?"

Alex recalled the men she'd seen lying on the ground and stepped away from Megan in order to hear the answer. "Old man Kilington and Mr. Frankel didn't make it, Mr. Dober and Mr. Millson were both shot but they should both be ok," Paul answered. "Ten of Murdock's men were killed, the rest scattered like the cowards they are. I doubt we'll be seeing any of them again now that their gravy train has dried up."

"I'd have to agree with that," Jarett said.

He wrapped his arm around Alex's waist and pulled her against his side. He wasn't willing to let her go for long after the events of this day. "Excuse me, excuse me."

The men stepped aside as Reverend White pushed his way to the front of the crowd. His eyes widened upon Alex as she leaned against Jarett's side. He rushed to stand in front of her. "Ms. Harris." He went to take hold of her hands but she only gave him the one. "My dear I am so sorry about the unfortunate events of this day."

"They weren't unfortunate Reverend; in fact I think the events of this day make for a very happy ending," she said with a pointed glance at Murdock in his cell.

The reverend gave her a pitying look that set Jarett's nerves on edge as his hand fisted. He wasn't about to hit a man of God but he was sorely tempted too. "My dear what you've experienced..."

"Nothing more than bumps and bruises Reverend," she assured him.

"Ah Ms. Harris, there are some things we do not like to face." Jarett realized it might not be him the reverend had to fear as Alex took a step toward the man. There was fire in her eyes as she glowered at him. Jarett kept a firm hold on her waist as the man took a startled step back.

"I've faced every horrible thing in my life Reverend. There are just people who prefer to believe things they shouldn't," she retorted. "God and I know the truth and believe me neither of us are liars, or *gossips*."

The reverend blanched as he released her hand. Pride slid through Jarett as he grinned at the baffled looking man. Hugh and Paul guffawed loudly, Megan elbowed Daryl in the ribs when he began to chuckle. "Oh... Ah yes, well that is good to hear my dear." He looked at Murdock before focusing on her again. "I understand if you'd like to postpone your ceremony."

"Absolutely not," she said fervently.

Even Jarett's eyebrows shot up at that one. She'd been insistent before that she wouldn't get married with Murdock's marks upon her. He'd completely understood then and had fully expected that it would probably be another month before she was ready to walk down the aisle.

"Are you certain my dear? I'm sure you will require some time to recover," the reverend said.

"I've never been more sure of anything in my life," she said. She glanced over her shoulder to where Murdock sat glowering at them from his cot. "I want him to still be alive when we get married."

Jarett grinned as he dropped a kiss on top of her head. The reverend looked scandalized but he nodded his head in consent. “I will see you soon then,” he murmured before turning and hurrying from the jail.

“Are you sure about this Alex?” Hugh asked.

“Yes,” she said as she turned away from the door. She met Murdock’s hate filled gaze unwaveringly. “It will be beautiful no matter what.”

“It will be,” Jarett agreed.

Alex closed her eyes and allowed herself to drift into the calming beat of Jarett’s heart. “I’d like to go home now,” she whispered and stifled a yawn.

“I’ll take the first watch here with Daryl tonight,” Hugh said. “I don’t think any of Murdock’s men will be back, but I think everyone should put on a bigger watch around their ranches tonight and for the next few weeks.”

“I agree,” Jarett said. “I’ll make sure there are more men on watch tonight.”

“Thank you.”

“I’ll ride back with you,” Paul said. “I have to get back to my father to make sure everything is secure for the night.”

Jarett nodded and bent down to sweep Alex into his arms. She curled up against his chest and rested her head in the hollow of his neck. Her warm breath tickled his neck as she nestled closer to him. The men all nodded to them and stepped aside as he carried her out of the jailhouse.

CHAPTER 26

"I cannot believe how many people are here," Alex whispered.

Her gaze scanned the clutter of wagons and people that had gathered at the ranch. To her alarm, and utter horror, the entire town seemed to have turned out for the wedding. "You've been the talk of the town for awhile now, and after the events of last week there was *no* way anyone was going to miss this," Megan replied as she fluttered anxiously around her.

Alex tried again to shoo her away, but Megan batted Alex's hand down to readjust her headpiece for the hundredth time. "Those people should mind their own," Lysette muttered.

Alex agreed with her, but she refrained from saying anything. She wanted to kill Megan and Hugh for inviting everyone, but they had insisted, and Alex hadn't actually believed that they would all come. People who had shunned her for years were here now, but then she had become even more of a spectacle recently.

Her gaze slid down to the right hand splinted and wrapped within some cotton bandages. It wasn't the typical accessory to go with a wedding dress, but at least the bandaging was white and Lysette had assured her that her hand would heal well if she refrained from using it. This last was told to her with an admonishing look that had made Alex promptly promise to take it easy. As she'd expected, Jarett had erupted into a rage at the sight of her hand, but between her and Hugh, they had managed to keep him from going after Murdock and killing him with his bare hands.

Daryl had put his job, as one of the town's blacksmiths on hold, when he'd been asked to fill the position as sheriff until someone reliable could be found that was willing to take the job on full time. The magistrate had already handed down Murdock's sentence to him; he was to be hanged for the murder of her father, and her kidnapping, in two days. Alex was relieved that everyone now knew the truth about her father, but she was surprised by how little pleasure she took in the fact that Murdock would be dead soon.

In fact, she had decided that she wasn't going to go to Murdock's hanging. Jarett and Hugh were going, but she planned to remain behind. She'd seen enough death and brutality in her life; she didn't wish to see anymore. It was time to move on and she looked forward to doing exactly that, she didn't need to see Murdock die in order to do so anymore.

Charges also could have been leveled against them for stealing, but no one in the area was willing to say anything against them, and the magistrate wouldn't listen to Murdock's testimony on the thieves. Though everyone in the area now felt that their suspicions about who the robbers actually were had been confirmed, no one said anything out loud.

Murdock's ranch had already been put up for sale. Some of the ranches closest to Murdock's had claimed different parcels of his land; the remaining ranchers would split the proceeds from the sale of his property amongst themselves. Though they could have taken land, Alex and Hugh had agreed they wanted nothing to do with it. When the ranch was sold, they would give their share of the money back over to the ranchers.

Jarett was in the process of looking into buying old man Kilington's land, as he'd had no family to leave his property to. Alex hoped they would be able to get it, as a piece of Kilington's land bordered theirs. She wanted to stay as close as possible to her family when the time came for them to move into their own home.

A loud bang from outside drew her attention as Perry fired his gun into the air and released a joyous shout. They'd found the young ranch hand in the woods after returning from seeing Murdock imprisoned. He'd still been unconscious from the blow he'd taken to his temple. It had taken Perry a few days of bed rest to recover from the blow one of Murdock's men had delivered to his head, but he was doing great now.

Alex turned away from the window and moved hurriedly away from Megan as she came at her with more pins. "Enough," she said firmly. "I've got enough pins in my hair."

Megan frowned at her, but refrained from making another move as she stepped back to survey Alex with a critical eye. A bright gleam came into Megan's eyes as she broke into a brilliant smile. "You look beautiful."

"Yes you do," Lysette agreed.

Alex moved to stand in front of the full-length mirror. It had belonged to her mother, but Alex had recently removed it from the attic where it had been stored since her death. Alex's breath froze as she stared at herself in disbelief. The low cut neck of the dress revealed a hint of her full breasts. It hugged her slender waist before flowing over her hips. The white of it contrasted beautifully with her bright copper hair and golden skin. Her hair flowed freely down her back, but Megan had made a crown of red and white roses and pinned it to her head. The bruises on her neck were all but gone and though there were still shadows on her cheek and her lips were still cracked, Megan had managed to cover up most of the remnants from her battle with Murdock.

Although she had hated all of the preparation that Megan had made her suffer through, she was now grateful for all of it. Tears sprang to her eyes as she turned to her best friend and pulled her into her arms. "Thank you," she whispered.

"I told you this day would come," Megan replied laughingly and stepped back to wipe tears from her own eyes. "No crying, you'll ruin your makeup," she scolded.

Alex glanced down the length of her dress. "Jarett's not going to recognize me."

"Probably not," Megan agreed. "Now, do I have to explain what will be expected of you on your wedding night?"

Alex laughed loudly as she wrapped her arms around Megan again. She was so grateful for her friend's loving and teasing nature. "Enough now, the ceremony is about to begin," Lysette admonished.

Alex turned to her surrogate mother. Despite Lysette's protestations, she embraced her and loudly kissed both of her cheeks. "Let's just hope that her betrothed does recognize her, I don't think you're going to want her back," Megan teased as Alex stepped away from Lysette.

"You've got that right," Lysette said but she dabbed at her eyes with her handkerchief.

"Come on," Megan urged and pulled at Alex's elbow.

Alex followed her down the hall and stairs; she paused at the front door when Megan pulled her back to fiddle with the crown again. Hugh appeared in the doorway, he stopped in midstride as his wide-eyed gaze landed on her. He snapped his mouth shut when Megan elbowed him in the ribs.

"You look beautiful," he whispered. "Just like mom."

Alex felt tears bloom in her eyes again as he came forward to take hold of her arm. "Thank you," she breathed.

"No tears." Megan shoved a bouquet of flowers into her left hand.

Alex held onto them as nervousness fluttered to life within her belly. She had no second thoughts over marrying Jarett, but the thought of facing all of the people outside made her want to turn and bolt. She knew what they would all be thinking, was certain that wagers had already been placed on whether or not there would be a child born in less than nine months, and on whose child it would be. She knew that most of them were not here for kind reasons, but to gossip and talk, and to watch the wild, loose, Alexandra Harris finally be tamed.

Like that will happen, she thought.

Hugh began to lead her forward; he carefully walked her down the stairs toward the arbor that had been set up before one of the pastures. The rolling hills made a beautiful backdrop to the wooden arbor adorned with white roses. She forgot all about the people ogling her as her eyes landed upon Jarett just before the arbor. He looked stunningly handsome in his elegant coat, and with his unruly black hair combed back. A small smile played at the corners of his mouth as he watched her. She smiled back at him and thrilled at the sensual gleam within his golden eyes.

Hugh squeezed her arm reassuringly before handing her over to Jarett. The last of her nervousness vanished when Jarett winked at her before turning to face the reverend. The ceremony slipped by in a blur that Alex barely remembered as all of her concentration was focused upon the man at her side. She was acutely aware of his warm body, and to her own chagrin and disgrace, she found herself becoming aroused. Though he had slept beside her every night of the week and a half since Murdock's attack, he had refused to touch her for fear that he would hurt her. Now she found herself eagerly looking forward to tonight.

She blurted her vows out. Jarett slipped a delicate gold band onto her finger before drawing her against him. It was only then she realized that they were now married. The thought had barely registered before he bent his head and kissed her. Alex forgot everything else as her body instinctively reacted to his touch and she pressed against him firmly.

Startled when he broke away, she took a stumbling step forward before he steadied her. A blush blazed into her cheeks as the crowd erupted into applause and whistles. Jarett smiled at her as he took hold of her arm and turned to lead her down the aisle.

"You look beautiful in a dress Alexandra," he whispered in her ear.

"Don't get used to it," she replied.

He chuckled as he wrapped his arm around her waist and continued to propel her forward. "You're always beautiful Love," he murmured in her ear. "But I rather prefer you with nothing on."

Her gaze shot to his as her mouth went dry and delicious shivers of anticipation coursed through her body. "You're incorrigible," she scolded.

He laughed again as someone began to play the fiddle. The crowd parted as Jarett swept her into the first dance. The day passed in a blur of dancing, laughter, music, and drinking that made her realize just how optimistic their future was. Alex managed to slip away after the second hour to change into a pretty, sapphire day dress that Jarett had bought for her to wear today.

The day was dwindling toward twilight, but the party showed no signs of stopping as Alex watched the people dancing. Alex leisurely sipped her punch as her gaze instinctively sought out Jarett. He stood with half a dozen ranchers, Paul, Daryl and her brother. Sensing her gaze, Jarett looked up at her and smiled as he waved.

"This has been a wonderful day," Megan said, drawing Alex's attention.

"Yes, it has," Alex agreed. "It seems that one of your dreams has been fulfilled."

"I only wanted to see you happy."

"I am."

She glanced around the large gathering again and smiled as she met Rachel's gaze. Dolly and Amy were with her, but their attention was focused elsewhere. Around the three of them was a growing cluster of young men who had consumed too much alcohol and were now eager for some female companionship.

Alex assumed that it wasn't at all proper to have the women from the saloon here, but she had made sure to invite them as well. Henry stood a small distance away from the crowd; a glass of whiskey was clutched in his hand as he surveyed the people gathered around him.

"I'll be back," she said to Megan.

Before Megan could reply, Alex lifted the skirt of her dress and hurried to her friend. Henry's pale eyes met hers, a smile spread over his lined face as she stepped next to his side. "You were a beautiful bride, Alex."

"Thank you Henry. Are you enjoying yourself?"

"I am."

Alex squeezed his hand. "Have you received any letters from Charlie?"

"No, but he'll be coming soon."

"Yes, he will," Alex replied, hoping that she was right.

"You should be with your husband, not conversing with an old man."

Alex laughed as she turned to survey the crowd again. Jarett's gaze drew her instantly. There was no smile on his face this time, but a smoldering look that warmed her to the tips of her toes. A delicious shiver raced down her spine at the promise in his gaze. She bit into her bottom lip as she lowered her eyes.

Henry laughed. “I think your husband misses your company.”

Alex couldn’t stop the small chuckle that escaped her. “He’s busy with his friends.”

“Trust me Alexandra; it’s your company he’s wanting.”

“Will you be staying the night Henry?”

He shrugged his stooped shoulders as he shook his head. “Nay, Rachel will be taking me back.”

Alex hid her disappointment from him. “Enjoy yourself Henry.”

“I will.”

Alex bent to plant a kiss on his weathered cheek. He blushed as he rubbed at his skin. “Congratulations my dear.”

“Thank you Henry.”

Her gaze met Jarett’s as she turned away from Henry. He was smiling at her with his eyebrow cocked in amusement. She returned his smile innocently as she made her way through the crowd toward him.

“Making plans with old lovers already?” Alex froze at the sound of the cold voice. Her eyes latched onto Suzanne’s malicious ones as she turned. She hadn’t even known that Suzanne was here. She should have known that Suzanne wouldn’t make her presence known until she found some way to try and ruin the day.

“What are you doing here Suzanne?” Alex inquired.

Suzanne lifted an elegant shoulder as she tossed back her brown hair. “The entire town was invited Alexandra. I wouldn’t miss seeing one of my oldest friends married off, and I had to offer my congratulations.”

“Thank you,” Alex replied crisply.

"Do you honestly think he'll remain faithful to…" Suzanne raked her from head to toe with a disdainful look. "*You.*"

Alex tilted her chin as she glared at the spiteful woman across from her. "Yes."

"Even after he realizes that you're carrying Murdock's child?"

Alex's fists clenched. "That isn't possible," she grated out.

"Come now Alex, you might as well admit it, everyone will know the truth one day anyway."

"You're not worth my time Suzanne," Alex told her.

She turned away from Suzanne but Jarett grabbed hold of her arms and stopped her before she could take one step away. A muscle in his jaw twitched as his gaze slid between her and Suzanne.

"What's going on here?" he demanded. He knew just how cruel Suzanne could be and he wasn't about to let anything or any*one* ruin this day for Alex.

"Suzanne was simply offering her congratulations," she informed him.

His eyes flicked toward her, but the muscle in his cheek twitched even more violently as he turned back to Suzanne. "Oh, look at this," Dolly cried as she sidled up to them, apparently oblivious to the tension in the air. "I'm glad that you were able to put your differences with Alex aside, and come to give her your congratulations Suzanne!" Suzanne scowled at Dolly while Alex fairly gaped at Dolly's statement. How she couldn't sense that something was truly wrong, was beyond her. "If I'm not mistaken Alex will be coming to your wedding soon too."

Suzanne frowned as she studied Dolly. "I'm not getting married."

"Oh?" Dolly smiled innocently as she tapped her chin thoughtfully. "Lyle Henderson told me that the two of you were quite close, *intimately* close. I only assumed that a fine woman such as yourself would be marrying a man she was *that* close too. Oh wait, silly me, Lyle left town last week, didn't he?"

Alex bit back a smile as Suzanne's face turned tomato red. "Lyle lied!" she spat.

"Perhaps he did, you know how men can be. I just assumed that since he said the same things about you as Jeremiah and Jed Barette..." Suzanne spun on her heel and stormed away into the crowd before Dolly could finish. "Bitch," Dolly muttered.

Alex burst into loud laughter as Dolly smiled at her and then Jarett. "Thank you Dolly," Alex said.

"You just have to learn how to handle her. Anger isn't going to help," she flicked a pointed glance at Jarett. "It's what she wants. I think she'll leave you alone from now on though."

"I think so too," Alex agreed.

Jarett grinned at Dolly as he slid a protective arm around Alex's waist. He glanced down at his wife as she laid her head against his chest, her small hand rested on his stomach as she continued to smile at Dolly. She was a complete mystery to him, someone who was friendlier and more comfortable with tavern wenches and drunks. He'd never met a woman like her and he knew that he would cherish every day they spent together for the rest of their lives.

Dolly disappeared into the crowd as Alex turned to Jarett. She smiled sweetly up at him. "I'd like to go to bed."

All the blood flooded into his groin area causing him to lengthen instantly. "You're hurt."

She pressed her breasts tantalizingly against his chest as she moved closer. "Not anymore and you don't have to be gentle."

She was going to be the absolute death of him but there was no way that he could say no to that. He would be gentle, but he couldn't deny her or himself any more. It had been too long since he had been inside her, too long since he had felt her moving against him. Leading her through the crowd, he ignored the loud whistles and shouts of encouragement as he swept her into his arms and carried her over the threshold. Alex wrapped her arms around his neck as he carried her up the stairs as quickly as he could.

"You didn't believe what Suzanne said about me cheating on you, did you?" he asked as he stepped into her room.

"No. I trust you completely Jarett."

He glanced down at her as he carried her across the room and deposited her gently on the bed. "Do you now?" he inquired.

"I do. However, if you ever think of breaking your vows, I can assure you that you will regret that decision for the rest of your days."

He laughed as he shook his head. "Trust me Alex; you are the only woman for me."

She rose to her feet. "Good. Now, if you'll excuse me, I have to undress."

"Which I fully intend to help you with."

He grabbed for her but she swiftly evaded his grasp. A sensuous smile played over her mouth as she shook her head at him. "No, you have to leave."

"Excuse me?"

"I have a surprise for you."

His curiosity was peaked, but his arousal was even stronger. "I'm sure that can wait until later."

"No," she said firmly. "It will only be a few minutes. Now shoo."

She pushed him toward the adjoining door of their bedrooms. Jarett groaned but finally relented; this seemed to be important to her, he could control himself for a few more minutes.

“Fine,” he said. He claimed her mouth and gave her a lingering kiss that left her breathless when he reluctantly pulled away. He was pleased to see the hazy desire in her eyes as she took a small step back. “Hurry.”

She nodded. “Of course.”

Jarett anxiously paced the suddenly small confines of his own room as he waited for her to arrive. Outside, a fire had been lit, and the flames were jumping high into the air. He strode to the window and looked down at the revelers that remained. The party had thinned down, but a few diehards were still celebrating. He watched their awkward dancing in amusement as he tried to ignore the powerful ache in his loins.

The sound of the door opening drew his attention away from the window. His breath froze as Alex stepped into the room and closed the door behind her. His gaze slid over her, he devoured her with his eyes as his erect cock jumped in eager anticipation. The nightgown she wore clung to every one of her delicate curves and emphasized the thrust of her luscious breasts; breasts that were completely bared to him, as was the rest of her, by the sheer material. She had taken her hair down to let it cascade down her back; it was the only thing that hid any of her skin from him.

Unable to stay away for even a second longer, he moved toward her and drew her into his arms. “It was well worth the wait,” he whispered huskily.

“Megan made it.”

“Remind me to thank her later.”

The robe he wore fell open as she rubbed herself against him invitingly; she was pleased to note the state of his arousal as it pressed into her belly. His eyes dilated as he bent his head and his mouth devoured hers with an intensity that left her trembling and weak. His mouth never left hers as he swept her up into his arms.

Alex mewled her eagerness for him as he placed her upon the bed and came down on top of her. He propped himself up on his hands, parted her thighs in one swift motion and settled himself between her. "It's been too long," he groaned against her ear.

Alex wrapped her legs around his waist and lifted her hips in invitation. She was already wet with wanting for him. There was a desperation growing within her that was nearly uncontrollable as he rubbed teasingly against her. "I need you," she gasped impatiently when he still didn't enter her.

His right hand enclosed her breast; he teased her nipple until it was hard before his mouth reclaimed hers. Alex shifted as the fierce longing in her body screamed to be fulfilled. Her left hand dug into his back as his tongue thrust into her mouth in deep strokes that stole her breath. Her patience was close to snapping when he finally slid into her. She breathed a sigh as he stretched and filled her.

"I love you Jarett," she whispered as she lifted her hips to meet his deep thrusts eagerly.

His eyes gleamed as they lovingly searched her face. "And I you," he murmured before taking her mouth again.

Alex gave herself over to the consuming pleasure of her husband's loving embrace.

EPILOGUE

Six months later,

Alex frowned thoughtfully as she gazed down the road and watched the dust that rose to fill the air. She stepped forward on the porch of the home that she and Jarret had moved into this month. They had torn down old man Kilington's small cabin after buying the property and used some of the wood to build a home closer to her brother's ranch. They had expanded the home, and the corrals, as Jarett had also bought some land from another neighbor of theirs to expand their lot. Everyone in town had come out to help them rebuild their new home and to celebrate.

She loved the land and was in the process of making the house a home by adding curtains and other decorative details she never would have thought of if Lysette and Megan weren't helping her. Now there were little knickknacks and dried flowers to go along with the afghans that Lysette had knitted for her. Thankfully, Lysette had offered to stay with them, otherwise she and Jarett would probably starve as cooking had never been her forte. Hugh came over every night for dinner, but he understood Lysette's choice to live with them for now.

Alex's hand drifted down to her belly as she stepped off the final stair and took a step toward the drive. Hugh wouldn't have come from this direction and neither would Paul. Megan was inside now, and Daryl was busy in town as he had agreed to become the full time sheriff after a lot of persuasion and encouragement from the townspeople.

Willy emerged from the side of the house and headed toward her. "Where is everyone?" she inquired.

"Hugh's in the north field, Jarett's in the hay loft."

"Please go get him Willy."

He hurried away as fast as his old, bowed legs would carry him. Alex shaded her eyes against the sun as the dust came closer to the ranch. She took another step forward as a wagon broke over the crest of the hill. A frown marred her brow when she spotted Henry in the passenger seat of the wagon, sitting beside a tall, broad man.

Recognition was slow in coming, but when it finally hit her who he was sitting next to, she let out a happy cry and started running toward the wagon. Charlie pulled up on the lines and descended the steps before she made it to them. She laughed as she flung herself into his arms and hugged him.

He swung her around before depositing her onto the ground again and stepping away to survey her. "My God Alex, I never would have recognized you!"

Alex laughed as she took a step back and her gaze traveled over the man before her. The lanky youth she recalled had grown into a devilishly handsome, solidly built man with twinkling brown eyes and disheveled dark blond hair. "Nor I you."

He grinned at her as his gaze traveled to her belly. She glanced down at the small bump that was just beginning to show. She had just entered the fifth month of her pregnancy. "And I never expected this!"

"I was beginning to get to the point where I wasn't expecting *you.*"

He grinned sheepishly as he ran a hand through his disheveled hair. "Well I'm back to stay now."

"I'm so happy to hear that Charlie, we all missed you, so much."

He took hold of her right hand and patted it reassuringly. The bones in it had healed well, but she always knew when it was going to rain now, as she would get a twinge in it hours beforehand. "I missed you all too. Now, where is that brother of yours?" he asked.

"Out in the north field. I'll send someone out to get him." Alex turned as Henry arrived beside her. The radiant smile on his face, and the joy in his eyes touched her heart and brought tears to her eyes. He was wearing the new outfit that Alex had helped him pick out what seemed like forever ago now, but it was still in good condition. He had even bathed, shaved, and brushed back his hair.

"When did you arrive?" Alex inquired of Charlie.

"A few hours ago."

Alex glanced over her shoulder as Jarett emerged from the barn, his eyes narrowed upon Charlie's arm draped casually around her shoulders. "Charlie, this is my husband Jarett," Alex said when he arrived at her side. "Jarett this is Henry's son, Charlie. One of my oldest friends."

"Hugh is older than me," Charlie quipped and Alex made a face at him. Charlie extended his hand to Jarett, who studied him for a minute before accepting his outstretched hand. "Pleased to meet you."

"You too," Jarett replied and released Charlie's hand. He wrapped his arm around Alex's waist and briefly brushed his hand over her swelling belly. "How are you doing Henry?"

"Good," Henry replied with a warm glance at his son.

"Well you must come in; Megan is inside with her daughter. Have you seen Daryl yet?"

"Yes," Charlie answered as they made their way toward the house. "He said he would be here for dinner later."

Alex laughed softly. "Of course he will. Willy?" Willy stepped forward. "Will you ride out and get Hugh, and could you ride over and see if Paul would like to join us for dinner?"

"I'll go right now," he said enthusiastically. "Hello Charlie, Henry."

"Hello Willy," they both replied, but Willy was already halfway to the new barn.

Jarett pulled the screen door open and held Alex back to allow Charlie and Henry to enter first. "Well, I'll be, if that ain't a sight for sore eyes!"

"Lysette!" Charlie greeted and ignored her protests as he embraced her warmly. "You're still taking care of these two monsters?"

"Someone has to," she muttered as she straightened the apron Charlie's hug had knocked askew.

"That they do," Charlie agreed and shot Alex a teasing grin. "I see you still can't get her to dress like a girl."

"Hey," Alex protested happily.

"And neither can her husband," Lysette said.

"She wore a wedding dress," Jarett supplied.

"That she did, and I was amazed," Lysette muttered.

"You weren't the only one," Jarett agreed.

"Okay, enough picking on me," Alex interjected.

"Who's here?" Megan demanded and poked her head around the corner. Her mouth dropped, she let out a little squeal before bolting forward and throwing her arms around Charlie. He picked her up and hugged her before placing her back on the ground. "You *are* still alive!"

"Har har," he told her as he poked her nose. "Where's the baby?"

"In the parlor, come on I'll introduce you."

They all moved into the parlor. Lysette brought them some tea and settled in to reminisce and catch up with Charlie. Laughter filled the house as Hugh, Daryl, Willy, and Paul arrived over the next few hours and they all exchanged stories and jokes. The candles were burning low when Alex lifted her head from Jarett's shoulder. Looking around she realized that their house was already a home, one that was filled with love and laughter and friends and family.

She rested her hand lovingly against her belly as she placed a kiss on her Jarett's cheek. He grinned at her as he pulled her closer and snuggled her within his embrace. Cocooned in the love that filled her home, she knew that this man had given her the strength she needed to love again, and to move on from the bitterness that had once encompassed her life. He was the last thing she had been looking for when he had walked into her life, turned it upside down, and stolen her heart, but in his arms she had most certainly found her home.

The End.